The Waking

Book I of the Elder Born

Willowsong Publishing

THE WAKING

BOOK I OF THE ELDER BORN

Willowsong Publishing

3004 Dahlgreen Road Raleigh, NC 27615

www.willowsongpublishing.com

First Printing 2018

ISBN-13: 978-0692400029 (Willowsong Publishing)

ISBN-10: 0692400028

LCCN: 2017908919

Map illustration by Alex McVey

For Jeff,

My beloved husband, who has seen me through my own Waking.

And for my boys, Joshua and Jonathan.

Special thanks to my parents, Robert and Ann Love, whose encouragement, support and enthusiasm helped me birth this book.

Acknowledgments

No book is written in a vacuum, and there are so many people who were part of this adventure for me. First and foremost I want to thank my husband, Jeff, whose support, encouragement, and belief in me helped me bring this book into being, and to whom I owe the wonder of my own Waking. My parents, Robert and Ann Love, who have followed these characters from initial inception, to the printed page, across many edits, highs, and lows. They are the ones who instilled within me the love of story, especially fantasy. My boys, Joshua and Jonathan, who have grown me as a person, and to whom I owe so much of my own perspective on life. Being a mom simply changes you! There are people past and present who have stepped into my life and encouraged my own Waking during the time I was writing this. To name just a few... Vicki Anderson, DeeDee Patron, Jessie May Wolfe, Kathleen Nelson Troyer, Lisa Pollard. And then there are the horses... my Halley mare, who challenged me to step out of my safe life and find out who I really am. Willow, who rescued me as much as I rescued her. Sensei, whose steady love lent me comfort more times than I can count. Neechee, who left an appaloosa shaped imprint on my soul, and Lizzie whose sweet nature brightened our entire farm. I am blessed beyond measure to be part of such a loving community, and to share the fruit of that here, in this book.

The Waking

Book I of the Elder Born

by Elizabeth Love Kennon

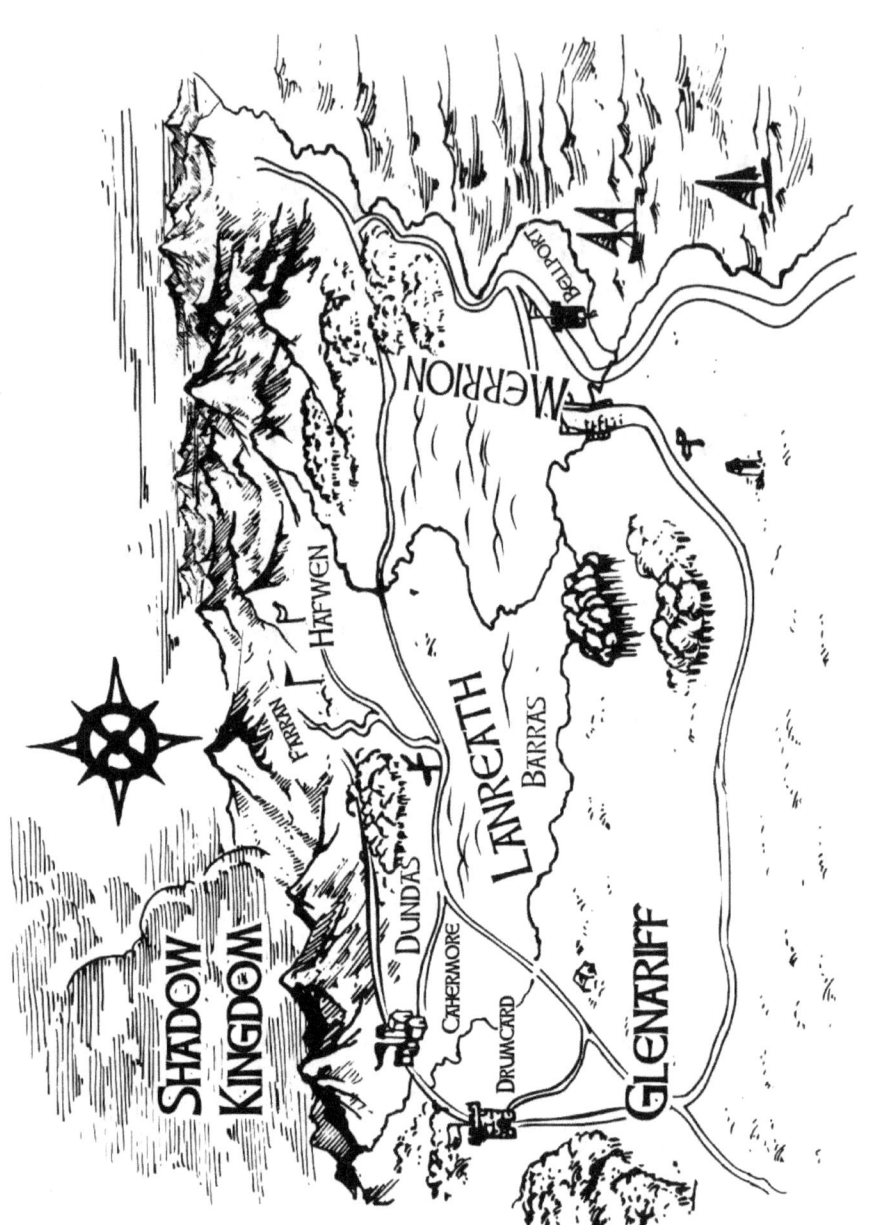

. Contents .

CHAPTER 1

THE LETTER

The inn door banged open. Elana glanced up from the parchment, her poised quill dripping ink onto the worn table, as she stopped to take note of the stranger. The light from the doorway framed the post rider, who paused at the entrance to the dark common room. There the regulars, mostly old sailors, whose arthritic limbs kept them land bound in changing weather, turned from their conversation, eyeing the newcomer. Only the scrape of a chair, and the clink of a glass on the high wooden bar broke the silence.

Farrell, the innkeeper, stuck his head out of the steaming kitchen, spotted the post rider and bustled over to him. Elana studied the rider as the two men talked. He wasn't from these parts, she thought, noting his cadence of speech. They rarely were. Maybe Bellport... the accent had a harsh edge to it.

A gruff voice interrupted her musings, pulling her back to the job at hand.

"Missy, you're ruinin' the board." The fisherman squinted across the thick table at her in the dim light of the oil lamp, his native distrust of anything or anyone different etched across his face.

"Where'd you say your pappy was?" The question was half accusation.

By now the villagers were accustomed to her father, even if they didn't entirely accept him. Hamilton was the only scrivener for miles. He spent his days sitting in the back corner of the inn, next to the small window, reading their occasional letters aloud to them and writing their responses, or drafting notes of ownership when the need occurred. They paid him in goods mostly - cloth, eggs, fish, vegetables, grain. It was a meager living, but their family was used to that. They hadn't settled in this coastal village to prosper. They came to find safety.

Elana managed a thin smile replying "He's helping Orvis with his boat."

The old man grunted.

She applied her quill to the parchment once more, all the while straining to hear Farrell's conversation with the post rider. It had been a fortnight since the last rider passed this way, and with her father out, she would be the one to read any incoming letters. The men's voices grew heated for a moment, and then the rider gave Farrell a single letter, turned on his heel and left.

Elana sighed. Precious little ever happened here. She turned her full attention back to the parchment and finished, surveying her work. Her letters formed small, neat rows that marched evenly across the page. She blew gently on the ink, making sure it wouldn't smudge, before handing it to the fisherman.

"Thankee, lass." The man's grizzled face softened. "Old eyes ain't what they used to be. I'll have the missus carry a basket up to the house before nightfall." He rolled up the parchment; a bill of sale for an old dinghy, tied it with a strand of twine and stumped out of the inn.

Elana shook her head as she watched him make his way across the empty street. How many times had she heard the excuses? Old eyes, shaky hands - it was the rare man who would willingly admit that a girl could read and write when he could not. Just one more example of how she didn't fit in...

Farrell, the innkeeper caught her eye from across the room and nodded to her. Finishing up with his customer, he wiped his greasy hands on his broad apron front and hurried her way.

The innkeeper was a big man, loud voiced and exuberant, with a beefy face that matched his red hair and bushy eyebrows. Even though he dwarfed the small-boned Elana, making her look like a child in his presence, he was one of the few who treated her with respect, and she enjoyed his company.

2

"That foreign fellow had a letter for your father," he said, pulling it from his apron pocket. An intricate blue seal marked the back of the heavy rolled parchment. "I told him I'd pass it along. He seemed a bit dicey about leaving it with me." He shook his head, a scowl creasing the heavy brows. "Foreigners," he snorted, handing her the letter. "Well, you be sure and take it to him, lass."

"Thank you. I will." She grinned up at him.

He smiled back and pushed open the swinging door to the kitchen where the smell of fish and boiled cabbage escaped its steamy quarters and rolled into the common room, mixing with the acrid smell of the fireplace.

Only a year ago they were the 'foreigners' in the village. Madelyn and Hamilton, her parents, had at last gained a tentative welcome. Her mother's knowledge of herbs saved a little boy's life last winter, when the fever and cough which racked his body left him gasping for breath. After his recovery, the women were kinder to Madelyn, though never quite friendly. They still regarded Elana with suspicion, though.

Now, at least, at Farrell's inn they were all welcomed. Farrell was extravagant in his courtesy toward them, and the stocky sunburnt fishermen followed his lead. Elana grinned. She didn't believe Farrell did anything in half measures. They were fortunate to have gained his friendship.

Unfortunately, his influence didn't extend to the womenfolk. Elana knew that her black hair and eyes, pale skin, and sharp features marked her as an outsider as much as her mountain accent. Worse than all of that though, was her independence. She had neither the ability nor the disposition to tend the sick. In that she was more like Hamilton, her father. He had taught her to read, write, and cipher numbers. Her mind was quick and she excelled at the work. Spending her days at Farrell's inn, she also had the opportunity to hear much of the village news. She learned too late to keep her opinions on what she heard to herself. It was bad enough doing a man's job, but to presume to act their equal on their turf... Elana still felt the sting of the women's indignation.

In the market, the plump fishwives whispered as she passed, and their towheaded children hid behind their skirts, staring at her with round blue eyes. They called her 'the witch girl' when they thought she couldn't hear them, though they were hushed by their mothers at once.

Just last week an especially bold young fellow took advantage of his mother's turned back and stomped over to her. With a firm tug on her tunic he made his presence known. His dimpled finger beckoned her down.

"Why does mamma call you a witch?" he demanded.

There was no embarrassment in his solemn blue eyes, only an honest question. She didn't know whether to laugh or cry. She gave him the only answer she knew.

"Because I'm different," she told him.

"Are you a witch?" he asked her.

"No, honey," she'd said, seeing his face fall at her answer. "I'm not nearly that interesting."

Rallying from his disappointment, he turned and called out to his mother and big sister, "She's not a witch. I just asked her."

Later, she shared a good laugh over that one with her parents, but the fear on that mother's face still haunted her.

The other problem in the villagers' eyes was, of course, that she was unmarried. All the girls her age were married with a babe at the breast, or a toddler clinging to their skirts. She shuddered at the thought. She couldn't imagine the prospect of marriage, and the thought of children of her own now, was enough to send her into hiding. So she kept her distance, did her job, and tried to swallow the loneliness that caught in her throat whenever a group of young folk stopped by the inn, talking and laughing together.

The ever-present smell of fish tugged her thoughts back to the cramped common room, and she wrinkled her nose at its reek which clung to the premises. It wafted up from the clothes of the regulars, from their boots, from the nets they brought in to mend while sharing yarns over numerous glasses of ale, and, if that wasn't enough, it floated out from the kitchen, where fish; baked, boiled, or fried, made up the bulk of Farrell's simple menu.

Farrell, who had lost his own wife years ago, had turned away all suggestions of remarriage, choosing instead to take full command over his domain. There wasn't much by way of decoration, at the inn. Homespun curtains hung on the windows and the old tables were scrubbed and clean. He went for function, not frills. That didn't bother the regulars though. They presided over the bar, perched on their three legged stools like old sea birds, exchanging speculations on the spring fishing, what with the last storm and the strong tides. She glanced back at the door through which the innkeeper had just disappeared. The inn was the center of life in the village, and Farrell was the center of the inn.

The kitchen door swung open again and the big man bustled toward Elana with a bundle of scrolls in his arms, his eyebrows working up and down in frustration.

"Could I have you do something for me, lass?" His question was apologetic. "That fool of a boy, who's been keeping my records, has mixed up the accounts beyond my patience to unravel."

The corners of Elana's mouth twitched. When things were slow, her father had made himself useful by setting up a system for the innkeeper to keep track of his accounts. In this way, he was able to teach the big man to read and write without offending his pride. Though Farrell was competent with his letters, he had little love for figures. He was forever trying to pawn off the keeping of his ledgers onto the serving boys who worked at the inn, most of whom possessed only a dim understanding of numbers.

"I'd be glad to. Just leave them here with me. I'll try and get them sorted out before lunch." Elana patted the table in front of her.

He dropped the scrolls of parchment on the table and sighed with relief. "Thank you. Now I can finish getting lunch out before it's time to start cooking supper." Mopping the sweat from his reddened face, he turned back to the kitchen, whistling.

Elana unrolled the ledgers and sorted them by date, checking the figures and reworking them. The work came easily for her. Her father had taught her well. The clarity of the numbers offered refuge from the twists and turns of life here in the Vale.

She finished before lunch, double-checked her work and then carefully rolled up each of the scrolls. Looking outside she noticed the sun had finally peeked through the bank of clouds that hung over the village all morning. If she hurried, she could run the post rider's letter up to her father and be back for any business before the lunch crowd dispersed. She replaced the stopper in her inkpot, carefully rolled her own parchment around her quills, and fitted the whole bundle into a worn leather sack. She tucked the post rider's letter, with its deep blue wax seal and intricate marking, into her tunic pocket. Getting up from the table, she slipped through the kitchen to Farrell's room and returned the ledgers to their rightful home on the big man's table.

He caught her on her way back through the kitchen. "Hold there just a moment," he said, waving to her as he seasoned a huge pot bubbling over the open fire. "I've got something for you. Just a little thank you." He opened a door of a tall pantry, pulled out a small bag of dried tea leaves and pressed them into Elana's hand, grinning like a boy. "It's the least I can do. You know I'm useless when it comes to numbers. Don't know what I'd do without you and your father. Enjoy it lass."

"Thank you," she said, her eyes widening at the gift. Tea was a delicacy and she knew that her work wasn't worth its cost. It had been months since she'd had any. The usual fare was goat's milk or weak ale. On impulse, she gave the big man a hug, which turned his face a deeper shade of red.

"Off with you now," he said, his eyes crinkling with his wide smile.

Elana waved goodbye and slipped once more through the kitchen doors to the common room.

The clatter of hooves on the cobbled street outside caught her attention - a man on horseback riding fast up the South road into the village. Maybe another post rider? She didn't want to miss it if it was. She glanced at the sun almost at high noon, and then back down the street. She would wait and see.

The man pulled his horse up in front of the inn. He was definitely a stranger to these parts. The group of children whose game of tag had spilled onto the inn yard, stopped playing and gaped openly at his outlandish garb - high leather riding boots and a long, hooded, black cloak that billowed behind him as he walked, revealing a sword in a carved leather scabbard belted underneath.

Elana watched him with a growing sense of foreboding. Something about him made her skin prickle. She could feel his presence as strongly as if he were standing right in front of her, and worse, she could have sworn that he could somehow feel hers, though he wasn't even looking her way. She suddenly wished she hadn't waited.

The man pushed open the door to the inn and the feeling grew until Elana felt like he was pushing her. Her first instinct was to push back but a nudging from the back of her mind stayed her. If she acknowledged him, if she responded in any way at all, he would know she could sense him. That would give her away as an Elder Born. The hair on the back of her neck stood up. She wanted nothing more than to crawl under the table and hide. She turned away so that he couldn't meet her eyes and focused on the small talk of the regulars, which had resumed after a brief pause.

"Yep, wind's been out of the north. It'll be rough rest of the afternoon. Not good for much." The old man nodded sagely and took a long pull on his glass of ale.

"They say Orvis' building a proper rig. Some captain out of Bellport asked him to do it. How he knew to find Orvis here's more'n I can figure though."

The leisurely conversation rose and fell.

Elana listened, using all her will to hold her attention to their talk, not to let it stray back toward the stranger; to ignore the pull she felt from him to reveal herself. Slowly the intensity of the stranger's presence diminished. She couldn't help noticing that Farrell had come out to welcome the man and ask if he could help him. The stranger's full intent turned toward the innkeeper and he studied Farrell before speaking. Elana felt a little safer listening in.

"Has the post rider been by here today?" His voice was smooth, easy to listen to, but his pale blue eyes were cold, hard as iron.

"He has, my friend, but with only one letter and no news to speak of, sorry to say," Farrell replied.

"Was he out of Bellport?" the stranger asked in an offhanded way.

"I believe so. Had a letter for Hamilton, our scrivener."

Elana froze for a moment, afraid that he would point the stranger in her direction. Farrell looked over toward the back table briefly and then turned away, as if changing his mind. "He wasn't here today, so the rider's moved on. Hope you didn't need him to take anything for you?"

The stranger looked at the innkeeper for a moment as if at a loss, then continued.

"Actually, I did. Do you know where this Hamilton lives? I might be able to catch up with the rider and have him send this letter for me." He tapped his tunic pocket. "I've an errand inland and don't have time to be chasing around the countryside." His smile gave Elana another momentary chill.

Farrell answered him quickly; his voice low. The stranger paused as though weighing his words, then tilted his head to Farrell, turned and strode out of the inn, his cloak billowing behind him. To Elana's surprise, when he re-mounted his horse, a large clean boned bay, he headed west, inland - away from her home.

When he was gone, Farrell hurried over to her for the third time that morning. The big man looked shaken. "I don't know who that rider was, lass, but if he was up to any good, you can boil me for a fish in my own stew."

She waited for him to continue.

"He asked after the post rider and I spoke before thinking. Told him the letter was for your father. Sorry. Something in me was shoutin' a warning, but I didn't catch it in time. He wanted to know where to find him - I sent him off in the other direction."

He laid a heavy hand on her shoulder. "You'd best be off with that letter. I hope I bought you enough time to make up for my blunder. I don't know what this fellow's after, but if you need any help, anything at all, you come see me. We take care of our own here."

Tears stung Elana's eyes at the warmth of his declaration. "Thank you," she said. "You know we'd come to you if we needed anything. I hope trouble doesn't find you on our account."

Farrell gave her a hug and a wry grin. "Don't you worry about me. I know your family's special. The way I see it, we'd be a lot better off to have more like you around."

Elana stared up at him. He knew. He knew they were Elder Born. Most of the Valefolk hated or feared them if they suspected, and so they'd hid. For five years they'd traveled the Vale, keeping their identities concealed, pretending to be one of the Valefolk, letting nothing more unusual show than her father's learning and her mother's healing abilities, until Elana had grown to hate hiding. Yet there was nothing to be done about it - it was a matter of survival.

But Farrell knew and didn't hate them. The thought worked its way to her insides, warming as it went.

"Thank you, Farrell. Thank you so much." Dazed, she returned his hug, gathered her things and slipped out the door, her mind whirling as she pelted down the sandy track behind the inn, to the ocean.

The salt wind stung her face as she climbed over the dunes that fell away to the shore. She felt safer along the sea than on the road and took off running over the packed sand, scattering sandpipers and angry gulls who screamed their curses down on her. Around the first bend she spotted her family's cottage nestled in the dunes, well outside the boarders of the village. The neat herb gardens her mother labored over bloomed with new growth, and on the other side of the cottage the vegetable garden stood, its early spring shoots peeking from the thin sandy soil. No smoke curled out of the chimney. Her mother was helping Granny Betts this morning.

Elana slowed down, clutching a stitch in her side and panting. Out over the breakers, a line of gray pelicans glided silently in perfect formation, rising and falling just inches over the waves, scanning the water for fish. Her eyes followed them until they vanished in the distance. She continued to gaze after them, all her senses keen and straining.

Still elated from her conversation with Farrell, she let her mind drift as her eyes reached further out across the water and then it was there - her Waking. It came more often now and stronger, that strange tugging inside of her that surfaced for every Elder Born during the years they moved into adulthood. It meant that her Elder Skills were unfolding, ready for training. They came in a torrent during the Waking years, as though they had to break through some invisible boundary that lay across the last threshold of youth. Her Waking had been late, she was eighteen and it only started this Spring. She had been worried that she might not have the Elder Born Skills, though her parents assured her that she had nothing to fear, it was just that Elder Born came to maturity somewhat later than the Valefolk. But nothing her parents had shared prepared her for the longing, the hunger, the yearning toward something indefinable, that it brought. Had they still lived back in Farran, the Last Colony of the Elder Born, where Elana had grown up, she would be starting her training now but the danger of their discovery, living here, in the Vale made her father put it off a little longer.

Elana wondered how much longer she could wait; her Waking was growing and sometimes she felt like it would sweep her away. Today it called to her, irresistible, beckoning her on and blocking out everything else around her. It felt wilder than usual, almost dangerous, but still gloriously alive. For the first time she was a little bit afraid to follow the call. She hesitated for a moment, debating if this was really a part of her Waking or something else, something darker. A picture of the stranger from the inn flashed across her mind's eye. She shivered, pulling back into herself. And then it was gone - her Waking, the picture, the sweet aliveness.

Only a faint imprint remained, like a watermark on the sand. Elana stood empty, shaken. The sun warmed her hair and the wind stung her face with its salt spray, but she was numb to it all. She had lost it. That moment of hesitation was all it took and it was gone. She felt deflated, like the better part of herself had evaporated with it, into thin air.

After waiting a while more, fruitlessly willing it to return, she turned away from the ocean and continued at a walk along the packed sand. Training - she looked forward to it. It would be good to have some control over what was happening inside her. Sometimes with her Waking she felt as if someone was calling her name from far away; sometimes it felt as if she could hear things that were going on in other places though she never knew where, and sometimes she saw things - things that she couldn't explain and could only half understand. Though always, she wrestled with the sense she carried from birth, that she could know what others were thinking, feeling - and what their intentions were. That wasn't so bad as a child in Farran, but living in the Vale, it could get unpleasant.

She shivered at the thought and trudged on toward Orvis' cottage. What would someone do who was Elder Born and didn't know it, didn't know what was going on? Even knowing, she felt at times that she was going crazy. She had heard of those Elder Born who grew up in the Vale and tried to silence their Skills. Before this, she never understood why anyone would try to push away their Elder Skills. She allowed herself a rueful grin; she was beginning to understand.

Around an outcropping of rock, she caught sight of Orvis and her father putting the final touches on a sailboat. It was bigger than the one man vessels that populated these waters. Curious, she broke into a run and waved. The two men stopped working, put down their tools and greeted her. Her father gave her a quick hug; Orvis grunted a brusque hello. Elana, used to his rough manners, grinned at the old sailor.

"I suppose you'll be coming and keeping us from our work now, will you lass?" Orvis knit his brows and returned her grin with a scowl.

"Only if you feed me some lunch."

He studied her a moment, chewing on his lip. "A scrawny thing like you could use some fattening up." He turned to her father. "What do you say, Hamilton? Shall we feed her?"

Elana's father gave her an appraising look, then nodded. "I think we'd better. It'd be a pity for her to get faint and not be able to return to her duties this afternoon."

Elana laughed. "Farrell gave me a bag of tea leaves for sorting out his ledgers. I'll put some water on to boil." She left them to finish up, and climbed back up the dunes to Orvis' cottage.

The cottage door stood open. Salt fish hung on strings from the rafters, and a round goat cheese lay wrapped in a cloth on the table. The fire was almost out. Elana added pieces of driftwood from the neat pile in the corner and poked the embers to stir up the flames. The kettle, when she checked it, was already full, so she hung it back on the hook over the fire. From the corner cupboard she took out three flat wooden plates and three wooden cups, worn and stained by long use.

The water was just boiling when her father and Orvis joined her, stooping to enter through the low door. Orvis broke off pieces of the salted fish while her father unwrapped a coarse loaf that he'd brought from home. Elana cut chunks of goat's milk cheese with a fish knife, then poured a cup of tea for each of them.

"So what brings you up here, besides the hopes of a free lunch?" Orvis asked her after they sat down.

She finished chewing her mouthful of bread and cheese and turned to her father. "The post rider came to the inn today with a letter for you. Farrell said the man wasn't happy about leaving it with him and that I should deliver it." She pulled the letter out of her tunic and handed it to him.

His eyebrows went up when he saw the deep blue seal on the back. "Reeves," he said, giving Orvis a knowing look. "Do you mind?"

Orvis nodded his consent.

Elana's pulse quickened as her father broke the seal and unrolled the parchment. She studied his face as he read. Sometimes she could almost sense what he was thinking, but now she felt him closed off, guarded.

He finished and carefully re-rolled the letter.

She held her breath, wanting to be included in what was going on. She wasn't a child anymore. Her father looked over at her and smiled, and she had a suspicion that he could tell all that was going through her head.

"Yes, you are old enough to know. I won't keep this from you any longer."

Elana blushed.

He reached over and gave her hand a squeeze. "It's alright. Your Waking is growing so powerful; it's hard to block you out."

He took a deep breath, gathering his thoughts, then said, "Reeves has found something. He's been in Bellport for years, searching the old records for anything that would give a clue to the whereabouts of the Silver Bells. They were the last of the Vale Gifts to be lost. As head of the Bells Eldership, that was his main purpose in settling at Bellport."

Elana watched her father, his face taut, words measured. She remembered Reeves from years ago, before they left Farran - flaming red hair and green eyes, always making music. She liked him. Everyone liked him. She never knew that he was head of the Bells Eldership though. She was glad that he was. She couldn't imagine someone more fitting. This was good news, wasn't it?

He cleared his throat. "Let me read it to you:

Dear Hamilton,

I found a roll of records and letters older than any thus far. Can't say more. My search has not gone unnoticed. The Black Knights are swarming over Bellport and there are rumors they'll head up the coast. There's been more activity from them this month than in the past three years. Even whispers of the Hunters. I'm afraid you, Madelyn,

and Elana may not be safe. Not with Elana's Waking. Had a letter
from Geri. She said to remind you and Madelyn about the Prophesy:

The three will rise to reunite

When the Shadow's arm grows long,

Together push the darkness back:

The Key, the Seed, the Song.

She knows something more. I believe it's the time. If you can, meet
me in Bellport. I will try to stay a fortnight more to wait for you. If not,
get to Geri at Farran. I will meet you there.

Peace to you.

Reeves

PS. Marek is in town. Courteous but closed. I know your thoughts,
but he is not beyond help. I am afraid for him. His danger is much
greater.

Again,

R.

Elana's head swirled. It felt like pieces of the old stories were coming
to life right in front of her, but what did it all mean? She looked up to
find her father's steady brown eyes on her. She didn't know what to
say. Words crowded together in her head. Then the other strange
events of her morning came rushing back as well.

"The post rider wasn't the only one to come to the inn." She told
them about the rider from the South, about his interest in her father's
whereabouts and Farrell's putting him on the wrong track.

Elana remembered the feeling that this man could somehow sense her
being there, or was trying to bait her into exposing herself to him. She
hesitated a moment, not wanting to sound cowardly, but decided that
it would be better to tell and look foolish than not, and regret it.

Quickly, before embarrassment stopped her, she told them about the uncanny pressing she felt coming from the man. She tried to keep the quaver out of her voice.

Her father and Orvis exchanged frowns.

"We have to move fast," her father said. "You did the right thing, Elana, by not rising to his bait. Had you pushed back at him, you would have revealed yourself at once. He feels your presence, but hopefully, he hasn't identified where it's coming from." Her father gave her a smile. "You did better today than many trained Elder Born might have done. I'm proud of you."

She looked at her father, afraid to ask the question that was pounding in her head.

His face was sober as he answered her unspoken thoughts. "Yes, the man was a Hunter. We have to leave as soon as possible. I think Farrell has bought us enough time to make some preparations."

Farrell. She'd almost forgotten. "Farrell knows about us. He said something about knowing we were in danger and wishing there were more like us around. He said he'd help in any way he could."

Her father nodded. "He's a good man, a leader with vision, the kind of man folks want to follow. I'm proud to call him a friend."

They sat for a moment, the lunch half-eaten, each lost in their own thoughts, then Orvis scraped his chair back from the table.

"No sense wastin' precious time. Hamilton, you make for Reeves in Bellport. Madelyn and Elana can stay here for now. I'll take them back to Farran."

Elana turned to him and nodded slowly. She'd known he was different from the other villagers, and had suspected that he might be Elder Born, but he was such an odd fellow, she never knew just how far she could trust her intuition about him.

A slow smile creased his wrinkled face. "Yes, lass. I'm Elder Born. Spent most of my life hiding it, but not any more. Not since your father came here. And it's been years now I've wanted to pick up and find Farran. My, well, my sister of sorts, Brenna, she had the Skills as well and left here twenty years ago for Farran. Hamilton tells me that she's been there many a year and thrivin'." Orvis' voice grew husky. "I'd like to see her again before my time comes. She was the saving of me when I was young and reckless."

Elana forgot her own worry as this news settled itself in her mind. She'd always felt safe with him, always trusted him instinctively, and never questioned that her parents let him into their confidence. He just felt like family. It had been so long since they'd been around others who were Elder Born, she hadn't let herself believe the signs that were in front of her. She felt the knot that had been tightening in her stomach unclench. It would be okay. Orvis would be with them, too.

She glanced at her father and saw that he was smiling at Orvis. "Thank you. You know I couldn't ask this of you. But neither can I refuse the offer. I am in your debt."

"No you're not. It's just time. You know it too." Orvis' voice was gruff, but Elana heard a catch in it.

They finished eating. She cleaned up the lunch things while her father and Orvis packed their tools. Her father decided against sending her back to the inn. With a Hunter about, they didn't want to risk another meeting. Orvis said that he'd go tell Farrell what was happening and see if he could find Hamilton passage to Bellport - call in on a favor from one of the local fishermen.

Elana and her father headed back to their cottage to begin packing. As they walked back down the beach, she asked him about her Waking. She told him what had happened on the way to Orvis' cottage and that the feelings were getting stronger. "Isn't it time for me to start my training?"

"It is, Elana. We would have started within the month, but now I'm afraid that it's going to have to wait a bit more."

She grimaced. "What do I do with all... this, then?" She waved her hands about, at a loss for words to describe the strange flood of perception.

16

Her father was silent for a while and Elana wondered if he had heard her question. Finally, he said, "Your mother and I hadn't said anything to you. There's been no need. But I think you should know something. Your Skills are stronger than any we've ever seen." He watched her face as she took this in. "I don't want to frighten you, but I am relieved that Geri has called us back to Farran. It's too dangerous for you to be out here during your Waking. Not with a Hunter around."

He paused, shook his head and then continued. "I don't understand it. For generations the Elders have watched their Skills dwindle, ever since the Betrayal. We don't usually speak of it, but there's no sense in hiding from the truth. Since the Ancient Ones' Gifts were lost to us, we have diminished. That is, until recently. Geri's power is akin to what the Skills looked like of old, and she says there are others as well. Darian's son - I met him when he was just a small boy. He's only a few years older than you are, and the Elder's power runs strong in him, too. I haven't seen him since Darian's death, so I don't know how his Waking went, or even where he is. Geri counseled his mother to take him into hiding. Reeves has hinted about another lad, also in hiding. I've never met him. And you…" He paused, pondering the idea, then turned to Elana with a sparkle back in his eye. "The Prophesy… Maybe it is time. I believe that Geri is on to something." He gave her a quick hug then lengthened his stride so that she had to jog to keep up.

That night Elana helped her mother pack clothes and food for their journey back to Farran. Her father had gone to the village to speak with Farrell about his ride to Bellport. They agreed that he would head off the following evening after seeing Madelyn and Elana safely to Orvis' cottage. Elana could feel the excitement in the air as they packed. She could almost forget that they were in any danger as the joy of returning to Farran washed over her.

Her mother stopped and kissed her lightly on the top of her head. "I know you're excited about going. I am, too. You've born it bravely,

Elana, living here in the Vale. It hasn't been easy for you. I'm glad we get to go home for your Waking."

She gave her mother a hug. Madelyn rarely spoke of the difficulties of Vale life but her eyes shone now with a brightness that Elana hadn't seen for years. They worked side by side, wrapping the herbs and infusions for her mother's medicine bag. Elana packed her quills and ink bottle along with the parchment that she had saved up. When they finished, Madelyn put a kettle of water up to boil and the two of them stepped out onto the dunes to watch the moon rise over the ocean.

With the sun down, the air chilled Elana and she slipped her arm through her mother's, sharing her warmth as they watched the ocean. Her thoughts swirled and she gave her mother a sideways glance.

"You're about to burst. What is it?" Her mother gave her arm a squeeze and turned to face her.

Elana didn't know where to start. One thing though, kept coming back to her. She blurted it out. "Reeves' letter spoke of a Prophesy and Father said that it might be time. Time for what?"

Her mother didn't reply for a moment. When she spoke, her voice was so low that Elana had to lean into her to catch her words.

"For the three Vale Gifts to be restored."

Elana stared at her. Was she serious? But that was impossible. The Vale Gifts - each the charge of one of the three Elderships, the Firestone, the Orchard Tree, and the Silver Bells - were dead, or lost for years beyond count.

"I thought that was just granny's tales - that they could all be restored." Her words tumbled out. "I know Reeves was looking for evidence of the Silver Bells being taken down, but I thought that was just to prove that they were ever there at all."

Madelyn sighed. "Sometimes truth is best remembered by the simple." She continued, "Even most of the Elders don't really believe it anymore. But a handful do."

"I don't understand."

"It was the Vale Gifts that kept the Shadow King out of the Vale, and only their restoration can save it now. Everything else can, at best, only postpone the inevitable." Her mother's voice grew stronger as she intoned the words of the Prophesy.

The three will rise to reunite

When the Shadow's arm grows long,

Together push the darkness back:

The Key, the Seed, the Song.

Elana felt a chill go through her, but not a dark chill like with the stranger at the inn. It was a whisper of promise that tingled through her entire body.

Her mother looked at her and nodded. "You feel it too, don't you? The Prophesy was set to song generations ago. What I told you is only the refrain. That's all that I know by heart. The rest of the song talks about the Bronze Key unlocking the hidden Firestone and a Seed from the Orchard Tree sprouting and growing to new life, and a song played on the Lady's Flute laying bare the deceits of the enemy and revealing the concealed Bells."

Elana listened to her mother and the longing and ache that marked her Waking stirred up in her again. She didn't interrupt for fear of stopping her.

Her mother continued. "Geri believes that the time is close. She shared it with a few of us in Farran before we left for the Vale. She has been leader of the Firestone Elders for many years now. I believe she knows much more than she lets on."

"And the Shadow King?" Elana's question hung half formed in the air. He was part of those old tales as well and Elana has always assumed that his relevance was limited to a historical anecdote.

"Unfortunately, he's real too," her mother answered. "The Hunters are his most feared servants - Elders lured into his service and turned dark, whose powers are augmented by his own - scouring the Vale for any Elder Born and turning them to his dark purposes, or else, if they refuse, killing them."

Elana shuddered. "But why do they go after the Elder Born?"

"The Shadow King knows that the Vale Gifts have been lost but not destroyed. From what we can tell, he is reading the signs and he too, knows the Prophecy. He seeks to destroy the Elders or turn their power to his own use, thus rendering the Vale Gifts useless to the Vale. Without the Elders to unlock them, the Vale Gifts are as good as destroyed - the result is the same. Then he will assault the Vale unchallenged. None will be able to stand against him."

Elana felt as if her world was tilting. She knew there was unrest throughout the Vale, and that her parents had left the safety of Farran to help the Valefolk, but she never realized the extent of the danger. She looked around half expecting a cloaked and booted Hunter to jump out from behind the bank of sea oats waving in the night breeze.

Her mother smoothed her hair and gave her a hug. "It's good that we're going back. We need to get you there soon. Your Waking isn't going to wait much longer."

They turned and walked hand-in-hand back to the cottage. The waning moon had just risen, huge and orange, hovering over the waves and sending tall pale shadows on before them. In the cottage, the water was boiling and Madelyn poured the remainder of the tea for them both. Elana lit an oil lamp and they sat around the small, round table sipping their tea.

There in the safety of their cottage, with the night shut out behind the curtains, it wasn't as alarming to think about what her mother said. She didn't know much about the Gifts, and found her thoughts returning to them. How could they be restored? Where would one look for them? She didn't say anything to her mother, but a wild notion had begun to play in her mind. Maybe she could help find them - her father said that the Elder power ran strong in her, maybe she could help bring them back...

"Could you tell me the story of the Vale Gifts being lost?" Elana asked her mother. She had heard it before, but it was one of those least repeated and she didn't yet know it by heart. To be truthful, she had believed it less than any of the others. Until now. Now it seemed crucial and she berated herself for not having committed it to memory.

"Okay," her mother said, "but that's all. Then we need to sleep.

Her mother's voice was smooth and to Elana's ears, almost sad as she recounted the story:

Long generations ago, a hunger for power crept in among the three Elderships. Some say that the Shadow King planted men in their midst, to corrupt the hearts of the Elders, but this has never been proved. Bannock the Proud, head of the Orchard Tree Eldership, gathered his nine brothers. Together, they laid siege to Laharan, city of the Firestone Eldership, seeking to capture the Book of Greening. That Book, rich in wisdom and power, contained records of all that the Ancient Ones did and said to the Elders in the age of the Waking of the Vale. Fiarella, head of the Firestone Eldership begged help from Valland the Eldest, head of the Bells Eldership. He came to her aid and in that conflict, Banock died.

Banock rode not to his own death only, but to the death of all that his Eldership had labored for on behalf of the Vale. On that day the Orchard Tree, Vale Gift of the Ancient Ones, for the blessing of plenty from the earth, for artistry, craftsmanship and the fruitful labor of people's hands, withered and died.

His youngest son, Baldor, who was peace-loving, took the last fruit of the tree, placed it in a golden box and fled. No one from the Orchard Tree Eldership ever saw Baldor again. Most believed he died in the Shadow Mountains. The box was lost.

With the Orchard Tree dead, the valley grew less fertile. The Ancient Ones gave the three Vale Gifts: the Firestone, the Orchard Tree and the Silver Bells, to work together for the blessing of the Vale. Without the Orchard Tree, the virtue of the Firestone and the Silver Bells diminished. When Fiarella died, the Book of Greening and the keeping of the Firestone passed to her daughter, Evana.

Her mother paused, looking at the dying fire. Elana felt her chest grow tight with a sadness that she'd never known before. It shouldn't have been like this. She watched the embers in the dying fire flicker, waiting for her mother to finish. Finally, her mother sighed and continued:

Evana counseled with Valland, the eldest, and they resolved to lock up the Firestone, talisman of power, wisdom and insight - fearing that it would become a source of contention. So they locked it up in Laharan, city of the Firestone, and by their arts concealed it. Evana and the Firestone Elders left Laharan and settled in the high hills of the Border Mountains. They rarely mingled with the Valefolk and no longer searched among them for those with the latent Skills of an Elder. With their removal to the Border Mountains, written language became a dying art and much history was lost. Superstition crept in where wisdom once held sway and so gradually, there was the Forgetting.

Within two generations, the Bells Eldership was scattered, the Silver Bells, heralds of joy, celebration and song, were stolen from the Bell Tower and lost to all record. With their parting, the last of the Ancient Ones' Vale Gifts were gone. Life in the Vale grew bleak. People struggled to eke out a living from the land and the sea, and their hearts as well as their hands, hardened.

Her mother stopped. "That is as far as it goes and it's not a happy story," she shook her head as if trying to clear her own thoughts, "but the end has yet to be told."

The fire was almost out. Madelyn yawned and stretched, pushing back from the table. "I'm done for tonight, sweetheart. We've got a big day tomorrow."

Elana gave her mother a hug goodnight and went to her small bed in the alcove at the back of the cottage. She curled up under the worn quilt, tossing and turning, unable to keep the questions from spinning in her head.

The story haunted her. To her thinking, it left way too much out; she wanted to know more. But it was more than that. Hearing the story sparked her Waking again. She lay in bed trying to stifle herself. The yearning and pull that accompanied her Waking felt almost painful. It seemed hours before sleep overtook her.

22

CHAPTER 2

FLIGHT TO BELLPORT

Moonlight snuck through the cracks of the shutters, pale and thin in the pre-dawn, outlining the edge of Elana's bed. She rolled over and blinked, trying to orient herself. At some point late in the night, like a dream, her father had returned home. Elana recalled her parent's whispered conversation, trying not to wake her. Now she was fully awake; the cottage silent except for the ever present pounding from the waves outside. Elana reached up and pushed open the shutters. Judging by the moon framed low through her window, it was still a good hour until sunrise.

She sat up, yawned and stretched, and tiptoed to her dresser, carefully working open the stuck drawers. Grabbing an old pair of trousers and an embroidered tunic that her mother made her for traveling, she slipped out of her nightgown and into the chilly clothes. Crawling up onto the window ledge, she threw her legs over the sill and dropped to the ground. Her feet ached in the cold sand. She followed the narrow trail by memory, down to the sea.

Elana climbed up the dunes, through sea oats taller than her head and out onto the beach. Goose bumps rose up on her arms at the damp breeze and sticky salt clung to her skin and hair. No stars lit the sky, only the waning moon shone fitfully through the mounting clouds, reflecting a dull yellow across the dunes and onto the surface of the growling ocean.

Her mind returned to the story of the lost Vale Gifts. It had haunted her dreams all night, crisscrossing through them, tracking her like a hound. She couldn't shake it.

When she reached the water, she turned north and started walking - her bare feet slapping out a rhythm on the wet sand while her mind mulled over the pieces she heard yesterday.

Geri said it was time - her father spoke of the Elders' power renewing, like in the days of the Greening.

Her steps quickened, the blood rose to her face - she was one, and Geri, and others - a boy, and young man, only a few years older than herself.

Maybe... her face grew hot at the thought, but she had too much momentum to stop now - maybe she was one of the ones to find the Vale Gifts?

Again, the tingling ran through her body and she did a little dance right there on the sand. Why not? Certainly, she'd need training first, to be able to control her Elder Skills, but then...

Her mind flitted over images of Geri honoring her in front of the entire Elder Colony, of people looking at her with awe and respect, of her parents smiling proudly from the side. No more mistaking her for a child and having to hide who she was - she was now the one people turned to for advice, for wisdom. She'd had to hide her identity for so long...

She stopped, and threw her hands wide toward the ocean. The wind kicked up as if in answer, blowing her hair back from her face and taking her breath away. Her Waking surged and she felt like a beacon shining on the beach. She could hear her name in the wind, "Elana, Elana, Elana," whispered over and over.

For a moment she saw a picture of Geri, standing alone on a mountainside, arms outstretched and then it shifted to a young man, looking out a window, listening to hooves pounding past outside, his fists clenched, jaw set. It shifted again and her parents were riding on horses in a band of men, galloping hard.

The visions faded and Elana stood, bracing herself against the wind, her heart hammering in her chest. She had never before seen things that clearly during her Waking. The visions, the surge of her Waking, seemed to converge, to affirm the hope that she was the one to find the Vale Gifts. She threw back her head and laughed aloud.

She wanted this more than she'd ever wanted anything. Her Waking coursed through her again. Her whole body shook with the power of it. She felt huge, like she could stride out over the rising waves, or spread her arms and fly. Without thinking, she raised her arms to the sky again, a light shining in the dark night, undiminished by the gathering storm.

The wind continued to rise, chasing the thick clouds in from the sea. Elana pressed against it, felt herself become part of it, riding its fierceness over the waves and then, like a deer senses the arrow in the moment before the kill, she felt it - a presence pressing back, the same one from yesterday afternoon - the stranger from the inn.

She gasped and froze. It couldn't be. Fear pierced her, knocking her off balance. Disoriented, the energy of her Waking ran wild and unchecked through her.

The roaring of the wind and pounding waves now whipped that fear into a frenzy. Spinning around, she cast a wild look up and down the beach, expecting a man in a black cloak to come striding out of the darkness toward her. The pressing remained and though her eyes couldn't make out anything, she didn't trust the waving sea grass not to hide a sinister form.

Too afraid to check further, she took off running toward the cottage, unseen horrors closing in, making her legs weak as she ploughed through the damp sand.

So stupid... how could I forget... supposed to hide...

The visions of glory were foolish now - vanity. How could she do this? Her breath came in gasps and she threw glances over her shoulder, half imagining the cloaked man in pursuit.

By the time she reached the dunes in front of their cottage, the surf crashed its rage onto the shore. Lightening forked down over the ocean giving Elana a momentary glimpse of the grasses waving in the thick darkness under the roiling clouds. Another bolt of lightening struck close - thunder cracking with the blue-white blaze. The hairs on the back of her neck prickled at the charge. Stumbling back from the spot, she struggled up the dunes, the wind grinding sand into her teeth, her eyes, lashing her hair across her face. The sky opened up and great sheets of rain swept down, making it all but impossible to see where she was going. She pushed her way thought the sea oats and topped the dunes, her hands and feet cut, bleeding from the sharp grasses. Her stomach felt like it had rocks in it, and for a moment she wondered if she was going to be sick.

She didn't know if she imagined it, but she thought she heard voices yelling on the wind. Another bolt of lightening flashed and she saw the cottage. Outside, milling in the vegetable gardens, were three horses and a man holding them. She heard pottery shatter inside, and before she could think what to do, her father's voice sounded clear in her mind.

"Get to Orvis!"

She jumped, whirled around looking for him, but she was alone on the dunes. Where had his voice come from? Lightening flashed again, striking the cottage this time. The thatched roof burst into flames. Elana screamed and lunged toward the cottage.

Just as she reached the gardens, the door flung open and two men ran out dragging her parents with them. Her father, hands bound, was bleeding from a knife cut on his face, and her mother appeared unconscious.

Her father shot a quick look at the place where she stood, his eyes blazing. "Go, NOW!" His voice sounded in her head again and Elana dropped to the ground and crawled back into the sea grass.

The man dragging him away paused for a moment and looked toward where Elana hid.

It was the Hunter.

She clapped both hands over her mouth, stopping a scream, and lay barely breathing, praying that the rain and the dark would cover her. The stranger waited a moment and she could feel that same pressing again. She willed herself to be invisible to him, to let no sign of her presence answer. Her heart beat in her throat and she tried to focus on anything but him and her parents. After what seemed an eternity, he turned back and dragged her father to his horse. The men slung her parents onto the saddles in front of them and without looking back, galloped off.

Elana crawled back out from the dunes her whole body shaking. She lay in the trampled garden, blinded by the rain and her tears, unable to move, with only one thought drumming through her head.

They were gone.

Her temples throbbed and pounded and the ground seemed to tilt. She scrambled to her knees as her stomach heaved its acids onto the broken earth. When it finally stopped, she sat back on the remains of her mother's vegetables, not trusting her legs to hold her.

Rain mingled with her tears, blurring her vision as she took in the smoldering cottage - a ruined wreck, smoking and hissing in the storm. Lightening flashed farther away, but she no longer heard it.

The storm blew inland. Behind her, over the sea, the rising sun broke through the clouds, blood red and huge along the horizon. It cast an eerie, unnatural light. The rain trailed off to a sprinkle and the winds died down.

Elana couldn't bring herself to go into the cottage. She couldn't face it. She forced herself to her feet, still shaking, and followed the path back over the dunes. Her father had told her to get to Orvis. She was sure it was him, though she still didn't have any idea how he spoke to her from inside the cottage. It didn't matter now. She had to find Orvis. She took a deep breath to steady herself, holding the queasiness in her stomach at bay. She didn't want to be sick again. Her mind felt numb. She couldn't think, couldn't figure.

Stumbling along the beach in a daze she let her feet carry her to Orvis' cottage, unaware of the morning breaking through around her, of the sand pipers gathering along the shore to hunt their breakfast of tiny clams in the wet sand. The last of the clouds blew away inland by the time she reached the cottage, leaving the sky a soft pink, but she barely noticed. It felt like someone else was walking in her body.

Orvis was climbing up from the beach with a stringer of fish in his hand when he saw her.

"Elana!" His voice sounded sharp, worried in the crisp morning air. "What happened? Are you alright?"

She shook her head, unable to form words, wanting only for it all to go away. Let it all be a bad dream. Let me wake up safe in my bed, in our cottage.

Orvis dropped the fish and ran to her. His strength hadn't diminished with age. He caught her just as she fell to her knees, unable to walk any further.

"What happened? Where are your parents?"

Like an outside observer, Elana watched him, noting how fear added a bite to his already gruff voice, and that his grip hurt her arms. She still couldn't find words.

"It's okay lass. Let's get you up to the cottage and we can sort everything out."

Leaving the fish on the beach, he scooped her up as though she were a child, carried her to the cottage and set her down in one of the old chairs.

Safe inside the cottage the words came tumbling out. "My parents - they took them, just now - the Hunter, three men, horses - they're gone!" Tears washed down Elana's dirt streaked face. "We have to find them - we have to get them back!"

Orvis gripped her shoulders, looked fiercely into her eyes, and let out a string of expletives that Elana had never used before. "What happened? You have to tell me everything, everything you can remember."

She took a long shuddering breath, trying to clear her mind. "I woke up this morning, it was still early." Her voice shook. "I snuck out, down to the beach before dawn. I do that a lot with my Waking. It was the story my mother told me last night, about the Lost Vale Gifts. I couldn't let it go and I got to thinking about it and thinking..." She broke off. She couldn't admit what she was imagining. "I was thinking about the story and my Waking sparked up, stronger than ever."

28

"Then I felt it, the same presence I felt at the inn and I was scared that the Hunter was there and would find me. I ran back home, but the storm broke out. When I got there, men and horses were there and they took my parents. I saw him - the Hunter. He had my father, but he didn't see me, though he was feeling for me with his presence. My father spoke in my head - I'm not crazy, Orvis, really. I heard him."

Orvis had started at this piece of information.

"He said to get to you. And he told me to hide. Lightening struck the cottage and it started burning. They took my parents and rode off." Elana stopped talking. She had gotten it out. She sat staring down, not wanting to meet the accusation she would surely find in the older man's eyes. She hadn't been able to help them. Worse than that, the thought that kept creeping back in - she'd let her Waking flow unchecked on the beach. What if that is what gave them away?

"They're gone," she whispered. "What am I going to do? Will the Hunters..." She couldn't bring herself to finish the statement.

Orvis' face clouded and he shook his head. "I won't lie to you. It's not good, but they're strong and you're here and there's two reasons to hope. Let me think a minute." He looked out the open cottage door to the sea and for a while was silent, lost in thought. Elana shifted, restless, wanting to be off, to chase after the men, not sit here talking.

After what seemed like forever, he turned back to her. "I wish I'd paid more attention to this Elder stuff when I was young, I might be more help now. But we've got to work with what we have. Your father was heading to Bellport to meet Reeves. That's a shorter journey than to Farran. Especially by sea. And less chance of unwanted company." A fierce grin flashed across his face and then was gone. "That's one thing I do know. And Reeves will know how to help your parents. If anyone can, it's him."

"That will take too long! By then..." Elana got up and started pacing around the cottage.

"Hold tight there lass. You're forgetting something. Those Hunters aren't after your parents. You're the one they're tracking."

She spun around and stared at him. "Me? Why?"

"I felt you out there this morning, gal. Your Waking's about the most powerful thing I've ever been around. It was like you were some lighthouse shining on the beach and I couldn't even see you my own self, just sense you there, if you know what I mean."

"You could feel me out there?"

"Lass, it would have been hard to miss you." His blue eyes bored into her and it felt as if he'd poured cold water over her. Her legs felt like jelly again. So it was true, she had drawn them.

"They know something's special about you. Your parents know it too. That's why they brought you to this forsaken place for your Waking - hoping to hide you from those who could feel it." He stuck a finger in her face and shook it. "You chase after them and you walk right into their trap."

She stared at him, uncomprehending.

"You gave them the slip this morning lass, but they'll use your parents for bait, lure you out after them. I don't believe they'll kill them with you still at large. It'd be stupid and they're not stupid.

"But how can I help? We have to save them!" Her throat tightened, making it hard to speak.

"We sail for Bellport. Today. You can't help them alone. We've got to find Reeves. Until then we have to do everything we can to keep you out of the Hunters' grip. I wouldn't give a brass coin for you parents' lives if the Hunters got their hands on you."

Orvis paced the floor. "I don't think it's safe to go back to your cottage, they'll be watching it." He studied her for a moment. "How do you feel about being a boy?"

"What?" Her mind was numb, making no sense of the question. Nothing seemed to matter anymore. Her parents were gone and it was her fault.

"You'll be safer traveling as a boy. I'll have to cut off your hair. It's a shame, but I don't see any way around it. You're small, so I'm hoping you can pass for a younger lad, maybe twelve or so. I've got some old clothes that might fit."

She could feel him grasping for something to do - some plan of action that would engage her, pull her mind back from the brink of despair. From a place that felt leagues outside of her, she loved him for it, though his choice of activities revealed how little he understood of females. He rummaged through an ancient chest and fished out a pair of sewing scissors. "Let's have a go at that hair. I hate to do it to you, so we'll get it over with quick."

Some more rummaging produced a comb, which from the looks of his own hair, hadn't seen much use.

Elana took it and automatically tugged through her tangled mass of long black hair. It reached to her waist and though she wasn't much for girl stuff, she was proud of it. Most of the Valefolk had fair or red hair, and she knew that her long black hair framing her pale skin was striking. She let out a small sigh. At another time she would have mourned its loss, but now it didn't matter.

Orvis picked up the scissors and started cutting at her shoulders, the thick hair dropping to the floor of the cottage. When he was done he frowned at her. "You're too damn pretty, that's what. You still look like a girl. Though not like any from around here. Let me get you some fisherman's clothes." He disappeared out the door and she heard him dragging something heavy back to the cottage.

"Used to be Brenna's," he said in response to the question on her face. "She would never abide by the rules. Knew the sea better than any man on the coast and went where she pleased, when she pleased. She was a little bit of a thing too, when she was younger. Don't know about now, of course."

He pried the lid off, revealing a jumble of assorted odds and ends - folded clothes, old fishing nets, some cracked and brittle boots, a roll of parchment tied with a blue ribbon, a tea pot, and other things peeking out from below, that Elana couldn't make out.

"She said she didn't need it when she left and I didn't have the heart to throw it out. Didn't make sense to keep it around though. I just boxed it up and kept it in the goat shed." He shook out a worn, hooded cloak, dyed indigo under layers of accumulated dirt.

"This should help some." He threw the cloak around her shoulders and pulled the hood up over her face. "There. Now for the rest." He shuffled through the clothes, coming up with two woolen fisherman's tunics, belted, with large outside pockets and the sail cloth half-trousers worn by all the men in the village. "I'll step outside. Try these on and see if they work."

Elana waited until Orvis was out of sight and then laid the clothes on the table. These were Brenna's. For the first time since the events of the morning she felt a brief stirring of her Waking as she tried to feel who this woman was. She hadn't heard of her before yesterday and for some reason she was drawn to the thought of her. Maybe she would get to meet her when they reached Farran.

She peeled off her own soaking trousers and tunic, which though unusual for a girl, were not cut in a boy's style. Tears burned her eyes as her fingers traced over the embroidered flowers that her mother had sewn - sweet pea and morning glory vines crawling up the front and over the sleeves. She hated to leave it, this last tangible contact with her parents, and laid it out to dry, hoping she could stuff it in her sack.

Brenna's clothes were still too big for her, but passable with one of the old boot laces wrapped around her waist to hold the trousers up. She took the other lace and tied her hair back into the low ponytail that apprentice boys wore, hoping that this would be an acceptable disguise.

Her mind flitted back to the Hunter. If only she could hide her Waking as easily as she could hide her gender. She stepped out of the cottage, willing herself to walk, to think, and waved to Orvis who was collecting the stringer of fish from the beach.

"How is it?" she called out to him.

He looked her over. "It'll do. You'll just have to keep you mouth shut. As soon as you open it, you'll spoil the whole thing."

Elana smiled at him, grateful for his efforts to cheer her, pressed her lips together in an exaggerated mime of silence and turned back to the cottage.

Packing took up the rest of the morning, and most of the afternoon, and Elana threw herself into the work. At least it was something she could do. She dug through Orvis' things, pulling out blankets for both of them, cooking pots, clothes and cloaks. Goat cheese and dried fish made up the majority of their food. She emptied the flour barrel and baked the last of the flour into flat loaves which she wrapped in serviceably clean towels. These would go on the tops of the packs, so they didn't crumble.

She was sure she would forget something important; her mother was always the one to pack for their travels and organization came easily for her, unlike Elana. Stepping back she cataloged the items before her, mentally checking and rechecking for omissions.

By late afternoon she was itching to be off. Hope that her parents wouldn't be killed as long as the Hunters thought they could lead them to her, gave her strength to keep going, and meaning and purpose to her activity. She would be out of their reach on the open sea.

The sun was sinking over the fields and woods inland when at last Orvis joined her, announcing that they'd take the sailboat he'd been making for the Captain in Bellport; it was seaworthy and he could get gold for it at delivery to help them make their journey. He'd worked all day getting it ready and now it was time, the tide had turned and they were leaving with it. He grilled her about the contents of each pack, nodding with approval at her efficiency, and brushed away her apologies for the state of his cottage.

"Ain't mine no more, I reckon," he answered. "Sometimes I'd get to thinking I'd stayed here too long, but now..." he let his sentence drop off. Turning away, he dug back through Brenna's trunk, and with surprising tenderness lifted out what looked to Elana to be a tarnished and dented old flute. She looked at him in surprise, he'd never struck her as the musical type.

"It was Brenna's," he said in answer to the unspoken question. "And Lars' before that, her father - like a father to me too. They both played it. She left it with me when she went, said something about my needing it more than her. Can't imagine why, seeing as how I've never played a note in my life, but I just can't bear to leave it behind. Maybe I'll get a chance to return it to her." His keen blue eyes softened for a moment and he placed his leathery hands on the equally worn instrument, covering the holes with awkward fingers.

Elana flushed and looked away, feeling like an intruder. She'd never imagined Orvis having a life beyond this cottage, in fact there was a lot she didn't know about him. She felt a momentary pang of nervousness - he was the only one in the world she had to turn to, and they didn't actually know each other that well. He was a friend of her father's, only peripherally in her world, until now. She ventured another glance and the nervousness evaporated. He was still wrapped in thought or memory. The years, and the roughness they brought, melted off his face.

Setting the flute down quietly, he looked past her for a moment as if he needed to give his mind time to come back to the here and now. "Sorry lass," he said. "It's been many a winter since I took that out."

He finished up the packing, throwing odds and ends that Elana forgot, into their packs and started carrying them to the boat. She picked up her pack and staggered a little under the weight of it, glad that they had the first leg of the journey by sea. She would have to be a bit more selective if they headed out from Bellport on foot.

Orvis fetched the nanny goat from the shed and half pulled, half carried her onto the boat. She looked none too pleased at the prospect of riding in that thing and Elana couldn't help but wondering if she wouldn't just jump out when they got started but Orvis tied her to the bow, and loaded the rest of their belongings inside.

"I'll need your help getting her out off the sand," he grunted, throwing his weight against the boat which scraped along the bottom in the receding tide. Elana pushed alongside him, straining and slipping on the wet sand until the boat jolted free. Elana fell forward and landed on her hands and knees in the salt water, soaking her tunic and trousers. Orvis laughed, the first laughter she heard that day. It sounded good.

"Hop in the boat there and find you some dry clothes to change into. I'll wait out here 'till you're through. It'll be chilly enough tonight without being soaked."

Elana scrambled in and pulled out the only change of clothes in her pack. Hunkering down below the seat she peeled off the wet clothes and scooted into the dry ones, fending off the goat who was trying all the while to eat her hair or her clothes or anything else she could reach. When she stood up and called to Orvis, he met her eyes with a twinkle.

"Don't worry about it. Happens to the best of us. You've got other Skills than the sea, lass. No one can do everything."

"Thanks." She guessed he was holding back more laughter. Oh well, she thought, at least we've started.

The old sailor swung lightly into the boat and manned the oars until they'd gone out past the breakers. He raised the sails while Elana laid her clothes to dry, out of reach of the goat. Silence filled the night, broken only by the slap of waves against the hull. Orange and red streaks still tinged the western horizon, but as she looked east the sky turned from velvety blue, to blue-black, to black, punctured only by white stars winking over the waves. The breeze carried the promise of a cold night. Elana pulled the cloak out of her sack and wrapped it around her.

She was too keyed up to eat so she just sat and watched the shore slip over the horizon. When it had vanished from sight she turned her gaze to Orvis. His white hair stood out in the starlight like a halo around his head and she realized that out here he seemed different. Her father had spoken of his Skill at sea and she knew it was legend in the village, but none of that prepared her for the change that came over him. The best she could describe it, she decided, was like how she felt this morning on the beach - like she was lit up and shining and powerful. He looked that way to her now, a part of the sea and the waves and the huge night sky.

When he sat back down, apparently satisfied with their course, she asked him about it. "Orvis," she began tentatively, not knowing how to phrase her question, "do you use your Elder Skill out at sea?"

He looked over at her, his eyes aglow and she realized that she had only seen a shadow of him until now. "Yes, lass. That's where my Skill always showed up strongest, since I was just a lad. Uncanny, people called it and I left home younger than you to get away from those who didn't trust what they couldn't understand. None of my people had it. I didn't know anyone who did until I met Lars and Brenna. Thought I was just a freak, never fit in except out here." He trailed off, remembering.

"It was easy enough to earn my way; the sea folk - fisherman, merchants, could see the use in it, though they never liked or trusted me. I just moved from village to village, working on boats, figuring I could learn everything there was to know and then I'd just live alone. Wouldn't need anybody, didn't have no use for anyone then. Still don't have much." His gruff laughter rolled out.

Elana ventured another question, hoping that he would keep talking. "How did you meet Brenna and Lars?"

A shadow passed over the old sailor's face and for a moment she regretted pressing him. "It was back in Elstead, when it was just a village. I'd come that far north, looking to get away from everyone and ran into Brenna, sailing on the ocean like a man. Well, she was unlike anyone I'd ever seen. She was bonnie and bright and all the lads had their eye on her but she would have none of them. 'I'm married to the sea,' she would always say, in her laughing way that left folks wondering if she was serious or jesting. I stuck around longer there, curiosity got the better of me and come to find out this lass could out sail any fisherman I'd ever seen. I'm not boasting now, but she was as good as me and I'd never seen anyone even close."

Elana listened entranced as Orvis spilled out the story.

"I heard someone chiding her for going out in a storm once and she answered them, 'I can never be afraid of the sea, it sings to me and as long as I listen to it, it won't bring me any harm.' I ran out of there needing to think things over. She'd just described what happens to me. I couldn't have thought of those words, but they were true. The idea jumped into my head that maybe she was like me. Maybe I wasn't some freak after all. I had to talk with her to find out."

The wind shifted and Orvis swung the sail around. "I thought that maybe I could work for her father and that would give me a chance to talk with her. I wasn't too good at speaking to gals, and when I saw her at the village there was always a crowd of lads looking for her attention.

"So I went to Lars, her father and offered my services to him. He looked me over and told me I could work and he'd let me sleep in the barn with the goats. That suited me fine and the next morning we set out fishing. It didn't take a week to figure out that whatever Brenna had, Lars had too and when I got up the courage to talk with him, he was the first to tell me it was the Elder Skills, though he warned me not to call it such around those who didn't have it. Not that I needed the warning. I told him that's why I wanted to talk with Brenna and when he figured out I wasn't trying to court her, he invited me in to the family. Said he never expected to meet another with the Skills in his life and that made us kin."

Orvis left off, a far away look in his eyes as he gazed out to sea. It was a while before he continued. "That was the happiest time of my life. We sailed together, worked together, never needed to talk much about what we were. I gave up my journey north and figured I'd settled for good."

Elana felt a pang go through her. She thought she had it hard these past five years, having to hide who she was from the Valefolk. It brought tears to her eyes to think of Orvis not having anyone until he met Brenna and Lars, living afraid that he was some sort of freak, feared and mistrusted by all those around him.

"What happened? I mean, you're not in Elstead anymore." She couldn't imagine leaving a home like that if she'd been the one to find it.

Orvis gave her a dark look. "Lars called it the Shadow. Said it was eating the Vale. He always said that the ocean was the only place clean of it, but for a long time it left our little village alone. It was ten years maybe, we lived like that, never really noticing the time pass. Nothing changed for us, but stuff was changing around us." He shook his head remembering. "Inlanders moving to the coast - news of trouble from the west. Some were right enough, but more than a few set about making Elstead over like one of the big towns - elected themselves a mayor and started making rules. The village grew and kept growing with farms on the outside and the old coast trail widened into a proper road. There were more inns and folks stopped there to trade their goods, not just at Bellport."

Elana had been to Elstead with her parents and now tried to picture the thriving town as a small coastal village. The only thing she remembered about it was the hostile stares her family drew from the Valefolk. Her father had decided to press on, unhappy with the idea of settling his family there.

Orvis' voice interrupted her musings, bitterness lacing his words. "The mayor came to talk to Lars. Told him that folks had been complaining about Brenna - sailing like a man, out in storms and unafraid of the sea. Said it wasn't natural and that it had to stop. The mayor was a little afraid of Lars and wouldn't come right out and say it, but hinted that people were calling Brenna a witch and that he couldn't be responsible for what might happen to her if she didn't change her ways."

"That night we talked and I told them that we could head north, up the coast and settle out of range of any villages. It was spring and I knew we could get a cottage built and snug before winter set in. We left that month in Lars' boat and sailed until we came to the spot where you find my cottage. Lars and I built that cottage and we settled there, with me sailing to the nearest villages to trade for what we needed. No one else even knew that Lars and Brenna lived with me. They thought I was a hermit, living alone off the ocean."

"Didn't you get lonely without anyone else around?" Elana asked him.

"I didn't. I don't need much from other folks, but Brenna got it pretty bad. It was like I could just watch the light in her die out. She wasn't made to be shut away from people, even to keep safe. It got so that the only time I saw her smile was when we were on the ocean or when she played Lars' flute. Then the old Brenna would come back for a time."

"Is that why she left?" Elana asked, her voice gentle.

"We carried on for another ten years that way, Brenna dwindling and Lars getting old. One winter Lars got sick and in a few weeks time he grew too weak to hang on anymore. When he passed and the mourning time had gone, Brenna told me that she needed to leave. Only her love for Lars had been holding her. She'd remembered stories from travelers back in Elstead of a Colony deep in the Boarder Mountains. Rumors, really. But she put things together and the way she saw it, those rumors pointed to more folks like us. When she said she was going I told her I would go with her, but she refused. The sea still called to me and she knew it. I couldn't lie to her and wasn't foolish enough to try and talk her out of it. She told me that I wasn't done here and left. Didn't take more than she'd need for the journey, everything else stayed behind, even Lars' flute. Said I'd follow one day and that maybe we'd meet again."

For the first time since they'd taken to the sea, Orvis looked old. His shoulders sagged and the light went out from his eyes. "When she left it felt like she'd taken the sun from out of the sky. I couldn't bear to see her things about the cottage, so I boxed them all up and tried to keep on alone. That was twenty years ago."

After a long silence he turned and looked at her, a ghost of a smile creasing his face. "Your father's the one who told me she made it to Farran and said she's become Geri's right hand. He taught me about the Elders, told me their stories." He reached out and gripped her arm. "We'll see your parents freed if it's the last thing I do. I promise you that."

Elana nodded, swallowing hard over the lump in her throat that made it difficult to respond, and looked up into the vast starry sky, making a silent promise that she would do everything she knew to help Orvis find Brenna again.

CHAPTER 3

AIDAN'S CALL

Night crept over the salt marsh; the spring peepers and crickets drowning out the last evening bird calls, and from somewhere in the distance a coyote howled its loneliness to the gathering dark. Among the ever-changing hillocks of grass, a fox barked sharp and clear, venturing out to hunt food for her hungry kits.

Aidan took in the night sounds as he made his evening rounds across the tiny farm. Moving with ease in his rangy body, he secured the chickens in their coop, tossed cut grass to the goats in their shed before closing them in, and walked down to the small pasture against the marshes where his horse, Kael, was grazing. The huge black horse trotted up, dancing his impatience. He spun and snorted at a noise in the marsh and Aidan, catching hold of Kael's mane and swinging lightly onto his back, willed his own calm to wash over the stallion as he quieted himself, listening.

He could feel it too - an unrest, something broken in the rhythm of the night. He turned Kael toward the barn and the horse covered the ground in great strides, eager to return to his stall. Aidan scooped dried oats into the trough and tossed some cut grass into the loose box before closing the door.

The hair prickled along the back of his neck, as he walked past the wattle and daub cottage that had been home for five years, and continued uphill to the top of the farm. There a dirt track led off into the miles of rich land that comprised his uncle's holdings. Five years ago, after his father, Darian's death, his Uncle Ulrich, the Lord of Glenariff, gave grudging consent to let Aidan, his mother, Bree, and his young sister, Arella, live as tenants on his land. His generosity extended only so far as allotting them this meager peninsula, with a broken down cottage that Aidan had worked to rebuild. Here, almost swallowed by the marshes, far away from any other homesteads, they wrested their livelihood from the scant three acres.

Aidan's face burned at the thought of his uncle. Ulrich had hated Darian since boyhood. Darian, the bastard heir, was taken in by their father as a child and adopted as his firstborn, for the love of the mother who died giving birth to him. Ulrich's mother had also died of fever and the boys were raised together. The whispers of his own mother's family poisoned Ulrich, embittering him against his elder half brother. They encouraged Ulrich's native ambition, hoping to one day return honor to his mother's name as the true wife.

No one realized that Darian's mother was Elder Born until Darian began his Waking. It was Ulrich's moment of triumph. He fanned the old flames of fear and hatred toward the Elder Born, blaming them for everything, from the poor crops, to the hostilities from the West.

Darian had always been the favorite of the people, but now they started looking askance at him. No Elder Born had ever held the Lord's Seat. It just wasn't done.

For Darian the answer was easy. Once his Waking started, he had no interest in ruling Glenariff. He made a formal abdication of the Lord's Seat to Ulrich and left quietly to search out Farran and training for his Elder Skills.

If anything, Ulrich hated and feared Darian even more now, with his Elder powers, always wary that he might return to try and take back the rulership of Glenariff. So, when Aidan and his mother showed up at his door, penniless and grieving Darian's death - Aidan was sure Ulrich relished the chance to help them only enough to keep them locked in poverty.

No one ever came down this way to the marshes, unless you counted his cousin Darcy who, each new moon, rode out on his fancy horses, arrayed in velvets and lace like some popinjay, arrogantly demanding their rent. Aidan grimaced at the thought, remembering the naive hope he'd clung to when they arrived, of the two of them becoming friends. They were the same age but Darcy lost no time letting Aidan know that he was above hanging about the son of an Elder Born bastard.

Hoofbeats pounding in the distance interrupted his musings. Leagues away, toward the West, hidden now in darkness, the ground lifted into knobby hills leading up to the Shadow Mountains. Aidan's skin prickled. From out of those mountains came the source of Kael's uneasiness, rolling in like some malignant mist that could be felt but not seen. It was strong tonight, stronger than usual; the clawing blanket of heaviness that pushed down from the mountains, creeping through the Vale. It was almost time...

With an involuntary shiver, he turned back to the cottage where the smell of venison stew wafted through the open window and into the night air. He could hear Arella, his younger sister, laugh as she played with the new kittens. For a moment his chest got tight. He'd always imagined that when it came time to leave they would all go together. Arella never knew her father, and Aidan was the closest thing to a father that she had. It wasn't to be that way though.

Last fall, an old traveler named Eli showed up at their door. He too, was Elder Born, from Farran, come with a twofold purpose: to round out Aidan's training, and to bring them a letter from Geri - the summons they'd been waiting for. He'd traveled there by way of the marshes to avoid the Hunters patrolling Ulrich's borders. It was the first contact they'd had with Farran since they'd arrived in this forsaken place. The letter said that when Aidan received the confirmation, he was to go ahead, alone. He had flatly refused to leave his mother and sister unprotected, but Eli promised, that after Aidan left, he would come back to take Arella and his mother to safety.

Light from the cottage spilled out through the window into the yard and he opened the door, stooping as he entered. His mother turned to look at him, her tawny eyes, so like his own, now sad, distant. She knew. She felt it too. He picked up Arella and swung her around while the little girl crowed with delight, then gave his mother a brief hug and a kiss on the cheek.

"I've packed food in your sack." She pointed to a dilapidated leather bag bulging at the sides. "You'll want to pack your clothes." She turned away from Aidan to stir the pot on the hearth, but not soon enough to hide the tears that welled up.

His heart wrenched. He realized that he'd been half hoping he was reading the signs wrong, but his mother's Skills weren't as strong as his and if she could feel it... His thoughts drifted off as he watched Arella play.

Eli instructed him to wait until his Uncle Ulrich had sworn allegiance to the Shadow King - that would be his confirmation. They had seen it coming for years. The Shadow King provided rich incentives for men to join his ranks, and the ruler of Glenariff was worth more than ordinary men. Once Ulrich swore allegiance, the Hunters that patrolled his boarders would concentrate themselves in Drumcard, the leading city. Only then would the watch on the boarders loosen long enough for him to get clear of Glenariff.

The purge would begin - the relentless flushing out of all who possessed the Elder Skills, or set themselves against the Shadow King. In the midst of that horror, the Hunters' vigilance would turn from the outlying roads, intent upon their quarry in the ancient city.

Aidan's jaw tightened, the blood pounding in his head at the thought; families running for their lives, looking for hiding places with none to be found. Few Valefolk would risk their own lives to protect the feared Elder Born. Ulrich had done much to deepen the mistrust of the Elder Born throughout Glenariff. With so much unrest, people were quick to believe his lies. It was easier to accept that the Elder Born - never quite fitting in, always a source of suspicion - were the source of their problems, rather than acknowledge that Glenariff had fallen prey to the steady infiltration of an enemy against whom they had no hope of prevailing.

So, with Ulrich's lies inflaming the generations of tension between the Elder Born and Valefolk, there was little hope for those left in Drumcard. He shuddered, trying to block out the picture of husbands arriving home to find their wives gone, children not returning from the market place, and fathers leaving in the morning to never come home again.

A pang went through him at the thought of his own father, Darian, who until his death, led the Elder Born's resistance to the Shadow King. As a boy he had watched his father leave time and again, rallying the Valefolk against the bands of Black Knights, searching for untrained Elders to bring to Farran, and coming home with stories of the people he met. Always between them stood the unspoken promise that after Aidan's training they would work together.

Then, five years ago, he didn't come back. After weeks of frantic searching, contacting everyone they knew, there was a knock on their door - Reeves. He heard news of Darian. Someone betrayed him to the Hunters. He was captured and after refusing to yield to the Shadow King, he'd been killed. Aidan's world crumbled that day. His dreams died. It wasn't until after his Waking that a new resolve rose up out of the rubble - to fill the place his father had left empty.

He'd been gone now for five years, and Aidan had chaffed under the knowledge that they were hiding here, on the backside of nowhere, from the very men who murdered his father. His mother, however would not be moved. Geri had told them to go into hiding until she gave word, so Aidan had waited while the unrest, and the darkness in the land around him, grew more palpable. Still no sign came, no call to step out and try to fill the place his father left empty.

Lost in his thoughts, he wandered over to his bed and started pulling clothes out of the chest he'd built the first year they spent here. He remembered the pride he felt upon finishing it, the first thing he made after his Waking. He loved the way his hands could feel the wood take shape; in every stage - from the tree he picked out to the finished chest - how the wood had seemed alive to him, showing him where to cut, where to plane, where to carve. He was happy building things, working with his hands to make his world better. He understood that.

His stomach knotted, driving away his appetite. He didn't want to admit it, but now that the moment had come, he felt a strange reluctance to go. It was a boy's dream to fill his father's place. What if he didn't have what it took? He sighed. There was no turning back now. It would be a matter of hours he guessed, before he received the final confirmation.

He rolled up his clothes and stuffed them into his pack: extra cloaks for the cold nights, tunics, breeches and the soft leather boots the shoemaker in the village taught him to fashion. Looking over the comfortable cottage, made so by his own hard work, he swallowed over a lump in his throat. These were things he knew, this was where he was sure of himself. What was he thinking of, to go traipsing around the countryside like some overgrown boy with delusions of grandeur?

Putting his pack by the door, Aidan joined his mother and sister. They shared a quiet supper of venison stew and early greens that he'd picked along the edge of the marshes. He caught Arella gazing at him, a knowing look in her dark eyes.

"You're going, aren't you?" she asked him.

"Yes." He was surprised at the quaver in his voice. "It's what we talked about. But I'll see you at Farran."

"Is Eli coming for us?"

Aidan was always amazed at how aware she was of what happened around her. It was hard to remember that she was only five.

"Yes, he'll come after I've gone. I'll be taking Kael."

"Who'll look after the farm?"

"The two of you until Eli comes. Then you'll take the goats and chickens with you. It'll be an adventure." His smiled flashed at the now serious child and then he dropped his own voice to match her tone. "I'm going to miss you, but you'll have to remember everything that happens so you can tell me when we meet at Farran." He wanted to give her something to do, some responsibility that would push back the sorrow of parting.

"I will," she said, her large black eyes solemn. "We'll see each other again, you know. You don't have to worry about us."

46

He felt the strange thrill that often happened around Arella. She was way too young to start her Waking, but there was something unnerving about how she could know things sometimes. In any case, her words comforted him, though he was vaguely ashamed that she should be comforting him and not the other way around.

After she went to bed his mother sat up with him, waiting. He was more like her than his father; quiet, serious, fiercely loyal. He didn't want to think about how much he'd miss her company. They worked well together, she'd never tried to hold him back or order him around. Her trust brought out the best in him.

"The Ancient Ones don't make mistakes when they bestow the Elder Skills."

He turned and caught her eye, surprised at the remark.

"I know," he answered, waiting to see what she was getting at.

"You'll make it there fine," his mother continued. "There's not a Hunter out there with your ability to read the land." She held his gaze, telling him in her quiet way that she knew the battle that was going on inside.

He shifted in his seat. "It's not the journey. Really. I won't do anything foolish, but I'm not afraid of them in the open country and I plan to stay off the larger roads." She lifted her eyebrows and he sighed. There was no use in dancing around the point.

"It's just that war is brewing. I can feel it pulsing through the land." He waved his hands and then they fell in his lap. He looked up, meeting her gaze. "I'm afraid Geri thinks I'm something I'm not."

There. He'd said it. The knot twisting his stomach loosened. He took a deep breath. The rest came pouring out.

"There's a hope, an expectation around me. I'd love to do whatever I can to help, I'm not afraid to fight if it comes to that."

His mother's eyes narrowed and he rushed on. She'd lost her husband, he knew she wasn't ready to loose her son.

"It's just that my Skills allow me to build, to create, to listen to the land, to animals - not wage war on the Shadow King or," he paused and shrugged his shoulders, "gather and rally people together. I think they're hoping I'll be more like Father."

"That would be their loss, not yours if they missed out on what you have to share. You are not Darian. You're not supposed to be." She placed a work hardened hand on his arm. "I loved your father for who he was, and I love you for who you are. And Aidan, you have something he never did."

A question stood out in his face at this last remark.

His mother ignored it. "Know that I believe in you," she said.

He met her gaze with a smile. Reaching over, he gave her a hug, and then froze, looking over her head out the window. From across the fields he heard them, closer this time - hoofbeats shaking the night. The distant yells of revelers carried across the fields. From the hills just to the west, torch lights flickered under the stars.

He released his mother and strode to the window, heart pounding, jaw set, fists clenched. He knew it was coming, but that didn't make it any easier to take. Ulrich had sworn allegiance. The men would lose themselves in revelry tonight; the Shadow King rewarded his vassals richly.

"It's time." His voice choked as he looked at his mother and then across the cottage at the sleeping form of Arella.

His mother nodded.

He walked over to the little girl and kissed her on the forehead. Her thin arms raised up and clasped him around the neck.

"I love you, Aidan," she said in a sleepy murmur and rolled over, asleep. He stroked her black hair and covered her up with a quilt.

His mother helped carry his things to the stall where Kael was pawing nervously. She stood back as he bridled and saddled the horse, strapping his bags to the back of the saddle. He fit his small bow and a quiver of arrows into one of the packs. He would need to hunt for his supper much of the time.

48

"Don't look back. We'll meet you there," she said when he stopped to give her another hug. "I love you."

He swung up onto Kael's back. "I love you, too," he answered, his eyes blurred. Turning the big horse east, into the marshes, he gave a wave over his shoulder as he guided Kael through the treacherous ground. When he craned his neck for one final glance, her slight form and their small farm had melted into the night.

They rode east all night, picking their way through the changing islands of grass, careful to avoid any unwanted encounters. Ulrich's land extended east for miles and he wanted to be well out of it before he left the marshes.

Eli had informed them that of the three main roads joining the cities of the Vale the Fairway was the least guarded. It ran east/west along the northern plains from Bellport, crossing the Gavril river almost in the foothills and dwindling away to a country track leading deep into the mountains in the northwest corner of the Vale. There were no major cities along that route, only towns and small villages dotting the rugged countryside.

The Greenway was the major trade route, connecting Bellport on the eastern coast to Drumcard in the southwest hills. Most of the Valefolk lived along the Greenway, with it's large towns separated by tilled fields, and The Hunters patrolled this road more than the others. They had formed bands of men, the Black Knights, who rode at the Hunters' command, roaming the roads, attacking those who looked like easy prey and making travel dangerous for anyone short of an armed company.

The Western Pass met the Greenway at Drumcard, the ancient city of the Orchard Tree Elders and ran north from there, through Cahermore, continuing parallel to the Shadow Mountains where it died away among the steep slopes of the Border Mountains. Legend had it that generations ago both the Fairway and the Western Pass led to the Firestone Peak where the Firestone Elders dwelled. There was nothing there now, though. Both roads ended in shifting tracks through the Boarder Mountains. It had grown desolate since the Forgetting; the Valefolk moved away from the hills under the Shadow Mountains, and now between the wild beasts and the Black Knights, no one traveled that way if they could avoid it.

Aidan was more cautious than scared at the thought of the journey. With Kael he could outrun almost any pursuit, and as long as he paid attention, the land would tell him in time to get out of the way of trouble. He just didn't know all the variables of the road, and didn't want to make any disastrous mistakes. The most direct route would have been to ride straight north to where he could skirt the Greenway and follow it west until he reached Drumcard. Then he could take the Western Pass north to the Border Mountains.

After hearing Eli's report though, he chose to ride East, to the coast, where he would follow the coastal track to the river Gavril, south of Bellport. He could follow the river inland in an almost direct route to the mountains below Farran.

At dawn he halted Kael and found a place for them both to rest while the sun was up. There was enough grass for the horse to graze, and Aidan foraged for his breakfast, bringing down a rabbit with his bow and lighting a small fire to cook the meat. Spring onions and wild thyme grew in abundance along the edge of the marshes and served to season his meal. He would save his supply of food for when he had no other choice.

The next three days passed quietly. He saw no other people, just the animals who made their home in the wilds of the marsh. The sky was clear, an endless blue by day and by night the stars and waning moon lit their path. A part of him wished this portion of the trip would go on indefinitely, but by the fourth day, the soil turned to sand and the breeze carried a salt tang. He turned out of the marshes and headed north; it was time to look for the coastal track.

The rumor of shadow in the air was fainter here along the edge of the ocean. Aidan had never seen the ocean before. Once he knew in what direction the road lay, he rode Kael east until the land ended and they stood before the vast blue-green water. His Elder Skills stirred in him as he heard a language that he'd never known in the wildness of the waves. Someday, he promised himself, if all goes well, I'll come back and spend time here. He knew that the ocean wasn't home for him, but its draw was irresistible nonetheless.

By the second day, heading north on the coastal track, he started passing signs of civilization; an old farmhouse here, a cottage set up on a hill, cows and sheep grazing in their pastures. They traveled by day, now that they were out of Ulrich's land. Aidan hoped to meet some of the people along the way, to get a feel for how they lived in the different parts of the Vale. For five years now, he hadn't traveled farther than the village above their farm. As the late afternoon sun cast the fields in a rosy glow, he got his wish.

A scrawny boy, not yet into his teens, scrambled along the side of the road, chasing after a herd of goats who were running in every direction. He had a shock of almost white hair that stood out from his head like a halo and his bony wrists and ankles extended well beyond the frayed edges of his patched jacket and trousers. The boy, sweating and panting, looked ready to throw his staff at the first goat he could reach. Fortunately for the goats, they were more nimble than the boy, letting him come almost within reach, only to dance off at the last moment.

Something about the boy tugged at Aidan, not letting him ride past. He hesitated a moment and then gave in. Evening was coming on anyhow, he wouldn't be loosing much time, and the notion that he needed to stop and help grew stronger. He pulled up Kael, stifling a chuckle at the scene before him. The boy spotted the huge horse, and abandoning his frantic chase, scrambled up the embankment beside the road. There he sat huddled in the grass, his arms wrapped about his legs as though trying to make himself invisible.

"I'm not going to hurt you lad," Aidan spoke to him in a gentle voice.

The boy just stared at him. He had the palest blue eyes Aidan had ever seen, almost like they were drained of their color. His skin, as well, looked almost translucent. He tried not to stare back, not wanting to make the boy uncomfortable, and cast about for something to say. He had the suspicion that he'd guessed wrong about the boy being frightened. Those pale blue eyes sized him up with a mixture of curiosity and defiance.

"It seems that you're in need of some help." It was a little stiff, but under the scrutiny of those eyes, it was the first thing he came up with. He swung down off Kael and looked up at the boy. "What's your name?"

The boy studied him a moment more and then answered, "Baird. Why do you want to know? Sir." He tacked on the last bit as if reciting a lesson in manners.

"Well, when I meet someone, I like to know their name. My name is Aidan. And this," he gestured toward his horse, "is Kael."

The defiance vanished from Baird's face as he stared openmouthed at the horse, making Aidan wonder if he'd ever seen one before. In the poorer areas, the farmers rarely owned even a donkey.

"If you'd like, I could help you gather your goats and bring them back to your home." He waited, watching the boy's face soften at his offer.

"Please, sir, I would like that right much. My granny's not well, and the goats only mind her. She'll be worrying about me if I'm not bringing them home soon." His voice had a pleasing lilt to it and Aidan found himself liking the boy more and more.

"All right then. What if I whistle them a tune that they'd like to follow and you can lead us all to your home?"

Baird smiled, bright as the sun and jumped up. The goats, now that they were no longer being chased, stood quietly grazing by the side of the road, watching Aidan out of their amber eyes. He began whistling a little tune, and one by one they turned and looked at him full on. As his eyes met each of theirs he caught impressions of their thoughts, full of grass, running and mischief. He silently invited each one to come with him, and fascinated, they followed. The whistling was a cover he'd learned long ago, to distract others from his ability to communicate with the animals.

As each of the animals turned to him, Aidan realized that they weren't the only ones listening to his song. Baird was studying him, his head cocked, pale blue eyes unfocused as he took in the simple melody. He caught Aidan's eye for a moment, grinned, and then joined in, whistling with him. After a few bars, he dropped the melody, and instead wove a harmony for it that floated up over and around the song. Aidan had some musical ability, but his eyes widened as he listened. He had to concentrate to maintain his melody line. The harmony haunted him, winding around his heart like a half remembered dream.

The boy seemed oblivious to the effect of his music and led the way, whistling a thousand variations on the original harmony, swinging his stick and whacking the tops off the grasses like he owned the world. Delighted, Aidan followed him. After a half hour's walking, Baird turned away from the road onto a footpath that wound through the low hills. A peace wrapped itself about this place, making Aidan think with a pang, of their own farm before the Shadow rolled out of the West. From the other side of the next hill, he could see smoke from a chimney spiraling into the air. The goats broke rank and gamboled past him to their home. One more hill and Baird's home lay before them.

Baird, still swinging his stick called out, "Granny, we're back!"

An aged woman raised herself up from the seat where she was sitting in front of a tiny ramshackle cottage. As she looked up toward where Aidan stood, he noted that the pupils of her blue eyes were milky white. She was blind.

She groped for her stick and made her way in careful steps toward him. "Welcome, Aidan, son of Darian," she said.

He stopped in his tracks, speechless and then took a step away from her, reeling as though he'd been struck. How did she know his name? How did she know his father?

Baird frowned and looked back at him. "Aw, Granny, you know him? I wanted to surprise you." She turned toward his voice and smiled at the boy but her words were for Aidan.

"I've been expecting him, Baird. Why don't you invite him in for supper?"

"Can you stay sir?" The boy's face was alight with anticipation. They obviously didn't see much company here.

"How could I refuse?" Aidan answered him, but his eyes turned to the old woman whose blind gaze was directed at his face.

"He has a horse, Granny!" the boy tugged at her sleeve, pointing to Kael.

"Yes, I heard him come up," she said. "We have a pasture for the milk cow that your horse could share if it isn't beneath him," she said with a hint of grin.

"Thank you, yes, that's fine." He found himself stumbling over his words; first Baird and his music and now a blind woman calling him by name and knowing his father... He was not at all recovered from the shock. He unsaddled Kael, rubbed him down and led him to the pasture where, unperturbed by the milk cow, the stallion rolled like a colt, stood up, shook the sand out of his coat and then started tearing at clumps of the fresh spring grass like he was starved.

Aidan smiled at his antics and then walked back to the cottage, probing, listening, gathering all he could from his surroundings. He didn't have the Skill that some Elder Born did, to immediately recognize other Elder Born, but even without it, he would have bet that this old woman was Elder Born too. Nothing else could explain her knowing. He wondered about the boy as well. Especially if he was her grandson.

Baird met him at the door and offered him a seat at their small table where a meal of coarse brown bread and vegetable stew was laid out in wooden bowls. The old woman walked in after Aidan, her stick in one hand, a bucket of fresh goat's milk in the other.

"I hope you don't mind our modest fare." She turned her head toward him and then inclined it toward the table.

"No, not at all. It's what I'm used to. Smells wonderful." Aidan blushed. He was still fumbling with his words. He might as well have been Baird's age instead of twenty-one.

The boy and his Granny each pulled up a chair and when the old woman folded her hands and bowed her head, Aidan followed suit. She spoke a blessing over the food, raised her head with a benevolent smile and gestured for them to begin. Aidan helped Baird serve the supper and was content to lay his questions aside while he enjoyed the simple meal. As they ate Baird kept them entertained with stories about their goats, and told his Granny all about meeting Aidan, apparently undaunted by her former knowledge of him.

The old woman only interrupted once. "I see you have some Skill indeed," she said to Aidan. "These goats don't follow a stranger."

He made no reply, wondering if she meant what he thought by 'Skill'.

After Baird cleared the table and set about washing the dishes, they moved to the porch where the stars winked into view one by one in the deep blue of the evening sky.

Aidan faced the old woman, whose strange milky-white gaze was blindly directed toward the open fields, and took a deep breath. "How do you know me?" he asked, "and my father?"

"How did my goats know they could follow you?" she countered.

Aidan paused a moment before answering. He decided to speak frankly. "You're an Elder Born too, then?"

"What do you think?"

He gritted his teeth. This wasn't going the way he expected. "Yes. I think you're an Elder Born and I obviously just told you that I am." The words came out with a little more heat than he intended. He took a another breath, bringing his emotions back under control.

"I'm sorry." It wouldn't do any good to fly off the handle, even if he was unnerved. He tried again.

"It's just that I want to know why I'm here, how could you have been expecting me?"

"Apology accepted." She inclined her head with the air of a queen granting pardon. "And I just needed to know that you were indeed who I thought you to be and not one sent to snare me." Her voice no longer sounded old and tired, but fierce, defiant almost.

"The Hunters?"

She nodded. "Even an old woman isn't exempt from their search. And they have searched for me long, without success."

"I'm not one of them. They, my father..." his voice trailed off for a moment. "Well, you must know what happened, if you knew him."

"Yes, I know." Her voice was low. "And one of his best friends betrayed him into their hands. You can never be too careful, Aidan. Never take anyone at their word. You must be sure before you give the gift of trust. Especially now."

"I don't understand."

"No, you wouldn't. But you'll need to." She was quiet for such a long time that Aidan wondered if she'd drifted off to sleep.

In the cottage he heard Baird finish up the dishes. From the sounds drifting into the night, the boy had taken out some sort of reed flute and started playing. The haunting tune stirred up the ache Aidan felt when he thought of his father's death. He wondered again why he was here - what was this all about. The old woman rocked in silence. He looked at her, wanting to ask her about his father, and then cleared his throat, finding himself at a loss for how to address her.

She turned, a grin creasing her wrinkled face. "You can call me Granny. I'm well old enough to be that to you, boy. There's no shame in it either."

"Granny," Aidan began, awkward at the use of such a familiar name, "How did you know my father?"

The old woman sighed. "Darian was the pride and joy of Farran. Who didn't know him?"

Aidan raised his eyebrows at her answer. He had begun to wonder if she answered anything directly.

She whistled tunelessly to the night, leaving Aidan to fidget in the chair next to her. As his thoughts began to wander down the path of Baird's playing, she faced him again.

"I was born like this, boy. Never seen the sunrise, nor the grass after the rain. Never seen the face of a loved one. But I see other things. I saw your father. And I saw you. Destiny's burdensome. Don't wish it on anyone you love. Not unless they've got a heart big enough to not be crushed by it."

He stared at her as though she were talking another language. Whose destiny? What? "I don't understand. Sorry."

She snorted. "I know you've got brains in there. Do I have to spell everything out?" Her chair creaked in time to the rocking. "Destiny. Me - for the sight I have, your father - for the work he started, you - for the path before you. Destiny."

The old woman rocked on without another word, her face stony, her brow furrowed. Aidan blinked. If this was spelling things out, he was in trouble. He didn't say any more for fear of angering her. He had a sinking feeling that this was some sort of a test and he was failing it miserably.

Baird came out to join them and they sat without speaking until the dark settled in around the cottage. Pushing herself out of her rocking chair, the old woman broke the silence.

"Time for bed. Aidan, you can sleep in Baird's bed. He'll take a blanket on the floor." She walked through the open cottage door and disappeared behind the rough linen curtain covering her sleeping quarters.

Aidan followed her inside the cottage and apologized to Baird. "Sorry to turn you out of your bed, lad." He grinned at the boy, rightly figuring that for him this was a wonderful adventure.

"Can I lay my blanket out next to your bed?" The boy's hair caught the starlight and seemed to glow like a nimbus around his head. Aidan resisted the urge to touch it.

"Of course. I'd love the company. Want to come with me to check on Kael?"

The boy jumped to his feet. Silent as two shadows in the night, they slipped into the cow pasture and up to the black horse. Kael turned to watch them, snuffing their scent in the air. He nuzzled Aidan's tunic for treats while Aidan showed Baird how to pet the horse. Aidan murmured soft and low to the animal who shifted nervously at the boy's touch.

"Kael must like you," he said to the beaming boy as they walked back to the cottage. "He won't let anyone touch him unless I'm there telling him it's okay, and even then, it's only been my mother and little sister." Aidan grinned in the darkness. "I pity the person who tries to lay a hand on him without my say so." Even in the dark Aidan thought he saw Baird walk taller at his words.

Aidan tossed and turned in the small bed that night. The old woman's cryptic hints disturbed him, following him into his dreams when he managed to drift off. He woke the next morning with the sickening feeling that he had lost something he needed, or was looking for something all night without success. He rolled out of bed, careful not to step on Baird who lay sleeping in the early morning light, a skinny arm thrown across his face.

The door to the goat shed creaked open and the old woman made her way out, her stick in one hand moving lightly on the ground before her, and a bucket of fresh goat's milk in the other.

She turned her face toward Aidan who stood on the porch breathing in the fresh morning air. "It's a good day for travel, boy," her voice creaked out. Before he could respond, she continued, "I have a gift for you before you go. Might come in handy along the way."

Aidan knew that he was being dismissed and hoped that this gift was something more useful than the cryptic messages of the night before - something he could at least recognize. He took a deep breath, a habit from his training, willing his pride to back down. It rankled, the way the old woman seemed to play with him, keeping him in the dark, giving him just enough information to confuse him. He didn't want to go without having his questions answered. Well, at least he would try.

"Last night," he began, as she climbed the steps to the porch, "you told me things, but only halfway."

She stopped climbing and put the bucket of goat's milk down on the step. "What would you have me say?"

Thoughts tumbled over themselves in his head. "Why did you tell me not to trust anyone? And what do you mean about destiny?" This last question touched the more painful spot. "I don't know what I'm supposed to do, but I don't think I'm what people are hoping I'll be. I'm just going back to Farran. That doesn't mean that I have the ability to fill my father's place." He could feel his face burning as he spoke. At least he was going to put it out in the open. She wasn't going to laugh at him behind his back.

"The Ancient Ones never make mistakes when they give out the Skills, boy." Her voice was low, almost sad. "It's just that we have other idea's about what's needed than they do. You're not supposed to take Darian's place. You're supposed to take your own."

He felt the heat drain out of his face. That was almost exactly what his mother said the night he left.

She walked the rest of the way up the stairs and took one of his hands between her ancient, wrinkled ones. "Aidan, I know what I see, but I don't see all ends. A word spoken out of time, misinterpreted, can prove disastrous. I can only say that you have a destiny before you and I'm not the only one who knows that." A smile flitted over her face, making it, for a moment, look almost impish. "It's no accident that your Skills can pass virtually undetected." She was serious once more. "For now, I will give you this piece of advice, though I fear that even here I may do more harm than good. Travel first to Bellport and find Reeves. The time is drawing near and the Hunters feel it to. I won't lie to you - Bellport is perilous for any Elder Born. I just feel that you both will have need of each other before your journey is completed."

Aidan's thoughts drifted back to the last time he saw his father's friend. Then suddenly remembering what the old woman said about his father's betrayal, he shot her a worried glance. "But Reeves isn't, didn't..." his question hung unfinished between them.

"No. Reeves is true. You can trust him with your life. But trust no one else. No one! The Hunters have many guises and many spies. Reveal your identity to no one." She released his hand and bent to retrieve the pail of milk. "There. I've told you more than I meant to, and more than I should have, no doubt, but lets pray that it works good and not harm."

Together with the boy, they breakfasted on brown bread, cheese and goat's milk.

"It's my job to milk the cow," Baird explained to Aidan. "And I get to take it to the miller just north of here on the coastal road. We trade milk for wheat and barley."

Aidan nodded. "You pull your weight around here, I can tell that. You've got the makings of a fine man." Baird swelled at this compliment, his pale face bright with pride. Aidan wondered as he watched the boy, what the future held for him. He was talented musically, but living out here, he'd never be able to develop that - unless it was part of an Elder Skill. He hoped that their paths would cross again; he genuinely liked the boy. When I make it to Farran, I'll see if there's any way I can help him, he promised himself. He knew how hard it was to grow up isolated from everyone... and he had his mother and sister. Baird had only his grandmother.

Aidan helped him with the dishes after breakfast and the boy returned the favor, helping Aidan pack his things up. He stood back a respectful distance while Aidan saddled Kael, only coming forward to stroke the huge horse at Aidan's signal.

The old woman was sitting on the porch knitting, her hands moving rhythmically in time to her rocking, when Aidan stepped up to take his leave.

"It's time for me to go, Granny," he said with genuine warmth. The crusty old woman had begun to grow on him. He would miss them both.

"Not before I give you something," she answered. She planted both feet, stopping the chair, and set her knitting down on a small table next to its arm. "It's an old woman's silliness, no doubt, but humor me." She pushed herself out of the chair and reaching for her stick, made her way back into the cottage. Aidan heard her opening a box and rustling through it. He couldn't imagine what it must be like to go through life without sight. He wondered exactly what her Skills were, because she seemed to manage better that he would have thought possible.

She emerged from the cottage holding a richly embroidered cloak over her frail arm. The body of the cloak was a deep forest green with bright yellow-gold braiding around its hood. Sewn into the fabric with what appeared to be gold threads were letters and symbols that merged, blended and danced together, giving them the illusion of movement.

Aidan sucked in his breath. He'd never seen something so rich, so beautiful. Even his cousin Darcy who strutted his finery in front of them each month when he came to collect their rent, had never owned anything of this quality. This cloak was fit for a ruler. It brought to mind stories of the Elder Born in the days of Greening, when their Skills flowed strong and proud throughout the Vale. It also brought to mind his conversation with the old woman. Destiny. That's what she'd called it. His stomach tightened. She stretched out her arms holding the heavy cloak out toward him. A part of him held back but he couldn't refuse. He lifted it off of her arms and spread the fabric wide, admiring the intricate lettering.

Something inside him stirred as the folds of fabric draped over his arm - an ache, a longing that was not entirely comfortable. For the briefest moment he saw a young man, his own age riding out in this cloak, one hand clutching to his chest a treasure that seemed to radiate from under the rich garment. He blinked and the old woman stood before him, with Baird at her side, both silent, waiting for him to speak.

"Thank you, it's beautiful, I mean I've never seen anything like this." He found himself stammering again. "Why are you giving it to me?"

She didn't answer, but instead motioned for him to kneel in front of her. Then, using her hands to feel where he was, she wrapped the cloak around his shoulders, her sensitive fingers tracing the patterns woven into the fabric.

Taking a step back from him as thought she could survey her work, she smiled and spoke one word. "Destiny."

CHAPTER 4

LORD GRATTON'S DAUGHTER

Aidan thanked the old woman and Baird, said his goodbyes, and turned Kael toward the Coastal Road heading north toward Bellport, still shaken by the visit. On either side of the road birds sang in the fields and the cool breeze carried with it the tangy scent of the ocean. Kael, well rested from their stop, pranced and jigged. The crisp air infected his senses and the long stretch of sandy road before him begged for a good run. His mood was contagious and it didn't take long for Aidan to give in, put away his musings and nudge the stallion forward.

The horse's long stride ate up the road, his pounding hooves beating out a rhythm more compelling than the worries that nagged and pulled at Aidan. The rich cloak snapped and shook behind him and his tawny hair whipped back over his shoulders. He blinked, his eyes watering from the force of the wind. By the time Kael was ready to slow down, Aidan's heart was lighter, his cares outdistanced, and for the time forgotten. They slowed to a trot, though even at this pace the miles flew past under them. The road was deserted, neither farm nor homestead lay along its length. The only signs of life were the occasional lanes, not more than grassy tracks leading, he guessed, to farms hidden from view among the sandy hills rising up to the west.

It was nearing lunch time before Aidan saw any sign of other travelers. Kael crested a hill. The road unwound before them - a thin white ribbon cutting its solitary path through the pale green grass until a dark band of forest below them swallowed it up. The sun, almost overhead, warmed Aidan's face, but he felt a sudden chill. For the first time since he'd left his home, he sensed something amiss in the land. The big horse halted, snorting and pawing. Aidan laid a hand on the stallion's neck.

He slid down off the horse, wanting to feel the ground under his feet. He'd never described it to anyone, it almost embarrassed him the way his Skill worked. It was as though in these moments he could hear the land speak to him. It was always easier to hear it when he was quiet and close to the ground. He squatted down, resting his palms against the warming sand. It wasn't the same wrongness as at home; where the darkness that could only be felt, rolled in from the West. This was more immediate, more tangible. A picture flashed into his mind - galloping horses, a chase. He stood up and surveyed the road below them. He could feel the hoofbeats now, not just with his Skill.

At the place where the road disappeared into the band of woods, a fine boned white horse sprung out, closely followed by two heavy set cobs. A woman rode sidesaddle on the white, her brightly colored robes billowing behind her. She didn't appear to be much of a rider, bouncing in the saddle and clutching the reins as though they were a lifeline. The men astride the cobs rode with swords drawn, gaining on the woman.

Aidan didn't wait to see more. He loosed his bow from his pack. A cold fury at the men's cowardice rose in him and swinging up onto Kael, he charged. The stallion, responding to his anger; bugled a challenge to the horses as he plunged down the hill. The men saw him coming and urged their mounts on. As soon as he was in range he took aim at one of the swords. Without knowing more, he wouldn't shoot to kill. The arrow was true, knocking the sword out of the man's grasp. The man's horse reeled as his rider yanked at the beast in an attempt to keep himself in the saddle.

Aidan notched another arrow and let it fly. Five years of hunting in the marshes to keep his family alive had made him an expert marksman. The arrow tore the second man's sword from his hand as well. Kael bore down upon them and as Aidan passed the white horse he caught a glimpse of the woman's terrified face. The two men pulled up their horses, eyes wide, fearful. He guessed that they weren't Black Knights, just opportunistic thieves. They hauled their mounts around and bolted back toward the woods.

64

Before he could follow, the woman on the white horse gave a cry. Aidan spun around in time to see her tumble out of the saddle. He abandoned the chase and galloped back to help her.

"Are you hurt?" he called out. He jumped off Kael and ran to her side.

She lay like a crumpled doll on the road. Her hood blown back, revealed green eyes flecked with light, under impossibly long eyelashes. Her skin was a honey gold and her heavy braids, the color of wheat, lay in the sand with bits of silk woven into them, sparkling in the sun like gemstones.

She didn't seem to have broken anything and her breathing, though shallow from fear looked like it came without pain. Aidan gathered her in his arms as though she had been Arella and set her down with care against a fallen log. He couldn't imagine why a woman of high station, would be traveling alone on the road.

"Thank you." She lifted her face to look at him. "You saved my life."

"Who were those men?" he asked her.

"I don't know. They cut off my path through the woods and all I knew to do was turn and run." Her voice shook and she covered her face with her hands.

"They're gone now." Aidan looked past her to the place where the thieves had run. The land felt clear again - he wasn't worried about them coming back. He wasn't fool enough though, to believe that this woman could ride alone without some other incident. Those two weren't the only ones watching the road for easy prey.

"Where were you going?" Aidan asked.

"To Bellport," she said. Her voice had a foreign edge to it, she pronounced her words in a crisp clear way that Aidan had never heard.

It only took a moment's thought. He offered himself as her escort.

"I'm riding to Bellport as well. I would be glad to go with you and see that you reach it safely." He waited for a reply. A long silence stretched out between them. Aidan felt his face burn. He realized that though she might appreciate being saved by a peasant, those raised to nobility were rarely willing to ride with one.

"My name's Aidan," he finally said, to break the silence.

She looked up, narrowed her green eyes and studied him. "Aidan, Aidan..." There was a pause as though she were trying to place him.

"We've never met," he said. "I certainly wouldn't have forgotten it. I mean..." His words stammered away into silence.

A wan smile flitted over her mouth, not reaching her eyes. "No. We haven't met. I'm Cecily." She extended her hand to him as the noblewomen did with the men of wealth, so that he could kiss it.

Aidan felt the blood rise to his face. He bent down, took her hand and brought it briefly to his lips. Their eyes met for a moment and he thought he saw her cheeks flush before she took her hand back.

He forced his mind to think. She was treating him like someone of importance. She must imagine him to be of her station. Then he realized that he was wearing the embroidered cloak and riding Kael. How could she know he was a no better than the poorest of peasants?

She seemed to weigh him before she spoke again. "You're not from around here, Aidan. My father is Lord Gratton, ruler of Merrion." She gave him a significant look as Aidan realized what that meant.

She was *The* Cecily - sole heir to the House of Gratton, and the Lord's seat of Merrion. The villagers back home gossiped about her - the flower of Merrion, she was called, and destined to be Darcy's bride.

He inclined his head in a half bow. "What are you doing traveling alone, lady? You must know that your life is endangered on the road. And your father - he would be sick with worry about you." He wondered briefly if she was that brave or just terribly naive.

"My father..." She turned away as if the word hurt her, then looked him full in the face. "Aidan, riding to Bellport, you must not know much of Lord Gratton. He wouldn't want his goods damaged. That is all I am to him."

Aidan shook his head. "Goods? What do you mean? What man would not cherish..." He blushed at his choice of words and let his question die unfinished.

Cecily looked away again. "My father left me at Ulrich's court, to marry his son, Darcy. But I won't stand for it. I will not be married off to that arrogant fop, even if it means that the sons of Airth take back what was theirs before my father drove them out."

Like a child who has kept a secret for too long, her words came tumbling out. "I lied to Lord Ulrich - told him I had a message from Marek, Lord Gratton's counselor and my guardian, commanding me to return home. I let him know it was an emergency. Marek sends messages by falcon to those who are close to him." She lowered her voice. "Some say he holds the bird in his thrall, that he has power over other's minds. He makes Ulrich nervous."

Aidan swallowed hard. Now that he'd met her, the idea of her being forced to marry Darcy was unthinkable.

Aidan nodded at her, but his mind was spinning.

"I don't believe it though. I've seen the falcon with him and they just love each other. He saved her you know, when she was just a fledgling. It's that simple." With a toss of her head she dismissed all rumors to the contrary. "But everyone who knows Marek knows his bird, so no one would question my tale. Even Ulrich wouldn't dare gainsay him. He sent me out with the first merchant traveling east."

Cecily paled. "The man was paid well to insure my safety. Yet, I overheard him plotting with his men last night to hold me for ransom. Marek always has me travel with a vial of sleeping powders. I offered to pour their wine this morning, and left them all slumbering at an abandoned farmstead back there." She pointed a shaking hand west into the concealing hills. "I was liberal with their portions. They shouldn't wake until midday tomorrow."

Her face clouded and her voice dropped to a whisper, desperation clinging to each word. "I have to get to Bellport and find Marek. He is the only one who could persuade my father to cancel the marriage agreement."

The tremor in her voice wrenched at Aidan. He couldn't imagine her being forced to marry that brute. He reached out and put a hand on her arm. "I know Darcy, I wouldn't send a dog I liked to him. Not that I'm calling you a dog," he blundered, his face burning as she looked questioningly at him, "but there's no way your father, Lord Gratton, can force you to marry him." He took a deep breath. "He has to see that!"

She turned to him, her eyes filled with tears. "Only Marek can make him see that."

"Please let me ride with you," Aidan said, throwing all caution aside. "I will see to it that you reach Marek unharmed."

"Thank you," she answered. "That is very kind of you." She gave him a quizzical look. "You're unlike any of the noblemen I've met. I feel like I can trust you, Aidan, riding to Bellport."

Aidan inclined his head to her in thanks, unsure of what to reply.

He caught her mare who was grazing with Kael, and helped her into the saddle. In a brief moment of looking into the mare's eyes he sensed the goodness of the horse - patient, proud to do her job well. She nickered to him, recognizing the connection and Aidan was glad of it. He would be able to direct her if they ran into any more trouble. It was clear that Cecily wasn't an accomplished rider.

He mounted Kael who was busy arching his neck and showing off to the mare, who ignored him entirely, and they rode in silence. He had never met anyone like Cecily - and not just her beauty, though rumors hadn't done her justice. Behind the brave exterior she seemed so lost. Vague thoughts of riding into Bellport and demanding that her father release her from this marriage ran through his head. He wished that she was Elder Born, though he doubted it, for he sensed nothing of the Skills about her. If she was, he could take her with him to Farran and she would be safe there. He tried not to focus on it but he couldn't help remembering what she felt like in his arms when he had gathered her up from her fall.

Thoughts of her drove out everything else for a while until Aidan felt his stomach begin to growl. He noticed that Cecily had nothing packed with her, neither food nor water. He had plenty to share and relished the thought of some more time to talk with the young woman. "Shall we stop for some lunch?" he asked, trying to match her speech in what he hoped was a proper sort of way.

She smiled and the light reached up to her eyes this time. "I would love to."

They rode to a spot where a huge oak overhung the road and there Aidan dismounted and helped her off her mare. He unsaddled both the horses and let them loose to graze. Kael would not wander off and he noticed with a grin that the stallion had taken to the white mare almost as much as Aidan had taken to her mistress. He threw down a blanket, unpacked his food sack, and set out the dark brown bread, goat's cheese and last fall's apples. It wasn't fancy, but then she might not expect that from someone traveling.

When they both were seated he broached the topic of Darcy again. "Cecily, I don't just know Darcy - he's my cousin." He'd been thinking and he decided that what he really needed to keep secret was his identity as an Elder Born and the destination of his journey.

She already believed him to be a nobleman and he was, in truth, of noble birth. He knew that the Elder Born didn't hold with such things, but had his father not renounced his claim to the Lord's Seat of Glenariff, he would be the heir, not Darcy. A clearer part of his mind knew it was foolish to even think about it, but he couldn't help himself.

"But Darcy is from the Tormey family," she said. "They rule Glenariff. How is it that we never met?" She lowered her eyes. "I wish my father had heard of you instead of him."

The piece of bread he was chewing on turned to sawdust in his mouth and he gulped, unable to swallow. He gave a little cough. "I wish he had too," he said. His heart raced. She liked him. He was sure of it. He looked at her delicate beauty, fine spun linen dress, the air of privilege... and then reality clouded the pretty dream. Would she even have looked twice if she knew he was without gold, without position in society - not to mention being one of the hated Elder Born?

Something inside prodded and poked at him. It was wrong to win her affections with a deception. He had to say something.

He looked down. The words stuck in his throat and he hated that he had to do it. "Cecily, I may be related to Darcy, but I'm not like him."

"Oh, I know you're not," she insisted. "You would never do the mean things he does. He is awful." She reached out, put her hand over his, and looked up at him, her eyes soft and shining.

His resolve cracked. He couldn't bring himself to say anything that would put the light out in those eyes. He sighed, giving up. There would be plenty of time later for that. He would find a way to tell her, he promised himself. Just not now.

They enjoyed a leisurely lunch together with Cecily carrying the conversation. She chatted on about people and things that Aidan knew almost nothing about. He was content though, just to hear her voice, to watch her face as she described her life in Bellport.

Occasionally Aidan would interrupt her, pointing out a bird singing close, or a deer grazing at the edge of the woods with a tiny fawn in tow. He was amazed at how little she noticed of the life all around her and how quickly her attention shifted back to whatever story she was telling. Maybe it came from being raised in the city, he thought, or maybe it was because no one had ever taken the time to show her.

As they were finishing lunch Kael wandered over to Aidan, nuzzling around him, in hopes of finding an apple core or a crust of the bread. Aidan offered some bread to the horse who took it with gentle lips. Kael stood by him while he ate, blowing into Aidan's hair.

Cecily turned her bright smile on the horse. "He's beautiful. Where did you get him?"

Aidan grinned. He wouldn't have volunteered the story, but since she asked, he was more than happy to tell her. "Actually, I won him from Darcy."

She looked up, laughter in her face. "Oh, do tell me," she said.

He settled back, stretching his long legs and soaking up her rapt attention. "Well, last fall a horse trader came through Ulrich's holdings and sold Kael to Darcy. Said he would improve his breeding stock. He sold him for a good sack of gold, but found out neither Darcy not their top horsemen could come near the animal. Word got out around in the court and Ulrich was incensed at his son spending gold on a horse he couldn't even touch, so Darcy announced that he'd give the horse to any man who could ride him. It made Darcy look like a hero, giving something of value away like that, and quieted Ulrich. He knows that goodwill translates into gold in his pocket. He doesn't mind looking like he's doing something nice if he'll profit from it."

Cecily was leaning forward, her mouth parted in a smile, following his every word.

Aidan continued, "Well, Darcy set the day and every man within leagues had a go. The horse was in a paddock and not one of them could catch him. Some would get close, but as soon as they laid a hand on him, he'd wheel off. Finally one man got a rope around his neck. It was like he got hold of a tornado. Kael dragged the fellow the length and breadth of the paddock before the man let go. Then Kael just galloped off... the rope trailing behind." Aidan shook his head remembering. "I wasn't going to be part of the whole thing - there's already bad blood between us and Ulrich's family. But I saw him there with that rope on and I just couldn't see him get hurt. So I walked up to the paddock and slipped between the rails and just waited. Pretty soon he stopped blowing and snorting and pranced over to see what I was made of. Well, I took one look in his eyes," he dropped his voice and looked again up at the big stallion, "and he caught me really. I'd never seen spirit like that in anything - man nor beast. I tried to let him know I'd never break that spirit and I guess he just understood. I took the rope off him, threw a leg over his back and away we rode. Felt like we were made for each other."

Cecily clapped her hands. "I wish I had been there to see it. I bet Darcy was furious. Serves him right, too."

"He was. If there wasn't a crowd there to witness it, he would've tried to weasel out for sure, but he was stuck, and I brought Kael home.

He's pretty tame now. Will let folks touch him and lead him, but usually only when I'm there. No one else's ever been on his back."

"You're both accomplished and brave. I saw you shoot the swords out of those men's hands. Where did you learn it all?" Cecily gazed up at him, her green eyes glowing in admiration.

Aidan blushed and brushed aside her flattery. Somehow he'd rather leave her with the impression of a well educated nobleman, than a dispossessed Elder Born having to learn to shoot so his family wouldn't starve.

"We'd better be riding again," he answered her. "There's still a lot of road between us and Bellport and I'd rather your merchant friends not catch up with us."

He encouraged Cecily to get up and walk around, easing the soreness in her legs while he packed their things away. When she got back he led the horses to a nearby stream to drink, saddled them and helped Cecily mount her mare. The remainder of the day passed too swiftly. She spent their ride telling him about herself, about her father, about growing up the only child of the Lord of Merrion.

Her mother had been a sickly woman who died in childbirth and Lord Gratton was too occupied with securing his newly conquered Lord's seat and the feud against the sons of Airth, to take much time with her. He left her instead to the care of Marek, his counselor. Though she had nannies and then later governesses who tended to her daily needs, Marek was her champion, always taking the time to call on her when he was in the city, telling her stories of his travels around the Vale. Her face lit up when she spoke of him - in her eyes this man could do no wrong.

Aidan felt a weed of jealousy growing in him around this Marek. He soothed himself by picturing him stooped, gray and wrinkled - a kindly old man, but not a suitor.

He told her about loosing his father when he was sixteen and that since then, he'd lived with his mother and younger sister, taking care of them on their farm. He didn't mention that they'd had to beg land off of Ulrich, imposing on his duty to a deceased brother, or that the farm was a scant three acres of mostly marsh. For the first time in his life, he was being treated with respect and he wanted to savor that, especially as it came from the most enchanting woman he'd ever laid eyes on.

All too soon evening settled in over the land, the sharp chill in the air reminding them that it was still only spring. Aidan wondered what Cecily would have done if he had not met up with her, having neither food, nor blankets, nor any change of clothes. Well, no matter, he thought. It gave him a welcome chance to take care of her.

A small grove of beech trees set back from the road presented an inviting spot to camp for the night. After starting a fire, Aidan took his bow and in a short time had shot two rabbits for their supper. Cecily turned away while he cleaned them. It never occurred to him that she might not have seen this done before. He roasted the meat on sticks over the fire and then when they had eaten, spread his blankets out for Cecily to sleep. He sat up against a tree, wrapped in his cloak. He watched as she drifted off into sleep and then tried to clear his mind as the fire danced, and the waning moon rose late over the trees.

Tomorrow they would reach Bellport. He was torn. He knew he must leave her to find Reeves and start on his own journey, yet he found himself devising excuses in his mind to postpone that moment. This day had been like a dream; a dream he didn't want to end. Well, at the very least, he would see her to her home, or to Marek's if that's where she wanted to go. His curiosity piqued at the thought of meeting this Marek. With an effort he pushed back all thought of what must come after, pulled his cloak more tightly around him and stretched out on the ground to sleep.

Aidan woke before dawn. Clear stars glittered against the blue-black sky and the moon cast pale shadows around their camp. The fire had burned down to embers. His body ached, stiff from the chill and the hard ground. Rising, he stretched and stomped, trying to entice the circulation through his long limbs. Cecily lay sleeping in his blankets, her golden braids with their ribbons catching the moonlight, shone faintly about her head. She turned over, murmured something in her sleep and smiled. He smiled looking at her then turned his attention to the fire, coaxing it back to life with the last of the dried wood, so that she would have a place to warm her hands when she woke.

She woke late, well after the sun rose and Aidan had already packed the horses for their ride. She warmed herself by the fire, eating bread and cheese that he brought before they both mounted up and set out for Bellport. Her chatter continued through the morning, picking up her stories where she had left off the night before. She seemed so glad of the chance to speak that Aidan wondered if she had any friends at home who cared to listen to her. He didn't always follow what she was saying, being unfamiliar with the names of the people and places, but it was delightful to watch the morning sun play over her animated features as she rambled on.

When they stopped for lunch he broached the topic of their arrival at Bellport.

"We will reach Bellport before supper if all goes well. I want to accompany you to wherever you're going. I don't want you to ride alone in the city."

She laughed at him as though he said something foolish. "Oh, no one would hurt me there." She looked away, quiet for a moment before adding, "I would like you to come with me though, if you will. I'd rather not say goodbye before we must. I plan on going to Marek's home. I'm sure he would be delighted to meet you." Her voice faltered for a moment.

"What's wrong?"

"It's only," she began, "I didn't think of it before I set off, but I do hope that he's at home. He travels a lot. I can't face Lord Gratton without speaking with Marek first."

Aidan felt his stomach knot in fear for her. He hadn't considered that complication. "I won't leave you until I know that you're safe," he assured her, with more confidence than he felt. He had very little gold and would need most of it to cross the Vale and find Farran. He took a steadying breath. He'd deal with that later.

By mid afternoon the lonely track of the Coastal Road had grown into a wide lane and the open land gave way to timber houses and farms with thatched roofs on each side of the road. Villages sprung up and then linked together into a sprawling town which led them to the ferry crossing, just south of Bellport. The rivers Gavril, from the North, and Naal, from the West, joined each other a little ways inland, south of Bellport, and flowed together to the sea. Along the Coastal Road the only crossing was by private boat or ferry. The river mouth was too wide and deep to ford.

Aidan paid the ferryman for both of them and they led the horses onto the boat. Kael snorting and pawing at the rocking craft, but Cecily's mare standing calmly, used to these crossings. Cecily fell silent as they neared Bellport; Aidan could see the worry gather in her eyes. She drew her hood back up over her head and retreated into it, hiding from the world. He wanted to say something encouraging to her, but his own mind was starting to spin. The worries, successfully forgotten on the road, waylaid him now at the sight of the city. The past two days were being torn from him, like a sweet dream, as they swept across the mouth of the river. He looked back over his shoulder, indulging in a last goodbye before turning to face the far shore and Bellport.

The town at the far shore extended to the very edge of the river, dirty and crowded, with weathered wooden houses worn gray by the salt winds. It was larger than any town Aidan had seen. Even as a young boy, their home had been in farm country tucked outside a small village west of Drumcard.

He knew how to listen to the land, how to read it's moods, understand the messages in the wind and the earth, but nothing prepared him for this. He could hear nothing here. Or, more accurately, he could hear too much, so that it sounded like a frantic jumble; the voice of the land muted beneath the swirling of humanity. It tired him, leaving him off balance, unnerved.

As they reached the dock, he could see the wall and gates of Bellport set above the river town, a monstrosity, lacking any grace. Fashioned from thick wood and crudely beaten iron, they stood silent, imposing; a frightened peoples' answer to the dangers of these troubled times.

The ancient city clung to the steep hill above the new wall and gates, rising to overlook all the land below. At it's pinnacle two stone towers watched over the city like sentinels of a bygone era. The sight of them, beautifully crafted and joined by an intricate archway that framed the empty sky, stirred Aidan's heart. He felt as though some memory were trying to surface from the depths of his mind. He couldn't imagine what, as he'd never been near here before. Laying the thoughts aside, he turned his gaze back to the river town.

The ferry docked and Aidan led both horses up the ramp to the riverbank, tying them at the hitching post before going back to escort Cecily. The light was extinguished from her face leaving her with a cold, aloof beauty, but none of the sweetness that captured his heart on the road. He wondered if the city did that to everyone - took the light and the life out of them.

They rode through the town without speaking, following the cobbled street up the hill to the gates of Bellport. Guards carrying short swords and cloaked in red with plumed helmets glinting in the evening sun, patrolled the gates, demanding from everyone who entered, their name and their business in the city. It seemed to Aidan to be a mere formality, for no one was stopped while he watched, though he wondered what he would do if they didn't let him in.

They waited in a short line for their turn to pass. After only a few minutes, the guards motioned them forward demanding that they state their names and business. Aidan was just working himself up to answer when Cecily rode in front of him, threw back her hood with a commanding look and gave them her name. She made no mention of any business. Abashed, they stepped back and bowed to her then hollered up ahead to clear the path so they could enter unhindered.

He rode through the gates behind Cecily, his face burning. Not that he doubted her when she said that her father was Lord of Merrion, but the more practical implications of that hadn't dawned on him until this moment. A wave of guilt and doubt washed over him. He still hadn't enlightened her about his standing in life. He had the sickening feeling that the chasm between their worlds was too great for affection alone to breach. Well, he told himself, he'd see her safely to Marek's house and then disappear from her life. She need never know. At least he could keep the memory of their ride together untarnished.

People in the streets made way for them as they approached - barefoot children scattered between the wagon vendors, faces dirty, clothes torn. Men and women hauling baskets of fish from the docks, and bales of cloth for sale, squeezed against the buildings lining the roads. Their stares held a mixture of fear and deference - though Aidan suspected it was because the two of them were mounted and not necessarily because they recognized Cecily.

They rode past broken down horses wending their way through the narrow streets, pulling carts of goods to sell or ship off at the docks - everything from copper pots, to fine fabrics. Wagons were set up in the streets where their drivers barked out their wares, but nowhere did they see other riders on the road.

Everywhere Aidan looked he saw the same gaunt, deadened expression in people's faces. They were faces that knew no joy, no hope beyond the grasping and striving for another day's bread. Even the rough houses and shops, weathered and dilapidated, mirrored the hopelessness that marked the lower city. His heart ached as he rode. In his worst nightmare he couldn't have imagined an existence like this. A foul stench rose from the streets: rotting fish, garbage, and waste - both human and animal, were dumped into channels lining the cobbled way. Aidan gagged at the fumes and pitied Kael who picked his way over the refuse, unwilling to step in the fetid puddles that collected in the road.

As they wound their way up the hill to the center of Bellport, the heart of the original city, they left the squalor behind. The houses here were larger, more luxurious, and though the cobbled streets were still narrow, in the older section of town the stone, wood, and intricate ironwork of the buildings stood in mute testimony to the glory of a time now gone.

For the first time since he crossed the river, Aidan felt the city speaking to him in one voice. Here it remembered something more than the grasping to buy, sell, and wrest a living from the crowded streets. It was almost as if he could hear a song running through the city, through the houses, the streets, the very earth it stood on; an ancient song, full of life and promise and joy. It brought tears to his eyes and for a moment he forgot about Cecily, about his journey, and wanted nothing more than to give the song a voice - to sing it out for all to hear. He caught himself in time and laughed. He was no singer and would likely make himself a fool in front of everyone, but the song remained, running faintly through the background of the old quarter, the crown of the city, like a life-giving stream.

Cecily led them up and around, through a tangled maze of streets and alleys, ever inward toward the center of Bellport. At last the ground leveled out and they stepped past a line of houses into a clearing. Rising up from the grass in the middle of the clearing were the two stone towers Aidan had seen from the ferry. His heart leapt and he looked over at Cecily to see if she felt it too. Her expression gave no indication of anything, if she did. This was indeed the heart of Bellport. The song he heard originated from the towers themselves. Tears stung Aidan's eyes at the beauty of the song, the sadness woven in harmony to the hope and joy. He was lost in it, in a place outside of time, a place where he knew his heart dwelt, though he'd never seen it before. He didn't realize that Cecily was speaking to him until she reached out and touched his arm.

"Aidan, are you well?" Some warmth broke through her frosty composure as she looked straight at him for the first time since they'd rode into the city.

"I'm sorry? Oh, yes, I'm fine, just looking around." His voice trailed off as he tried to drag his mind back to where she sat. The pull of the towers' song here, on the hill, was stronger, more real than the woman next to him. He shook his head, trying to clear it.

"Marek lives in a house down this lane." She pointed to their right, down a steep cobbled way lined with ornate houses. "Lord Gratton hates it up here, so I knew I wouldn't run into him following this route. He lives on the other side of the city."

Aidan followed her gaze, across the tower circle and down to the north side of the hill. He nodded. It made sense, with what she'd shared about her father, that he'd dislike this place. Even if he couldn't hear the song, perhaps some of it got through to him. He turned Kael with reluctance and followed Cecily away from the towers, down the lane to Marek's house.

They passed house after house along the old street, each could be a small castle - their walls formed from cut granite with intricate carvings, scrollwork, and animals over the windows and doors and on the corners of the homes. The ironwork on the gates was equally ornate, the product of lifetimes of study, work and refinement; its art now lost. Aidan looked longingly around him. He thought of the men and women who built this city, of the Skills they had and the secrets now forgotten. Everywhere the mark of the Elder Born was stamped upon the ancient city. What he would have given for a month with one of the old master craftsmen! He thought of the simple things he'd built on their farm in the marsh and sighed. Would he ever live to see a time of peace where his Skills could be put to use?

Cecily slowed her mare in front of the largest house on the street. The huge front, with windows taller than two men, towered over the lane. Looking up and down the quiet street to see that no one was watching, she motioned for Aidan to follow her up a side alley to the back entrance of the house. The sun had sunk below the horizon leaving a pale gold light lingering in the western sky. The alley lay shadowed between the houses, and the horse's hooves echoed on the cobblestones. Aidan felt his throat tighten as they approached the servant's entrance. What if Marek wasn't home? What would happen to Cecily? How could he help her?

He smiled ruefully. There were no good outcomes here. He equally dreaded the thought that Marek would be home and he would be dismissed, no longer needed, and the dream would be over. Well, it had to end sometime. He took a deep breath and steeled himself for the inevitable.

Cecily dismounted and he followed suite, holding the two horses as she snuck up to the back door, but before she could ring the bell cord the door opened and an elderly servant peered out into the gathering darkness.

"Cecily? Is that you?" His thin reedy call was cut short as he almost ran into her.

"Braxton, I'm right here. Please let me in!" Cecily threw back her hood again and the light from the house shone on her face. The old man smiled and held out both arms to her. She rushed to him, like a child to her father and he hurried her inside.

Aidan stood bewildered outside the door. He didn't know what to do, he supposed he should find the stable and put her mare up; he rather hoped he'd have a chance to say goodbye. He was still debating the right course when her voice floated out into the evening.

"Braxton, I have a friend with me. I met him on the road and he escorted me safely here."

The old man returned to the door and peered shortsightedly into the dark.

"Hello sir," Aidan ventured. He didn't want to startle the fellow.

"Good evening," the man answered in a stiff voice. "We thank you for seeing Lady Cecily to our home. Would you like to come in and take some supper before you continue on your way?"

Aidan's face grew hot. It was clear that he was an unwelcome extra to this party. "No, thank you. If you'll point me to the stables I'll return her mare there and be off."

"No need for you to do that, young man." The servant looked at him suspiciously. "I'll ring the stable boy to fetch her. The falcon flew in just an hour ago with a message from Marek telling us to expect our Lady's arrival."

It was Aidan's turn to look surprised. "How did he know? Cecily didn't tell him she was coming."

The old man smiled smugly. "Nothing escapes Marek's notice. And Lady Cecily holds a special place in his heart." He continued to look down his sharp nose at Aidan. Cecily was long gone, ushered into the house by another servant.

"I'll be taking my leave then," Aidan said, with as much dignity as he could muster.

"Yes. Goodbye." The old man closed the door firmly in Aidan's face.

He turned and threw himself onto Kael, resisting the urge to growl and pound at the door. Of all the rude, demeaning, insensitive... His thoughts trailed off as he turned out of the alley and back toward the lane. Taking a deep breath he tried to put it behind him. Had the man known he wasn't wealthy? Why did he spirit Cecily away and turn him out without so much as a kind word? He let Kael make his own way down the lane and back toward the lower city. His head throbbed and he had a hard time thinking straight.

He pushed back the questions that crowded his mind. It was better this way - hard, but better. He had no business with someone like Cecily and it wasn't like he was even free to court her. He was Elder Born and she was nobility. The two don't mix.

He swallowed hard, as though the motion could suppress his bitterness, and rode out of the old city, away from the song that animated it, and into the new quarters where a night's lodging wouldn't dwindle as much of his gold. Along the oceanfront he found a shabby inn with a broken down stable and yard in the back where he could rest Kael. After he had seen to his horse's supper, he shouldered his bags and trudged up the inn steps under a creaking sign that read, The Rusty Tub.

The innkeeper was a pleasant enough fellow, broad shouldered with a thatch of wavy blonde hair and bloodshot eyes. He looked like he enjoyed his ale as much as his customers did, but he was free with his talk, telling Aidan news of the city as he dished out a thick fish and potato stew onto a wooden plate for him. The inn was quiet and Aidan decided to risk asking the man's help in finding Reeves.

"I've come looking for an old friend of the family," he started, not sure yet how much information he would need to divulge. "I haven't seen him in years and don't know the best way of finding his whereabouts."

The innkeeper gave him a knowing look. "I'll need more than that to go on, lad, if I'm to help you."

Aidan, sensing no malice in the man, continued. "He was an accomplished musician the last I heard, though I don't know how he earns his bread these days. He is known by the name, Reeves."

He watched as the innkeeper sorted through a mental list of acquaintances. "Sorry lad, I've never heard the name before, but I'll put the word out for you if you'd like. And you're welcome here 'till you get hold of him. Maybe you should try the inns in the old city. Some pay a pretty bag of silver for a tune. Folks up that way have it to spare. Down here by the wharf, a bottle of ale's all the consolation we have."

Aidan smiled his thanks. He was glad for a direction to start his search in the morning and what the man said made sense. He finished his supper and retired to his sleeping pallet in a tiny upstairs room. Bone tired and weary of heart, he was asleep as soon as his head touched the blankets.

It felt like moments later when he awoke suddenly, all his senses straining. Something was wrong. He wasn't sure if he'd dreamed it or not but he thought he'd heard a girl cry for help. His first thought was Cecily, but that didn't make sense. He heard shouts outside his window - sounded like a drunken brawl. Dazed and exhausted he staggered to his feet and flung open the shutters.

There, just below, three men were closing in on what looked like an old man and a boy. He caught the flash of a knife and the old man crumpled to the ground, the boy running to his side. Aidan yelled, hoping to startle the attackers.

The man with the knife stopped for a moment, looking for the source of the noise. In that instant the boy drew himself up. Aidan wasn't quite sure what happened next. With his mind he heard a girl's voice shout

"NO!"

He was knocked back from the window by what felt like a battering ram. When he crawled back up to see what happened, the men were running toward the wharf. In a moment the attackers disappeared into the darkness. The boy knelt on the cobblestones, cradling the old man's head in his arms.

At the entrance of the alley he heard hoofbeats and another man's voice. A tall, well built man, with a commanding air, ran to the scene of the fight. He lifted the old man with great care and called back to the street for help. From out of the darkness he heard cart wheels grating on the stones. He murmured something to the boy which seemed to comfort him and then carried the wounded man out of the alley, the boy at his side.

Still dazed from whatever had hit him, Aidan sat back down on his pallet. Clearly, the old man and the boy were now in good hands, and there was nothing that he could do to help. He shook his head, trying to piece together what just happened. Where did the girl's voice come from, and who or what hit him? He stared out at the starless sky without any real hope of answers. The predawn carts were rolling over the cobbles when Aidan finally lay back down again to finish his night's sleep.

CHAPTER 5

THE COUNSELOR

After two days on the open sea, Orvis turned their boat toward shore. A stiff wind drove them in over the crested waves, the white sails snapping. The weather remained fair, much to Elana's relief, and Orvis had taken them far enough out to sea that they saw no signs of any other craft. Straining for a sight of land, Elana watched with anticipation as the outline of rocks climbed over the horizon, a welcome change from the rolling green water. She hadn't said anything to Orvis; she could see how much the ocean meant to him, but her body ached for the feel of solid ground under her feet. He was right about the sea not being a part of her. Not that it didn't stir something in her; she just felt out of her element. Thankfully, she didn't suffer from seasickness, but the monotony of endless waves grew tiresome.

The coast, as they neared the shore, became rugged. The grass covered dunes gave way to jagged rocks that loomed above the water, their high craggy faces frowning at them, impenetrable and almost, it seemed, menacing. Elana's stomach turned queasy at the sight. Her Waking tugged at her. She took a deep breath, stood up, and let the focus of her eyes soften, hoping to catch a glimpse of whatever was disturbing her.

With a surge that made her grip the sides of the boat, her Waking flared. Now as she looked along the shoreline she saw the jagged rocks, still there, but blurred, indistinct, engulfed in a shadow whose roiling, malignant presence spread groping tendrils out to the very edges of the coast. A presence reached out toward her, seeking, but not seeking blindly. It reminded her forcefully of the Hunter. She clapped her hand over her mouth, biting her palm to stifle a scream. She'd heard her parents and now Orvis talk about it, but that didn't prepare her for seeing the Shadow herself. Knees shaking, she sat back down in the boat, her Waking seeping away.

The knot in her stomach clenched tighter, making it impossible to choke down the breakfast Orvis offered. She shivered and pulled her cloak higher around her shoulders, as if by this she could ward off the presence within the Shadow.

By midday they rounded a sharp bend and entered the harbor. From here, Elana caught sight of the old city high on the hill overlooking the sea, its arched stone towers rising from the center like an ancient crown. For the first time since her glimpse of the Shadow that morning, her stomach unknotted. Hope rose once again at the sight of the city, and she squinted her eyes for a better view. Somewhere in Bellport dwelt Reeves and with him, she breathed a silent prayer to the Ancient Ones, help for her parents.

She sat, taking in the activity and bustle of the crowded harbor as Orvis navigated their boat, searching for an available dock. Fishing boats of all sizes vied with each other for space at the docks, and merchants' ships cut through the harbor waves, heavily laden with goods to sell or transport up the coast. At the wharf, grayed storefronts and inns, shabby and in need of repair, serviced the sailors whose shouts carried across the harbor. Fights broke out, starting and ending without anyone slowing their work to take notice or intervene. Beyond the wharf, she could hear the faint cries of vendors barking their wares. As the old sailor butted up to an empty dock and tied the small ship, the putrid smell of rotting fish, and the acrid scent of tar, assaulted her senses.

"You'd best keep silent lass," Orvis counseled her. "I'll do the talking for the both of us. This is no place for the likes of you."

Rough looking men, shirtless and tattooed, some with missing teeth, eyes, or limbs, leered at her and she pulled her hood down over her face, remembering what Orvis said about her still looking too pretty to pass for a boy. She stuck close to him, keeping her eyes down and trying to keep her Waking in check as well. She didn't want to imagine what would happen if her Waking burst out here. She willed herself to be inconspicuous, not worth anyone's attention, a mouse running between the paws of a lion.

Orvis paid his silver for the privilege of docking the boat and the two of them, shouldering their packs and dragging the nanny goat by a short rope, set off for the port town.

"It ain't safe to leave anything on the ship once it goes to dock," he told her. "Not without a man standing guard who's handy with a piece of steel. We'll sell the goat and then see about finding the Captain so we can get our gold and move on."

Elana nodded, struggling under her heavy pack. People pushed and shoved them from all directions in their rush to get where they were going. The cobblestones under foot were slick where the shopkeepers emptied buckets of filthy water and wastes right onto the road. More than once Elana stumbled, scrambling to keep herself from going down in the greasy muck.

Orvis stopped at an inn a few blocks off the waterfront, eyeing the place in silence. He nodded to himself, turned and gave her a wink, and then, before her eyes, he bristled up, like an old dog readying for a fight. The scowl lines in his face deepened and a warning glint lit in his eye.

"This is as good a place as any." he growled. "Don't stare and remember, let me do the talking."

They picked their way around to the back of the inn where Orvis waylaid the innkeeper coming through the kitchen. His already gruff voice and mannerisms grew hostile as he bargained, snarling back and forth with the man over the price of the goat. When they'd settled the deal, a fair amount more silver than Elana imagined they'd get, he stumped off down the street muttering something about finding the Captain.

She followed him in silence, trudging inland and uphill. They pushed their way through the crowded new quarters that spilled down from the old city like so much scum boiling over the rim of a pot. In the streets ragged children begged for food, picking through scraps with

86

the dogs. No one smiled as they passed; grim faces looked through her, drawn tight into themselves. She tried to avoid the faces marked with over bright eyes and the false cheer brought on by too much drink. The very air around them seethed with anger and unrest. She looked over at Orvis to see if he felt it, but he had shut himself away, still dark and bristling. Hoisting her pack higher on her back, she plodded after him.

After what seemed like hours weaving their way through the twisted streets, he stopped at a derelict inn with filthy windows and a broken sign swinging from a single chain over the door. The sign was weathered and cracked, the paint peeling off. Elana couldn't make out the name of the inn.

"Stick close to me," Orvis told her. "This ain't the nicest establishment you'll ever see. But I'll get news of the Captain's whereabouts here if I'm not mistaken."

She tailed him into the inn; it seemed a glorified name for this dingy room with an old bar and handful of broken down tables, encrusted with dust, and smelling of mold and strong drink. Orvis walked straight up to the bar. A wiry man with stringy gray hair and tattoos covering his arms stepped up. Elana didn't know if he was there to help them or to run them off. Orvis grunted his question in the man's direction. The man answered him in tones too low for Elana to overhear and apparently satisfied with the answer he got, Orvis muttered a farewell and turned to leave.

Before they'd crossed the short length of the floor, another tattooed sailor with a silver ring in his nose stood up, knocking his stool back and sloshing some foul smelling brew down his bare chest.

"What'll ya take for the lad?" he slurred.

Elana shuddered. He was talking about her. She stuck tight to Orvis who ignored the man and reaching the door, pushed it open. The man lurched out from behind his table and made a grab for her. Before she realized what was happening Orvis wheeled around, steel flashing from his hand and the man, who had just caught hold of her sleeve, fell back bellowing.

"Your slit throat if you don't keep your hands to yourself," Orvis growled. With a firm hand he steered her out the door and into the open air.

"Who was that?" she asked, trying to keep her voice steady.

"Low life. This city's full of 'em. You all right?" With a quick flick, he wiped the blade of his knife on his trousers and sheathed it once again.

Elana nodded in answer. "I didn't know you carried a knife."

"Tools of the trade. Wish it weren't so, but I'd rather have it to use, than need it and be without." He turned away from her and headed back down the hill toward the port.

"The Captain's due in this afternoon. With a little luck we can get hold of him before he's been too long in the taverns, and get our gold. Then we'll be quit of this rat hole. Unless I'm much mistaken, I don't figure we'll find Reeves here. We'll go up there to make our search." He pointed up to the towers on the top of the hill.

Elana followed his finger; once again, the sight of the arched towers stirred something inside her. They stood tall and majestic, like an outpost against the Shadow. Almost, she imagined, they were the heart of all that was once good and beautiful about this city. Reluctantly she turned back down toward the squalid wharf. They still had to finish their business before they were free to climb the hill and look for Reeves.

After half a dozen inquires, Orvis found the dock where the Captain was to land. He slipped the guard some coins and they climbed over the ropes that sectioned off the landing docks from the rest of the port. There they waited on the empty pilings, isolated for the moment from the bustle all around. By the time the ship arrived, the sun was sinking behind Bellport. Orvis met the Captain as he came down the gangplank.

The man seemed kindly compared to the other characters Elana had seen that day. He gave orders for his men to unload the ship and then asked Orvis to lead the way to the fishing boat. With eager hands he inspected every inch of the boat, running nimble fingers over the smoothed boards and checking all the joints and fittings. When he was satisfied he paid them gold on the spot, clapping Orvis on the shoulder and thanking him in a hearty voice.

As Orvis shook hands with the man and tucked the bag of gold into his tunic pocket, Elana noticed three men watching from inside an old schooner docked close by. One of them, a huge man with a black eye patch, caught her looking and yanked the other two down out of sight. The skin on the back of her neck prickled as they walked off the docks. She was glad when they were safely quit of the wharf and heading back into town.

"Let's find a place to get some supper before we head up to the old city," Orvis suggested. Elana, her stomach growling and her legs weak from hunger, agreed. He led them to an inn along the waterfront that looked better kept than most. The sign, newly painted and hanging straight above the door, announced to all that the Golden Keg was open for business. Inside, the smells set her mouth watering.

Orvis found them a table in the back, away from curious eyes. They ordered fresh fish - its thick white meat flaking off the bones, hot bread, carrots and potatoes, and boiled greens, all drenched in butter. They ate in silence, relishing a cooked meal after days of slim rations aboard the fishing boat. It was dark by the time they had finished, sated from their meal and weary from the afternoon's walking.

"We'd best be off and find a place to lodge for the night. Tomorrow'll be time enough to head up the hill. Nighttime's no time for hanging about these streets." Orvis squeezed through the crowded room and paid the innkeeper for their meal.

Sitting alone, Elana felt the back of her neck prickle again and turned to find a man watching her while Orvis and the innkeeper talked. She looked quickly away and pulled her hood down over her face. When Orvis came back he said that there were no rooms here but the innkeeper had recommended a lodging house down the street. She followed him to the door, keeping her hood low until they were outside.

"Just down the street here and take the last alley on the left." Orvis recounted the innkeeper's directions. He scanned the storefronts on either side, making sure they were heading the right way.

In the dark the streets were less crowded, though the groups of sailors that passed seemed louder, wilder than in daylight and most of them smelling strongly of drink. They turned at last into a narrow alley that came to a dead end just in front of the harbor. Ahead of them they saw an inn, its light spilling into the alley from an open door.

"That must be it," Orvis said and quickened his pace.

"Hey you!"

The shout shattered the silence of the alley. Orvis spun around at the sound and pushed Elana roughly behind him. "Get to the inn," he barked.

She didn't mean to disobey. But she couldn't move. The blood stopped in her veins. Her legs froze, rooted to the spot. Booted steps pounded down the alley from the street and even in the dim light of the streetlamp Elana was sure she recognized the huge man from the schooner.

Without stopping to think what she was doing, she cried out with her Waking, just as her father had called to her without a voice, speaking directly inside her mind the morning the Hunter attacked. Before she could wonder how she did it, from somewhere out in the night, she felt a faint response, then another. Hope flashed momentarily in her mind and then, as she looked up the alley, it died. Two other men materialized out of the shadows, flanking the huge man with the eye patch; all of them with knives drawn. Wherever those responses came from, she was foolish to believe that they could find her here in time, even assuming they would want to help.

They'd never make the inn door before the men caught them. Orvis seemed to have drawn the same conclusion. He threw down his pack and stood his ground, his knife glinting dully in the dim light. Only his rapid breathing betrayed any trace of fear. She stood with him, facing the men, her heart beating wildly, hands clammy. She took a deep breath, trying to steady herself, wishing that she had some weapon at hand.

In a moment the men were upon them, circling like starved wolves, their eyes cold, unfeeling. The man with the eye patch spoke first. "We saw you take a bag of gold from that Captain on the docks, Grandpa. Hand it over now and you just might get out of here alive."

Orvis reached into his tunic as though searching for the gold and Elana heard the clunk of the heavy pieces. The men drew closer, hungry for their prize, greed etched across their faces, eyes gloating. They circled close enough for her to smell their sour stench, unwashed bodies, drink, and tar from the shipyards. Slowly Orvis pulled the sack from his tunic pocket. Elana's heart sunk. She knew he had to give in - it was three against one, but that gold was to get them to Farran.

Then, as the one eyed man grabbed for the sack Orvis jumped back and whipped it across his face, knocking him off balance. Before the other two realized what had happened, he'd slashed his knife clear through the man's shoulder, severing the tendons. The big man howled, clutching his limp arm as his companions watched, dumbstruck.

Elana wanted to cheer. She was just as surprised as the men, who looked like they'd lost their taste for a fight. Orvis reached down to pick up his bags and Elana, her legs obeying her again, started running for the inn. She heard Orvis following, when behind her, with a roar like an enraged animal, the man with the eye patch flung himself at Orvis. She spun around in time to see the old sailor crumple to the ground, a dark stain spreading across the back of his tunic. She screamed and ran back, collapsing over the old sailor, trying to shield his body with her own.

The one-eyed man closed in, his companions behind him now; faces mad with vengeance, ready to finish the job. From an open window overhead someone yelled. Her attacker hesitated for a moment, glancing up and Elana followed his gaze. A young man with tawny hair and eyes was hanging out the window, yelling. When he turned toward her, their eyes met. For a wild moment, Elana was sure she knew him, but the impression was lost as she turned back to Orvis' attacker.

She had no weapon with which to face him, but this time Elana stood up, rage pounding through her. She stared the man down, seeing uncertainty, then fear spread over his face. The power of her Waking built in her like a wave - feeding on the anger. She focused it on the men.

With everything in her she cried, "NO!" and unleashed the wave.

The men slammed against the cobblestones. She heard one of them shout, "It's an Elder Born witch! Run!" Panic in their eyes, they crawled to their feet and bolted past her. In seconds they were lost in the shadows that clung to the harbor. Elana's Waking drained out.

From out on the street cries sounded and hoofbeats rang on the cobblestones of the alley. Elana saw a man galloping toward them. She had a fleeting realization that she'd just given herself away as an Elder Born and then all thoughts of the world around her gave way to worry about Orvis.

She sunk to her knees cradling Orvis' head, oblivious now to everything but his face, gray with pain, and the hot red blood seeping out of the gash in his tunic. Please don't die, she begged silently, brushing the old sailor's white hair back from his face. The man on horseback was upon them before she knew he was there. He jumped off his horse and shouted back to the street for help. In a daze she registered footsteps running to obey his command. With gentle hands the man peeled off Orvis' tunic and inspected the wound. Orvis opened his eyes, struggling to get away.

"Lay still, my friend. That's a nasty gash. I've sent for help." His voice was strong, used to giving orders, and his piercing eyes reminded Elana of a hawk. Orvis lay back, his breathing labored.

The man turned to Elana. "I've called for my carriage. We can move him to my house and I will have my physician tend to him." His eyes probed hers while he spoke. There was something familiar about him; she just couldn't place it right now. She turned back to Orvis, forcing herself to think, to answer.

"Thank you, sir." She choked out the words. Now that her Waking was gone, she found herself shaking. "I can't lose him, he's all I have."

The man picked up her hand in a gesture of sympathy and looked at her. She forced herself to meet his gaze, tried to manage a weak smile of thanks. For the briefest of moments his presence was there, just a flash, but there in her mind. She jerked her hand away, startled by the intrusion and looked down. Had she imagined it? Her heart pounded. What if he was a Hunter? She'd just given herself away and now he had Orvis too. Panic rose, threatening to drown out all clear thought. Breathe, she commanded her body. She took a deep breath. Her head cleared a little.

She snuck a glance at the man but he made no sign of having felt anything strange. Yet a lingering familiarity hovered over the place where she had felt his presence. Then she placed it. He had been one of the ones to answer her cry for help. Relief washed over her. From out in the street the rumbling of carriage wheels brought back her fear for Orvis once again, and drove all other thoughts from her mind.

"I'm going to have to carry him," the man said. "Will you be able to walk to the carriage?"

"Yes. I'm not hurt."

Her knees trembled and she forced herself to take small steps, following the man, with Orvis in his arms, until she reached the protection of the carriage. There she collapsed onto a seat while the man stretched the wounded sailor out on the opposite side. The carriage lurched forward and she closed her eyes, wishing it could all be a nightmare and she could wake up to find the rocking of the carriage was their boat, and they were still safe at sea.

A groan brought her back and she sprung forward, reaching out for Orvis' hand. "I'm here Orvis," she whispered. "This man's going to get you help."

His fingers squeezed hers and she stayed by his side, sitting on the carriage floor, aware of the stranger's keen gaze upon her. She realized after a long silence that she didn't even know the man's name.

"I'm sorry sir, we are in your debt and I don't even know your name."

"I am Marek," he answered, as though he'd been waiting for the question. "And you are?"

She took a moment to answer. Her mind was racing. Marek! Reeves spoke of someone by that name in his letter. This man knew Reeves. "My name is Elana," she said, throwing away all thought of pretense. She remembered Reeves saying something about him being in danger. He would understand then. She looked up at him, curiosity in her face. What brought him to the docks on this night? He must be a good man to offer help to strangers so willingly.

Maybe they would succeed. Orvis would recover - he had to, and they would find Reeves and he would help her parents. She clung to these shards of hope, gleaning whatever small strength she could from them.

"I'm honored to meet you, Elana," Marek said, inclining his head toward her. "And who is your companion here?"

"His name is Orvis."

"I won't lie to you," Marek told her, his voice sober, "he is gravely injured, but you're both lucky to be alive at all. My physician is the best in the city. I will do all in my power to see that he recovers."

"Thank you, thank you so much," Elana breathed out. She sat, back against the seat of the carriage, and closed her eyes, squeezing back hot tears, not wanting to let Marek see her cry.

Night masked their destination as the carriage lurched and turned, winding ever upwards until the noise of the lower city was lost behind them. Finally, only the wheels on the cobbled streets, and the horses' hooves, sounded in the dark. Orvis' grip on Elana's hand weakened until, at last, she lost him to unconsciousness. Unwilling to relinquish his hand, she clung to the old sailor, her hope waning with each turn. Marek rode in silence beside her.

After what seemed an endless ride, the carriage jolted to a stop. Hands reached in, prying Orvis' hand out of her grip, then someone helped her navigate the step down.

"There now, you must let the physician tend to your companion. Marek will see that he gets the best possible care." The voice belonged to an elderly man who held a lamp up as he peered down his long thin nose at her. His scant hair was parted and combed with precision across his shining head. He steadied her as she stepped out of the carriage and steered her into a massive house. Once inside, he rang a small silver bell hanging in the entrance. A serving woman bustled up.

"Marietta, see to it that our guest lacks for nothing."

The plump serving woman curtsied.

"Oh, Marietta, please be sure that no one disturbs her. She has had a most difficult evening. These are Marek's express wishes."

"Certainly, Braxton," the serving woman replied and, and with a warm smile, gestured for Elana to follow her. Braxton turned on his heel and walked off.

"But what about Orvis?" Elana turned back toward the door where two more serving men bore Orvis through to another room.

"My lady?" Marietta's glance lingered on her unusual garb. "In this house, indeed in most all of Bellport, the Master's word is law. If he said that he'll help your friend, than rest assured that he will, and don't go meddling when it's time for you to step back."

Elana's face reddened.

The serving woman shook her head, clucking under her breath. "I'll peek in through the night. If it looks too bad, I'll make sure you can bid your respects. It's a nasty business, mixing with those sailors down by the docks. You're lucky to be here at all. Now, let's get you to your room. A proper bath wouldn't hurt you, neither."

Exhaustion overcame Elana and she gave up, allowing herself to be led down a winding series of halls, into a lavish room. Marietta rang a bell in the room and another serving girl appeared. Before long Elana found herself in a hot bath with Marietta scrubbing her down as though she was a small child. She was too tired to protest. Another bell rang and clean clothes were brought, finely spun linens trimmed in lace, and satins in jewel-bright colors. Elana had never seen such richness. She tried not to think of her cropped hair and coarse appearance in the midst of such luxury. Once out of the bath, Marietta had her dried, dressed and tucked into bed before she could utter a word.

"Now you sleep, dearie. You've had a bad day and that's for sure. Let's hope the night brings better news." She set a cup of steaming hot tea down on a night table and stood over Elana while she drank it.

The tea gave off the faint smell of sedative herbs. The smell brought back memories of helping her mother care for the sick and wounded. Tears stung her eyes. She finished the bitter tea and was sleeping before she laid her head on the feather pillow.

Whether it was the tea, or the events of the day, dark images stalked her dreams: the Shadow crawling over the coast, Orvis crumpled on the cobblestones, the crimson stain spreading over his tunic, and a man with hawk's eyes swooping down and pulling her up in his talons. She tossed and turned through the night, grateful, when morning brought a reprieve.

Slipping out of bed, she threw open the curtains and searched in vain for her pack. Instead of her own clothes, she found a pale blue, linen dress spread over the chair by the window. She felt awkward wearing such finery, but it was better than roaming the house in a borrowed nightgown. She pulled it on and laced up the slippers that were set neatly under the chair, surprised that both were a near fit. She was smaller boned than most of the Valefolk, and was used to clothes hanging on her. With a blue silk ribbon that Marietta left, she tied back her hair, making a striking picture in the glass on the wall.

Now that she was fully awake, she studied the room around her. Whatever else Marek was, he was certainly rich. Didn't Marietta say something about his word being law in Bellport? She scowled, trying to figure that out. Lord Gratton was ruler of Merrion, and the Lord's Seat was in Bellport.

Her father had spent hours teaching her about how the Valefolk ruled themselves. She racked her brain, trying to remember.

There were three main Lordships, which long ago, corresponded to the three Elderships. Merrion spread out along the coast, with Bellport as it's main city, controlling the trade up and down the shore as well as along the mouth of the rivers Gavril and Naal. The Bells Eldership used to dwell in Bellport, with Elders renowned for both song and sailing.

Glenariff, the largest of the Lordships, controlled the richest land in the Vale, from the Shadow Mountains in the West, down to the salt marshes in the South. From what her father had told her, their ancient boundary line lay along the lower river Naal, running from West to East across the center of the Vale. In recent years, with Lord Ulrich sitting in the Lord's seat, Glenariff's borders had been creeping north, across the river, challenging the Freefolk of Lanreath.

Drumcard was home to the Lord's Seat of Glenariff, established long ago, by the Orchard Tree Eldership. It had been, in it's prime, the center for all craftsmanship, for fine art, and for the making of ingenious devices, whose usefulness spread throughout the Vale. The Elders' Skills with the land and their ability to fashion things with their hands, brought great wealth to Glenariff, which, while the Elders remained, was renowned for its peace and prosperity.

The third Lordship, Lanreath, was home to the Freefolk. The smallest and least arable of the three, it lay between the rivers Gavril and Naal, extending north into the Boarder Mountains and west to the Shadow Mountains. Much of its land was rocky, mountainous, and forbidding. The Firestone Elders dwelt long ago in Laharan, city of the Firestone. There, set in Firestone Peak, the most powerful of all the Ancient Ones' Gifts kept watch over the Vale, protecting it from the Shadow's threat in the West.

Elana grimaced. Few believed those tales anymore, and since the Elders locked up the Firestone and fled Laharan, even the Freefolk abandoned that place. It was said that the city was now hidden, lost in the trackless hills. The Freefolk dwelt in three clans, each responsible for the well-being of its members, and mingling with the other clans only to trade their goods. The wealthier clans lived along Glenariff's boarders, fighting now to maintain their traditional land rights. That was all Elana could remember.

So where did Marek fit in to all this? She puzzled over it a moment more and then laid it aside. She'd keep her eyes and ears open while she was here. Now though, she needed to find Orvis. At the thought of him, fears that she'd managed to keep at bay since she woke, rushed in.

Creeping into the darkened hallway, she tried to recall any scrap of memory from last night to help her find her way.

"You are up, my lady."

Elana jumped at the voice. Behind her, Braxton seemed to have materialized from out of nowhere.

"Yes, thank you sir. I was hoping to find my friend, Orvis." She took a deep breath, trying to keep the panic out of her voice and asked the question she feared. "Is he - did he - he's not..." She couldn't finish. In spite of her effort, a tear slid down her cheek.

Braxton's somber face warmed for a moment. "No, my lady. He is with us still, though it was touch and go throughout the night. The physician believes that no vital organs were pierced. He has ordered strict rest for your friend and given him a dose of curatives that will help him sleep. He has a long road before him to regain his strength."

Elana sighed in relief. "I should like to see him if I may," she asked. "I know he's sleeping, but it would ease my own heart to be near him a while."

The older man inclined his head. "Certainly, my lady. Follow me." He led her through a maze of corridors, some broad with intricate benches resting under windows twice the height of a grown man, some darkened and narrow, with only an occasional wall sconce giving off a guttering light, up steep steps and down again, until Elana had lost all sense of direction. They stopped at last in front of a small door. Elana pushed it open, her hands shaking.

In the center of a gracious room, Orvis lay sleeping on a freshly made bed, his face pale in the morning light. His breathing came in gasps, ragged and shallow, as though the act of drawing breath pained him. She knelt by the bed and reached up, touching the old sailor's white hair. He looked smaller here, so frail.

Footsteps sounded in the hall behind her. "Elana."

She turned to see Marek enter the room. Braxton bowed and backed out, closing the door as he left.

"The Ancient Ones smile on you. You are fortunate indeed to have your friend with us still." Marek took her arm and led her to a low bench along the far wall. At his touch, she again felt the pressing of his presence - not threatening, but powerful. She accepted it as a part of him, afraid to do anything that would seem ungrateful. Looking around, she felt humbled at their debt to him. Without his help, Orvis would have died in the night.

"I don't know how to thank you," she began, "You've done so much for us. We could never begin to repay you."

He waved aside her words, his keen eyes holding her own. "We are of a kind, you and I." He paused, letting the implication of his words sink in.

Elana swallowed hard, then nodded. She knew that he was Elder Born. She had never been around anyone, save the Hunter, whose Skill presence was this powerful. However, being this open about it took some getting used to.

Marek's face softened for a moment. "Ours is a life of hiding," he said, half to himself, "of covering up who and what we are. One longs for others with whom one can stop pretending." His words carried with them a vulnerability that seemed at odds with his controlled demeanor. Her heart warmed toward this man who seemed to possess everything and yet have no one to share it with.

On impulse she whispered, "I would never betray you. I promise. Our lives are indebted to you. And..." She paused, unsure of whether it was rude to say more.

"Yes?" His eyes held hers, a suppressed eagerness lighting them.

Elana jumped in. "I am very much in need of your help, as an Elder Born." She blushed at her own forthrightness, and then added, "If you are willing."

He nodded for her to continue.

"I must be honest with you though and tell you that even by helping me last night, you draw trouble to your own house."

"I am not afraid for myself, Elana. But I am afraid for you. If you would confide in me, I will do everything in my power to help you."

Tears of gratitude stung her eyes. "Thank you."

He smiled at her and stood, beckoning her to follow. "It's best not to wake your friend. Let's breakfast together in my private garden. There we can speak without fear of being overheard."

He led the way back through the maze of corridors until they came upon a door leading into a high walled garden. Elana stepped through the door and gasped at its beauty. Flowering vines climbed the stone walls and an arched trellis laden with early blooming roses formed an alcove, within which sat a small stone table and benches. A breakfast of fruit, golden bread, soft cheese, and spiced wine was laid on the table.

Marek gestured for her to sit and then joined her, serving her deftly as though it was his honor. As they ate, his questions drew out the entire story of the letter, the Hunter, her parents' kidnapping, and their flight to Bellport. She tried to remember everything relevant to her parent's rescue, fearing that any caution on her part now would only thwart Marek's ability to help her.

He listened attentively, probing at several points, each around her Waking. When she recounted the fight in the alley he stopped her.

"Have you had any training?"

"None," she answered. "My parents thought it safer to wait until we reached Farran."

"How were you able to block those men with your Skill?"

"I don't know. I was so angry at them for hurting Orvis, my Waking surged up in me and when I shouted at them, it seemed like all the force of my Waking hit them." She shook her head. "I didn't know that sort of thing was even possible. I don't think I could do it again, though."

Marek nodded, thoughtful, his eyes never leaving her. "Your father is right about the power of your Skills. I know of no untrained Elders, and almost no trained ones, who could send a mind cry and overcome three armed men. What you have is extraordinary... and dangerous." His eyes narrowed and he shook his head. "It's no small wonder that a Hunter is on your trail. They can feel the power. The docks will be crawling with Black Knights today. I wouldn't give a brass coin for your life if you had stayed down there through the night."

The hair on the back of her neck prickled. In her fear for Orvis' life, she never considered the consequences of using her Waking. "What will I do?" she asked him, desperate now. "I have to get to Reeves."

Marek remained silent, looking past her, seemingly lost in his own thoughts.

She shifted in her seat. If Marek couldn't, or wouldn't help her...

Almost as though he'd read her thoughts, Marek shook his head and smiled at her. "I do know Reeves, and I will send word to him, if he remains in Bellport. With the Hunter searching for you, he may be forced to leave. They have long been on his trail as well." He paused, studying her, and Elana could feel tension under his calm surface.

"You are so young," he began. "I don't want to burden you. Yet..." His words trailed off.

Elana leaned forward in her seat.

"What do you think of the prophecy?" he asked.

A chill passed through Elana. She had not spoken of her desire to be one of those to fulfill it. Yet she felt Marek's mind jumping beyond her words to that point.

"It stirs something in me," she began, not wanting to appear presumptuous. I can't put it down."

Marek's voice intoned the prophecy:

The three will rise to reunite

When the Shadow's arm grows long

Together push the darkness back:

The Key, the Seed, the Song.

At his words, her Waking surged again. The garden, the table, even Marek grew indistinct. She saw a woman standing before her, holding out an intricately wrought bronze key. There were rugged mountains in the background. The woman was speaking but Elana couldn't make out her words.

As suddenly as it appeared, the vision vanished. Marek was sitting across from her, gripping the table with both hands; his face pale.

"Elana, are you okay?"

She nodded, unable to speak yet.

"I'm sorry to have pressed you like this. All my questions can wait. What can't wait is your training." He came around to where she was and knelt before her. "It shouldn't have to be done this way, but I fear for your life if you leave this place. I have never offered this to another…" Here he paused. "But would you be willing to entrust me with your training?"

Elana's heart hammered in her chest. He would be willing to train her? This was more than she dared hope for. Thoughts crowded and pushed each other in her mind and there, in the midst of her excitement, the image of the man with hawk's eyes, returned unbidden, from last night's dreams. Fear knotted her stomach. Was Marek that man? Was the Hunter? How could she know? She wanted the training… knew she needed it.

Traditionally, all training was done, either by an Elder of the same gender, or by a parent. All the Elder Born went through the same early training, and then if they had the desire, once they had mastered their Waking and begun to use their Skills, they sought out a leader among their own Eldership to pursue further training, specific to their Skill abilities. She had harbored the hope that if she lived in Farran, then Geri, the head Firestone Elder, might consider taking her on for advanced training.

She looked over at Marek, feeling his Skill presence. A new thought formed itself in her mind. He was powerful enough to take her training beyond the early levels, and if he could, then maybe she would be able to fulfill the prophecy. That tipped the balance. She needed all the help she could get, and if Marek had meant to harm them, why would he go to such trouble to help them. Her resolve gained momentum. She pushed all her fears and cautions aside.

"Yes, thank you. I never meant to ask so much of you." She met Marek's keen eyes for a moment, before looking away. His presence was still unnerving.

"You are of the Firestone Eldership," he said. "I am as well. We are fortunate. I would not be able to do as much for you if our Skills were not compatible." He continued, "Orvis, for example, is of the Bells Eldership. So is Reeves. Neither one could equip you properly for what lies ahead. Elana, I will not lie to you. Your Skills exceed any I have seen. But before we can focus them, we'll need a way of hiding your power from those who would harm you."

She nodded, remembering the Hunter, and the Shadow crawling over the coast.

"The only way I know of accomplishing this, is extremely advanced." He weighed her in his gaze. "I don't know if you will be able to do it. Most Elders are unable to develop their Skills to that level."

She bristled and drew herself up, ready to prove that she could meet any challenge. "Try me. I have never had a direction to channel my Skills before. I will do whatever it takes."

Marek's laugh rang out. "I couldn't ask for more than that." The laughter died and he grew serious again, holding her with his eyes. For a long moment he remained silent. When he spoke, his voice was sober. "What I am speaking of is a mind link."

Elana looked down, feeling the blood rush to her face. Her boast taunted her. This was the last thing she imagined. A mind link left the people joined, perilously vulnerable to one another. It was considered the most advanced, and one of the most dangerous of Skill practices, reserved for the leaders of the Elderships, and used only in times of grave danger. It was the abuse of Skills like this that gave the Valefolk cause to fear and hate the Elder Born. The Valefolk had little defense against such power if the Elder Born used it to control them.

"I know it breaks all tradition and propriety," Marek spoke, his voice low. "But it's the only way I know to place myself between you and the Hunters." He waited, giving her time to think.

Her face grew hot again, this time ashamed for doubting him. He was offering to put himself at tremendous risk to shelter her. It was foolish of her to turn away.

"I'm sorry. I just never imagined..." she faltered. "But you are so kind to risk this for me. I am willing." A cold knot tightened in her stomach. This was not the way it should be, but then, neither was her parent's capture, nor Orvis' wounding. If she was unable to adjust, she would likely end up dead, or worse..."

He smiled. "I understand."

"What do I need to do?"

Marek rose and motioned for her to do the same. "Stand here in front of me." He held out both his hands, palms facing her. "Place your hands against mine."

She took a deep breath, willing her hands not to shake, and raised them up until she was touching his palms.

"Now, look directly in my eyes and try to keep your mind open. Do not look away. You needn't do anything, just be willing to receive the contact."

Elana looked into his keen eyes, forcing herself not to draw back at his intensity. Her hands grew hot from his touch. Suddenly his presence flashed in her mind.

"Elana."

She started and pulled away from him, breaking both their eye contact and touch. It was gone.

"Oh, I'm so sorry." She was mortified that she'd pulled back. "I was surprised. I won't do that again." She hoped he wouldn't loose patience with her.

He nodded, his face inscrutable, and she placed her hands against his once more. It only took holding his gaze for a moment, and he was there. His presence overwhelmed her; burned against her mind. She felt dizzy, disoriented, like there wasn't enough room for her inside her own head. This was worse than when the Hunter was pressing in on her. She reminded herself that this time it was to help her, to protect her. She wondered briefly if Marek could hear her thoughts, and reddened, trying to shut her own voice down.

"Elana." His lips never moved. His voice was in her head.

"Yes," she answered, also with her mind.

"Excellent. You are truly amazing. You have done what most Elders will never be able to do."

She smiled in spite of her discomfort. It was true. They had forged a mind link.

"Put your hands down, but don't look away. Let us try and maintain the link without touch."

She obeyed him. The burning of his presence diminished, but he remained in her mind. She grinned, the heady feeling of power raising her spirits. "We did it." She felt him recoil slightly at her words, surprise maybe, but then he answered.

"Yes. Well done. Now let us each take a step back."

They both stepped back. Elana felt the link waver for a moment, then hold strong.

"Now," Marek spoke into her mind, "I want you to turn and face away from me."

Elana turned. The link diminished yet again in intensity, but held. "You are still here."

"Yes. Now, let us each walk about the garden and tell the other what we see."

With the intensity diminished, Elana felt more like herself again. She reveled in this new direction for her Skills, chatting to him through their link about the flowers, the trees, the birds, the patterns of sun and shade. Even when he didn't answer directly, she could feel his pride and approval of her. She was grinning so hard her cheeks ached.

Long before Elana was ready, Marek called an end to the day's training.

"I don't want to strain your abilities," he told her. "We will meet each morning before breakfast, here in this garden, and practice together." He caught her eye and Elana felt again, the burning of his presence. She set herself against the disorientation, refusing to look away, and held his gaze, matching his intensity with her own. Surprise flickered in his eyes and then he looked away. "You have much to be proud of, Elana." He spoke out loud this time, though she could still feel the echo of his thoughts in her mind.

She smiled at him, suddenly aware of her exhaustion. This took more out of her than she realized.

They walked to the garden door. Before opening it, Marek paused.

"I will try and keep a loose contact with you throughout the day. It may help you adjust to the rigors of this Skill. Also," he stopped, taking time to choose his words, "it goes without saying that this is to stay between us. There are many who pass through this house. Only Braxton knows of my identity. He is of the Valefolk, but completely loyal to me. Yet, I would not trust even him with this. Or, as much as it pains me to say it, Orvis. You must understand that I do not know him myself, and I cannot risk betrayal."

Elana nodded. She would never dream of revealing her training to anyone of this household. She swallowed hard at the thought of hiding this from Orvis. Maybe by the time he grew strong enough for them to talk together, Marek would grow comfortable with him. She understood that he risked his safety and reputation to help them. It was the least she could do to respect his wishes.

"One more thing," Marek continued, "there is a certain guest here. Lady Cecily. Lord Gratton's daughter and heir. I am her father's counselor, and her guardian. Unfortunately, they are provincial in their understanding of the Elder Born. It is best that she not know of your presence. She is very jealous of my time and attentions. I'm afraid that she would treat you most unkindly if she knew of our time together. She has a sweet side, but there is much of her father's willfulness in her. I don't want you to suffer at her hands. I will see to it that her stay is brief. I must clear up a misunderstanding between her and her father before I can send her home again."

Elana stared at him. He was counselor to Lord Gratton? No wonder his word was law in Bellport. It would be law in most of Merrion! She had heard rumors of Cecily; her beauty was the subject of many stories. She would have liked to see her for herself, but it was no loss to avoid contact with Lord Gratton's daughter. Aside from them being of similar age, they would have nothing in common. Cecily was royalty. Elana was Elder Born, and the daughter of a simple scrivener and a healer. She agreed with Marek. It would be better that way.

"Go now and rest. You'll find you need it after your exertion this morning. Braxton will make sure that all your needs are met."

Marek led the way out of the garden. No sooner had he closed the door, then Braxton came down the hall.

"My lady," he said to Elana. "I will gladly show you to your room."

Elana nodded to Marek and followed Braxton through the maze of corridors, back to her room. She closed the door behind her, dizzy with excitement and exhaustion. They had done it. Marek's presence lingered in her mind. If she focused on it she felt it grow. She frowned. Right now she didn't want that. She wasn't sure just how much of her mind he had access to and she needed a moment to be alone with her thoughts. She hoped she was thinking quietly.

She walked over to her window, looking out over the rooftops of the neighboring houses. Her room was high enough up to have a view of the old quarters of Bellport. Only a few blocks away, the Bell Towers stood, graceful against the blue sky. They tugged at her with a force stronger and more compelling even, than the mind link; a connection to the ancient past, a now mute testimony to the truth of the Prophecy.

If the mind link could keep her safe, the first chance she got, she promised herself, she would go see the Bell Towers. She might even find Reeves there. She knew that Marek was a very busy man and he was already taking so much of his time to help her. If she could find Reeves herself, that would save Marek the trouble. She felt his presence stir in her mind and quickly changed her line of thought. She had a suspicion that he wouldn't want her to go out. But she couldn't just remain locked in the house. Anyhow, she rationalized, it wasn't like she would be going down to the docks.

She looked back out at the Bell Towers. Somehow she couldn't picture a Hunter being comfortable spending much time around them. Even empty, they exuded a virtue and a strength unlike anything Elana had ever known. It wouldn't be hard to slip out and just go for a quick visit. She'd give it a little while, get to know the routines of the house and then she'd go. As long as Marek was only loosely linked with her during the day, no one need be the wiser.

CHAPTER 6

THE BELL TOWER

The sun glared through Aidan's window, waking him from a troubled sleep. He threw off the covers and hurried down the stairs, hoping to grab a bite to eat before beginning his search for Reeves.

"I see you're up, young man." The innkeeper looked up from his table, worry clouding his face. "You missed the excitement." Aidan looked around the empty room.

"Where is everyone?"

"Seems there was somewhat of a to-do outside here last night. Heard a scuffle in the alley myself, but didn't pay it any mind." He shrugged his shoulders. "You get used to that sort of thing around here."

Aidan nodded.

"By morning though, the place was crawling with," he cast a furtive glance at the now abandoned tables, "Black Knights."

The hairs on the back of Aidan's neck stood up. He remembered the mind cry and being thrown off his feet. By what? Had those men in the alley attacked someone in league with the Black Knights? He had heard stories of the Hunters' Skills, developed to control and dominate others. Who other than a Hunter could have thrown off those attackers, and him? There had been a boy out there, but the voice he heard in his head was a girl's. It made his stomach turn to think that Elder Born children were being culled and trained as the Shadow King's tools.

The innkeeper lowered his voice. "They're after another of those Elder Born."

Aidan struggled to keep his face impassive.

"Pity for them," the innkeeper rambled on. "They can't help being born what they are. Still, it gives me the willies. The fellow in black, what came in this morning, said that at least one was on the loose around here. One turned bad. Using their powers to attack the Valefolk. He asked me if I'd seen it." He shook his head. "Almost wish I had. The fellow offered a pretty piece of gold for any word of it. Seems they vanished from the premises right after the attack. The Black Knights will take care of it to be sure." He looked over his shoulder at the closed door. "I don't know which is worse, the Black Knights or the Elder Born. I'd steer clear of both if you know what I mean." He nodded, a knowing look in his bloodshot eyes. "If we don't bother them, it's a better chance they won't bother us."

All Aidan could do was nod. He'd heard this sort of thing often enough from the villagers near their farm. It rankled him, but pity for the man won out over anger. The innkeeper didn't choose to be born and raised in ignorance, and his views were more kindly than many Aidan had been subjected to. Grateful that he hadn't walked in on a Hunter's search, or a room full of Black Knights, he ordered a hot breakfast and ate it alone at a table near the window. The innkeeper vanished into the kitchen.

Aidan thanked the Ancient Ones that his Skill presence was hidden to any but the most powerful of the Elder Born. He remembered as a child, his parents taking him to Geri, concerned that he lacked the Skills. She had the ability to recognize Elder Born, even before their Waking. She was the one who told them that though they hadn't presented in the usual way, his Skills were more powerful than any she had seen; some sort of throwback to the time before the Forgetting.

"Just be patient with him," she told them. "He'll develop in his own way and in his own time."

For now, that was a blessing. He'd have to be on guard though, going out through the city. It would be better if he didn't return to this inn. After finishing his breakfast, he packed his clothes, thanked the innkeeper, and paid him the silver he owed for bed and board.

Out in the stable, Kael was restless, eager to be off. He was unused to being confined and the noise and the smells of the docks made him edgy. For the first time since he started the trip, Aidan wondered if it had been wise to bring the stallion. He caught the attention of everyone around. He had never meant to come to the city. He had imagined following the less traveled roads and cutting across barren stretches of countryside. Slipping by, undetected in Bellport, was a fool's hope.

He deliberated as the horse cleaned the last of his oats out of the manger. The innkeeper had suggested searching in the Old City for Reeves. He hadn't silver to spare, but with the Black Knights combing the docks, he was safer up the hill. There too, he wouldn't stand out as much. He allowed himself a wry smile at the irony of it. Aidan, the peasant, would fit in best among the gentry of Bellport.

He pulled the green cloak from his pack, where he'd folded it away. He would play the part of a nobleman for a while longer. He brushed Kael until he gleamed, saddled him and swung up on the big horse, riding tall out of the yard; Kael's hooves clattering against the cobblestones.

They wound their way ever upwards toward the Old City. Aidan's heart lightened as they left the squalor of the docks and the lower sections. He strained his Skills, listening for the song that emanated from the empty Towers, visible now, against the sky. The land still remembered it, and in quiet corners a harmony rose close enough to the surface for Aidan to discern. It drew him, beckoning, calling to him, until it became his sole focus. It crowded out all concerns about the Hunters, about the Black Knights, the sting of parting with Cecily, even all thoughts of finding Reeves. These things dissolved into the background. Only the ancient song remained.

He rode on, oblivious to the glances he drew as he followed the paths where the song was clearest, hungry to find himself at its source. When at last he guided Kael into the grassy courtyard that formed a crown over Bellport, the sun stood directly over the Towers. It was empty here, the outward silence permeated by the song. Even Kael seemed to feel it, for he let out a great sigh and set to grazing, his body visibly relaxing for the first time since they boarded the ferry.

Aidan dismounted, his feet eager to contact the green earth. From either side of the Towers, low stone buildings skirted the courtyard of grass where he now stood. The craftsmanship of both the Towers and the stone buildings spoke of an age long past. With the last remaining space in his mind, he focused on the Towers, the emptiness between them framing the cloudless sky. The song consumed him. Its bittersweet presence overtook him and he sank down into the grass, closed his eyes, and let the song that ran through the land fill his entire being.

Shadows lay long across the courtyard when Aidan opened his eyes. Kael, who'd been nuzzling him with his sweet, grassy breath, snorted. Aidan sat up, heart pounding. What time was it? How long had he been laying there? He climbed to his feet, dazed and disoriented, trying desperately to clear his mind enough to think. The song flowed on without ceasing from the Towers, but whether he had grown accustomed to it, or whether his fear made it less consuming, Aidan didn't know.

He'd just remembered that he was supposed to be looking for Reeves, when Kael spun around, placing himself between Aidan and the Towers, his ears laced back. Measured footsteps sounded on the flagstone walk. Aidan pulled his bow out of the pack on the stallions back, fit it with an arrow, and peered around Kael's haunches.

A man, cloaked and hooded, approached them from the shadows of the stone buildings. His face remained hidden, but Aidan could sense no disruption of the song at his presence. He lowered his bow. Kael's ears swiveled around as though he were trying to hear something that eluded him. The man stopped a dozen paces from them. Aidan stepped out from behind Kael, waiting for him to speak.

"You are a stranger to this place. What is your business here?" His voice was low and melodic, and though his words were courteous, there was a hint of a challenge behind them.

Aidan deliberated before speaking. He wished in vain that he possessed the Skill to read others' intentions. He had to go on what he had. All he knew for sure right now, was the song, and that flowed out unchanging.

"I'm looking for someone," he answered, careful to give as little information as possible without causing offense.

The man withdrew further into his hood. "What makes you think you will find them here?" He couldn't read the man's tone.

"I didn't think I would find him here specifically." Aidan weighed his words. He decided to reveal a little more. "I'm from the country. This is my first time in Bellport, and I was drawn to this quiet place. I didn't sleep well last night at the inn, and I must have dozed off. I had no intention of intruding." As the words left his mouth, he remembered that he was trying to pose as a nobleman. His face burned at the blunder. A nobleman would have stayed as a guest in someone's home, welcomed and well cared for.

"Who are you?" The cloaked man asked.

That was the one question Aidan was hoping to avoid. He hadn't worked out a clear answer to that one yet. Kael took a step closer to the man, neck arched, ears forward. Aidan had never seen him so solicitous toward anyone new. That was a good sign.

The thought of pulling off a ruse exhausted him. Anyhow, he reassured himself, if the man tried to do anything to them, Aidan was armed, and Kael could outrun any horse in the city.

He took a deep breath. "My name is Aidan. I'm from Glenariff. I am indeed a stranger to these parts."

"Aidan, from Glenariff..." the man's voice gentled. "I have an old friend who lives in that Lordship. I haven't seen her since she was widowed five years ago." He pushed his hood back from his face. Even standing in the shadows, the man's red hair seemed to glow of its own accord. Level green eyes met his own. "Welcome, Aidan, son of Darian."

Relief washed over Aidan making his legs go wobbly. He'd found Reeves.

"How did you know?" he began.

Reeves smiled at him and Aidan felt like the sun had just broken out of the clouds. "Where do I start?" He chuckled. "You are the image of your mother, Eli told me you would be traveling soon, riding a great dark stallion, and you are wearing the cloak of succession, Baldor's cloak. You found Granny.

"Cloak of succession? How did you know I met Granny?"

"She's been keeping it for you. It's hard to understand what goes through her head. But I've never known her to be wrong. She sees more without eyes than most see with them. If she didn't tell you more, than I won't either. I'm not Skilled in the Sight like she is."

Reeves threw his arms wide in an embrace. "It is good to see you again, Aidan. I've looked forward to this day."

Aidan's throat tightened as he embraced his father's old friend. He knew now what Granny meant by, "You can trust him with your life." In finding Reeves, he felt like he had stumbled upon an oasis.

"Granny told me to find you before I traveled to Farran." He looked down, embarrassed to meet the other man's eyes. "She told me a lot, but I don't think I understood it."

Reeves laughed. "You aren't the first, and won't be the last. Don't let that bother you." He linked his arm through Aidan's, drawing him back toward the low stone buildings. "Let's move out of the courtyard. There's a stable with a grassy paddock behind the Towers where your horse will be comfortable. I keep a small room here that will be adequate shelter for tonight. I'll feed you before I tire you with questions."

Aidan smiled gratefully back at him, his spirits rising. Who could stay unhappy in this man's presence? Feeling safer than he had since his father was alive, he followed Reeves to the stables, untacked Kael, fed him a ration of oats and turned the horse out to graze. All the while Reeves leaned back against one of the stone walls. Taking a set of reed pipes from his cloak, Reeves played them softly; the notes picking up themes from the Towers' song. The setting sun broke through a low bank of clouds, streaming the day's last golden light over the threesome. Aidan wished with all his heart that fate had allowed him to remain here. He had never been anywhere more peaceful.

Images from the song swirled through his mind, stronger now that Reeves played bits of it on his pipes. He watched in silence as the sun sank below the horizon. At last, Reeves put the pipes away, the images they conjured dissolving with the last of the light.

"I did promise you supper." He motioned for Aidan to follow him and led the way to a half buried side door in one of the old buildings. Stopping before a flight of steps that seemed to lead down into the ground, he retrieved a wrought iron key from a notch in the rail. Aidan followed him down the steps.

"Welcome to my humble abode."

He wasn't simply being modest. The room was only big enough for a bed, a fireplace and a table and chair set under a tiny shuttered window high up in the wall. The thick stone walls retained moisture from the earth, exuding the smell of wet stone and brown dirt. If Aidan were to judge on appearance alone, it looked more like a prison cell than a dwelling, though the song from the Towers permeated the entire structure. It was even more powerful here than in the courtyard, filling the cramped, dank room with a richness unequalled in the finest homes of Bellport.

Aidan realized that Reeves was watching him. "It's not much to look at," he began.

"But the song..." Aidan interrupted him, whispering so as to not interfere with the music that rolled out of the stones.

"You can hear it?"

"Of course! How could I not? That's what brought me here."

Reeves' smile grew broader. "Geri's right about you. Not everyone can, you know."

"What is it?"

"It's the song of the Ancient Ones." Reeves face grew wistful. "The song that the Silver Bells played when they hung between those Towers. The stones of the tower, the old buildings, and even the earth itself still remember it. But without the Bells, it's lost to the Valefolk who have built their lives here. And they need it the most."

"But you played parts of it on your pipes. Can they hear it then?"

"Only while I play it aloud. That's one of the reasons I've stayed here all these years. I couldn't leave them with no one to give voice to the song." Reeves face sobered. "I must leave now, though. Even here, in the Towers, it has become too dangerous."

Aidan's thought traveled back to last night, and the words of the innkeeper this morning. "Something happened just outside the inn where I was sleeping," he said. He told Reeves about what he heard and saw, and what the innkeeper told him.

Reeves listened, his face inscrutable. "I honestly don't know what to think. I don't know who that could have been or why the Black Knights are after them. Unfortunately, it's not always clear who are our friends and who are our enemies." He stared out into the dark beyond the open door.

Aidan waited for him to continue.

He let out a sigh and turned back toward Aidan. "Let's have some supper. After we eat I would like very much to hear your whole story."

From a pack in the corner, Reeves unearthed some still fresh bread, a wedge of pale cheese, some dried fruit, and a bottle of wine. He set the food out on the table, but left the fireplace unlit. "It's not safe to build a fire here anymore. I'm afraid it would draw the wrong sort of attention."

Reeves sat on the bed and Aidan pulled up a chair and bowed his head while Reeves blessed the food. The bread and cheese filled his stomach, and the wine warmed him sufficiently to compensate for the lack of fire. With his hunger sated, he recounted the events of the past few days. He blushed as he spoke of Cecily, their time together, and their abrupt parting. What kind of fool had he been to even entertain thoughts of her?

At last he finished. "So, here I am, with no clue as to why I was to seek you out, or what I'm to do when I reach Farran." He frowned. "I feel so out of place."

Reeves sat silent for a long while. At last he spoke. "I don't know why Granny sent you to find me, but I will tell you all I know." He rose and cleared the leftover food from the table.

Aidan waited.

"Your father was one of my closest friends. He was a brilliant leader; a powerful Elder Born. People were drawn to him... trusted him instinctively. His vision was to build a bridge between the Elder Born and the Valefolk, to reintegrate the two peoples so that each could strengthen the other. He saw the Shadow overtaking the Vale and this was his answer to it." He looked Aidan in the eyes. "This wasn't the only answer, nor the complete answer, but it was the piece given to Darian to accomplish." Reeves turned away.

"He was cut down before that dream was realized." Bitterness laced the words. "Betrayed. There have been conjectures, accusations, but never proof of who revealed Darian's whereabouts to the Hunter. With him gone, the struggle against the Shadow was driven underground." Reeves paced the small room.

"There were four of us - invincible in our own minds until that day: Darian, the youngest, leader of the Orchard Tree Eldership, Hamilton, a gifted teacher from the Firestone Eldership, Marek, powerful and brilliant, born and raised in the Vale, who found his way to Farran as a young man. He was also from the Firestone Eldership. And me. I was from the Bells Eldership. We were inseparable; dreaming of grand things, hoping to restore the Elder Born to their place within the Vale.

"Is that the Marek that Cecily spoke of?" Aidan asked.

Reeves nodded. "Marek traveled with me to Bellport, where I hoped to uncover any clue as to the whereabouts of the Bells. Once in the Vale, differences that I had failed to recognize started showing, and almost from the moment we arrived in Bellport a wall rose between us."

Worry deepened the lines around Reeves' eyes. "Marek was always ambitious. Having grown up in the Vale, he knew how to attain power and how to wield it. He was hungry to prove himself. His Skills bordered on dangerous. He went through his Waking untrained, and though Geri trained him herself when he arrived at Farran, he still practiced Skills that many feared to learn. I've heard rumors that he uses his powers to control others' minds. I wish I could say it weren't so. His Skills are far beyond the range of my own."

Reeves sighed. "I miss him. Or maybe I miss the young man I knew many years ago. He arrived in Farran right after my older brother left for the Vale, and stayed with us the years he spent there. We were like brothers." He sat pensive, fingering the pipes in his cloak pocket. "I'm afraid for him. There are temptations to those who openly wield power, that I think he would find hard to refuse. He sees to it that our paths rarely cross."

A whinny from the paddock interrupted their conversation. Aidan jumped to his feet. "Kael - someone's here!"

Reeves snuffed out their lantern, plunging them into darkness. In the silence that followed, Aidan heard it; the shift in the song. Discord broke up the subtle harmonies, sending chills down his spine. Reeves' hand gripped his shoulder.

"A Hunter." His hoarse whisper confirmed Aidan's fears. "Take Kael and fly from here. I'm sorry I couldn't be of more help."

Aidan's heart hammered against his chest. "Will I see you again?"

"If I am able, I will meet you here tomorrow, at sunset. That will give me time to put them off my trail. If you don't see me, leave here at once." Again the hand squeezed his shoulder. "Don't trust anyone, Aidan. Promise me that. Take no companions along the road. Tell no one of your destination. If the Hunters knew that you existed, they would scour the Vale for you."

Kael whinnied again.

"Go, now! And may the Ancient Ones be with you."

Aidan sprung for the door, pausing for a moment to listen to the land. He felt the malevolence of the Hunter, but from farther away. Pulling the door open, he sprinted across the grass toward Kael.

With shaking fingers he strapped on the horse's saddle, fastening his packs, and slipped the bridle over Kael's head. The stallion pawed the ground, anxious, ears swiveling, nostrils distended. When all was in place, Aidan leaped up on the great horse and urged him with the lightest touch through the gate. They crossed the grassy courtyard in the blackness, Kael prancing and jigging. Clouds covered the stars and the moon had not yet risen. Not until they made the street did Aidan let the horse loose.

In that moment, he felt, like fingers reaching to grab him, the Hunter's intent turned his way. The groping evil reached out for him, and just when he was sure all was lost, it turned away. Not waiting to question his good fortune, Aidan urged Kael on, down the road, into the darkness and the unknown.

Night swallowed them up as Aidan guided Kael down the cobbled lane, through the now deserted streets. Kael's hoofbeats echoed in the darkness; the sound bouncing off tall stone houses that loomed over them. He headed west, away from the docks, trying to put as much space as possible between himself and the Hunter. This part of the city wasn't as populated as the east side, toward the sea. No lamps lit the streets. No inns, with the promise of food and a bed, beckoned to travelers. Aidan despaired of finding any place with a room and a stable.

Before he realized it they had ridden up to the City's wall. It stood closer to the crown on this side; Bellport's inhabitants spilled down toward the sea, with only a token few dwelling here against the hills. As they neared the wall, houses stood empty; decrepit shells of a time long gone. Chills raised up along Aidan's neck. He tried not to imagine dark forms creeping among the abandoned homes. He took a deep breath, reining in his imagination. He needed to explore the area. He could sense no actual evil here, only the pounding of his own heart. This just might prove an ideal cover for the night.

It was behind one of these deserted homes that Aidan found refuge. Set back from the street, the house had a high stone wall enclosing a tangled and overgrown garden. A wooden gate, hanging askew on rusty hinges afforded the only entrance to the garden. With much coaxing he pushed the gate open.

The old moon was rising, its light milky through the thin clouds. Aidan could make out the forms of trees and overgrown gangly shrubs, gnarled with age. There wasn't much room to move around, but he unsaddled Kael, letting the horse browse on whatever edibles he could find. He spread out his own blanket and sat down, staring out into the shadows, trying to make sense of what had happened. The moon was high in the sky before sleep overtook him.

At first light he rose, saddled Kael again and slipped out of the garden. Still remembering the feeling of evil groping for him, he was fearful about remaining too long in any one place. It was his plan to stay moving until sunset. Then he would travel up to the Bell Towers. He had no idea what he would do if Reeves wasn't there. He had to leave, but by what road? He had been hoping that Reeves could help him with that. All roads leading to Bellport were watched and heavily guarded.

Once in the marketplace, he spent a brass coin on a loaf of fresh bread. He and Kael wandered through the streets, watching the inhabitants, cautious for any signs of being followed, his ear ever tuned to the faint harmonies of the Tower's song. For the first time since he left Cecily, he now had the leisure to think of her. He hoped she was safe, and that she was freed from her engagement to Darcy. He missed her company. The blood rushed to his face. He knew he should put her from his mind, but each time he saw a woman with golden hair he spun around, hoping it was her.

He wondered too, about this Marek. Both Cecily and Reeves seemed to care a great deal for him, though he guessed that Reeves' concern ran deeper than the man had let on. Certainly, if Marek was after power, he had attained it. He wasn't disposed to trust the man. He had never known one of the Firestone Elders well, and the thought of a powerful Elder Born using his Skills to control others... Well, he was inclined to side with the Valefolk on that one. His own Skills operated so differently.

The day dragged on. Aidan worked his way along the hill, ever alert to any change in the song that might signal danger. There was none. He formulated a loose plan. If he couldn't find Reeves he would stop by Marek's house and see Cecily one more time before leaving. Even if he ran into Marek, the encounter would be brief, and given that he'd been the one to see the girl home safely, there was no justifiable cause for fear.

Someone of Marek's stature wouldn't likely be relaxing at home, waiting to entertain uninvited guests. The truth was, he would more likely have to deal with the old butler again. A frown crossed his face. He just wanted to say goodbye to her. Who knew if he would ever see her again once he left for Farran?

He argued back and forth with himself as he steered Kael toward the Towers, finally promising himself that if Reeves wasn't there, he would go straight to find Cecily, say his goodbyes, and then leave Bellport that night. It would be some compensation for not getting to finish his time with Reeves.

The sun was sinking below the rooftops when he arrived at the Bell Towers. The song flowed out, uninterrupted. It was safe. But Reeves was not there. A knot tightened in Aidan's throat, conflicting emotions vying with each other for preeminence. He turned Kael to leave, when footsteps sounded from the direction of the underground room. Nudging the stallion forward he trotted through the Towers, the hope that Reeves was indeed here, washing over him.

"Reeves," he called. "It's me. I just got here."

He heard someone scramble to shut a door. A cloaked form appeared halfway up the steps to Reeves' room. It wasn't Reeves. He clapped a hand over his mouth - too late.

"Who are you?" A girl's voice spoke from within the hood. It sounded familiar to him, and for a moment Aidan's heart pounded in the vain hope that it was Cecily.

"Aidan," he answered, hoping to see her face and have this turn out alright.

"Who were you talking to?" the voice asked him.

It wasn't Cecily. And he'd just given his name and Reeves', to a complete stranger. His stomach clenched. He had to get out of here. He turned to leave and then stopped. Was she alone? Was this a trap? He decided to play along a little longer... try and get some information out of her.

"What are you doing here?" Fear put a rough edge on his voice.

The girl threw her hood back and looked at him, her black eyes blazing. He started. He had thought she was a girl, but her dark hair was cut at the shoulders like a boy's, and as he looked closely, he realized that she was dressed like the fishermen from the docks. She was too pretty to be a boy, though.

He frowned.

She looked him straight in the eyes. "I'm looking for Reeves, and by the sound of it, you were expecting to find him here too." Her manner was commanding, almost fierce.

Aidan bristled, and then felt for a moment that he would be sick. Whoever she was, she knew too much. "I don't know what you're talking about," he lied.

She tipped her head and squinted at him. "Yes you do, and you're a bad liar. I've seen you before, but I can't think where." She studied him, lips pursed.

Aidan watched her, not wanting to speak, afraid to give anything else away.

"Were you," she began. "No. It couldn't be. Look at me," she ordered. He would have laughed at being ordered around by someone so small, except that she exuded a strength, a force of will that caught him off guard.

When he caught her eyes he felt a burning of her presence in his mind. He gasped and pulled back. What was she?

"You are!" Triumph rang in her voice. "You looked out the window the night Orvis was attacked. You gave me that moment to fight them off."

Aidan's insides went cold. That's why she was familiar. It was her voice that sounded in his head that night on the docks. She was the one who had used some sort of power to knock out the three men and himself. She was the one that the Black Knights and the Hunter were after. Or was she in league with them? Were they trying to avenge her?

The reins were slippery in his hands. He though of what Reeves said. 'Those who wield power have temptations that would be hard to refuse.'

What was she? What had this girl done? Was she able to control others' minds? He didn't want to stay around and find out.

"I must be going." He spun Kael around.

"Wait! You only just got here and I know you'd be able to help me." Her voice trembled, the air of command evaporated.

Aidan hesitated.

"That's a beautiful horse you have."

It was clear she was trying to start again on a better foot. He wasn't sure that he wanted any of it.

"Thank you," he answered, his voice stiff. He cursed again the oddity of his Skills that enabled him to hear so much from the land, from animals, from inanimate objects, yet never illuminated people, their thoughts and intentions.

Kael turned back toward the girl and nickered. She reached out a hand toward him. "I wouldn't pet him," he snapped at her. "He bites."

She gave him a funny look and withdrew her hand. Kael continued to strain toward her.

"Have it your way," she said. "It's really important, though, that I find Reeves. Marek said that he'd look for him, but I thought that I'd check myself, too." She looked up at Aidan, her dark eyes blending in with the dusk. "Please, if you know anything about where he is, I must know."

She knows Marek? He frowned. After what Reeves shared about him, this didn't exactly recommend her.

Kael stirred under him and he reached out in his mind toward the horse. He sensed her presence with his horse. What would she do to his horse?

"I'm afraid you've mistaken me for someone else." His words came out clipped. "I must be going."

"No. You can't just leave." Desperation edged her voice, pulling him back. "Aidan, I'm an Elder Born. I know you are too."

Now, his head swam. No one but Geri had been able to discern his Skill presence. He'd heard stories about the Hunters' abilities to detect the Skill in the Elder Born, no matter how faint. The Shadow King had given them the ability to track Elder Born, like dogs following a scent. Reeves' final words came back to him. 'Don't trust anyone, Aidan. Promise me that. Take no companions along the road. Tell no one of your destination. If the Hunters knew that you existed, they would scour the Vale for you.'

He didn't wait to hear any more. He pulled Kael's head around, the stallion snorting in protest, and galloped through the towers, across the grassy courtyard and down the lane that Cecily had followed. His heart pounded and sweat trickled down his back in spite of the chill in the wind.

That was too close a call. His mind swirled in turmoil. Thoughts of the girl haunted him. She reminded him of Arella, fragile looking, with her dark hair and eyes, and fair skin. He shook his head, remembering her presence in Kael's mind. Looks can be deceiving. He reached out toward the horse once again. This time it was only Kael there, sniffing the night air, listening to the sounds, without a thought for the girl they'd just encountered at the Towers. He stroked Kael's arched neck, trying not to think about what he would do if something were to happen to his horse.

Shadows from the huge houses spilled into the streets. Aidan let Kael pick his way over the cobblestones, as he searched his memory, trying to place which house belonged to Marek. How was this girl connected with the man? He seemed to know everyone. After riding past the house once and turning around again, he determined that it indeed was the one Cecily had entered. He drew a deep breath. He would go up to the house, see if he could speak to Cecily, say goodbye and leave. Aidan clung to the shreds of this plan with desperation, willing some normalcy to return.

His heart pounded in his chest. He forced himself to breathe more slowly. Closing his eyes, he took a moment and listened for the Towers' song. Relief washed over him as he heard the song again, flowing out clear, undisturbed through the evening. Strange, he thought; none of his own discord was echoed in the song.

He moved Kael deeper into the shadows, giving himself time to calm down. "I do want to see Cecily," he thought. It was the one bright spot that had kept him going through this trying day. "I'm not going back on that now."

He dismounted and pulled out the green cloak, which he had tucked back into his saddlebags while he was trying to hide from the Hunter. He shook it out and fastened the clasp around his shoulders. After a brief inspection of the side alley, he resolved to go straight to the front door. He looped Kael's reins around the hitching post along the lane, breathing a prayer to the Ancient Ones, that no one would try to harm the stallion. Straightening his shoulders, he marched up to the massive wooden door and rang the bell.

Footsteps sounded, boot heels on a stone floor, and then a serving man pulled the door open. Aidan recognized the man, Braxton was his name, who had welcomed Cecily so warmly and then turned him out. He took a deep breath.

"I'm here to see Cecily."

Braxton looked down his long thin nose at Aidan. "I'm sorry. The Lady Cecily is not available."

"When will I be able to see her?" He hoped he sounded bolder than he felt.

Braxton looked him over. "What is your business with her?"

Aidan bristled at the older man's tone. "If you would know," he said in his most lordly voice, "I saved her from common thieves who were chasing her down on the road, and then saw her safely back to Bellport. I wished to bid her farewell before I take leave of this city."

Braxton's face twitched and Aidan wondered if the man was laughing at him. Before either could speak again, a door to a side passage burst open.

"Aidan! I thought I heard your voice." Cecily's face shone, her green eyes seeking out Aidan's.

"My Lady." Braxton bowed his head, his lips clamped in a thin, disapproving line.

"Cecily!" Aidan caught her outstretched hands in his own. His throat tightened. Memory had not done her justice. Her hair was swept up above her head, with loose wisps of gold framing her face. A deep green dress set off her eyes, the pale honey of her skin, the red of her lips. Half formed plans to prolong their time raced through his mind.

Cecily shot a guilty glance at Braxton and then looked up, smiling at Aidan. "Marek told me to keep it a secret that I'm here, but as you're the one who brought me, I couldn't possibly be disobeying him." She tucked her arm through his. "I missed you," she whispered. "Marek said he'll try to talk Lord Gratton out of making me marry that awful cousin of yours."

Braxton started at this. The servant gave a half bow and exited through another door. Aidan tried to put him out of his mind.

"I have to leave the city, Cecily," he said. "I couldn't bring myself to leave without saying goodbye to you."

She colored at his words. "I thought you'd had enough of me when you ran out the other night."

It was Aidan's turn to be surprised. "No. That fellow, Braxton, acted as if I were an unpleasant addition to your party. I didn't want to intrude."

"You would never be intruding." She leaned against his arm.

Aidan's throat tightened. His heart pounded and he tried to take a deep breath to steady himself.

"When are you leaving?" she asked.

"I was going to leave tonight, after I said goodbye to you." The prospect seemed bleak. He pushed away thoughts of the road.

"Well," she paused, biting her lip, "if you could postpone your travel until the morning, maybe we could spend some more time together."

Aidan's pulse quickened. "I'd love to spend more time with you. Really." He returned her smile and then looked back at the door where Braxton exited. "But I'm not welcome in this house and I have no place to stay. Braxton..." His words trailed off.

Cecily waved her hands, brushing aside his objections. "Braxton's just protective of me. He's alright. He's Marek's right hand."

Aidan made a mental note to watch out for the man.

"What I'm trying to say is that I have to leave Bellport in the morning. Marek thinks it better if I'm out of the city until he's smoothed things over with Lord Gratton. He's arranged for me to check on some business of his in Rivergate, along the Greenway. He said it was good for my education, if I'm to one day rule Merrion." Her voice was flippant. Aidan had trouble picturing her in the Lord's Seat.

She rushed on, "If you waited, maybe we could travel together." Her chatter halted abruptly. "Where are you going, anyway?"

He shifted and looked away. What could he tell her? How much of the truth should he reveal? "I'm traveling on family business," he said. "It's complicated."

She frowned, obviously not used to having her questions avoided.

"But," he continued. "I'm free to choose my own road, and if you're heading out the Greenway to Rivergate, then I would be honored to accompany you." With a sweeping gesture of his arm, he bowed.

She clapped her hands, her face alight once more. "Splendid. Then I will see to it that Kael is stabled here and a guest room is prepared for you. We can go talk to Marek. He's just in. I'm sure he will be delighted to have you accompany me. I've told him all about you."

Aidan's throat went dry. Meet Marek? Now? He wasn't prepared for that. Everything was happening too fast today.

"Let me go and stable Kael. He's not great with other people." Aidan played for time, his mind racing. What would he say to this man? Would Marek be able to tell that he was Elder Born?

"Bring him around to the back," Cecily ordered. "I'll have the stable boy show you a clean stall. Then meet me at the side entrance. We'll talk with Marek and then get you some supper."

Aidan nodded and slipped out the front door. Kael nickered a greeting and Aidan flung his arms around the stallion. The horse's solid warmth calmed him. He was in it now. He couldn't just leave Cecily. He didn't want to. They navigated the cobbled alley in the dark and found the yard around the back with the stables. There, the stable boy showed Aidan a large box stall, with fresh hay in the manger. Once Kael settled in, Aidan put up the saddle, bridle, and pack, giving the boy strict orders to let no one in the horse's stall. He measured out a generous helping of oats for the stallion's supper, refilled his water buckets and with a last look over his shoulder, said goodnight to the horse and headed back to the house.

As he crossed the yard, the lit windows from the house illuminated a small figure scurrying into the alley. Instantly all his senses heightened. Was someone trying to break in to the house? He slipped into the shadows where he could watch, unseen. The figure stopped at the side entrance, slipped the hood off its cloak, and turned toward the stable for a moment, before opening the door and disappearing inside.

Aidan froze to the spot. It was the girl from the Towers. She had said something about Marek, but was she now going to tell him about

Aidan? Did Cecily know her? He couldn't picture Cecily in league with anyone like that. If he hadn't just seen Cecily's eyes shining up at him, he would have run back to the stable and fled the City with Kael. He couldn't disappoint her, though.

He waited, giving his heart a chance to resume its normal rhythm. He would meet Cecily, keep on his guard, and see what happened.

CHAPTER 7

MANY MEETINGS

The door clicked shut, blocking out the night. Elana leaned against the wall, her breath coming in short gasps. She meant to get back from the Towers before dark but after finding Reeves' room, and then the man from the docks... She had searched every cranny for something to make it all make sense.

"Never mind," she told herself. Maybe tomorrow she could slip out again. Part of her wanted to ask Marek about it all, but she didn't want to risk his displeasure.

Once inside the house, she felt his presence in her mind, questioning. "I'm okay," she sent to him. "Just out taking some air."

A lingering question remained from him, and then the presence faded. She felt him preoccupied, troubled. She didn't pry, didn't want to draw any more questions. There were enough of her own to wrestle with.

Light footsteps sounded outside the hall door. Before she could even take off her cloak the door burst open. A stately young woman with golden hair and a green velvet dress trimmed in lace, flew into the hall, eyes shining, hands outstretched. Elana stepped back. The woman gave a small cry and flushed. Anger sparked in her eyes.

"I'm sorry," Elana began. "I didn't mean to startle you."

"Who are you? What are you doing here?" the woman demanded.

"My name is Elana." Her mind raced. This must be Cecily. She didn't know of any other young woman in the house. Quickly, she had to come up with some excuse for her presence here. "I'm a... I've just been..." She looked around, desperate to find a source of inspiration. Voices drifted into the hall from the kitchens.

"I'm a servant here - only just."

Cecily took in the cropped hair and fisherman's clothes, her disdain undisguised. "What are you doing lazing about in the hall? I've ordered a special supper. I suggest you get to the kitchens and help with the preparations." Her eyes flashed cold fire as she studied Elana's garb. "I don't know what you're playing at, wearing those rags. Marek doesn't keep wharf rats for his servants. You'd better be grateful for your place here. There's plenty others to replace you if you're not competent for the job. I'll speak to Braxton about you, and have my eye on you tonight"

Elana felt her own temper rise and struggled to contain it. Remembering her promise to Marek, she inclined her head in a bow, and retreated through the door toward the kitchens. She felt Lady Cecily's gaze following her.

What was she to do now, prepare a special supper? She'd never served anyone of a higher class than her parents or the occasional villager. What she really wanted was to pour a pitcher of curdled goat's milk over Cecily's head. She grinned at the thought of the lumpy milk running down over the green velvet dress. That would cool her off some.

Marek's presence pressed in on her again, questioning. She figured she'd better tell him the truth about this before she made a bigger mess of things.

"I just ran into Cecily. I'm so sorry," she sent to him.

Worry came back to her in waves.

"I told her I was a servant and she ordered me to the kitchen. She said she'd be keeping an eye on me tonight. I think I really blew it." The picture of Cecily with curdled goat's milk dripping off of her danced before her eyes. She grinned again, in spite of herself.

"You didn't!" The shock in Marek's tone made Elana laugh out loud.

"No... no. I just wanted to." She felt Marek's laughter resound with her own.

"I'm so sorry." His tone was remorseful. "No one should ever treat you like that. I'm sending her away in the morning. I've devised some business that should keep her out of trouble. Would you..."

Elana felt the rest of the unspoken request. She nodded, even though she knew Marek couldn't see her. "I will. It's just one night. And it's my fault. I shouldn't have been about at this hour."

"Thank you, Elana." His relief washed through her mind.

She didn't want to do anything that would compromise him. Not after all he was doing for Orvis and her.

She pushed through two sets of swinging doors. A huge stone fireplace that she could have stood up in, dominated the kitchen. Cured meats hung from the rafters, as well as dried herbs and vegetables. Servants bustled between wooden work tables, cutting a leg of beef, spicing bowls of fruit and vegetables, kneading bread. She stared at them all working so efficiently. Where would she fit into all of this. A side door opened into the kitchen and Braxton entered.

"My Lady," he said. "The Master said that you would have need of this tonight." He held out a black and white servant's outfit. "It may be a little large for you, my Lady..." His voice drifted off. He looked away, apologetic.

"Thank you, Braxton. You always seem to know just what I need." She looked up at him, trying to catch his eye, hoping that he could illuminate her as to her duties for the night, but the older servant simply handed her the outfit, bowed, turned on his heel and walked back through the door.

Elana looked around for an inconspicuous place to change. A door on her left stood ajar and pushing it open, she saw that it lead to a flight of steps going down. She ducked inside and hurried down the steps. By a dim lamp in the wall she could just make out the room at the bottom. Wine bottles filled it floor to ceiling, stacked in wooden racks, some clean, some thick with dust.

It would do. She squeezed between two racks and stripped off the clothes that Orvis had given her. Her thoughts lingered on the old sailor. Right now, she would have welcomed the chance to sit and talk with him, but even if she didn't have to go through with this charade, the physician only let her visit him once a day while he hovered in attendance. It shamed her to admit it, but in a way the short visits had been a relief. Her promise to keep Marek's identity and their mind link hidden hung upon her like a weight.

Sounds from the hall above broke into her thoughts. Half undressed, she struggled to cover herself, crouching between the high shelves. Footsteps thudded on the stairs, and a lively whistling broke the stillness of the cellar. Elana could just make out the bulk of a man's silhouette. She tried to melt into the shelves.

"Mountain Vineyard - one bottle of his finest. A lordly gift for their afternoon repast." The man broke off whistling and chuckled to himself. Elana recognized the cook from the kitchens. "I hope our noble guest has a strong constitution."

He walked straight past her, stirring up the dust with his feet. She didn't breathe. Moving directly to the object of his search, he tossed the bottle into the air with a deft throw, caught it with a flourish and wiped it clean of cobwebs.

"What's this?" He acted out a quick pantomime of shock and dismay. "Our young hero caught sleeping on the job?" He twirled the bottle in his hand, holding it now like a sword. With a deep bow to an imaginary opponent, he said, "Beware, good sir, he's bested better men than you, and for much less affront." Flipping the bottle over and laughing out loud, he jogged back up the stairs.

Elana took a deep breath. Her heart pounded and her legs shook. She didn't want to know what he was talking about. A suspicion nagged at her that given his position and power, Marek might, at times, have to act in ways that involved more intrigue than she was used to.

There was enough to think about right now, without meddling in this. She pulled the servant's outfit over her head, grateful for the belt that tied the over-large garment to her waist. Braxton had even thought to bring a pair of shoes for her. Her feet swam in them, but they would suffice. She stowed her clothes between the shelves and dashed up the stairs, peeking through the door to be sure no one saw her exit.

The cook was hovering over a serving girl, showing her how to arrange the meat on the platter. Elana approached him with caution.

"Excuse me," she offered.

He spun to face her, heavy brows creased into a frown. "Who are you?"

Elana started to answer, but he cut her off.

"You must be the new servant. No one warned you to steer clear of Lady Cecily, eh?" A momentary grin flashed across his face. "She's a law unto herself. Only Marek can keep that one in hand."

Elana nodded, only partially relieved by his joviality.

"Braxton told me about you. Said to have you help serve the dinner." He gave Elana a once over. "Now why did you go and cut your hair off like that? You trying to look like a boy or something? It doesn't work."

She blanched at his question.

"No worry, lass. I won't go prying into your business. But I could have used a pretty thing like you to brighten up this place." His leering grin made her want to run back to the wine cellar. Serving at the dinner was starting to look better.

"Where do I go?" she asked.

"You're to wait out there," he pointed to a door that led, she guessed, into one of the dining rooms. "Help them get seated, pour their wine, serve the food, and try to stay invisible." He shook his head. "Bad business, sending you into deep water with nothing but a rowboat. Didn't they tell you anything?"

She shook her head. It was an apt expression. Though, as the cook looked her over once more, she decided that she'd take the 'deep water' over staying here with him. She hurried over to the door.

"I'll be here all evening, if you'd be wanting some company." His voice followed her out.

She slipped through the door and shut it tight behind her, her heart hammering against her chest. Taking a deep breath, she practiced the technique that Marek showed her to keep her Waking in check. After what happened at the docks, she was wary of letting herself get too angry or afraid. She understood now, that her Waking fed on strong emotion. She needed to get better at subduing it.

"Are you okay?" Marek's question interrupted her thoughts.

"Practicing," she sent back to him.

"Good for you. I've arranged to dine with Cecily and her guest tonight, so you won't have to be alone."

Relief flooded her and she took the first easy breath she'd taken all night. "I've never done anything like this before."

"Don't worry. Just follow my instructions. Everything will be fine." A calm washed in on his reassuring tones. "You may want to look over the table and make sure that everything is in place. We'll be there shortly."

Elana scanned the table, too embarrassed to say that she'd never seen a formal table before, and she wouldn't recognize something out of place unless it jumped up and bit her. It all looked sumptuous to her; white linens, silver, porcelain plates, more forks, knives and spoons than she could imagine using in one meal.

She took up her place in the corner as the door opened. Eyes down, she willed herself to remain invisible. Marek led the way, followed by Cecily, who was laughing and chattering to someone who followed after her. Elana stiffened at the sight of her. She could obviously be charming when she felt like it. She followed Cecily's gaze to the object of the Lady's attentions. It was a young man. She risked a more direct look. Not just any young man, it was the man from the Towers, from the docks - Aidan.

Her Waking surged unchecked before she could try to wrestle it under control. Marek shot her a warning glance.

"Careful." The word hung in her mind.

Elana's head swirled. What was he doing here? With Cecily? Why had he run away from her at the Towers?

Marek's instructions cut through her thoughts. "You must seat everyone. First me, then Cecily, then our guest, Aidan."

She moved, numb, pulling out the chair for Marek. He sat without acknowledging her. She turned to help Cecily, who arched an eyebrow at her before turning back to her companion. Last came Aidan. Elana reached tentatively toward him in her mind, trying to figure out what he was doing. He recoiled from her thoughts as though he'd been shocked, and jumped back away from her, knocking the chair out of her hands.

"I'm sorry," he stammered, his face reddening. "Clumsy of me." He refused to look at her.

"What are you doing?" Marek's question seared across her mind.

"I'm sorry," she sent back to him. "I wasn't thinking."

"You know him?"

"I think I've seen him before."

"We'll speak of this later." A wall came up between them as she saw Cecily turn toward Marek.

Elana picked up the chair and Aidan sat down. She could feel his turmoil. He turned back toward Cecily, but Elana could feel his mind guarding itself against her presence.

She followed Marek's terse instructions as she served the meal, hardly able to focus on the conversation, with the effort of playing her part. Cecily's eyes followed her every move, the light fading out of them, as soon as she turned toward her. When the dishes were served she had a chance to melt back against the wall and listen to their talk.

"It would set my mind much to ease if you were to accompany Cecily on her trip to Rivergate." Marek's voice was warm, resonant, though Elana felt none of that warmth resound in his thoughts. He was no longer walled to her and she found that she could feel an echo as it were, of his emotions.

"It would be my honor," Aidan answered him.

He was still completely guarded, and had not for a moment let down the fierce wall that crackled through the air in the room. Worry, fear and secrecy swam around him. When Elana tried to discern who or what he was, all she could see was a mountain shrouded in clouds. What did that mean? She stopped trying. Why bother, as he so clearly didn't want anything to do with her.

"I don't think Cecily appreciates how dangerous travel on the roads today can be," Marek continued their conversation.

Cecily shot her guardian a rueful glance.

"After all, if it weren't for you, I may have lost her on the road back to Bellport." Marek gave her a reproving look. "She fancies herself grown up now, and dares to put herself in jeopardy without even taking the time to consult those who are in a position to help her."

Cecily hung her head. "I'm sorry Marek. I didn't think. I won't do anything like that again."

"I forgive you, dear one." He patted her hand. "You know that I'm always here to help you.".

Elana felt warmth pour out of Cecily.

"I will have everything ready for you both to set out in the morning. Aidan, I insist on compensating you for taking care of my sweet girl."

Aidan nodded, clearly uncomfortable at receiving this generosity.

"I will have Braxton pack all the supplies that you'll need for the road." Marek pushed his chair back from the table. "There is much still for me to do tonight. I'm afraid that I must leave you two. When you are ready," he looked at Aidan, "the guest suite is prepared for your comfort." He kissed Cecily's hand and inclined his head toward Aidan.

Aidan scrambled to his feet and performed an awkward bow.

Elana reached out in desperation to Marek. "What am I to do?"

"They should leave soon. Bring the dinner things into the kitchen and then you're free to go back to your room," he responded. Without looking around, he strode from the room.

She wished that the floor would open up and swallow her. Anywhere seemed better than here right now. Looking up at the couple, she stifled a grimace. They were too perfect together; Cecily with her pale gold hair and bright green eyes and Aidan's tawny eyes and hair. She blushed thinking of her shorn locks and baggy servant's garb. Something in her wanted to like Aidan, but she pushed it down fiercely as she felt the walls around him holding her at bay. They deserve each other, she thought, remembering Cecily's contemptuous disdain. Tomorrow morning couldn't come too soon as far as she was concerned.

Cecily slipped her arm through Aidan's. With a whisper to him and a quick look back at where Elana was standing, the two of them floated out of the room together.

Elana's face burned. Cecily's laughter rang out in the hall and their footsteps died away into silence. She took a deep breath and began piling up the dishes.

The cook met her at the door to the kitchen, opening it with a wink and a flourish.

"There now, it looks like you made it back into safe harbor."

That would not have been her way of describing it. More like, 'out of the frying pan, into the fire.' He kept looking at her like she was a tasty morsel he'd like to try. She put the dishes down and hurried back to the dining room to pick up some more.

"You don't have to run away from me, lassie," he drawled. He followed her into the dining room, deftly clearing the heavy serving plates off the table. "Have a seat and rest a moment. It takes some getting used to, standing through a meal, serving others, and watching them eat, without so much as a moment to rest yourself." He produced a clean plate from the kitchen and before she could protest, he cut her a portion of the uneaten meat, served it up with the spiced vegetables and a cup of wine.

"Here you go," he said. "We look after our own here."

Her defenses dropped a little and she awarded him a smile. It was hours since she'd eaten and she was starting to feel shaky.

"Thank you..." she looked at him questioningly, realizing that she didn't know his name.

"Hayes," he answered. "And you are?"

"Elana."

He turned his head and looked at her, this time the leer was gone. "Not the Elana who came with the wounded sailor?"

She flushed, appalled that she'd just given herself away. Hayes was shaking his head, a half-grin playing across his face. "It's okay. Your secret's safe with me. But why this?"

Elana risked reaching out toward him, trying to discern if it was safe to tell him any more. Aside from his attraction to her, she felt nothing that gave her cause for alarm.

"I ran into Cecily in the hall tonight. Marek thought it better if she didn't know of my presence here, so I told her I was a servant."

Hayes threw back his head and laughed. "You'd been caught red-handed and then you had to play it out 'till the end." His face sobered. "Lady Cecily's a piece of work and there's no doubt about that. I'd hate to have her looking over my shoulder. Good thing for you she's headed out in the morning with that young gentleman. I'll place my silver on it that he's got a mind to waltz off with her Ladyship's hand - and get more than he bargained for with it. He's likely got his sights on the Lord's seat. Poor fool."

He poured himself a cup of wine and raised it in a toast. "Here's to them both leaving the house."

Elana raised her own glass to his in a hearty salute.

Hayes downed his wine and motioned for her to stay seated while he finished up the cleaning. When she had finished eating, he cleared her place as well.

"Forgive me, Elana, for being a bit forward with you." His eyes still twinkled, belying the apology. "I didn't realize that you were a guest here."

It was her turn to laugh. "Forgiven. And thank you for a wonderful supper." She reached out her hand in a peace offering. Hayes shook it respectfully, and then winked and brought it up to his lips for a quick kiss.

"If there's ever anything you need, I'm at your service."

"Thank you, Hayes." She didn't know just how far Marek's protection carried, but she made a note not to wander into the kitchens alone again.

She made sure he had returned to his duties before she ventured down the steps into the wine cellar. She slipped back into her own clothes and bundled up the servant's outfit under her arm. The tension of the evening on top of using her Waking so much left a pounding in her head that made it hard to think. All she wanted now was find her room and her bed. She stumbled down the maze of hallways that were slowly growing more familiar. Finding her room she collapsed on the freshly made bed.

"Elana?" Marek's voice dragged her back from the edge of sleep.

"What," she answered, trying to hide her resentment at being awakened.

"I need to talk with you about Aidan."

"Now?"

"Yes. It's important."

"Can we talk face to face? My head aches."

"Meet me in the garden. I'll be waiting for you."

She pulled on less conspicuous clothes before making her way through the great house to Marek's private garden. The house lay still, and for all her straining, she could hear no signs of life as she crept through the shadowed halls.

After the darkness of the house, the garden glowed in the starlight. Her eyes immediately picked out Marek's form, pacing under the trees by the far wall. Agitation rolled off of him in waves. When he turned toward her, she resisted the urge to step back.

140

"What's wrong?" she asked.

"Tell me what you know of this Aidan." His voice was clipped, his brow furrowed.

"I believe that I saw him the night Orvis was attacked," Elana began. She hesitated, something inside her going off in a warning.

"Really?" Marek gathered himself in, gracious once more. "Where was he?"

"He looked out a window above us and yelled. That gave me time to block the attackers with my Waking."

"So he saw you do that?"

Elana felt her face flush. "I guess so, though I never saw him look out again." A thought took form in her head. Maybe her Waking had blasted him as well. That might explain why he mistrusted her so. What must he think she was?

"Have you seen him at any time since then?"

She was cornered. She hadn't wanted to tell him about going to the Towers, but she knew she couldn't lie to him. He would sense it.

"I saw him again this evening." She looked down, unable to meet Marek's probing gaze. "At the Towers."

She felt a jolt of emotion shoot through him, before he collected himself again.

"I didn't know you had gone out there. It's dangerous, very dangerous, for you to travel through this city." He grabbed her by the shoulders. "Elana, do you know what might have happened to you?"

"I'm sorry. It's just that they were calling to me. I had to see them."

"You could have asked me, and I would have accompanied you, kept you safe."

"You're right. I just didn't want to bother you." Elana felt like a small child again, in trouble for some misdeed. She took a deep breath and met Marek's reproachful gaze. "I won't do that again."

"I'm glad to hear it. You're a very special young woman and I don't want anything to happen to you." He turned away and continued his pacing. "Did you know that a Hunter searched the Towers yesterday?"

Goose flesh rose up on the back of Elana's neck. She had no idea. "I didn't think they would... in a place like that..."

"They're searching for you."

She could see in her mind again, the shadowed tentacles reaching across the water, toward her. She shivered trying to close her mind to that image.

"Tell me about tonight." Marek's voice brought her back to the present.

"It was," she paused, searching for words, "really strange."

Marek stopped pacing and faced her again. "Tell me everything that happened," he said, his voice tight, controlled. "This is very important."

She swallowed over a lump in her throat. As best she could, she recounted her conversation with Aidan and his abrupt departure. "I don't know why he seemed so afraid of me," she finished.

A half-smile played over Marek's face. "So he is Elder Born." He nodded at her. "He must know that he couldn't possibly be a fit suitor for Cecily. And he's kept this from her. Not exactly noble behavior, do you think?"

Elana nodded. She had not thought of the implications. Elder Born rarely married Valefolk. Most Valefolk feared or hated them. To marry one of their leaders... He would never be accepted as a candidate for the Lord's Seat. Cecily would have to relinquish her claim to rulership if she were to wed him.

Marek studied her, and she could feel him there with her thoughts. "I wonder what our young hero has in mind?"

Elana's face burned. She remembered the words she overheard from the cook in the wine cellar. Was Aidan the one he was speaking of? Something in her wanted to reach out to him, but she berated herself for it. It was just as well that he was leaving. She would let Marek worry about them. There were more important things for her to worry about.

Marek turned to her with kindness in his eyes. "It's late," he said to her. "Go to your room and sleep now. Meet me here before dawn. I need to see about something."

Aidan grit his teeth as he and Cecily left the dining room. His head pounded from the effort of keeping the girl from the Towers at bay. What was she doing in that house? She was no servant. Between her and Marek, he felt like he'd been in battle. He could feel Marek pressing against him in the same way - probing, questioning. He'd refused to acknowledge it. It was probably too late, but he didn't want to let Marek know he was Elder Born. He didn't trust the man any more than he trusted the girl.

Cecily chattered on as she led him down the hall. It amazed him that she could be so unaware of all that was happening. Innocent, he corrected himself. She wasn't Elder Born. There was no way she could know. He smiled, laughed, and attempted to go along with her. It was wonderful to see her again, no mistake about that. Only now, he began to think, the trip here was a fool's venture.

"I told you Marek would be thrilled to have you come with me," Cecily leaned against his shoulder, looking up at him with her brilliant green eyes.

He couldn't help but warm to her. She was exquisite.

"I can't wait to be on the road with you again," he said. At least they would be leaving in the morning; out of the reach of either Marek or the girl from the Towers.

"This time we won't have to sleep outside, or eat messes cooked over a campfire." She wrinkled her nose at the thought. "Marek knows every innkeeper from here to Drumcard. He'll let us know the best places to stop. All I have to do is give our names and we will have the finest service these rustic towns can provide."

Aidan's smile slipped from his face. The image of playing the hero again for Cecily faded with the smile. He was more like a livery boy; tagging along to keep her safe and amused. Marek's comment at dinner about compensating him, rankled. He felt bought and paid for.

The walls of the house seemed to close in on him. He just wanted to be gone. He took a deep breath, steadying himself. Marek would want him to feel that way. He could sense the man's displeasure at Cecily's fondness for him. He wouldn't be run off. Tomorrow the two of them would set out together.

Cecily showed him to his room and promised to see him first thing in the morning. When she left, Aidan closed the door behind her. He sighed and lay back on the bed, trying to sort out his jumbled thoughts. His mind raced like an animal caught in a cage. He had to get out of the house for a while, just to think.

Opening the door, he checked that no one was watching, and made his way back down the hall until he found the side door. He would tell anyone who might ask, that he was checking on Kael. In truth, he was going out to the stallion, but it was more for himself.

Outside under the stars, the song from the Towers surged through him. He hadn't realized it, but it had been barely audible in Marek's home. Peace rolled in with the song, soothing his mind, his nerves. He made his way across the yard to the stable, where Kael's whinny welcomed him. Letting himself into the big horse's stall, he rested his head against the stallion's neck, breathing in his warm, sweet smell. He let his thoughts drift along with Kael's; filled with hay, mingled night smells, and the song from the Towers running through it all. Funny how animals hadn't blocked themselves off from hearing things like that. He'd never met anyone until Reeves, who had even spoken of it.

He thought of his father's old friend, wondering if the Bells Elder was still in Bellport, or if he'd left the city. He hoped he'd get a chance to see him again soon. A nagging sense of failure hounded him. The only reason he'd come to Bellport was because of what Granny had said about finding Reeves. He was pretty sure he was supposed to do more than just say, "hello," to the man.

Well, he couldn't find him now, and it was too dangerous to stay here and wait. He needed to work out a plan. Cecily was traveling to Rivergate, and he would accompany her there. After that, he and Kael would take to the open country. That's what he'd wanted to do all along. This had been a long diversion from his intended path. It was time to get to Farran.

The thought was bittersweet. He didn't want to dwell on the final parting with Cecily. Even though this was stolen time, he could pretend for a little longer that they may have had a chance together.

The night was still and as Aidan settled into that stillness, the Song of the Towers slowly drove all thought from him. He curled up in the fresh bedding of Kael's stall and let the Song carry him over to dreaming.

Before the first light of dawn, Aidan woke, uneasy. Kael shifted, restless in the stall. Outside, hushed voices whispered.

"Be sure she is unharmed."

"What about…"

"You know what to do."

Aidan crouched beneath the stall door, peering through the cracks in the wood. A man on horseback turned and wheeled out of the yard. Another, his face covered by his hood, hurried back to the house.

Was the 'she' Cecily? Was it someone else? The girl from the Towers? He would have sworn that the hooded man's voice was Marek's. Aidan shivered. He took a deep breath. The music of the Song was faint, discordant. He wanted to run in the house and tell Cecily, but that was foolish. What could she do? Anyway, Marek dealt with other people than just her. It was really none of his business. He glanced at the sky. It would be morning soon.

He fed Kael his breakfast early, made sure his bags were packed, and stole back inside. He made it to his room just before Cecily arrived.

"You have straw in your hair," she said, picking the offending pieces out.

"I went down early to feed Kael." He hoped no further questions would come.

"Oh." She seemed distracted, like part of her mind was elsewhere.

"Well, shall we?" he asked.

Her smile returned. "I'm ready." She slipped her hand through his arm and led the way to the kitchens for a bite before they left.

The cook, who served their breakfast, kept glancing over at them, a leering smile on his face. Aidan shifted in his seat. He didn't trust anyone here. Cecily was uncharacteristically quiet.

"Are you well?" he asked her.

"Me? Yes. Only a little tired. Marek had some last minute instructions for me before bed." She laughed, but none of her brightness animated it. "I'm not used to late nights and early mornings put together." She placed her hand over his. "I'll be fine." She met his glance for a moment and then looked down.

Aidan found he was hungry and finished his food with relish; sausage and eggs with hearty bread and a hot, bitter drink with a strong aroma that he'd never encountered before. Cecily only picked at her food.

He pushed back his plate and she rose right away. "Let's be off," she said.

He nodded, glad to be quit of this place.

At the stables, Marek held her mare, already packed and saddled. A commotion sounded from the direction of Kael's stall.

"Damn horse, won't let anyone near him." One of the stable boys came limping out into the yard.

Aidan's eyes flashed.

"We would have had your horse ready for you," Marek intervened, "but as you see…" He pointed in the direction of Kael's stall, where two other stable boys sulked off, nursing minor wounds.

"He doesn't suffer others to handle him."

Marek smiled, enigmatic. "You have a way with animals, I see."

Aidan stiffened and walked off to check on Kael, who had emerged unscathed from the scuffle. He saddled the horse, calming him with his touch and voice, and the special way they spoke without words. In a few minutes they were set.

"You have enough food packed to take you through two afternoons on the road. Follow the Greenway and you should make Rivergate in that time. Tonight, I suggest you stop at Pikeman's Crossing. It is the halfway point between Bellport and Rivergate. Look for the Thistledown. It is the only decent inn you'll find there." Marek nodded, almost to himself. "Mention my name to the innkeeper and you'll receive the best of care. He owes me a favor and will be glad for a chance to repay it."

Cecily nodded up at him, her eyes bright with gratitude.

"Once you arrive at Rivergate, there is some business that I have asked Cecily to look after. A man by the name of Parkin will meet you at the Three Oaks. He will give her further instructions." He turned to Aidan. "I cannot thank you enough for going out of your way to see to my dear girl's safety. I pray that the rest of your trip be smooth and profitable." Reaching into his cloak, he pulled out a small leather bag, and handed it to the young man.

Aidan's jaw tightened. By the feel of the bag, it was gold. He tried to appear grateful, but his stomach churned. Bought, paid for and dismissed; he was nothing more than a hired servant here.

He nodded at Marek, not trusting himself to speak.

Cecily gave the man a kiss on the cheek and a brief hug. Marek settled her into her saddle and fussed over her tack. When he was finished, Aidan swung up on Kael, spun the stallion around and trotted from the yard. It wasn't until they left the street that Aidan turned to look at her.

She looked back at him, her eyes pleading. "Don't be mad at Marek. He's always been protective of me. He's more like my father than Lord Gratton. You don't know how highly he thinks of you - entrusting me to your care for such a journey."

Aidan reddened. He didn't want to cause her pain, or to act like an offended apprentice.

"I'm sorry," he said. He slowed Kael, letting Cecily's mare come alongside. "I behaved badly. Please forgive me. I'm not used to such ways."

Her face lit up. All signs of her earlier moodiness vanished. "Of course I forgive you. Let's enjoy these two days." She reached out her hand to him, almost unseating herself.

"You be careful! We'll have more fun if you don't fall off."

She laughed, and it was as though the sun came out for the first time that day.

Her high spirits were contagious. Soon Aidan was laughing and talking with her as though they were the only two people in the world. He never even noticed the smiles they elicited from passersby. Before midmorning they were outside the gates, leaving Bellport and all its worries behind them.

Merchants and travelers frequented the Greenway, and even in these dangerous days, it was well traveled between Bellport and Rivergate. Lord Gratton had, in fact, posted his own guards along this stretch of road; not so much as to insure his people's safety, as to see to the safety of the goods that made their way to and from Bellport. Without this trade, Bellport's prosperity would be short lived.

Each time Aidan and Cecily passed a company of guards, the men saluted Lord Gratton's daughter. She smiled and waved to them, delighted with the attention. Aidan caught, on more than one occasion, stares and whispers directed at him. There would be plenty of conjecture tonight at the inns, over Lady Cecily's traveling companion.

At midday they stopped beside the road for a meal. Aidan unwrapped fresh bread, meats, cheese, fruit, and a flask of wine. There was enough food packed for a feast. He spread out a blanket on the fresh grass, untacked the horses and helped Cecily to her meal. She ate with relish this time, and he joined her. The food was excellent, and he even enjoyed the wine. He was unused to drinking fine wine, and found this to be light, not too sweet, and altogether pleasing.

When they were finished Aidan packed everything back up while Cecily dozed on the blanket. He woke her when the horses were saddled, but she was groggy, disoriented almost. He knew that she drank more wine than he had, but assumed she was used to it and now hoped she was well enough to ride. He felt his own senses clouded from the wine and berated himself for indulging.

They made their way slowly up the road, letting the horses choose their own pace. Aidan's head grew fuzzier, not clearer as he rode and something inside him was starting to panic. This wasn't the wine. Even strong drink wouldn't effect him this way in such a small quantity. His ears rang and his head pounded. It was hard to stay on Kael.

He heard a thud just behind him and turned to see Cecily lying on road. Her face was pale and her eyes closed. The white mare stood over her quietly. He slid down off Kael and stumbled over to her. The ground came reeling up to meet him, and he was aware of footsteps running toward them at the same time he heard Kael's scream.

He forced himself upright and turned to see half a dozen men; black cloaked and booted drawing toward them. Below him, Cecily moaned. Kael reared, striking at the nearest of the men. He heard hooves crushing bone, and the man crumpled. Aidan knew he could outrun them on Kael, but he couldn't leave Cecily here.

He pulled his hunting knife from his belt. The white mare was dancing now, nervous. One of the men rushed in, grabbing her bridle. Kael screamed again, savaging the man's horse.

The rest of them circled, none getting in striking range of the stallion's hooves. Aidan's head swam. Everything was moving in slow motion. He felt like a deer he had seen once in the marshes, surrounded by wolves. Gasping, he hauled Cecily up, trying to get her onto Kael's saddle. She slumped over the stallion's neck. He started to climb up himself when one of the men stepped in front of Kael.

He threw back his hood, looked straight into Aidan's eyes and a voice exploded in Aidan's head, "NO!"

Kael stumbled and fell, throwing both of them to the ground. Aidan lay there frozen. From where he looked up, he could see nothing except the man's eyes. He couldn't move. The man's presence filled all of his mind, hating him, pressing in on him, leaving no room for him there. Everything started spinning. Footsteps sounded to his right and he heard a man carry Cecily off. Another led away the mare. The man with his hood thrown back still stood over him, his eyes boring into Aidan's head.

Next to him he heard Kael struggle to rise. The man took his eyes off Aidan and turned them on the stallion. Aidan felt the horse's mind reeling from the man's invasion. And then Kael was gone. He couldn't reach him anymore.

He yelled and launched himself at the Hunter. "Not Kael!" He couldn't take his horse. Someone struck him on the head. The world exploded into pain. The slow laugh of the man whose presence still burned in his mind, was the last sound he heard before blackness took him.

He didn't know if it was hours or days later that he woke. He couldn't move, and something lumpy was poking into his side. Dried blood cracked on his lips. When he opened his eyes it was as black as with them shut. His heart hammered in his chest. He forced himself to breathe, to still his thoughts. He closed his eyes again to focus. By the feel of it he was lodged against some rock or tree, in the woods somewhere. The ground seemed to tilt away below him. Small insect sounds and tree frogs nearby indicated that it was night. So he hadn't lost his sight.

His hands were tied behind his back, his shoulders twisted to the breaking point. His feet were tied as well and he felt as if he had been beaten all over. There was no place that didn't hurt. He concentrated on breathing, stilling the panic that rose up. They had left him here to die.

What about Cecily? Kael? Where were they? He had no answers, and if he couldn't free himself, he would die here, never knowing.

He tried to move, to inch his way around. The bonds on his wrists bit into his skin. He shifted his position, and suddenly whatever was supporting his weight gave way and he rolled, bouncing and skidding down a steep embankment. He crashed into a rock, cutting his face afresh and stopping his plunge. The hot blood was salty on his swollen tongue. The rock's jagged surface pressed cruelly into his body. He was afraid to shift again, lest he fall further into the unknown blackness. A lump pounded on the side of his head.

Slowly, his eyes grew accustomed to the darkness. Clouds that had covered the stars blew away west. By their faint light, Aidan took stock of his position.

Above him he could make out the outline of the top of the cliff. Far below, he could hear water running; a stream by the sound of it. The boulder that broke his fall was huge. He was lucky it hadn't killed him. He rolled over, trying to put the massive rock at his back. His arm caught on a broken point, and for a moment he was afraid he would wrench his shoulder out of joint. He felt his skin tear on the rock's teeth and blood ran down his wrists as he broke free.

That gave him an idea. He pressed himself along the rock until he found the sharp edge again. Straining to raise himself up, he hooked the ropes binding his wrists on the edge of the rock. The muscles in his shoulders and legs burned and cramped as he tried to work the rope back and forth over the rock. He couldn't feel anything give. Panting, he paused, his legs trembling with the effort of holding himself up. If he gave up, he would die here.

He tried again. Nothing. He tried until his strength gave out and then half hung there, his mind whirling with pain. Again, he roused himself. This time, as he was ready to give up, he felt one of the cords snap. He renewed his effort. Sweat drenched his tunic. The rope broke free, sending him face first into the hill.

Tears ran down his cheeks, mixing with the dirt and leaves. He tried to move his arms, but both were too numb to respond. He lay there, his arms at his sides, his legs still bound, and sunk into unconsciousness.

CHAPTER 8

THE WESTERN ROAD

Elana sat alone in Marek's private garden. Pale stars studded the blue-black sky. A huge yawn burst out of her and she rubbed her eyes. Her mind felt numb, sleep clouded. Behind her the door scraped open and Marek entered. Stifling another yawn, she stood to greet him.

"Sit, please." His voice in her head sounded gentle, controlled. Beneath that control, a riptide of anxiety jolted her into wakefulness.

She sat back down. "What's wrong?" she sent to him. It struck her as odd, that she could sense that much from him in just a moment.

A strained smile softened his face. "The worries of a man who's seen too much to trust easily." He sat down next to her.

For a moment it seemed to Elana that the walls in his mind wavered. A picture of him formed: Marek as a statue, powerful, commanding - except that when she looked closely, there were cracks running throughout. Her throat tightened, her eyes stung. Incongruous as it seemed, pity for the most powerful man in Bellport, welled up in her.

"I'm so sorry," she sent back to him. She reached out her hand for his. He held it a moment, and she could feel him draw strength from her touch. It was good to be able to give something back, even if it was only a little comfort.

"Is there anything I can do?" She looked up at him, holding his gaze, letting the intensity of his presence burn into her without pulling back.

He remained silent, but his eyes bore into her mind; testing her, weighing her.

She absorbed it, meeting him with the calm he had taught her in these few days of training. She wasn't afraid of him.

Finally, he dropped his gaze. "Elana," he spoke to her mind, "We don't have as much time as I'd hoped."

"What do you mean?"

"I told you a Hunter searched the Towers."

She nodded.

"Reeves has been forced to leave Bellport."

Her heart dropped. How would she help her parents?

"Courage, dear one."

She felt strength coming from him.

"There is a way, but things are moving faster than I imagined. I wanted more time to train you, to help you get ready."

Her Waking stirred.

"Remember when we first talked and I spoke of the Prophesy?"

The hair on the back of her neck stood up. The last traces of sleep fled.

"I believe that Reeves has information about it. That's why the Hunters are searching for him."

Blood pounded in Elana's head. It was hard to hear what Marek was sending to her. Her Waking surged, beyond her control. Images flashed before her eyes, too fast for her to make sense of them.

Marek's hands on her shoulders brought her back. "You have to control it," he spoke to her mind. "I can't send you out there if you let it out like that."

The fear in his voice stilled the last of her Waking.

"I'm sorry. I don't know what happens. It's whenever you talk about the Prophesy. It doesn't happen at other times like that."

"I know," he said. There was a long pause. He spoke the next words out loud. They sounded huge in the still night air. "It's because you are meant to fulfill it."

The garden spun around Elana. She forced herself to concentrate on the rhythm of her breathing, controlling this time, the surge of her Waking. He was right. She knew he was right, and it wasn't just foolish pride or wishful thinking. She blinked back tears and met his gaze.

"I know," she whispered. "I think I've known since the letter."

"That's why the Hunters are after you. That's why they took your parents. It's not just that your Waking is so powerful. It's that they have to stop you. Or turn you to their side."

Elana's stomach clenched. "But Marek, what am I to do? I don't know the first thing about the Prophesy. I was hoping that Reeves could help me."

He was silent a long while. Finally, he spoke, "I don't know the things that Reeves knows, but I will help you all I can." He grasped both of her hands. "Listen carefully to me. I believe that this is the only hope for your parents. You won't be able to do anything for them short of fulfilling your part of the Prophesy."

"My part?"

"Yes. That is my best understanding, after years of searching and study. Remember the Prophesy:

The three will rise to reunite

When the Shadow's arm grows long

Together push the darkness back:

The Key, the Seed, the Song.

Think about it. 'The three will rise,' refers to the three Gifts of the Ancient Ones: the Firestone, the Orchard Tree, the Silver Bells. They're not spoken of directly, only by those things that will help bring them back." His eyes lit with a hunger Elana hadn't witnessed before. "There are stories. Not many know of them, but I searched them out while I lived in Farran; of the Firestone being locked up, hidden somehow, and that some token is needed to unlock it. I believe that's what 'the Key' refers to."

The vision she had the day Marek started her training... The woman with the intricately wrought Bronze Key... She pulled her attention back to Marek's words.

" 'The Seed' is clearer. There must, somewhere, be a seed preserved from the Orchard Tree. I don't know as much about that, as it isn't my Eldership." He waved his hand as though brushing it aside. "'The Song' I suspect refers to the Silver Bells. The Bells Elders were often Gifted musicians. My guess is that there is either an instrument, or a Song, or maybe both together that will lead to the Silver Bells. This is the part I believe, that Reeves has more answers to."

The excitement in his voice fanned her own. He continued, "But from what I understand, the Firestone is the key to the Gifts. It is the most powerful of the three. That is the Gift that you are called to restore. It is the ruling Gift."

Her head swam. It took her a moment to find her voice. "Marek. There's something I didn't tell you." She described the vision she had a few days ago; of the woman, of the Bronze Key.

Marek gripped her, his fingers bruising her arms. "This is it! Elana, you are closer than I imagined. Do you have any idea where this woman is?"

"There were mountains, rugged ones. Not like around Farran. But that's all I know. I get visions sometimes, but they don't always come complete."

Marek frowned. "Rugged mountains, you say? I've traveled most of the Vale and the only place that sounds like that is up around the Empty Hills. There are stories from around those parts, strange stories about a land that's not fully part of our world. Some say that's where the door to Laharan lies."

"Laharan?"

"The Island. Some sort of place between this world and the home of the Ancient Ones. An old legend has it that when Evana, locked up the Firestone, the Ancient Ones took Firestone Peak to Laharan. Removed an entire mountain from the map."

Elana stared at him.

"There's no hole, it's just not there. They say that there is a door. Of course many Elder Born have searched in the place where Firestone Peak was supposed to be, but no one has ever found a trace of it. And no door. Most who travel to that area find themselves so disoriented that they have no memory of the land or how they got back out again. The Valefolk believe that part of the Border Mountains is cursed."

Elana's stomach knotted. "How am I to find a mountain that isn't there?"

Marek frowned. "That is a problem. But it's not our first problem. For now, I have to get you out of Bellport. It's too dangerous here for you. I will have to create a diversion, draw the Hunters off your trail. Then, if all goes as planned, I'll be able to meet you on the road. Together, we can look for the door to Laharan."

"Where can I go? And what about Orvis? He's not well enough to travel yet."

Marek touched her cheek in a gesture of sympathy. "I know that Orvis is a good friend, but Elana, he is unable to help you in this. If you wait for him, your parents will suffer for it." His voice whispered in her head, "I'm so sorry, so many hard choices before you. I know you've been through much, but you must be strong now."

She nodded, swallowing down the bile that rose in her throat. She didn't want to think about saying goodbye to the old sailor.

"This afternoon, a company of men in my employ leaves for Rivergate. I was going to send Cecily with them, but I felt it would be more expedient for her to travel with Aidan. I would like you to be among the men when they leave. I'm afraid that for now, it is safest to maintain your appearance as a boy. The leader of the company, Gaius, will know of your identity. He will see to it that you arrive at Rivergate in safety." He lowered his voice, "The success of this plan, depends almost entirely upon your ability to control your Waking. Until I am with you again, I cannot shield you from the Hunters. And they are ever vigilant."

A chill crept up her back once again. She forced her fear down and met Marek's gaze. "Who are these men I'm to travel with?"

Marek laughed. "Well, you should ask. I'll tell you, as you will figure it out for yourself, shortly. They are cutthroats and thieves. Desperate men, against whom the doors of this world have slammed shut. They are dangerous men, not to be trifled with. I used to be one myself, before I stumbled upon Farran. I have a soft spot for those who live by their wits and nerve." The glint in his eye confirmed his words.

Elana caught a glimpse of memory from him, young, powerful, dangerous, always on the run, answering to no man, master of all he saw. Marek cleared his throat and the vision was gone.

"I have learned that it is better for all, to give such men a legitimate place. Put them to work where their particular skills will serve, and then see that they are well rewarded. Befriend such a man and you have a loyalty that no gold can buy."

"How many are there?" Elana felt herself cowering at the thought of such riding companions.

"Only a handful will go with you. There are many more, but they are needed elsewhere." Marek chuckled. "As my special friend, you will find no safer traveling companions."

She did not doubt him. In a twisted way, she saw the genius of it. This man was a born leader. She pitied anyone who stood in his way.

Hope rekindled. "When do I need to be ready?"

Marek smiled at her. "After the noon meal. I will have Braxton pack appropriate clothes for you. Can you ride a horse?"

"Yes." She loved to ride, and hadn't since they'd come east to the sea.

"Take your noon meal in the kitchen today, and then meet me at the stables. We will find an appropriate mount for you."

Clouds from the east caught the first light of dawn and painted it, red streaked, across the sky. It brought to mind the fishermen's warning about a red sky at dawn.

"Orvis," Elana sighed. Excitement about the trip warred with her guilt over leaving him. She cast about for some way to explain all this without exposing Marek. There wasn't any way. Marek would have to forgive her. It felt like betrayal to leave her father's friend without telling him what was happening. She decided at last, that she would tell him of Marek's being Elder Born, but not of their mind link. Orvis wouldn't expose him. Marek had saved his life, and Orvis knew what it was to live in hiding.

Her feet found their way to his door too quickly. After a gentle knock, she pushed the door open. The old sailor lay in his bed, eyes alert for the first time since they'd arrived.

"Elana." His voice sounded rusty. The morning light shone around him, lighting up his silver hair. His face was still gray, gaunt.

"Orvis." She ran up and knelt beside the bed, taking his hands in her own. "How are you feeling?"

He grimaced. "Death isn't claiming me yet." His breathing was still harsh, labored. "How are you doing? Are they treating you well?"

She could feel the old mistrust of strangers, under his words.

"They've been wonderful to me, Orvis. Marek has been so helpful."

He closed his eyes. Sweat stood out on his forehead.

"You're in pain. What can I do to help?"

A bowl of water and a cloth sat on the table beside his bed. She wet the cloth and wiped the old sailor's face.

"I'm sorry." Orvis' eyes opened and met her own. "I'm no help to you like this, lass. Any word of Reeves?"

She nodded. "Marek knows him. He's left the city right now, the Hunters were on his trail."

"Is Marek..." He left the question unfinished.

"Yes."

"I thought so. Good."

"But no one here save Braxton knows," Elana rushed on. She didn't want him to think he could talk about it freely.

"I'm no fool, lass. The man saved my life. He won't hear anything from me."

Blood rushed to her face. "I'm sorry Orvis. He made me promise I wouldn't say anything. But I can't hide it from you."

"Nothing to be sorry for," he gasped out the words. His weathered hand patted hers.

"Orvis," Elana paused, not knowing how to broach her leaving. "Marek has offered to help me. He thinks it's too dangerous for me to stay in Bellport. The Hunters are looking for me here." She took a deep breath. "He's arranged safe passage for me to Rivergate. He hopes to meet me there."

"And do what?" The old sailor squinted.

"Marek believes that I am one of the ones to fulfill the Prophecy." It sounded crazy to her now, even as the words left her mouth. She pushed on. "He thinks that it will be the only way I can help my parents. That's why the Hunters captured them, trying to get at me and... and stop me."

Orvis lay quiet for a while. Finally he spoke. "Your father mentioned something of the kind to me. Not in those words exactly, but hinting around to it. He didn't want you to carry that burden yet." He shook his head. "And how does Marek plan to help you?"

She didn't have a clear answer to give him. "For now, just to get me out of Bellport. He's studied the Prophesy. He said that what I have to do has something to do with a Key, and a door to a place that isn't there. That's where the Firestone is."

"Lass, you aren't making sense. Find a door to a place that isn't there?"

"Yes." Elana realized how ridiculous this sounded. "He called it Laharan. The Island. A place between our world and the Ancient Ones' world. The Ancient Ones took the mountain with the Firestone to Laharan and left only a door."

160

"So you're going to go traipsing around the wilderness with a man you barely know, while the Hunters are on your trail, looking for a door to a place that isn't there?"

This wasn't going well.

"Yes."

Orvis sighed. "I should have been there for you, lass. I know I owe my life to this Marek, but I hate to see you go off with someone we don't know the first thing about. Call me old fashioned, but I just don't like it."

"I don't either, Orvis," she said, "but I don't see any alternatives. I'd like to be back home with my parents, and the only way I have any hope of seeing them again, is to do this."

"I know. I just wish it were different. I wish I could go with you."

"So do I," she whispered. He was her last link to home. She didn't want to say goodbye to him.

"I've tired you out," she said. "You rest now. Maybe when you get well, you can follow."

His eyes lit up at her words. "I'll do that. You watch for me. I'll find you again if I have to cross the entire Vale on foot."

Closing the door to Orvis' room, Elana hurried to her own. Marek said that Braxton would pack clothes for her, but there were a few things she didn't want to leave behind. When she got to her room she found clothes laid out.

They fit her well enough, the breeches and tunic were finely crafted and comfortable for travel, and strong leather boots would serve her well in the wilds. More sensible, she noted than a woman's costume. She tied the deep blue arm band over her right arm; the symbol of one of Marek's personal servants. In this entire house, only Braxton wore the band. Each wealthy house had a color or pattern that they used for their highest servants' bands. It was considered an honor to be a banded servant; tied to that household for life.

Even so, Elana rankled at the thought. She knew Marek was only trying to help her, but she was unused to such things. She couldn't think of herself in those terms.

Trying to put away those thoughts, she rifled through her own pack and pulled out the tunic that her mother had embroidered for her. This wouldn't stay behind. The stained cloak that had belonged to Brenna came out with it; the only keepsakes from her old life. Packing them in her new bags, she surveyed the room. Braxton had been thorough, she didn't need to add anything else, and she'd rather not carry more than necessary. It was still early for the noon meal, but she thought she'd visit the kitchens and get to the stables early.

Hayes greeted her with a grin. "I hear we're loosing the pleasure of your company as well," he said.

"Is there anything you don't hear?" Elana asked.

"Not much. Lady Cecily and her gentleman friend left this morning. Seems the party's moving to Rivergate."

"That's where I'm going." Her throat went dry. "This time I know to steer clear of her."

"It may not be as hard as you think."

"What do you mean?"

"Heading for a destination, and arriving at that place are two different things," he said with a cryptic smile.

"Are they running away... going to elope or something?"

"I can't go telling all of my secrets now, can I?" With a wink, he left to fill up a plate and bring it back for her.

"Whoever thinks you'll pass as a boy, doesn't have eyes."

"Well, I'll just have to do my best."

"You'd be well served to not speak too much."

The smile faded off her face. "I know. That's what Orvis said too, when we were coming to Bellport."

"You're going to miss that old sailor, aren't you?"

162

"Yes."

"I'll keep an eye on him, make sure he's not wanting for anything. Any friend of yours is a friend of mine."

"Thank you." Elana caught his eye and smiled.

"Anything for you, my dear." He bowed with a flourish, then left her to eat her meal.

Though she arrived at the stables early, Marek was already there, giving instructions to a lean, fair-haired man in weathered traveling clothes.

"Elana, come here."

The fair-haired man watched her like a cat watches a bird.

"Gaius, this is Elana. Elana, Gaius. I wanted you two to meet before the others joined us."

"Gaius inclined his head toward her.

Elana could sense the man sizing her up. "I'm honored to meet you," she said and bowed to him.

A cold smile tried to break the severity of his face. "Marek, you'll never pull it off. This one won't pass for a servant, let alone a boy."

Elana reached out to Marek, questioning.

"Don't do anything to offend him. He'll be your greatest ally on the road," Marek's voice sounded in her head.

"I'm afraid you're right, Mr. Gaius," she answered. "I don't play the part well enough. Do you have any suggestions? I'd be willing to try anything."

The man considered her, studying her up and down. "A servant too bold, or a boy too pretty will only draw attention. The question is, how can you travel, without others taking notice?"

Elana looked at Marek, who was nodding, considering the man's words.

"The Barras." Gaius said.

Elana gave him a questioning look.

"They dwell in the eastern plains of Lanreath, between Merrion and the mountains. You've heard of the Freefolk?"

She nodded, searching her memory for something to make this all fit together.

Gaius elaborated. "They are one of them. They answer to no Lord, ruling themselves, for as long as story goes back." He gave a rough laugh. "The Lords stay out of their lands when they know what's good for them. They don't take kindly to visitors. But more to the point, they don't keep their women tied to the house like most of the Valefolk. The women ride and fight with the best of the men. Only, they don't travel often."

"How does that help us?" Elana asked.

He ignored her question and fired back one of his own. "How are you with a horse?"

She felt Marek's mind close in on the man's idea.

"I'm good with them, only it's been a while," she answered.

"Yes. Very good, Gaius. The golden mare. As a gift, with her handler." A slow smile spread over Marek's face. "And as such, she would be untouchable to any. Excellent."

"Elana," he said. "You will take the filly, Devi, with you. She will be your mount."

"I don't understand," she said.

Gaius elaborated. "The Barras breed the Vale's finest horses, only they don't part with them easily. If they do sell a horse, someone who's handled the horse travels with it to see that it is well cared for. As such, they are treated as an honored guest wherever they go."

In her head Elana heard Marek ask, "Have you ever contacted an animal?"

She started at the question, and paused to think about it. "Yes," she answered. She had reached out to Kael, Aidan's horse and he received the contact willingly. She had also had a link of sorts with other

164

animals she'd known. She'd never thought of it in those terms, though.

"You may need to contact this one to tame her. She's a young mare, and only just trained to saddle. But she's worth a Lord's ransom and I planned on offering her to Lord Ulrich to appease Cecily's refusal of Darian."

Out loud she said, "That will be perfect." She risked a smile at Gaius. "Thank you for your help."

He returned the smile, though she couldn't read what he was thinking behind his pale eyes.

Marek untied the blue band from Elana's arm, and she let her hair fall free around her face.

"Can I keep these clothes? They're so much better suited for travel than a woman's."

Gaius grunted. "Aye. The horsewomen of the Lanreath ride astride, just as the men." He narrowed his eyes, studying her. "You don't look like them, they're fair and tall, as a rule, but no one's going to risk offending you by pointing that out." He laughed without mirth. "Offending one of the Barras shortens your life span. No, you'll pass untroubled."

She could feel him probing her. This one was Elder Born, untrained probably. Whether he knew it or not, she could feel his Skill reaching out toward her mind. With very little effort, she diverted his thought, felt him cast about for a moment, disoriented and then return to the conversation.

"That is, if you can handle the horse."

"I'll do my best," she said.

At a word from Marek, one of the stable boys brought a young mare into the yard. Her coat shone a rich gold in the afternoon sun, setting off her flaxen mane and tail. Elana had never seen her like.

Gaius whistled low. "She is worth a Lord's ransom. I'd hate to part with her if she were mine."

The mare pranced, tossing her head, and then went straight up on her hind legs, jerking the lead out of the stable boy's hands. She let out a high whinny, spun, and raced around the yard.

Elana's heart was in her throat. She had ridden as a girl, but this mare was wild. The stable boy, waving his hands as he ran after her, only served to egg her on. Elana could feel both Marek and Gaius' eyes on her. She had to do something.

Tentatively, she reached out with her mind to the mare. A blur of images, feelings, swept through her: bright sunshine after the dark stable, exhilaration in her pounding legs, annoyance at the flapping two legged creature she so easily outran, smells and sounds clamoring for attention, the sweet grass beckoning at her feet. Alana kept her mind very still, not wanting to frighten Devi with her presence. After a moment, she felt the mare acknowledge her, push toward her. She felt the wordless question, "friend or foe?"

"Friend." Elana couldn't send her words, but she sent feelings: peace and safety, the comfort of companionship, the joy of a morning run, the contentment of good food. She sent a picture of herself and watched as the mare slowed and looked around. Devi turned to face her, ears forward.

Marek frowned at the stable boy and he fell back.

With uncertain steps the golden mare approached her. Elana looked away, not wanting to threaten. She stilled her breathing, feeling through the mare, how anxious she was. After a few minutes, the mare's soft nose blew against her cheek. She let Devi take in her scent, all the while staying close in her thoughts. When she reached up her hand to touch the velvet face, Devi rubbed her head vigorously against her shoulder.

"She'll need to learn some manners, but she's sweet," Elana said out loud.

"Aye, she'll play the role," Gaius said, and turned to fetch his own mount.

"Excellent." Marek's beamed at her.

Pride softened his voice in her mind. "Your Skills are stronger than I imagined. It is unusual for a Firestone Elder to be able to contact an animal. I did it with Vian, but I had rescued her as a fledgling, so the bonding was more natural.

"I'm still not sure I can ride her," she sent back. "It's not like I'm controlling her. It's more like I'm trying to talk with her, to be her friend."

"Give it a try. I think she'll let you."

Elana took a deep breath and reached again toward Devi. She sent a picture of her riding and questioned. The mare snorted and pranced away a few steps. Elana waited for her to come back. She sent the question again, feeling the mare's puzzlement at her request.

Slowly, she approached Devi and took hold of the lead. It was just a halter, but Elana led her alongside a low wall, climbed up and slid a leg over the golden back. She felt Devi stiffen and reached out to her with calming thoughts. The mare took a deep breath and let it out in a sigh. Elana stroked her neck, remembering to breathe, herself.

They walked around the yard together, Devi reaching out to her for reassurance every few steps. By the time the other men began to arrive, Elana had moved the mare into a trot and even cantered some, holding onto the flaxen mane so she wouldn't fall off.

She brought her back to Marek as the men were saddling up.

"I think I'd like to have a saddle for the trip," she said, her voice shaky.

Marek smile lit up his face. "Good girl. I knew you could do it."

He brought her a soft saddle and a bridle which Elana fitted to the mare herself. She tied her pack behind the saddle and mounted up once more.

"Elana," Marek spoke in her mind. "It will be more dangerous because you are contacting Devi. Try to use your Skills with her as little as possible. It is harder to detect contact with an animal, so I am not as worried about that, but even so, please be careful."

"I will," she promised.

"Ride with Gaius. You'll camp along the road the first night. Gaius has business to attend for me in Pikeman's Crossing in the morning. You should reach Rivergate by the second night."

"What about Cecily?" she asked silently.

"She will be ahead of you and staying in a different place. I've taken care of that." Marek answered in kind.

Elana nodded. "Will I be able to reach you from that far away?"

"You should be able to, but don't try too often, it will draw attention to you. But if you really need me, don't hesitate to call. I'll help you in any way I can. No matter what, Elana, don't leave Rivergate until I get there. It's more dangerous than you realize. And remember, the less you say, the less you mingle with the men, the better."

Tension crept back through her body and she felt Devi shift restlessly in response.

Gaius blew a low, pulsing note on a horn that hung by his side. The men rallied round him. He motioned for Elana to join him and then, raising a hand in salute to Marek, he wheeled his bay gelding and cantered out of the yard.

Elana was almost unseated as Devi spun to follow the big bay. She didn't have time to think about anything else as she was swept up in the mare's senses. It was all she could do to keep the flighty creature earthbound; she wanted to run, outrun the city, the smells, run back to the fields under the mountains, where she had played with her dam.

Bellport passed by her in a blur. It took all her Skills, concentration and ability to keep the mare underneath her. By the time they left the main gate behind, Devi had stopped spinning every time something new crossed their path.

She rode alongside Gaius, the other men keeping their distance, though she wasn't sure if it was due to Gaius' orders, or their desire to protect their mounts from Devi. Now that she had stopped spinning and wheeling at every new sight, the mare had taken to lacing her ears back and lunging at any horse who came near her.

"You're just the pampered princess, aren't you?" she whispered to the pointed ears that swiveled back to catch her words.

They rode throughout the afternoon without incident. The weather remained fair and warm, and everyone they passed on the Greenway stood aside for them. It was so different from her life before, that Elana felt as though she were riding in a dream. She remembered countless times traveling, when she and her parents hid off the road to avoid unpleasant encounters with the Valefolk. Always before, she had looked down when she met someone, not wanting to elicit hostility. Now she could ride with her head up, unafraid to draw the stares of the farmers, merchants, and travelers. Devi was eye catching, and everyone they passed watched them until they rode out of site.

It wasn't until after dark that two of the men scouted out a clearing near a stream to take their evening meal and rest for the night. Gaius called the company to halt. Elana had counted fifteen men on horseback plus herself. With gratitude, she slid off Devi's back, the muscles in her legs protesting from the extended ride. She unsaddled the mare and took her to the stream to drink. Gaius strung a high line between two trees with some rope and motioned for her to tie the mare. Elana fed Devi, rubbed out her saddle marks, and only then approached the circle of men around the campfire for her own meal.

Marek had provided them with a rich feast: cooked meat, flat bread, cheese, fruit, and wine. She ate off by herself, remembering his warning about not mixing or speaking more than necessary. She could feel the stares of the men, but at a look from Gaius they would find something else to be busy about.

Now that they had stopped riding, she could focus on something other than her horse. She felt Gaius' thoughts around her, not pushing, but questioning. She blocked him without his knowing, feeling each time his frustration at a thought that slipped away. He seemed safe enough, but she wasn't going to take any chances.

Night deepened as the fire burned down to embers. No moon showed her face, only stars filled the sky. One by one the men dropped off to sleep. Elana checked on Devi, took out her cloak from the pack and wrapped it around herself. Gaius was walking around the camp. He stopped at her spot and knelt down.

"Best if you sleep over by me," he whispered. "I can't vouch for the men out of my sight."

Elana grabbed her cloak, scrambled to her feet and followed him to the edge of camp. He pulled out a huge knife in a leather sheath, from his pack and tossed it to her.

"Never hurts."

"Thanks," she said, staring at the knife and hoping with all her might that she wouldn't have call to use it. She leaned back against a tree and watched the embers flicker. Sounds of snoring filled the camp, and the rustling of men and horses bedding down.

Looking up at the sky, she wondered where her parents were. Were they still alive? The ache from missing them, worrying about them, twisted her stomach into knots. It was a long time before she drifted off to sleep, clutching the awkward knife in her hands.

Jagged mountains reared up, their tips lost in a cloud filled sky. She was looking, looking for something, but she couldn't remember what. She called to Marek, but instead of his voice, she saw another face; a young man with tawny hair and eyes - Aidan.

Elana woke with a start, heart pounding. It was just a dream. She stilled her breathing, not wanting her Waking to surge out of control. At the edge of her mind, she heard Marek's voice.

"Are you alright?" Worry laced his words. "Why did you call?"

"It was just a dream. I'm fine," she answered.

"I'm glad. Remember, you can reach me if you need anything."

"I will."

The sky lightened to a flat gray. Next to her, Gaius' spot was empty. She could hear sounds across the camp of the men waking. Tucking the knife into her belt, she wrapped her damp cloak around her. The wind had shifted in the night, blowing clouds in from the east. A heavy dew clung to her clothes and hair, sticking them to her with clammy fingers and making her shiver in the morning chill.

Breakfast was a hurried affair, consisting of leftovers from the night before. Elana grabbed a hunk of bread and cheese, forcing herself to eat. She couldn't afford to be weak from hunger. Already, her legs complained at each movement, unused to the exertion of yesterday's ride. She'd get used to it soon enough.

She checked her pack, fed and watered Devi and saddled the mare by the time the men were gathering up.

Gaius blew the low pulsing note on the horn once more, and they headed off. The fog rolled in thicker, rising up from the coast and overtaking them as they rode. Gaius didn't seem to notice and set a demanding pace.

After an hour's ride, they came to the outskirts of a town.

"Pikeman's Crossing," Gaius told Elana. "I have business here. The men will go on ahead and wait in the woods on the other side. It's best that you come with me."

He had words with a man from the company and the rest of them veered off the Greenway. In a moment, they were lost in the fog.

Elana steered Devi after Gaius' bay. The horses' hooves sounded hollow on the packed dirt road; amplified in the stillness of the morning.

"I'm to meet a man at the Broadside Inn. You'd best wait with the horses in the stable. No one will question you being with them." He sneered. "Folks here see too much to rest easy. They're almost as scared of the Free Folk of Lanreath as they are of the Elder Born. Some say there's no difference." He looked sideways at her and again she felt the questioning from him. She closed her mind to the contact.

Together they rode into town. A freshly painted wooden sign hung along the main street announced the Broadside Inn. Gaius pointed her toward the stable yard in the back, vaulted off his bay and handed her the reins. Without a glance back he strode inside. Elana dismounted Devi and led the two horses around back, hoping that Gaius was right and that no one would ask her any questions.

The stables were quiet, except for the steady chewing of horses eating their hay. An old hostler with white bristly hair moved slowly among his charges, cleaning out their stalls. He stopped when he saw her and gave a half bow. Elana could feel his love for the animals, and their comfort in his presence. She smiled at him.

"She's a lovely mare. I've rarely seen her like."

"Thank you. She's a gift for one of the Lords. I hate to part with her, though."

"The Lords may own their bodies, but we hold their hearts." He nodded; an enigmatic smile playing across his face.

She looked up at him, surprised at the candid remark.

Before she could think of an answer, a commotion broke out in the yard. Men's shouts and horses' whinnies broke the peace of the morning. Elana's heart pounded. Not knowing what to expect she ran into the yard, dragging her two horses behind her.

A rough looking man, black cloaked and booted, riding a thick-limbed chestnut galloped into the yard shouting curses at a horse he was pulling behind him. The horse went up on his hind legs, bugling a challenge. Elana gasped. It was Aidan's horse - the huge black stallion she had seen with him at the Towers. There couldn't be two like him. The stallion pinned his ears back and struck out at the man, catching his leg with a hoof. Terrified of the attack, the chestnut leaped aside. The man fell with a thud from the saddle, blood seeping through his legging. The black horse rounded on him again, pulled back at the last minute by the rope around his neck which was still connected to the chestnut's saddle.

Without thinking of what she was doing, Elana dropped the leads of her horses and ran between the stallion and the wounded man. With all the strength she had, she reached out to the black horse. The power of his rage threatened to sweep her away, but she held to herself, breathing, willing her Waking to stay in check, willing the horse to recognize her. Fragmented images flashed across her mind - men attacking Aidan and Cecily, beating Aidan, tying ropes around the horse, dragging him away from his friend.

Elana sent back images of Aidan, from her own mind, trying to comfort the horse, let him know she was his friend. His feet came back down to the ground and he turned away from the fallen man. She felt him much more aware of her than Devi was, almost able to communicate. She sent him a picture of the two of them finding Aidan. The stallion's ears pricked, and he gave a low nicker. He walked over to her and rubbed her face with his nose. She could feel his panic subsiding. All she got from him were flashes of Aidan. The devotion of this horse brought tears to her eyes. He sent her pictures of the man, and then the sound of his voice; soft, reassuring; speaking words that she couldn't understand, though she made out one that sounded like 'Kael', over and over. She guessed that it was the horse's name.

"Kael," she said in a soft voice.

The stallion nickered again.

Behind her, she heard the man struggling to his feet. Before she could turn, Kael screamed, and charged past her. She heard a thud, and then the clatter of a knife hit the ground. He had tried to attack her!

Her own rage matched Kael's as she spun to face the man.

"What do you think you're doing with this horse?" she asked, her voice low, a cold fury upon her. She felt the man quail under her assault.

"I know this horse, and I know his owner, and you should be hung for a thief or worse." She fixed him with her gaze, cowing his mind with the force of her Waking.

The man scrambled backwards, desperate to get away.

"I don't know what you did to Aidan, but you will tell me right now where he is and you will return to me the gold you took from him as well." This last was in response to the picture that flashed through the man's mind of stealing a purse of gold from the pack.

"You're a witch!" the man hissed. "How could you know that!"

"It doesn't take magic to spot a thief," she replied, "and I could let the horse finish you right here. I'm the one who stopped him."

The man turned gray. "Please, no!" he begged. "Here..." He reached into his tunic, pulled out a purse of gold and threw it to her.

She saw in his mind, the picture of a green cloak being tucked into his saddle bags. "I hope you don't mind," she turned to him. "But I am going to check your bags for any other valuables that may have found their way in."

The man dropped his head, defeated.

She pulled open the bags, and relieved him of a beautiful green cloak, as well as a purse of silver, and a wallet of food. "Lord Aidan will have need of these, I think."

She untied Kael from the chestnut, who moved as far away from the stallion as possible. Walking up to the black horse, she loosened the ropes from around his neck, careful not to rub the open sores left by them. His bridle was still on, the reins hanging down in front of him. She picked them up and led the horse back to the man.

"Where is Aidan?" she asked, fearing the worst.

"Back along the Greenway toward Bellport. I left with the horse before they were through with him."

She narrowed her eyes and looked at him. "What about the Lady he traveled with?"

The man cast about, as if looking for a place to run. "We had orders not to hurt her, or her horse. She's been taken, but she's safe. I guess they wanted her for ransom."

Elana's heart dropped. "If Aidan's been killed, I will return and demand your life in exchange."

"We'll hold him here, my Lady," said a voice from behind her.

She turned to see the old hostler, holding both her horses and staring down at the man with contempt.

"We don't take lightly to horse thieves," the old man said. "And he's in no condition to ride."

She smiled at the man, grateful for his support.

From out of the inn, a fat man bustled into the yard. "What's this?" he shouted. "Knife fights in my bar and horse thieves in my yard!"

The hostler stepped up and spoke a few quiet words to the innkeeper.

"We'll retain him here, Lady, until you return with news that all has been mended." The innkeeper frowned at her, his eyebrows working up and down in distress. "Bad news, bad news all around. Were you traveling with a fair haired fellow?"

"Yes."

"I'm afraid he'll be unable to travel for at least a fortnight. Another customer came after him and he pulled his own knife. He's cut up, pretty bad, though the other fellow won't live to see tomorrow's sunrise. Handy with a knife, that one. Wouldn't cross him, myself. Seeing as how he was attacked in my inn, I've offered to keep him here and tend him 'till he's well."

Elana took a deep breath, steadying herself. "That is very kind of you."

"He told me to look for you here, and tell you to ride on alone. Leave his horse though. He'll be on his way as soon as he's able."

"Thank you sir. I will do that. Thank you for everything." She graced him with a smile that turned his ears red.

"It's my pleasure. Always ready to help our guests." He grabbed the wounded horse thief by the arm and half dragged, half carried him back to the inn.

The hostler bowed to Elana and handed her Devi's reins. "Peace to you, my lady," he said. "You've done a good turn today."

She swung up on Devi, tied Kael's reins to her saddle and trotted out of the yard back toward Bellport. Everyone stared as she rode out of town, but no one made any move to stop her.

Out on the Greenway, Elana felt lost. Her Waking was spent and she could hardly believe that she'd cowed that man out of the stolen horse, goods, and gold.

Devi and Kael had sorted themselves out. After her first few attempts to bite him, he tore into her neck, leaving teeth marks along her creamy mane. She behaved like a lady after that, not even pinning her ears back when he drew up next to her.

The sun burned off the morning fog, leaving the road clear except for patches of mist in the low places and under the trees. Elana rode back down along the track she came, calling out Aidan's name every few minutes. She tried to look for signs that might lead to him, but realized that she had neither the training nor the Skills for that sort of thing. Desperate for some way to reach him, she called out in her mind to him.

From far off she felt a faint echo and then the walls going up. She hugged Devi. He was alive. They rode on, with Elana calling out, all morning. As it drew near to lunch, Kael grew restless. She saw pictures from him of Aidan.

"Do you know where he is?" she asked, not expecting any answer.

The horse tugged her toward the side of the road. She untied him, fastened his reins around his neck so he wouldn't hurt himself and let him lead them. The stallion took off through the woods, whipping through the trees at a pace that Devi could hardly keep up with. They trailed him to the top of a steep hill that ended in a cliff.

Kael stopped and whinnied, his nostrils flared as though trying to pick up a scent. From part way down, Elana heard a groan. She scrambled to the edge of the drop off and called out Aidan's name. Another groan helped her locate the crumpled figure wedged against a boulder.

CHAPTER 9

CHANGE OF PLANS

Aidan slid in and out of consciousness, never sure if the nightmares or the waking were real. Losing Kael hurt more than the beating he took. It seemed at times that he could feel his horse reaching out for him. He gathered his strength to answer back, but the one time he felt Kael, the girl from the Towers was there, too. Bitterness rose up in him and his mind wandered in a black haze.

It was the earth that wakened him. It's rhythms, strong and solid, carried him back to consciousness. With consciousness came pain. Every muscle hurt. His head felt numb, his stomach queasy, his body beaten. What had happened? The last thing he could remember before he found himself here, was that man's laughter burning into his mind. The Hunter. He took Kael, took Cecily...

Aidan tried to shift his arms and found that they moved. They shook from the effort, but he was able to push himself up to kneeling. Daylight shone through the trees, illuminating the drop down the cliff. Now that he could see, he braced his bound legs against a jagged edge of the boulder, sawing the rope in increments until it gave way. The task took the remainder of his strength, and he lay back, exhausted, unable to attempt the hill. Hunger, thirst, and the abuse at the hands of the black cloaked men, were taking their toll.

His eyes threatened to close of their own accord. He struggled, trying to force his mind to focus on some sort of plan. Nothing came. His swollen tongue stuck to his mouth and his body shook from the effort to stay awake. What was the use? They hadn't been kind enough to kill him quickly. They'd left him here, instead, to die. His thoughts grew dark and he sunk again into semi-consciousness.

From somewhere above him, a tree branch broke. He stirred himself, fearing the worst. Footsteps sounded; horses, and a person. He tried to bury himself in the leaves, hoping that they would go away.

A lone whinny split the silence. Aidan's heart leaped. Kael. He knew that whinny anywhere. He tried to call to him, but all that came out was a groan. He lifted himself up and the world spun around him. Kael whinnied again, insistent.

"Aidan?" A girl's voice called his name.

He knew that voice. He groaned again, defeated. It was her; the girl from the Towers. She must be in league with the Hunter. How else did she get Kael?

"We're going to help you," she called down to him. "Stay put. Don't try to move. I'm going to find something to pull you up with."

It wasn't like he could go anywhere even if he tried.

He heard her rummaging through the packs, talking to the horses, and finally, sliding down the slope, clinging to a rope that was tied somewhere at the top of the cliff. She stopped next to him, panting and disheveled.

"What happened?" she asked him.

"Maybe you could tell me," he growled.

She looked away, biting her lip. After a pause she said, "All I know is this. A man rode into Pikeman's Crossing this morning with your horse. I recognized him, and accused the man of thieving. Your horse almost killed him. I think the man was relieved to be rid of him. Is his name Kael?"

"Yes. How did you know?"

"Well, you can't run away this time, can you?" Her black eyes flashed. "I'll say it clearly, so we both can hear. It's because you and I are Elder Born."

Aidan winced as though she'd struck him. "You can't know that."

"Yes I can. That's one of my Skills. I'm from the Firestone Eldership." She offered that last bit in an attempt at a friendly aside. "And you are...?"

"Can't you tell?"

"No," she answered with candor. "If I had to guess, it would say, Orchard Tree Eldership. Your horse is very bonded with you. He led us here, you know."

"How can you tell?"

"I can reach him, though only with a lot of effort, and even then it's blurry. I can reach Devi, too. Only she's much harder. You can tell that Kael's had practice."

She looked at him, questioning. "Why do you hate me? What have I ever done to you?"

The night at the docks came back clearly to his mind. There was no use pretending anymore. He had nowhere to run to and no strength to run even if he did.

"I saw what you did... at the docks," he said. "You used your Skills to attack. I thought you were a Hunter, or in league with them." He studied her. "To be honest, I'm not sure that I was wrong, but you have my horse and I'm stuck here, so trusting you seems to be my only option."

Her face clouded. She offered no explanation. "I could just leave you here, you know. Except that I couldn't live with myself. I don't know why I bother. Come on. Let's get this rope around you."

She tied the rope around his waist. He recognized it as one he packed from his farm. He grit his teeth, holding back a comment about her going through his things. He couldn't explain to himself why she rubbed him so wrong.

After she had satisfied herself that he was secure, she used the rope to climb back up. He felt the rope being untied and for a moment feared that she would let him fall the rest of the way to his death.

It was Kael's presence that assured him. Aidan caught pictures from Kael's mind of the rope being tied to his saddle. He breathed a sigh of relief, trusting his horse implicitly.

At her word, the stallion backed step by step until Aidan found himself laying at the top of the hill. The cuts on his face and arms reopened. Blood ran into one of his eyes and he could taste it in his mouth. His relief at being here was soured at watching her with Kael. Once again, he could feel her presence in the stallion's mind.

The big horse walked up to him, snuffing his hair, his clothes. Aidan rolled over onto his back and hugged Kael's nose, hiding his tears in the horse's cheek. The girl untied his rope from the saddle and stepped back, waiting.

After a minute, Aidan gathered himself and turned to her. "I don't know your name," he said.

"Elana."

"Well, thank you, Elana. You saved my life." He was beginning to feel ashamed of his earlier behavior. There were still questions about her he would like to have answered, but for now he was content that she meant him no harm.

"You're welcome." She gave a half bow, like a servant would do. "I took the liberty of searching the thief's packs. I think I recovered a few of your valuables as well." She showed him the purse of gold, the cloak, the purse of silver, and the wallet of food.

For the first time since he'd woken Aidan smiled. "Well, I do thank you, and I must say that you lightened his load as well as returning mine."

She gave him a puzzled look.

"The cloak and the gold are mine, but the silver and the wallet belonged to him, or maybe to some other unfortunate soul that got in his way."

180

She smiled with him, her face lighting up. "Well, I can't say that I'm sorry. After what he did to you, you should receive some compensation." She sobered again. "What did happen?"

Aidan paused, trying to remember. "It's hard to put together. It felt almost like a dream. Cecily and I had stopped for lunch and when we rode on I thought that maybe we had drunk too much wine, though it's never affected me that way before. She fell off her mare and when I went back to get her, we were surrounded." His face clouded. "There was a Hunter there. He invaded Kael's mind. And mine also." He studied the ground at his feet, not wanted to meet her gaze.

"I'm so sorry," said Elana.

"Then someone hit me and when I woke up, I was here, alone."

"They left you here to die?"

"That's all I can figure." He was silent awhile, remembering.

"I asked the man who stole Kael what happened to the lady you were riding with," Elana offered. "He said they had orders not to hurt her, or her horse... turn her in for ransom, he guessed. He wasn't a Hunter. I would know." She paused. "He wasn't actually very bright either. He was pretty scared of me. But I was angry." She shrugged and looked through her pack for a flask of water. "Here, drink some of this. You must be parched."

Aidan took it and drank. He thought he'd never get enough.

"It's okay, you can finish it," Elana said. "I have another, as well as a flask of wine. And I can refill this one at a stream."

He finished it all and lay back, feeling his strength return. He watched the girl as she rifled through the packs pulling out food for lunch. Now that he'd allowed himself to think of her as a friend, he found her at least a little intriguing. She was so different than Cecily; small and dark, intense - all angles and sharp pointed questions, with a flash of temper he could feel just under the surface. He was reminded again of Arella, and had to smile, imagining the two of them together. Arella would like Elana. He was sure of that. They were of a kind... just not his kind.

She came back offering him flat bread, cheese and fruit. Aidan ate hungrily, his appetite returning as well. It had been a day since he'd eaten or drank anything. While he ate, she tore strips of linen from a shirt in her pack.

"We're going to have to bind those cuts," she said. "Let me clean them out first and then I can bind them properly. My mother was a healer, though I must admit I inherited none of her Skills."

Aidan raised an eyebrow at this last piece of information.

"I don't have the Skills for it, but I do know what needs to be done," she retorted, her hands on her hips. "Now, let me just wash these out."

She poured water from the other flask on one of the makeshift bandages and began dabbing the dirt out of one of the deeper cuts on Aidan's head. He winced, but held still. He too, knew that this must be done.

He was grateful, at least, that none of his bones had been broken. Cuts and bruises wouldn't keep him bedridden. His mind, clearing now, jumped to Cecily's predicament. He had to find her, rescue her from those men.

"There." Elana stood back and surveyed her work. "That's the worst of it tended. You're fortunate, you know, that nothing was broken. Though this would have been sufficient to finish you off, if Kael hadn't found you."

He winced as he tried to move his right shoulder. "I know. I did say, 'thank you'."

"What are you going to do now?" she asked. "I don't think it's wise for you to travel too soon. Those men might still be out there."

"I need to find Cecily. I can't leave her."

She nodded, raising an eyebrow at him in question.

"What about you?" he retorted. "What makes it safe for you to travel alone?"

She looked away, all traces of swagger gone. "I didn't think of that when I rode out. All I knew is that I had to find you." She fiddled with the laces on her pack. "I wasn't traveling alone. Marek sent me out with a company of men. The leader looked after me, but he received a knife wound in a fight at Pikeman's Crossing. I was supposed to ride straight to Rivergate and wait for Marek there." She met his gaze. "I took Kael and searched for you instead."

Guilt over Elana's situation and worry about Cecily battled in Aidan's head. "Look," he said. "What if I were to take you back to Pikeman's Crossing? Could you manage your way to Rivergate from there?"

"You don't have to do that, you know. Actually, if you would be so kind as to show me back to the Greenway, Devi and I could manage perfectly from there." Her tone turned stiff and formal and she busied herself with the golden mare. "There is other help available to me, you know."

"No, I didn't. But if you say so..." Pulling on a tree limb to steady himself, Aidan hauled himself up on his feet. The world spun around him and he clung to the tree, waiting for the ground to stop moving. He could feel the life flowing through the tree, steady, affirming; strengthening him. So strange how his Skills presented, but he wouldn't trade them for anything. He called to Kael and the horse moved his body next to Aidan's. With great effort he struggled up into the saddle.

Elana finished packing up, untied Devi and mounted with grace. He sensed the mare's trust in her and regretted his own suspicion. She followed behind Kael, and Aidan wondered what it must be like to ride blind through the world. He could read the life in the land, in the air, the changes that spoke of running water, or stagnant marshes, of roadways where many people travel, or fields where animals graze. He pitied Elana. It must be terrifying to so easily become lost.

Remembering her water flask, he stopped by a fresh stream and rested while she refilled it.

"What brought you to Bellport?" she asked, as they sat by the stream.

The question sent a tremor through his body. He heard again Reeves' warning to tell no one of his mission or destination. Casting about for a plausible answer, he came up with, "Family business."

"Really." She shook her head. "Don't talk then. I didn't mean to pry."

She busied herself with her bags. Aidan could feel her curiosity burning. After a long silence she turned back to face him, her hands on her hips.

"Did that business have anything to do with marrying Cecily?" she blurted out.

"No," Aidan said, and then laughed out loud at the look on her face. "Meeting Cecily was entirely an accident. She was running away from an arranged marriage and I happened to be riding along the road when she was attacked. I drove off the attackers and escorted her to Marek's house."

"So, getting attacked is a regular thing for her then." Elana's voice was acid.

"No, I don't think so." He shook his head. "She's led a really sheltered life."

"Until you came along and swept her off her feet."

"Look, none of this was planned, if that's what you're getting at." He could feel his cheeks getting red. "I was doing for her what I would have done for anyone."

He saw her face soften. "I'm sorry. It's just so..." She looked away, the corners of her mouth twitching.

"I know." The absurdity of it hadn't escaped him in the retelling either. "She's probably got every eligible Lord in Merrion, and most of those in Glenariff as well, trailing after her."

"You really care for her, don't you?" Elana asked, her voice low.

"I think she's special. I've never met anyone like her before."

"Does she know about you, being Elder Born I mean?"

184

It was Aidan's turn to look away. "No. I haven't told her. I assumed that I would never see her after this trip, and so it doesn't really matter."

She nodded. "It's usually better that way."

He met her eyes, grateful for the understanding there.

She stood up and brushed off her tunic. "Well, we'd best be off," she said with a wink. "You've got a damsel in distress waiting to be rescued."

Forcing a smile that looked more like a grimace, he got up in stages, his body screaming in protest. The road lay just ahead, and though he was anxious for Cecily's well being, he didn't savor the thought of a fight right now. He hadn't even thought of a plan to rescue her.

He climbed back on Kael and set off at a slow pace.

"So, what are you doing, traveling in these parts?" He returned Elana's question back to her.

"My parents were taken by a Hunter. I need to help them." Her voice was tight, hard.

"Are you just out here alone?"

"No. I have help. It's not something I can talk about." She looked over at him. "I'm sorry."

"I understand." He paused. She looked so young up there on the golden mare. So alone and out of place. "I hope you find them," he said.

"Thank you. So do I."

They rode the rest of the way in silence. Elana looked surprised when the trees finally opened up, revealing the cleared sweep of empty road.

"Thank you for getting me back here," she said as they stepped out onto the Greenway.

"You risked yourself to save me, and you reunited me with Kael. I'm sorry I suspected you." He reached out his hand to her.

She took it and smiled. "Forgiven."

"Pikeman's Crossing is ahead to the right, and beyond that, Rivergate. May the Ancient Ones be with you."

"May your paths be paths of peace," she finished the traditional salutation.

He watched her ride off on the golden mare until only their dust rose in the distance. Then he turned his back to them and headed Kael toward Bellport. If what Elana said about using Cecily for ransom was right, then they would have brought her near there.

He reached the gates by sunset. Everywhere he looked the city was crawling with guards.

"You there!" An armed guard with a red plumed helmet pointed his spear at Aidan and Kael.

"Yes," Aidan answered him. He knew his appearance would raise suspicion. Both he and Kael looked terrible. The horse was mud splattered, caked in dried sweat, with rope burns around his neck, and he was bloody and bandaged.

"What's your business here after dark?"

"I must see Lord Marek."

"You and half of Bellport." The guard sneered. "Wanting to pledge your honor to rescue the Lady Cecily no doubt. Well, not but a few hours ago, our Lord Marek snatched her from the clutches of the notorious Black Knights." He pushed back his helmet. "They say he let her ride out under the protection of some brave young Lord from Glenariff." He spit on the ground. "The idiot rode her straight into a trap. Wouldn't wonder if he wasn't in on it himself. I hope for his sake, he'd dead. At least he'd have the honor of dying trying to protect her. Anything less, and I'd not show my face round these parts."

Aidan felt the blood drain from his face.

"What happened to you anyway?" the guard asked. "You're in no condition to perform heroics."

He thought fast. "Someone along the road insulted the Lady Cecily's virtue. I made a point of teaching him a lesson."

"Looks like they taught you one, but well done. Your heart's in the right place. I recommend you find yourself lodgings by the water. We're under orders to keep the gates closed until daybreak."

"Thank you."

He spun Kael around and headed for the Greenway. He had no intentions of spending any time nearer Bellport than he could help. His face burned. Did she and Marek think him a traitor or a fool? It was over now. His best course lay in putting her out of his mind and resuming his original plan. She could never have been his anyway, he tried to console himself. It was a sweet dream, but a dream none the less.

As soon as they got far enough from Bellport to find open country again, they would turn off the road and find a spot to sleep in the woods. Aidan didn't know who had seen Kael with the Black Knights, and he didn't need any questions.

The first sliver of the new moon had long since set by the time they left the outlying towns behind. All he could think about was sleep. At the first promising turnoff, they left the road and melted from sight in the thick trees. He found a stream and led Kael up along it's bed. Better to leave no scent if anyone were tracking them. At a partial clearing, Aidan turned Kael out of the water and up the steep bank. He slipped off the horse's back, unsaddled him and fed him a small portion of the oats he had packed from home. They both drank their fill, and then with the stars shining through the leaves, Aidan wrapped his old cloak over his aching body and lost himself in sleep.

Elana hurried down the Greenway on Devi. It wasn't the same, traveling alone. Without Aidan or Gaius' company of men, she had time to dwell on just how dangerous her position was. Since this morning, she had used her Waking with Kael, with the thief, and in searching for Aidan. Images of the Shadow reaching out to find her, haunted her path. She cringed every time a new party rode past, exchanging only the barest pleasantries. Devi, unused to riding out alone, picked up her nervousness, shying and spinning once again at every strange sound.

The evening sun cast a gold light through the trees as Pikeman's Crossing came into view. Her plan was to stop by the inn, check on Gaius, and let the innkeeper know that she had returned the horse. Exhausted from the day's effort, she looked forward to spending the night indoors. Thoughts of a hot supper and a soft bed kept her going. Come morning she would ride for Rivergate. She had lost only a day.

No travelers passed her along the Greenway as they drew closer to town. She pulled Devi up short. Something wasn't right. A turn in the road revealed her first glimpse of the town and before her the streets of Pikeman's Crossing lay empty. An oppressive silence shrouded the place and a chill crept up her spine. She backed Devi away, suddenly sure that someone was watching them.

"My lady!" A voice called from the thicket lining the road.

Devi leaped and spun, nearly unseating Elana.

"Who's there?"

A shock of white bristly hair emerged from the thicket, followed by the face of the old hostler. "My lady, get off the road!"

She didn't need to be told twice. Crashing the mare through the nearest opening in the hedge she tore through the brush, bloodying her face and hands. Safely hidden on the other side, she made her way back to where the old hostler's head had appeared. The man popped out before them.

"I've been watching for you," he said. "You must not go into town."

"Why not? What happened?" A cold knot drew itself tight in her stomach. She knew what she was about to hear.

"This afternoon a man rode down the Greenway from Bellport. Full of his own importance, all dark looking in a black cloak and tall boots. He was asking questions... uncanny like. Mighty interested in what folks had to say about you and that black horse. Said he had business with you, but wouldn't give any name. He pressed your friend at the

188

inn for your whereabouts and when the man wouldn't speak, he threatened him. The innkeeper heard the cloaked man say if he ever ran into your friend some dark night on the road, no one would be the wiser for what he'd do." The old hostler held his hands out to her as though she were a child. "I don't mean to scare you, my lady, but the man didn't feel natural, somehow. Felt like he was pressing into my thoughts, trying to read them or something."

Elana tried to swallow over the lump in her throat. The Hunter. She had drawn him here. It was her fault.

"What am I to do?" She asked the hostler, not really expecting any answer. "I have to make it to Rivergate. Marek said that he'd meet me there."

His eyebrows went up at the sound of Marek's name. "It would have been better for you, had you headed out this morning." He gave her a wink and a nod. "I wouldn't have thought as much of you, though. You did the right thing by that animal. Did you find his master?"

"Yes." She shook her head. Sometimes she wondered about herself. It was a fool's errand, but she couldn't bring herself to regret it.

"It'll take a full night's ride if you follow the Greenway, to make Rivergate. And day or night, the Greenway's not a place that I'd be keen on traveling, were I you."

"What choice do I have?"

"If you're willing, I can take you there by the river. I have my donkey tied down the road apiece. I was planning to make the trip today. My sister lives there and I visit when I can. I thought I'd wait though to see that you came safely in."

The knot in Elana's stomach loosened a degree. "Thank you. That's so kind." She didn't need her Waking to sense that there was no hidden intent in this man, no deception. With only the barest of effort, she touched the outline of some old sorrow, now an empty ache in him, but nothing to cause her alarm.

"I am Gwyth," he stated, reaching out a work worn hand to her.

She took it, surprised at the gentleness in his touch. "I am Elana. Thank you so much Gwyth."

Relieved to have found an ally, she followed him, leading Devi until they came upon a clearing where a small brown donkey slept, tied to a tree. Devi snorted at the creature, who only opened a lazy eye and looked up at her, uninterested.

Gwyth untied the donkey, whispered something unintelligible into her long, furry ears, and climbed up on her back. Elana mounted Devi and followed them. The donkey picked her way down the steep rocky trail with care, never putting a small hoof out of place. Behind her, Devi blundered, slid, and crashed through the woods, making a racket that Elana was sure would alert the whole town. As the night closed in under the trees, they reached the river. A foot path wound along it's high banks, wide enough for them to ride side by side.

"Where did you get her?" Elana asked the hostler about the donkey.

The hostler smiled and rested a work hardened hand on the donkey's soft neck. "The innkeeper gave her to me. Some fellow didn't have the silver to pay his lodgings and had left her there. Stubborn girl. No one could get her to do a thing. The innkeeper said she was an embarrassment and I was welcome to her if I pleased." He stroked her absently. "Jenny and I get on just fine now. I couldn't ask for a more faithful friend. She just needed a little understanding."

The donkey's ears swiveled back to catch every word.

"It's like she's listening to you," Elana said, laughing.

"Aye, she is. They know more than you give them credit for." The look he gave her made her think that he might be talking about more than just donkeys.

They rode in silence. The stars reflecting in the River lit their way. Elana's head began to nod.

"There now, we can't have you falling asleep on your mare." Gwyth's voice jarred her awake. "Hop off and lets walk a while."

Elana's legs protested at having to carry her. She led the mare, half supporting herself with the reins.

"If you don't mind my asking," he said, "how'd you come to be mixed up with that black cloaked man?"

A sudden wariness drove back her fatigue. She glanced sideways at the old hostler. "It's a long story."

"We've got a long ride."

She deliberated, sorting out what she could honestly share. She owed this kind fellow some explanation. She'd try to keep it brief.

"That man, or one like him, came after our family. They captured my parents. I escaped by chance. They're still looking for me."

"You're not from here, are you?" His question was gentle.

"No."

"You hear stories at the inn, folk like to talk, tell tales. Not everything you hear is true, but you can sift out the nuggets after a while." He gave her a slow wink. "That wasn't the first time a man like that's rode through. Hunters, they call 'em. Say they hunt down the Elder Born. Have some old grudge against them. Most folks don't know who to fear more. Figure they're safest staying out of the business. They'd rather turn their heads when a neighbor disappears, than say anything and risk drawing attention to themselves. "Feared that the Elder Born will curse 'em, or the Hunters will kill 'em outright."

Elana's mouth went dry.

"Fools. The way I see it, if you don't stand up to help your neighbors, there'll be no one left to stand up and help you when the time comes. Anyhow, I've never heard of an Elder Born cursing no one. But I've known more'n a few folks who disappeared to those Hunters." He gave his donkey another pat. "Anyhow, I'm partial to anyone who treats their animals well. Precious few give 'em more than half a thought." He smiled at Elana, who smiled back.

"Well, I'm grateful to you," Elana said. She hesitated, and then on impulse blurted out, "I am Elder Born, you know. Though I've never imagined cursing anyone. It's enough to get by without folks hating or fearing you."

Gwyth laughed. "I know darlin'. I saw you with that stallion, and the thief. No girl I know could have done as much. I'm honored to help you any way I can." There's stories that some still remember. Talk about a time when the Elder Born and Valefolk lived happy together. Before the trouble came from out of the West." His face grew pensive and he walked without talking for a while.

Elana felt the sorrow in him well up. She began to wonder if he had dropped the conversation, when he continued.

"I knew a man once. Believed that if anyone could, he could bring it back again. He was a bastard son of the House of Tormey. They're the ruling family of Glenariff, you know. Actually, he was the elder son at that, though they hushed that up. Well, this man gave up his right to the Lord's seat to go wandering through the Vale on a mission of his own. He was Elder Born too." He gave her a look and a nod. "His mother was an Elder Born who kept it hidden. She died in childbirth, so no one realized he was Elder Born until he was close to grown. He'd inherited it from her. The House of Tormey tried to disown him over it. More's the pity, seeing as how Ulrich took the Lord's seat in his place." The hostler spat on the ground as though the name left a vile taste in his mouth.

"Who was he?" Elana's curiosity piqued.

"Name was Darian. Fine fellow, born leader. Folk flocked to him, both Elder Born and Valefolk. That's where I heard much of the old stories. He didn't stand on ceremony with anyone. Everyone who knew him loved him."

Elana probed her memory. She'd heard the name before. Yes. Her father's friend was named Darian; the one who died right before they came down to the Vale. She turned her attention back to Gwyth.

"Well, some fifteen years back, he came down from the mountains with a wife and young son. Traveled the Vale stirring up the folk to stand together against the Darkness from out of the West. Brought hope - that's what he did." Tears glinted in the old man's eyes. "Gave us something to look toward, to be proud of."

"What happened to him?" Elana asked, fearing what she already suspected.

"About five years ago someone betrayed him to the Hunters. Must have been someone close, from what I can figure. They captured him one night. Thought they'd turn him to their own purposes. Well, word got back that he wouldn't turn. He's not with us anymore." The tears spilled down the old man's cheeks, and he wiped them away with an impatient hand. "His wife and son disappeared. They say she went back to Farran. I don't know, myself. Wouldn't blame them if they had."

"He was my father's close friend," Elana said, her voice subdued. "They knew each other in Farran. I know he misses him terribly."

The hostler reached over and patted her on the shoulder.

"What did you do after that?" she asked him.

"I left Glenariff. Too many memories there. My sister lived with her husband in Rivergate, so I came out here. Got a position at the Pikeman's Crossing Inn. Been here ever since."

The path opened up, its sandy track shining white in the starlight. The hostler mounted his donkey and suggested that they make use of the clear road to trot.

Now, fully awake, Elana remounted Devi and they set out. She moderated the mare's pace to stay alongside the donkey. Her thoughts strayed back to her parents. The hostler's story caused her hope to ebb. What reason did she have to believe that her parents were still alive? The rest of the journey passed in dark musings.

A few hours before sunrise, Gwyth pulled up.

"Rivergate lies just beyond this bend. We made better time than any who might have taken the Greenway. It follows the long way 'round. You are welcome to join me at my sister's home. It's nothing fancy, but you'll be away from prying eyes there."

Elana agreed, hoping this would buy her time to reach Marek.

"Thank you so much. In all likelihood, I owe you my life."

He inclined his head. "It's my honor."

She followed him up, away from the river toward the town. Rivergate was sleeping. Not a sound came from the empty streets. Gwyth made his way to a small house on the edge of town. Opening the back gate, he led his donkey through and beckoned for Elana to follow.

"I planned on waiting here in the barn. I didn't want to wake my sister at this hour. I hope that doesn't offend you."

Relieved, Elana shook her head. "No. I'm more comfortable with Devi than around most people."

They unsaddled their mounts and put them each in a small stall. The hostler found fresh hay, and after feeding the animals and watering them, he made a bed for Elana at the back of the barn. He sat outside, leaning against the old building, his silhouette visible in the starlight.

The sweet smell of the hay beckoned to Elana. Every muscle ached and her eyes felt gritty. She yawned so wide her jaws hurt.

"I have to reach Marek," she thought. If I don't contact him now, I might not have the chance later. It had dawned on her that without Gaius she had no idea of where Marek would meet her.

"Marek." The call was tentative; as soft as she could make it. She didn't want to broadcast her whereabouts to the Hunters.

"Elana?" His reply came back strong and loud. She hadn't woken him.

"I'm okay. I've just got to Rivergate though and I don't know where to meet you. Gaius was wounded at Pikeman's crossing and I've had to go on without him."

"What happened?" Worry came flooding in from him.

"I can't talk now. The Hunters traced me to Pikeman's Crossing and I had to leave via the river." She remembered about Cecily, and as much as she disliked the girl, she felt obligated to tell Marek what she had heard. "Cecily was captured. We heard about it at the town. I hope that you can help her." The last part was added out of politeness.

"I have her safely home. Don't worry about that. It's you I'm worried about."

There was a long silence. Then Marek went on, "At daybreak, find the inn called The Three Oaks. The innkeeper goes by the name, 'Stoney'. Tell him that I will join you there tomorrow. He will offer you a room on the ground floor. Tell him that you'd rather have one higher up. That is our password. You can trust him to take care of you. Don't venture out once you're there. That is very important. I am on my way directly."

Elana yawned again, and hoped that she could remember all that. She didn't worry about wanting to go out. It would be enough to find a bed where she could sleep.

"Goodnight," she sent to him, and was asleep before he had a chance to reply.

It seemed like moments later when Gwyth's voice woke her.

"It will be morning soon. Best be on your way, before the town wakens. Both you and your mare are too memorable to be seen safely."

She shook herself awake, forcing her mind to think. With numb fingers, she saddled Devi, led her out of the yard, and mounted up.

"Thank you for everything. If I ever have a chance to pay you back, know that I will."

He smiled at her. "Where are you going?"

"The Three Oaks. I don't know how to find it, though."

He pointed toward the main section of town. "It's just past the open market. You can't miss it. It has three huge old oaks standing out front. Quite a fine place. May the Ancient Ones be with you."

"May your paths be paths of peace," she answered.

Turning Devi toward town, she waved goodbye and set off for the inn. The day promised to be fair and bright; the first streaks of sunlight outlined the treetops against the cloudless sky. The only sounds to break the stillness were the occasional crowing of a rooster and the lowing of cows waiting to be milked. In different circumstances she would have enjoyed spending time here. She found the inn without difficulty and led Devi around back to the stables. A young groom her own age came to meet her, still tousled-haired from sleep. She asked for a stall for her mare, and said that she would be down later to take care of her. If she was going to play the part of one of the Free-folk, she might as well do it right.

The young groom showed her a roomy stall and ran to fetch fresh hay and water. She left the mare there, and took her belongings with her into the inn.

The common room stood empty, none of the guests had risen. The sounds of someone preparing breakfast, as well as the mouth watering smell of sausage issued forth from the kitchen. Pushing the door open with a tentative hand she peeked inside.

A hard looking man, with iron gray hair and black eyes strode up to her.

"May I help you?"

Elana swallowed hard. She hoped she had remembered everything correctly. "I'm looking for Stoney."

"Well, you've found him. Who are you?"

His manners didn't make it any easier. "I'm a friend of Marek's. He's planning on meeting me here tomorrow. He told me to find you and wait here for him."

The man looked her over, narrowing his eyes. "Well, I can offer you my very best room, right here on the ground floor."

Bracing herself, Elana answered back, "Thank you so much, that's very kind, but I would much rather have a room higher up."

The man's face broke into a smile. "Then so you shall. You'll excuse my suspicion. There's those who aren't above claiming more of a connection to the Lord's Right Hand than they actually have. Vian flew in yesterday, with news to expect you. I thought you were due in before nightfall, and with a company of men. You'll understand why I needed to be sure."

She let out a huge sigh. "I understand. It's just good to have gotten here at last."

He led her upstairs to her room and left with the promise of breakfast upon his return. The room faced the street, with a clear view of the market. It was simply, but tastefully furnished, with a bed, a chair, and a desk. There was a bowl and pitcher for washing, and thick towels folded neatly beside them. Elana filled the bowl and scrubbed the dirt from the road off her face. A proper bath would feel wonderful, but she would take what she could get.

A knock at the door warned her of Stoney's return. He entered, carrying a tray laden with eggs, sausage, fresh bread and milk. Elana's stomach growled audibly. Stoney ignored the sound.

"It'd be best if you stay put here in your room. I'll see to it no one disturbs your rest." He set the tray down on the desk, gave a half-bow and backed out of the room, closing the door behind him.

Once she was alone, Elana sank into the chair, tore off a hunk of the fresh bread and stuffed it into her mouth. The sausages smelled even better up close. She forgot everything for a while and enjoyed her breakfast. With her stomach full, her fatigue returned. She closed the thick curtains and lay back on the bed, asleep in an instant.

The smell of supper cooking downstairs woke her hours later. Elana rose, freshened up, and ventured out of her room. She checked on Devi first. The mare was content, and glad to see her. Surprised at how tired she still was, she stopped by the common room to ask Stoney if she could get supper in her room. He brought up a bowl of beef stew, fresh bread, and a some wine. Elana finished all of it, stacked the dishes by the door and gratefully fell back asleep.

The clatter of horse's hooves in the street below wakened her. Dazed, she sat up, rubbing her eyes and trying to piece together where she was. The room was dark. Slowly it all came back. She rolled out of bed and pushed aside the curtains. The predawn sky was a dusky blue. She peered through the dim light, up and down the street, looking for the source of the noise.

He was standing there, at the entrance to the inn. The Hunter. She sucked in her breath, willing her heart to stop pounding. Keeping herself hidden, she watched. He stood outside, making no move to enter the premises. It was the same one that she saw in Farrell's inn. She wouldn't soon forget his face. It took a moment before she realized that she didn't feel him trying to push in on her mind. Leaning back against the wall she focused on her breathing. This was no time for her Waking to surge out of control.

Another set of hooves rang out against the stones on the street. She looked again. It was Marek. He galloped straight to the inn, pulled his horse up and swung off. Without hesitation, he strode up to the Hunter as though he were expecting to find him there. She saw them exchange words, though she couldn't hear what they were saying. After a moment, the Hunter untied his horse, mounted, and galloped off.

Elana sank to the floor, dizzy. She waited there, numb inside, trying to erase the scene she just witnessed. She had to trust Marek. Who else did she have? Where else could she go for help?

A soft knock sounded on the door. Scrambling to her feet she called out, "Come in."

Marek entered, smiling. He carried a lit oil lamp in one hand and held the other out to her.

"I'm so glad to find you well. I was afraid for you, my dear."

She felt the warmth of his affection reaching out to her mind. For the first time, she braced herself against it.

"I saw the Hunter outside. You talked with him." She lacked the energy to dissemble. "Why?"

"Did you think..." He squinted at her. "No, no. I've hidden my identity from him. Elana, as counselor to Lord Gratton, I am forced to deal with some undesirable characters. I try to make the best of it, using these connections to accomplish whatever good I can. Tonight I was able to send him away on a worthless errand, and divert his search for you."

Probing his thoughts ever so gently, she felt a stiffness, a caution that wasn't there a moment earlier. Just as soon as she felt it, it was gone. He smiled, and the warmth returned.

"But enough of this talk about me. How are you? How did you fare? Tell me everything."

She laid aside her fears for now, and related the story of Gaius and finding Kael. When it came to talking about Aidan, she realized that she was hesitant. She knew Marek didn't think highly of him, and she was no longer inclined to agree with him on this count. She hurried through, feeling Marek's penetrating gaze upon her. When she reached the part about the hostler, he raised his eyebrows.

"The man was waiting for you?"

"Yes. And he warned me about traveling on the Greenway."

"The Ancient Ones are indeed watching over you. Was he an Elder Born?"

"No. He knew one though - Darian."

At the sound of that name, Elana felt a shock go through Marek. His mind became a walled fortress, allowing her no access.

"What's wrong? Are you okay?"

"Fine, I'm fine," he answered stiffly.

"You knew him, didn't you."

"Yes, but it was a long time ago."

"Do you know what happened to him?"

"Only that he was caught by the Hunters. No one ever found him after that. He was a dreamer. Unfortunately, it brought him to an early death."

The force of Marek's will, keeping her from his mind, surged through Elana. She changed the topic, hoping to stop the assault.

"The hostler was very kind. He's the sort of man who almost makes me believe that the Elder Born and the Valefolk could live together peaceably again."

Her hope was ill placed. Marek turned away, visibly angry. "That's rubbish. The prattle of idealistic fools. It's fine for the Elder Born to sit in the safety of Farran and speak of returning the Vale to what it was when my grandfather's grandfather walked this soil. But let them be raised here, by the Valefolk, like I was. Let them live among them, at their mercy, scoffed at, hated, feared. No doubt, there are exceptions among them. Valefolk of immense worth. I have known some myself. But cherish those few, and as for the rest, I say that the Elder Born would do well to take up their place and rule the Vale once again. The pride of the Lords has opened the door for the Shadow from the West to darken this land. The Lords' power was never meant to be unchecked, but answerable to the Eldership of that land."

His eyes blazed, and the walls that had been pushing Elana out, vanished. She was in danger now, of being swept away by his passion.

"I have lived here, studied these people, and through Lord Gratton, even ruled them. I know what they are made of. They will not easily relinquish their power to the Elder Born again. If we hope to have a place here, we must wrest it for ourselves. Only then, can we dare dream of living at peace."

He paced back and forth, the flame from the oil lamp flickering in his hand. Brows knit together, dark eyes alight with fervor, his power filled the room. For the first time since she met him, Elana realized why the Valefolk that spoke of him, spoke with fear. It troubled her that she also had this kind of power. He looked to her, like she felt that morning on the beach, before the Hunters came. Except that there was anger, dark and smoldering, that fueled this passion. An anger that she didn't begin to understand.

CHAPTER 10

NEW COMPANY

Morning brought no reprieve for Aidan. No matter how many times he resolved to turn his thoughts to Farran, images of Cecily cluttered his mind. The guard's words last night haunted him. Cecily must think he had betrayed her, or think him the fool for walking her into a trap. Eager to put distance between himself and the memory, he ate a quick breakfast of brown bread and cold meat from the thief's wallet. He mounted Kael and set off across the countryside toward Rivergate.

The trip should take something less than two days and by that time he would need to replenish his supplies. Once he crossed over into Lanreath, land of the free-folk, towns were fewer and farther between. Food for himself, and grain for Kael would be harder to come by. Anyway, two days would allow some of the rumors about Cecily's capture to be set to rest with actual news. He might learn something more of what happened.

The ride proved uneventful, much to Aidan's relief. His cuts and bruises, though starting to heal, were still shocking enough to elicit questions. He made sure he encountered no one.

Alone now, he turned to the land for solace. He had been so preoccupied with thoughts of Cecily, that from the time they left Bellport, he hadn't used his Waking. Away from Bell Towers, the Song that had drawn him in, sounded faint and thin, like an echo. He missed it. As he traveled farther from Bellport it faded, until it was barely a whisper.

Out here, the land pulsed with fear. Whenever his path drew closer to the Greenway, he felt its discord grow, throbbing, its undercurrent poisoning the air. The wild places weren't as contaminated by it, but there was no place that it left untouched.

Kael responded to it, shifting nervously, snorting at strange sounds, his ears constantly swiveling; vigilant for signs of danger. By the second day, as Rivergate drew into sight, Aidan was heartily sick of the discord. His only thought was to get his supplies and make for Lanreath in as direct a line as they could find paths to ride.

He skirted the town, hoping to get a better sense of the place before riding in. It seemed pleasant enough; an open air market dominated the main street, where several taverns and a large inn, boasting three huge oaks, lined the road. As a border town, it made its livelihood servicing those who traveled the Greenway. It distinguished itself as being the only landmark where the three Lands - Merrion, Glenariff, and Lanreath met. It was situated just inside Merrion, at the joining of the two boarder rivers, the Gavril - whose turbulent waters raced down from the Border Mountains in the north, and the Naal - which flowed wide and placid from the west. Ferries were employed from dawn until dusk, carrying travelers across the "Big River" as it was called after the joining. The people here were less provincial than in most towns this size, accustomed to strangers coming through, and didn't take more than a passing glance at Aidan as he rode slowly through the market.

The sun was sinking golden in the west by the time he'd finished bargaining for the last of his supplies. He'd gotten oats for Kael, twice baked flat bread, cheese, salted meat, and an extra water skin for himself. It was enough to hold him for the next few weeks if he was very careful and used every opportunity to hunt along the way. The only thing he hadn't been able to find was a map of the surrounding area. He wanted to avoid walking blindly back into Glenariff, and risking any entanglement with his uncle. Though the Naal River was the ancient border between Glenariff and Lanreath, he knew Ulrich had mercenaries fighting to seize the land north of the Naal, and his men patrolled the lands once belonging to the free-folk of Lanreath.

He stopped at a watering trough, letting Kael drink as he pondered where he might find a map. Lost in thought, he didn't notice the older man leading a donkey down the now quiet street.

"Excuse me," the man said.

Aidan jumped up. The man, whose bristly white hair stood out from his head, held out his hands apologetically.

"I didn't mean to startle you. I just recognized your horse and wanted to offer my congratulations on his safe return."

Aidan tried to swallow, but his throat felt like it was coated with dust. Who but his attackers would recognize Kael and know that he had been stolen? He backed away from the man, reaching for the horse's reins.

"You misunderstand," the man said. "My name is Gwyth. I work as a hostler in Pikeman's Crossing. Just a few days ago, I saw your horse dragged to the inn by a man who was no match for him." His eyes twinkled at the memory. "There was a young lady just arrived on a golden mare. She walked up to this man, all flash and fire, accused him of thievery, and took back the horse and any valuables on his person. Then with no thought for her own safety, she rode out with her mare and this stallion to search for the animal's rightful owner." Here he gave a solemn bow. "Seeing as how the beast is calm and willing with you, I imagined you to be his owner."

Aidan let his breath out with a sigh and managed to swallow. "I am. Elana saved my life as well as returning Kael." He blushed as he said it, remembering how he'd suspected her at first and then in the end, left her to travel alone so he could go find Cecily.

Gwyth nodded. "I had the honor of accompanying her here after she returned your horse. I believe she's still at the Three Oaks. She said that Marek was coming from Bellport to join her." He gave Aidan a significant look. "Don't ask me what a man of his station wants from her that he's going this far out of his way. I didn't have the heart to say anything, poor lass. She was exhausted as it was. He may very well be able to keep her safe from more pressing trouble."

"What do you know of Marek? What other trouble?"

Gwyth looked up and down the street. A tinsmith in a towering cart drove past the water trough. Pots and pans, candlesticks, buckets and cutlery clattered and clanked as they swung above the open window in the cart.

He leaned toward Aidan and lowered his voice. "There's Hunters seen here. I worry for the lass."

"But Marek. He's here? With her?"

"That's what they say. Though I can't imagine they'll stay here long."

"Where are they going?"

"I don't have any idea." Gwyth shrugged his shoulders. Then, as though he were speaking to himself, he said, "Seeing her stirred it all back up in me. I came out here to get away from it all - five years I've hidden out, trying to forget, and she brought it all back in five minutes."

Aidan frowned. "I'm sorry?" He didn't want to offend the man, but he had no idea what he was talking about.

Gwyth looked him over, studying his face as if searching for something there. He shook his head. "The ramblings of an old man. I shouldn't be talking with you about any of this. My apologies." He turned as if to leave.

"Wait!" Aidan called. "Please, don't go."

The hostler turned back. "It's a fool's hope. Nothing more. And I've played the fool too many times for one my age." His eyes hardened and the lines in his face deepened.

"What are you talking about?"

"I came here, left my home, five years ago, running from a broken dream. I promised myself that I wouldn't think anymore beyond the day's work. I was done hoping."

Aidan felt the air tighten with anticipation. "What dream?"

Gwyth let out a slow sigh. "It's nothing to do with you, boy. Go live your life. Enjoy your position. You have everything in front of you."

"I don't know what I have in front of me," Aidan faltered. "My dreams died when I lost my father, five years ago. I've been piecing them back together, but they don't seem to fit." His face flushed at this admission. Looking at Gwyth, he felt suddenly alone, too young, too inexperienced against the growing threat. He wished in vain that he'd been able to speak more with Reeves. It was Reeves he needed, not an aging hostler who most likely knew nothing of the Shadow, or the Elder Born.

The hard edge melted from Gwyth's face. "I'm sorry, lad. It's hard on a boy to loose his father." He stared off beyond Aidan, focused on some scene from the past. "I don't know why an old man's troubles should interest you. But, I'm from Glenariff. Grew up on a farm outside of Drumcard."

The air around Aidan tingled.

"I figure it was ten years ago I first met Darian. He was a young man, not yet thirty, but with a fire in him that I'd never seen."

Aidan held his breath.

"He had a vision - of a better way of living, and folks followed him, believed in him. He never met a stranger. Everyone that knew him, loved him." Gwyth's voice trailed off.

"He was murdered." Aidan spoke the words that shattered his world.

"Yes." Gwyth studied him, a frown playing over his face. "How did you know?"

Aidan turned away. He wasn't supposed to tell anyone who he was. Reeves had warned him. An ache spread through him. Since the day he lost his father he'd never spoken with anyone outside his small family about his grief. He looked over at the hostler. Kael was snuffing the man's white hair, and Gwyth had a gentle hand on the horse's face. He threw caution aside.

"He was my father."

Tears welled up in the old man's eyes. "You're Aidan?"

Aidan nodded, unable to speak.

Gwyth held out his arms and embraced Aidan as though he were his own son.

"I had no idea. I thought your mother took you to Farran. I'm so sorry..." His voice trailed off and he released his hold, suddenly self-conscious. "It must have been so hard on you."

Aidan tried to answer, but his throat was too thick to form words. He swallowed hard and tried again. "I miss him so much." His eyes burned and he looked away, blinking back tears. Kael nuzzled his face.

Gwyth stood silent, giving him a chance to compose himself.

"I'm trying to return to Farran now. Only I've been sidetracked and nothing seems to be going as I planned."

"How can I help?" the old man asked.

"Right now, I need to find a map. I don't want to cross over the boarders into Glenariff."

"There's a map hanging in the common room of the Three Oaks. They serve travelers mostly. That's where Elana is staying. You might look her up while you're there."

"I met Marek in Bellport. That was enough for me."

"I wasn't talking about him, now was I?" Gwyth gave him a shrewd look. "She risked herself for you, didn't she?" He waited for his words to sink in. "The Falcon looks out for himself. That girl's got more trouble than a body should have, and only him to turn to. Doesn't seem right."

Aidan squirmed under Gwyth's level gaze. He wanted to argue with the old man, to tell him that he'd had enough of saving ladies in distress, that it was just that thinking that landed him in his current predicament. His insides wrenched. He was supposed to be on his way to Farran. The more time he spent on the road, the more he felt like a failure. This was just another wild goose chase, leading to who knows what trouble.

He looked away. The truth was, Marek scared him. There was something about the man that made his blood run cold. He didn't know what or why, but he didn't relish the idea of taking up with him and Elana. Finally, the voice in his head sputtered and died out. Raising his head, he met Gwyth's gaze.

"I'll go. If I can help her, I will, but I'm not promising anything. I'm no match for Marek."

Gwyth beamed. "You've your father's courage, and there's not many who could say the same. Thank you, lad. You've set an old man's heart to rest. If there's ever anything I can do for you, you've but to name it. I'm at your service."

Aidan found a seat in an inconspicuous corner of the winding bar and ordered a bowl of stew and a glass of ale from the iron haired innkeeper. The spacious common room with its gleaming tables and imposing fireplace, was filling up. His eyes scanned the faces, bent over their bowls or merry at their drinks, searching for Elana. There was not a female face in the room. He sat back, half relieved, and waited for his supper. A carefully drawn map of the surrounding area covered the wall behind him. He swiveled in his seat and gave the map his full attention, taking the opportunity to commit its lines to memory. By the time the innkeeper returned, Aidan was restless. The fear that he'd felt along the Greenway, was magnified in this immaculate establishment. As he looked, nothing seemed out of place, but Aidan felt discord pulsing through the room. It made it hard for him to think clearly. He struggled in vain to come up with some sort of plan to locate Elana. He finished his supper, paid for his meal, and still, nothing.

He left the common room to go check on Kael. True to his word, he intended to spend the night in this place if needed, and find Elana. After what he'd sensed there in the main building though, he would sleep easier in the stall with his stallion, than in one of their rooms. The growing weight he'd felt in the common room lifted. Here, the rhythm of the animals ,steady, trusting, honest, pervaded the grounds. Kael nickered his welcome as Aidan slipped in the stall. He breathed in the scent of the stallion's coat, and dried grass, forgetting himself for a moment in its sweetness.

The door to the inn swung open, flooding the stable yard with a yellow glow. In the momentary borrowed light, he made out a lone figure approaching the barns. He watched, confident that he remained unseen in the dark of the stall. The inn door opened again, and someone called out into the darkness. The figure answered. Aidan's pulse quickened. It was Elana.

Apprehension warred with excitement. He had devised no plan yet - no plausible explanation of why he wanted to help her now. He knew he could still leave if he wanted to, but something held him. It was more than his promise to Gwyth. Kael stretched his neck over the stall door and nickered.

"Hey there, handsome," Elana said, as she stroked his nose. "What are you doing here? I thought you and Aidan had a damsel to rescue."

The shadows sharpened her already angular face. She looked strained, weary.

"He's with me," Aidan answered, standing up inches from her.

Elana jumped.

"Don't do that!"

He tried to suppress his grin. "I'm sorry. We're out of the damsel rescuing business. Didn't pay well, and no appreciation."

"I'm sorry to hear that." Nothing about her looked it.

"I see you made it to Rivergate in one piece."

"Yes. Though it was close." Her face sobered. "If it weren't for the help of a man I met in Pikeman's Crossing, I might not be alive right now."

"Gwyth. He's a good man."

"How do you know him?"

"I met him here this afternoon. He told me you were staying at the Three Oaks. Recognized Kael and came to pay his respects to the horse."

"Yes, he would." Elana smiled, the angles of her face softening.

"So did you come here just to see me?"

Aidan fumbled, the easiness of their banter had carried him farther than he'd planned. He was a dreadful liar and he knew it. If he were to do this, he'd have to tell the truth. She was free to refuse his offer.

"Yes, I did. Gwyth mentioned something about you being in a tight place, and I felt bad riding away the other day."

She raised an eyebrow at him. "What about your 'family business'?"

Aidan felt his face grow hot. He was grateful for the darkness. "I am traveling back to Farran. Geri has sent for me. I was warned not to tell anyone who I was or where I was going. But the one person who might have been able to help me was forced out of Bellport by the Hunters."

"Oh..." She looked away, her fingers tracing the worn wood of the door. "It's a generous offer, but I already have a companion."

"Sometimes it's risky to place your entire well being into the hands of one person. Even if that person is Marek."

Her sharp intake of breath let him know he'd hit the mark.

He continued. "I'm not trying to pry, but what is it that you're doing?"

She turned away. "I can't say. It's not that I don't trust you. I do. It's just that I promised..." her voice trailed off.

"You promised Marck you'd keep his secrets."

"And mine!" Her eyes flashed as she spun back around. "My parents are out there somewhere, and this is the only way I can think that might help them."

"Maybe I can help." He spoke softly, as though to a wild animal, willing her not to run from him.

The fire in her eyes went out. "I don't know. I don't know anything anymore."

Aidan sensed something tugging at her, pulling her away from him. She was silent, her eyes unfocused as though she were deep in thought. A frown puckered on her face.

"I have to feed Devi." She turned abruptly and walked away from the stall.

Aidan opened the door and followed her. "You can't just walk away like that."

"You did. Twice. In fact, the first time you ran."

"I didn't know who you were. I thought you were one of the Hunters."

She spun to face him. He stopped short to keep from running her over. "That's the point. It's the Hunters who are after me. I need someone who's NOT scared of them. I'm sorry, Aidan. I'm not your next damsel in distress. If you'll excuse me..."

She walked off to the other barn, the air crackling around her. Something wasn't right. Aidan played the conversation over in his head. Halfway through she'd changed. The more he thought about it, the surer he was. He followed her across the yard.

"Elana, wait."

She was measuring grain for her mare.

"What happened?"

"I don't know what you're doing here, but this isn't going to work."

"I'm sorry for not trusting you before. I already said that. I don't know what to say, except that I have this feeling that I'm supposed to ride with you. I can't even tell you why. I'm not trying to save you. It's not like that. I was sent to Bellport to see Reeves. Nothing came of that, except for one thing. Meeting you. And then you found me on the road. I wouldn't be here if it weren't for you. Hardly a damsel in distress."

A flicker of a smile played around her mouth.

"I don't know what you're doing, but I'm supposed to come with you." He took a deep breath. "Can't we at least try?"

She looked long into his eyes and he felt again that pushing on his mind. He forced himself not to block her out.

210

"You can ask Marek. He'll have the final say."

Elana tossed in her sleep that night. Long fingered shadows pursued her through her dreams. Falcons and tawny haired young men with gold-flecked eyes dogged her steps, beckoning for her to follow. The dreams drove her from her bed before dawn and she sat by the window, hugging her knees in her arms as she watched the sky turn from black to iron gray. Heavy clouds rolling in from the east, obscured any sunrise. She shivered, wishing in vain to be back safely at her parent's cottage on the shore.

Marek's outwardly gracious invitation to Aidan didn't fool her. She could feel the older man seething every time he thought of Aidan. Was it because of what happened with Cecily? He did seem protective of her. Elana shook her head. It was more than that. It had to be. The enmity she felt from him went too deep. She was stunned when he agreed to have Aidan join them. His warning to her still burned in her head.

"Confide nothing to him beyond what you've already disclosed. Especially our mind link. He must not know, Elana."

The thought of the day ahead left her with a cold weight in her stomach. It was difficult enough to be traveling with someone she barely knew, but to be traveling with two men who had trouble being civil with one another... She sighed and let her thoughts trail off into gloomy speculations. All her hopes of finding the Ancient Ones' Gifts and saving her parents, now seemed childish. She swallowed over a lump in her throat. It would be accomplishment enough to make it to Farran alive.

"Good morning, Elana." Marek's thoughts interrupted her musings.

"Good morning," she answered, her own thoughts listless.

"Are you alright?" She felt him pressing on her, and the weight inside grew heavier.

"I'm fine. Just didn't sleep well." She braced herself against his presence, wishing for once that she could have her thoughts to herself. Since he arrived in Rivergate, she'd felt him there on the edge of her awareness; watchful, concerned, attentive to any changes in her mood. In another circumstance, she might have been flattered, but she was too weary for that now. Her head felt fuzzy, it was hard to think clearly.

"I sent word to Aidan that we would meet him in the common room for breakfast. I'd like to see you before we go down."

Arguing seemed too difficult. "That's fine," she answered.

Moments later, the door opened and Marek entered. He paced back and forth across the wooden floor.

"Today we set out," he spoke aloud. "The rain will help cover our trail." He stopped and placed a hand on Elana's shoulder. "I need to be honest with you."

The power of his emotion threatened to sweep her up with him.

"I wouldn't have chosen for Aidan to come with us, but if he has a mind to follow, I'd rather have him where I can see him. I knew his father. Darian was a powerful Elder Born. Unfortunately, Aidan has almost no discernible Skill. I don't trust him. Not after what happened with Cecily. I don't know what his interest is in you, but I won't allow him to interfere with you accomplishing your mission."

It was hard to think. Elana felt her mind embracing Marek's thoughts. The fuzziness lessened when she allowed him in further. She took a deep breath, relieved. It was easier this way.

"I don't want him alone with you. I made you a promise that I would help you in any way I could. I will keep that promise. You can trust me, Elana."

He held both of her shoulders and looked into her eyes as he spoke. His conviction burned into her. Why had she ever questioned him? All worries about him dissolved as his eyes bore into hers.

Power, that's what she needed. That's what would keep her safe, help her find her parents. Marek had power. He would share it with her.

212

When she thought of Aidan, he seemed young and foolish. She wondered why she had ever been sympathetic toward him.

"Good girl," Marek spoke into her mind. "Together, we can overcome anything. No one can stop us."

He continued to hold her eyes. She felt power flowing from him into her, making her dizzy with its force.

"Let it in," he spoke into her mind. "I won't hold anything you need back from you. You'll need this, Elana. Open up to it. Let it in."

Something in her fought it, didn't want him in that close. It felt, in some last corner of her mind, like she was loosing a part of herself. She faltered.

"We need to take our mind link deeper." Marek's eyes held hers, reading the fear in her mind. "You have not yet begun to be challenged. If you would have my help, you must follow me here. I know of no other way to help you save your parents. We need to have access to each other always. There's too much at stake to back out now."

'Each other.' The words struck something in her. She was not just giving him access to her, but she held equal access to him. Her thoughts cleared. She would risk it. It was no more than he was risking.

"Alright." She met his gaze full on and opened her mind to him. For a moment she lost all sense of herself. She was Marek, thinking his thoughts, feeling his feelings. He was everywhere. Panic threatened to overtake her. She gasped, tried to think. No, that wouldn't work. She reached out with the Skill she had since she was a small child. That ability to read people, to know what was happing within them. It was as natural as breathing to her.

Suddenly she saw behind Marek's outward face. Pictures and emotions flooded her: a small boy hiding in a damp cellar, listening to footsteps creaking above him, wincing at the force of a beating, biting his lips to hold back the cries, anger, deep and powerful like a river threatening to carry him away. And there were pictures of Farran, of Reeves, her father, and a tawny haired man that reminded her of

Aidan, standing on the outskirts of a crowd, bitterness, an ache that gnawed at his bones.

Elana slid through the maze of images, no more noticed than a whisper. All of Marek's concentration was focused on her, pouring himself into her. If she met him there, either to resist him, or to welcome him, she would be lost; helpless before his will. She stayed here, sifting through his memories as they filtered into her mind, trying to still her own thoughts, desperate to remain hidden. A part of her pitied him. She never imagined that someone so powerful could have been so tormented. She couldn't make out his story, just the imprint of pain that it left on him. Reeves' letter came back to her mind. "He is not beyond help". She hadn't any idea what he meant at the time, but now she was glad to remember it.

"Very good," Marek's voice sounded in her head.

She could feel him testing her.

She nodded, unsure of how to respond. What would he do if he knew what she had seen? She was no longer afraid of him. What she saw in him did that much, but neither did she trust him implicitly as before. He wanted something from her, she could feel it pulsing through him. Until she knew what that was, she didn't want to alienate him. Whatever it was, it was more important to him than life itself. His whole person vibrated with it, how could she have missed this before? This was why he was protecting her, and for now she still needed that protection.

Marek presided over breakfast, outwardly high spirited and magnanimous. Aidan maintained a polite but guarded demeanor, and Elana sat in silence. Marek's presence never left her mind. She could taste his bitterness toward Aidan. Once, she caught the image of the tawny haired man she'd seen earlier in his mind. He looked like he could have been Aidan's older brother.

When Marek suggested that she gather up her things from her room, she complied without any question. She felt him pressing on her, willing her to agree with him as he talked, to obey him when he asked something of her. Is this what he'd done with Cecily? With Lord

Gratton? A picture of Braxton came to her, his unquestioning obedience and uncanny knowledge of what was needed. She smiled a grim smile. So this was why. What she couldn't figure was why it didn't work with her. Instead of controlling her, he'd let her in past his mask. Maybe it was because she was Elder Born. All the others had been Vale Folk. She would play along for now. It was better that he didn't know.

It was easier when he wasn't right there. Back in her room, she packed up her things, remembering now how growing up, she'd only have to look at her father or mother to know what they were thinking or feeling. It was this ability that made living with the Vale Folk so hard. She had no defense against their hatred and suspicion. They might smile at her face, but she could feel their thoughts as though they'd shouted them. She'd always wondered how they could be so rude. For the first time, it occurred to her that they had no idea she could read them. She pondered this as she made her way to the stable.

They left the Greenway as soon as they were out of the town. Marek took them North, out of Rivergate, following the east bank of the Gavril. Riding single file along a deserted track, they saw no one the entire morning. A relentless drizzle, which had begun as soon as they mounted, soaked Elana to the skin. Thick clouds obscured all but the ground around them. Traveling in a cocoon of mist and rain, Elana lost all sense of direction and time.

After what felt like hours, it still wasn't any lighter than when they set out and the hollow feeling growing in her stomach remained the only indication that at least one meal had been missed. Marek remained ever-present in her mind, his intensity setting her on edge. Only Aidan seemed unperturbed as they rode, wrapped in his own thoughts. She tried to ignore him, afraid that even a thought in his direction would bring trouble with Marek.

Instead she focused her Skill toward Marek, entering his mind through the link they formed. Images of power rolled through his thoughts; people bowing before him, Marek sitting on a high seat, a circlet of gold about his black hair. Elana worked hard not to inject her presence into his thoughts. He held the images of power, fondled them, as a child would cherish some talisman of comfort when his parents were gone. Except this was no child. The hunger in him threatened to overwhelm her.

They stopped at last for a quick bite to eat.

"If all goes as planned," Marek told them, "we should reach the Gavril fords before sunset. We can cross the river there and be safely into Lanreath by nightfall."

Elana caught a glint in Aidan's eyes. He was pleased. She wondered why.

She watched Aidan tend to Kael, unsaddling and watering him, before he took his own meal. Following his lead, she untied Devi and Marek's big bay, took off their saddles and led them down to the river to drink. Marek was studying a map he carried in a bag about his waist.

"Thank you," he spoke absently into Elana's mind.

"I'm glad to," she answered him. A smile played about her mouth. He was used to being waited on. This was a good way to gain some space. He wouldn't question her motivation.

Mud from the rain turned the riverbank into a treacherous slope. Aidan led Kael upriver to a shallower spot. Devi tugged at the reins, eager to get to the water. She followed Aidan's path and her two horses half slid down the bank to the Gavril.

Aidan didn't look up at her.

"Aidan?" Her voice was a whisper.

He turned, his tawny eyes accusingly. "If you don't want me to come along, you can just say so."

"It's not that. I do want you to." She felt for Marek and received only images of a map and thoughts about travel. Closing her eyes, she breathed slowly, willing her emotions to settle.

"I'm glad you're here. I just don't want to rouse Marek's suspicion. I don't want him to do anything to you."

"He wouldn't..."

216

"I don't know that. I don't know what he's capable of. He's complicated."

"Then let's leave. We can go off together without him. Elana, I don't trust the man. I don't know why you're with him."

I can't do that. It's hard to explain. I need to find out more. I just wanted you to know that I'm glad you came. I didn't want you to think I was sulking."

"Well, I'm glad you said something. I sure wouldn't have guessed it." His mouth curved into a smile that never reached his eyes.

Elana reached out and touched his arm. A simple gesture, but as soon as her fingers brushed against his sleeve, a jolt went through her.

Instantly, Marek was there. "What was that? Are you okay? Aidan didn't do anything to you?"

"No, I'm fine. Don't worry. It was just my Waking. It does that sometimes." She hoped that partial lie would pass. It was true that her Waking did that. It just didn't do it this time.

Marek's presence eased off.

"Elana?" Aidan was looking at her, worry lines creasing his forehead.

"I'm okay. Just thinking." She wanted to laugh at the ridiculousness of having to tell two different lies to two different men over the same incident. She wasn't okay. All she could think of was getting out of there without having to answer any more questions.

Aidan's eyes tried to hold hers, but she turned away. It was too dangerous. Just looking at him set off the same tingly feeling. Her face burned as she busied herself with Devi's bridle strap. She felt like a fool. She'd seen the village girls her age acting absurd around the older boys, but she'd sworn that she would never behave like that. It never occurred to her that they might not have had much of a choice.

"Why couldn't Aidan have been another girl?" she bemoaned, under her breath. "That would have made it all so much easier." Well, she wasn't going to think any more about it. Not now, with Marek peeking in on all her thoughts. The horror of that image cooled her completely. She'd never considered that complication when they forged the mind link. She blushed all over again, grabbed the horses' reins and dragged them up the muddy bank and away from Aidan.

CHAPTER 11

LANREATH

Lunch was a distant memory and Elana's stomach was gnawing on itself when Marek allowed them to stop for a cheerless supper of bread, cheese, and cold meat. Elana ate in the drizzle, hurrying to finish her food before the rain soaked it completely. Since her conversation at the river with Aidan, she had tried not to think, not to feel. It was too risky.

Marek remained preoccupied and had not questioned her. She meant to keep it that way. She never realized how difficult it was to not think of anything. The very things she tried not to think about crowded her mind.

She grimaced. Marek remained ever present in the periphery of her mind, like the sound of the sea in her old village, never distinct until focused on. His thoughts and feelings left traces; footprints, that if she chose to follow, would lead her to him. She resisted awhile, resenting the intrusion, and then more out of exhaustion than inspiration decided to follow their trail. There at least, she could think of something, without it raising suspicion.

It took a moment to gain her bearings. The brooding intensity of his thoughts threatened to carry her out with them. Excitement, goaded on by something darker: anger, fear, no - revenge, churned through him. Images of his falcon formed, almost as though he were calling the bird, and behind it all, passing notions left only a ghost of an image, fleeting shadows, some darker, some lighter. It gave her the impression of overhearing a conversation in the next room. Only those things spoken loudly and forcibly were discernible. The rest was a droning, sometimes animated, sometimes soothing, but none of it clear.

That gave her hope. If she could only make out the thoughts he focused strongly on, then maybe he faced the same limitations toward her. She still had to find a way to discover what he wanted from her, and she wasn't keen on his knowing about her prying.

They finished their meal and saddled the horses. Marek was determined to make the Gavril fords before dark. The rain stopped and a rent in the heavy clouds revealed a blood red sunset. Elana thought it an ill omen.

Marek's navigation was true, and before the light had left the sky, they arrived at the Gavril fords. Kael and Marek's bay crossed easily, but it took all of Elana's presence of mind to convince Devi that the swirling black water would not wash her away. By the time she reached the other side, crossing over into Lanreath, home of the free folk, only a faint trace of purple remained above the tree line.

"We'll find a place to camp," Marek said, "get a good night's sleep and start early tomorrow morning."

A grove of old oaks at the bottom of the hill offered shelter for the night. Exhaustion flattened Elana. It was no longer an effort to subdue her thoughts. She was too fatigued to think or feel. It was getting harder and harder to hold onto a sense of herself. Everything was Marek. It was his thoughts she was thinking, whispers of his feelings that stirred through her.

What little bit of her mind remained lucid wanted to panic. It took too much energy, though. Sleep, that's what she needed. That would help her. As soon as she was done tending to Devi, she wrapped herself in her cloak and slid into a dreamless sleep.

Sometime in the night, the sound of wings woke her. Blackness engulfed the camp. Elana couldn't see her hand in front of her face. They had lit no fire before sleeping, so there were no embers giving off their dying glow. It took her a moment to remember where she was and why. Then she felt him.

It wasn't words, but pictures. In the darkness, with no distractions, she saw the images Marek sent; a picture of a man, black cloaked and booted, galloping on a raw boned bay, a company of ruffians, a wooded track, isolated, with a huge bolder standing just off the road, and Aidan astride Kael. She heard the rustle of parchment and again, the flutter of wings and a falcon's lone cry.

His satisfaction nauseated her. The cloaked man, she recognized, he was the one from her village, the Hunter who kidnapped her parents, the one she saw him speak with in Rivergate. But what did this have to do with Aidan?

She felt Marek reach toward her, tentative. Mumbling something incoherent, she rolled over, hoping he would think her dreaming. His thoughts left. Her mind raced. He hadn't approved of Aidan as a companion for Cecily and they were attacked on the road, Aidan left for dead. He didn't like Aidan traveling with them now.

She lay awake, trying to let her thoughts drift until Marek's breathing leveled out. Reaching toward him, she tested to see if he was awake. No response greeted her. Good. Sitting up, she tried to come up with a plan. There was no way she could let Aidan be attacked again. It no longer mattered if she didn't know why Marek was protecting her. She hadn't thought him capable of that kind of betrayal. They had to leave.

By morning her conviction was solidified, but still she had no clear plan. She would talk to Aidan at the first opportunity. Together they could think of something. The attack could come at any time.

When the two men woke, she made a point of taking Devi and Marek's bay to water. Aidan followed her with Kael. She felt Marek's thoughts with her as they headed out, and then something else distracted him. This was the chance she was waiting for.

"Aidan," she whispered, "you're in danger here."

"No kidding. We all are." He didn't bother to look at her.

"No. I mean you, especially. Marek is going to have you attacked again. I believe he's the one who set up the first attack."

He turned toward her, his eyes hard. "I wouldn't be surprised. But, how do you know?"

Elana frowned. She still wasn't comfortable talking about the mind link. "I can't tell you right now. Only I know that you were right about having to leave."

"Well, let's go now."

Her blood raced at the thought. But then, they had no supplies, no saddles, even. They wouldn't get far with no food and no silver. She said as much to Aidan.

"Do you have any other ideas?" he asked.

"No."

Marek's bay stumbled and Aidan, who was behind her called for Elana to stop.

He left Kael standing and took the big horse's reins, asking him to walk out, all the while watching his feet. The horse stumbled again and Aidan walked around to his hip, bent and picked up one of the massive hind feet.

"This boy deserves better," he muttered, stroking the bay's hip as he set the foot down, "and I think we can give it to him."

Elana moved back to look. Aidan showed her where the iron shoe that protected the foot was twisted. A rock had become lodged in it, and the nails were pulled out from one side. She could see where the hoof had cracked under the strain.

"I should have noticed." Aidan looked remorseful. "We need to find a village or a farm where Marek can trade him in for a mount that's sound. He won't be doing any riding on this one."

"I'm sorry for him," Elana said, stroking the bay, "but if Marek has to find another horse..." she left the sentence unfinished.

"That's all well and good," Aidan answered, "so long as we don't get attacked first."

"I didn't think of that."

"If we see any signs of it, we run. Follow me, I don't get lost easily. With Marek unhorsed, we still have some advantage."

"But what about the Hunter?"

He shrugged. "We'll have to trust to our mounts. I doubt there's many horses that can outrun either of these two."

That wasn't exactly comforting, Elana thought.

All the while Aidan was talking, he worked the offending shoe off the bay's hoof. The horse limped now, but no longer stumbled. Satisfied that he'd done all he could to help the beast, he handed him back to Elana.

Marek's presence interrupted her thoughts.

"Where are you? Are you okay?"

"Yes," she answered him silently. "Your horse had a twisted shoe and Aidan removed it before it could do more damage to his hoof. I'm afraid he can't be ridden."

Marek's frustration assaulted her before he gained control of himself. "Well, I'll just have to buy another at the next farm. These things happen."

"Do you know where we're going?"

"I have an idea, but it's not been proven yet. Hurry back, we're already late."

Late for what, she wondered, but kept the thought to herself. As far as she was concerned, late was good.

When they returned, Elana suggested that they pack the bay's supplies onto Devi and Kael, so that they could travel as quickly as possible. Aidan took out a knife and trimmed the crumbled edges off the injured hoof with care.

"You have a way with animals, Aidan," Marek said. He made it sound like an insult.

"I grew up on a farm. It's just a part of who I am."

"Yes, I suppose that would do it." Marek turned away, leaving Aidan standing with his face red.

They seemed to creep along, now that Marek traveled on foot. Elana felt his impatience build. They ate their afternoon meal while they walked, and the whole day dragged out like a punishment. The late afternoon sun turned the land golden when Marek spotted a grassy path that led away from the track. Here were plowed fields, and a farmhouse was just visible over the rise. Marek's face lit up. He halted, peering up the path for any sight of the farm's occupants.

"It's not advisable for us to be seen all together. One person traveling alone elicits fewer questions. I will go up here and see if they would be willing to sell me a horse. I know the track that we're on. It would be better if the two of you travel ahead. Not too far from here there is a large boulder standing at the edge of a wood. It is hard to miss. I will meet you there as soon as I'm done."

Elana's felt herself turn to ice. She remembered the picture from last night.

"Trust me," his voice sounded in her head. "No harm will come to you."

She nodded, not trusting herself to answer.

Marek turned and walked the bay up the path.

"Aidan, that's the place. I know it."

"What do you mean?"

"That boulder. It's the place of the attack."

Aidan grinned at her. "Well, we'll just have to disappoint them." He turned Kael off the track, pushing him into a canter through the high grass.

Elana followed on Devi, a smile breaking over her face for the first time in days. Aidan led them through the countryside, doubling back through streams, skirting woods, and avoiding all signs of people. He seemed to be in his element. Elana found herself hopelessly lost.

"How do you know where you're going?" she asked when they stopped to let the horses drink.

"It's a part of my Gifting." His voice was flat and he looked away. "The land talks to me if I listen."

"Like the animals?"

He turned his back on her.

"I didn't mean it the way Marek did. I think it's wonderful."

"Right." He spun around to face her, tawny eyes flashing. "My father gathered the people together to stand against the Shadow King, and I listen to the land and talk to animals. Some help that is."

"I think it's a lot more helpful than my Gifting. At least yours doesn't do harm."

"Why do you say that?"

Elana busied herself mounting Devi, so she wouldn't have to look at him. "I need to tell you something, but I don't think you're going to like me much after I do."

"Try me." Aidan's voice softened.

She took a deep breath, not sure why she was doing this now. "I hear people if I listen."

His eyebrows went up in question.

"Not what they say, but what they're thinking. And when my Waking is strong, I can influence their minds."

Aidan nodded, as though putting pieces of a puzzle together. "Like that night by the docks?"

"Yes. Only I'd never done it before and that surprised me as much as anyone."

"I bet it did." He grinned at her, then his face grew serious. "It's not the Gift, but how you use it. That would be scary in someone who wanted power over others."

Elana's face burned. "That's not all. Marek found us that night. He saved Orvis' life. He also offered to help me." She struggled, trying to find the right words. Why was this so hard to say? "He said that the only way he could protect me from the Hunter was if we forged a mind link." Her body was shaking. She so wanted Aidan not to hate her for this. She needed his help, but more than that, she wanted his good opinion.

He nodded, his face inscrutable. "I didn't know that was still possible. I thought it was just used by the leaders, before the Forgetting."

"I know," she answered, miserably. "And I see why it should be. But I had nowhere else to turn. I trusted him then. He did know my father." It was a feeble excuse and she knew it.

"So now? Are you still..." Aidan left his question unfinished.

"Yes. I haven't heard from him yet, but I expect when he finds we've gone, he will try and track me. And Aidan," she paused, "when I use my Gifting it seems to draw the Hunters to me."

He rolled his eyes a moment. "You wouldn't want to make it too easy or anything, would you?"

"You don't hate me?"

"No." He arched an eyebrow at her. "But do you understand why I thought you were dangerous?"

"I don't blame you. I guess you were right."

"A weapon... but in whose hands?"

"What do you mean?"

"Nothing. It just came to me." He looked around as though expecting unfriendly eyes to be peering out at them. "Lets get moving."

He swung up on Kael and led the way through the woods. Branches reached out to grab at them and shadows took on the form of horsemen in Elana's eyes. Devi picked up her nervousness and starting spooking at every strange sound. Kael strained his head, nostrils flaring, trying to catch some scent.

All at once Elana felt Marek's presence slam through her mind. There was no question, no articulation, just rage.

"Run!" she shouted.

Devi and Kael exploded into a gallop, racing single file through the narrow wooded path. Aidan checked Kael for a moment and then turned sharply to the right.

"They won't expect us to leave the cover of the woods."

In a few more strides, the trees thinned and then open fields greeted them. Elana crouched over Devi's mane, her eyes streaming tears from the wind. She couldn't see anything except the setting sun as they rode due west.

Lanreath, she thought. She didn't know why, but the name gave her hope. The land of the Free Folk. The Valefolk here managed their own affairs, owing allegiance to no Lord. No trade routes ran through the land between the rivers, only local roads, and from what she remembered her parents saying, the Hunters rarely bothered to cross these borders. Marek's position with Lord Gratton would give him no advantage in Lanreath.

His presence in her mind lessened by degrees as they ran west. They pulled up their lathered horses as the sun slipped below the hills.

"I think they've given up pursuit for now," Elana said. "I can't feel him as strongly."

Aidan was still, listening. "The land is clear. We're safe for now."

Dismounting, they led the tired horses, letting them cool out before they stopped. They walked in silence, each lost in their own thoughts.

Darkness crept in from the east; the shadows lengthened along the hills and the first evening star winked in the sky. A far off howl sent Devi snorting and whirling around Elana, ears straining into the night.

"We'd best find a place to camp," Aidan said. He paused, intent on the land around them. "There's a hollow over this hill that will serve."

"How do you know?" Elana asked him.

"I just do." He shrugged. "It's my Gifting." He shot her a sideways grin. "Not as dramatic as yours, but it's come in handy now and then."

"I'll say." She followed him to the hollow where an ancient stand of trees offered shelter from any prying eyes.

Unwilling to light a fire, they ate more cold meat and bread for supper. Aidan took out his cloak and wrapped himself in it. Elana got out blankets from her pack and made a makeshift bed between two gnarled tree roots. Exhaustion made every movement an effort, but sleep eluded her.

"Aidan?" she asked.

"Yes."

"Do you have any idea where we're going?"

He rolled over to face her. "Only guesses. You've been pretty close about your plans."

Her cheeks burned. With all that happened, she never had been honest with him about what she was trying to do. "I'm sorry," she said. "There was so much going on with Marek..." she trailed off.

"I'm not sure what to believe now," she continued. "I feel like a fool."

Aidan sat up and pulled the green cloak close around his shoulders. "Why don't you start at the beginning?"

Grateful for the darkness, Elana began the story, starting with the letter. The words came out with halting steps. The details that haunted her sleep were hard to speak out loud. She forced herself to be honest - about her hopes of finding the Gifts, of finding Laharan, about what happened with Marek, and about how quickly she became caught up in what he could do for her. Until she heard herself saying it, she hadn't realized how guilty she felt about leaving Orvis, or how much faith she had put in the thin thread of Marek's promises.

She tried to keep her Waking in check as she spoke, but in spite of her best efforts she felt it pulsing through her. When she was done she sat huddled in her blankets, torn between the surge of her Waking and despair.

Long after Elana drifted off to sleep, Aidan sat next to her, staring up into the night. He had held his peace while she talked, but his insides churned. He glanced at her pale face, outlined in the starlight, and troubled even in sleep. Had things been different, they might have grown up together. Her father had been close friends with his own. He recognized Hamilton's name from his father's stories of Farran. The thought of this man and his wife being swallowed up by the Shadow, of Elana being left without family without a home, burned in him.

He had felt her Waking shine as she spoke of the Gifts, and though he said nothing, his own stirred as well. There was no question of doubting her, only the question of how best to help. A slow grin spread over his face. His Skills may not help in open warfare, but they were better suited to finding the hidden land, taken from this realm by the Ancient Ones. It wouldn't be easy with Marek and the Hunter on their trail. He worried about the mind link Elana shared with Marek. He shared a link of similar kind with Kael, though he had never called it that before, but what could the man access through her?

His thoughts rolled round and round. He would need help if they were to navigate Lanreath successfully. The only thing he knew about this land was that it was divided among three different peoples, dwelling peaceably, each within their own respective borders. The Barras, renowned herdsmen, raised horses, cattle and sheep, following their flocks along the rolling hills and moors of eastern Lanreath, from the Border Mountains down to the fords outside Rivergate. They were known throughout the vale as master weavers as well, creating wool tapestries the likes of which could not be found elsewhere. They were a reclusive people, welcoming few into their midst. Aidan had the suspicion that Kael was bred here. He didn't know anything else about them though; how they governed themselves, whether they traded with the other clans, or with the people of Merrion. He'd heard rumors that they were fierce fighters, but he'd never met anyone from the Barras before. They were traveling through the Barras' lands now, and he wished his education had included something more than hearsay about these people.

Aidan tossed his thoughts back and forth, unsure of their next steps. Long after Elana's breathing stilled, he managed to lay down, and give into sleep.

Morning dawned bright and clear with a promise of a warm spring day. They started out early, eager to put more distance between themselves and Marek. Elana kept to herself through the morning, looking pale and drawn. Aidan let her be, focusing his Skills on the land, listening for any sounds of discord, any breath of enmity. There was none. It was as though Marek and the Hunter had vanished into the blue spring air. He wasn't complaining, but neither did he trust it.

At lunch, Aidan broke the silence between them.

"You remind me so much of my little sister, Arella," he said. "I hope you get a chance to meet her."

She gave him a funny look.

"I'm eighteen," she said.

"I didn't mean that you were little. Well, you are small, but not like that..." The blood rushed to his face. Why did she have to twist what he said?

"I'd like to meet her, Aidan." Elana gave him a look of apology.

"Right." It came out more brusque than he intended. He didn't feel like talking anymore.

They rode on, Elana growing more withdrawn as they went. He remembered riding down the road with Cecily. She may have been too engaging, it kept him from paying attention to the land around him, but Elana seemed insensible to his presence. It was like she wasn't there, her mind was elsewhere. He missed Cecily's light chatter and the way she looked up at him when she spoke.

Every time he glanced over at Elana, she was staring straight ahead, jaw set, eyes locked on the path before them. He wanted to say something to comfort her, to cheer her, but all words died unspoken at the hard light in her eyes. Though the land around them remained clear of any danger, he sensed a growing darkness around her. He was worried about her link with Marek. Was he tracking them through her? Why wasn't she speaking about it?

Their riding had taken them deep into Lanreath. Where before only woods and meadows bordered the road, now isolated farms dotted the countryside. Sheep and cattle grazed on hilly pastures and freshly ploughed fields broke up the new green with patches of dark brown earth. The people they passed seemed suspicious of them, hesitant to return his greeting. Aidan imagined not many strangers came through this way. Elana didn't make things easier, hardly turning to note them at all. By nightfall, he noticed that even Devi grew restless, taking on whatever shadow Elana wrestled with.

"What's happening with you?" he finally asked, as they made camp for the night.

"What do you mean?" Her voice was defensive.

"I mean your silence all day and the darkness around you." His voice carried the frustration he'd been holding back.

"I'm sorry that I'm not like Cecily," she quipped and turned away from him.

"That's not what I'm talking about and you know it. How can I help you if you're not honest with me?"

"There's nothing you can do to help me with this." Her voice was bitter, resigned.

"What do you mean?"

"Marek."

"Has he been tracking you?"

"He's been reaching out to me all day."

"How?

She gave him a look.

"Can you tell if he's nearby?"

"I'm not exactly having conversations with him." She lapsed into silence again.

Aidan left her alone. He took care of both their horses, reaching out to Devi as he did. The mare was as irritable as Elana, not willing to respond to the calming thoughts he was sending her. He finally gave up and drew comfort from his bond with Kael, grateful for the horse's steadfast companionship.

Elana just sat, staring off into the evening sky as he got dried meat out of their packs for supper. He was still unwilling to risk a fire if it wasn't necessary, and tonight felt milder than the past few nights. When he was finished, he found Elana staring at him, her eyes haunted.

"He misses me."

"What?"

"Marek. I can feel it. He's hurt. He trusted me."

"To do what? Follow him into the Hunter's arms?" Aidan didn't know where this was going and he didn't like the sound of it.

"What have I done?"

"Elana, you've taken care of yourself. You heard what he was going to do. How can you wonder about this?"

"You can't understand. You've never had a mind link." She flung this last piece back at him. "It's not that simple."

"It's pretty simple to me. He was trying to get me killed, and he wanted you for something, and I'd lay gold down that it wasn't about helping you. He knows how to take care of himself. All too well, I'd say."

She glared at him. "I know that."

They ate their supper in silence, the animosity crackling between them. Aidan was grateful for nightfall and the chance to wrap himself in his cloak and at least pretend to sleep.

Sometime in the night the sound of muffled sobbing woke him. He rolled over and squinted, trying to make out the dim outline of Elana. He knew she was crying, but he didn't want to brave her anger to find out why. He shifted and turned on the hard ground, finding sleep elusive now. When at last sleep pulled him in, strange dreams of a great dark bird hovering over them, just beyond sight, followed him through the remainder of the night.

When he woke to a gray morning, Elana was still sleeping, wrapped in her cloak, her face at peace. He rose and saw to the horses, taking care not to wake her. It would be best if she could rest as much as possible. By the time he returned she was awake.

"Good morning," he ventured.

"Good morning. I'm sorry about yesterday."

He nodded, sure that anything he might say would be the wrong thing.

"Marek left me last night."

"What do you mean?"

"He asked me if I really wanted him to leave. I told him yes. He said that he was worried about my safety and was afraid that you had kidnapped me. I told him I was fine, but I had to travel without him. He said that he wouldn't impose himself on me, but if I ever needed him, I had only to call and he would be there." A queer look, almost of triumph crossed her face. "I know he's not to be trusted, but he isn't all bad. I've seen more of him than that."

Her face relaxed for the first time since Aidan met her. "Anyway, he's not trying to track me through our link anymore. We're free to go."

"Well, that's good news," he ventured. He kept his doubts to himself. It was good just to see her happy. He would take that for now and keep his eyes and ears open.

The road took them into the midst of larger farms. It seemed odd to Aidan that they passed no villages. He sensed that more people dwelt here, but they encountered no signs of it. Those that they passed looked at them with downright hostility. The anger in their faces was echoed through the land and in the air.

"Elana, I don't know who these people are, but we need to go carefully. This place is seething with anger."

Underneath him, Kael began to get restive. As Aidan reached out to him, he caught impressions of horses running together over open fields, of nights grazing and resting under the stars, and then of men chasing them, snaring them with ropes, dragging them from their herd.

He knew nothing of Kael's past and wondered for the first time if Darcy had acquired Kael through less than honest means. It wouldn't be out of character for his cousin to do that. Spending a bag of gold big enough to feed a small village on some whim, wasn't out of the question for him either.

The sound of a fast running stream broke into his thoughts. Trees closed in on the narrow dirt road as it twisted and dipped down toward the water. Aidan felt a twinge of warning that they were not alone, and loosed his bow from his pack, readying an arrow, should it be needed. The underbrush cracked up ahead. Aidan aimed his bow at the sound. He heard the sharp intake of Elana's breath and felt more than saw Elana and Devi draw up beside them.

Before Aidan could get a good look at who or what was waiting for them, Kael let out an exuberant whinny. It was answered by a horse that could have passed for Kael's full brother. While Kael was black with no marking on him at all, this one was black with a small white star on his forehead. A man sat astride the horse with an easy grace that did nothing to hide his air of command. His blond hair was pulled back, and his dark blue eyes studied them while a mocking smile played around the corners of his mouth.

Aidan sized him up while Kael jigged underneath him, stretching his nose out toward the man's horse. The man was older than him; Aidan guessed, by maybe ten years. He was tall and, armed with a long sword and a bow, though he made no move to pick up either. There was no sense of evil surrounding him. Aidan breathed a sigh of relief about that. The steel behind those blue eyes made Aidan decide this wasn't someone he would want to face in a fight.

"Well, what do we have here?" The man broke the silence, his voice low, taunting.

Aidan bristled.

"We are travelers, seeking safe passage through your lands."

"Travelers? How quaint." He waited, the twisted smile now taking up full residence on his face.

"Yes, we're just passing through."

"Ah, are you and your lady friend," here he paused, his eyes taking in Elana appreciatively, "traveling anywhere in particular?"

Beside him, Aidan could feel Elana's hackles rise. Before he could motion her to be quiet she spat out, "Lady friend! What exactly do you mean by that."

"My, my. I wouldn't think I'd have to spell it out for you. Though you do seem a little young. He shook his head at Aidan. "Did you have to promise her you'd marry?"

"How dare you!" Elana retorted. "That's not what we are."

"Elana..." Aidan shook his head at her.

"So, the spitfire has a name. Hello Elana." The man tipped his head to her. "We're not children here, there's no need to pretend. Unless of course the man isn't capable..." He let his words trail off and cast an appraising look at Aidan.

"That's not the case," Aidan replied through clenched teeth.

"I'm glad to hear it, for your sake." The stranger gave him a wink.

"Who are you?" Elana demanded, her face flushed, though Aidan couldn't tell if it was from anger or embarrassment.

"They didn't teach you much of anything where you come from, did they. How things are between a man and a woman, manners..." He shook his head, a grave look on his face. "But I like your spirit, so I'll excuse your ignorance. My name is Faris." He made a sweeping bow from the saddle. "You are the fair Elana, and your friend," he gave the word special emphasis, "is?"

"Aidan." Aidan gathered whatever shreds of dignity he could muster. This wasn't going at all well.

"Well, Aidan, you're a bold pair to come riding through our lands on horses that were stolen from us. Our memories are not that short. Or were you planning on returning them to their families?"

"Kael belongs to you?" His heart dropped to his stomach, as his fear was confirmed. "I didn't know..."

"I'm sure you paid good gold for him didn't you? Hoping to improve your breeding stock? That filly you've got," he pointed at Devi, "is the result of generations of meticulous breeding. The family who bred her lost their only daughter to the Black Knights. She died trying to protect their horses."

Elana blanched, all the fire gone from her bearing. "I had no idea. Marek gave her to me to ride. I didn't know how he came by her. I'd be glad to return her, though I know that can never replace their daughter."

"No, it can't. But the sentiment is appreciated." Faris' eyes hardened. "You know Marek?"

"Well, I just met him a few weeks ago... It's a long story, really..."

Aidan interrupted before Faris could reply. "Black Knights? What do they have to do with it?"

Faris raised an eyebrow. "Where have you been, boy? What part of the Vale are you from anyway? It's the Black Knights who've been thieving our best animals and selling them off to the wealthy of Drumcard and Bellport. To keep one of our horses is to enter into a blood feud with the Barras. Now, you don't seem to have the skill it takes to be a horse thief. At least not one who keeps his head on his shoulders. Had I believed that you'd stolen them, you'd both have been dead before we'd exchanged names. I do hate killing someone once we've been properly introduced."

Aidan didn't doubt his ability to carry out the threat. His throat tightened, making it hard to speak. There was nowhere to run to, nothing he knew to do. He couldn't imagine being separated from Kael, yet looking at Faris' own mount who was trying to sniff noses with Kael, he recognized the veracity of the man's claim.

"Just be glad it's me you met and not my cousin. Wirt would have swung first and left any questions unanswered. He's not the inquisitive type. Now me, on the other hand, I love a good story." He looked the two over and laughed out loud. "In that area I'm sure you won't disappoint."

Aidan cast a sideways glance at Elana. Her jaw was set and her eyes flashed dangerously.

Faris continued, "Unfortunately for you though, you'll need to tell that story to my uncle Varen, Wirt's father. He's the leader of the Barras, at least until Wirt completes the rites of succession. Much as I might like to, I don't have the authority to spare your lives."

Aidan swallowed hard over the lump in his throat and nodded. "Thank you for that chance."

"My pleasure, Aidan." The mocking smile disappeared from his face. "I have some questions of my own that I'm hoping you might answer."

Aidan and Elana followed Faris across the stream and then through the woods on a path that Aidan had taken for a game trail. He saw no sense in running, as Faris' horse was every bit a match for Kael and more powerful than Devi. He wished that he could have a moment to talk with Elana, to decide what they were going to tell this Varen. As much as he mistrusted the practice of a mind link, he had to acknowledge that it would come in handy right now. He glanced over at Elana, who rode beside him in silence, her face inscrutable. She might as well be across the Vale for all he could read her.

The sun started dipping down toward the west before Faris stopped them in a small clearing. Protected from the wind by the surrounding trees, it was warm and still; the only sound besides the occasional bird call, and evening frogs, came from a shallow stream that cut across one corner.

"We can eat and water the horses here and still reach the Clan House by nightfall." Faris dismounted and unsaddled his horse, letting him graze at will.

Aidan followed his example, unsaddling Kael and turning him loose. He trusted the big horse not to wander away. Kael immediately went up to Faris' mount and the two sniffed noses, squealing and pawing the air. Devi watched them with interest.

"It's been over a year since Shay has seen his brother." Faris' voice was low as he watched the two horses play together.

"Was he yours?" Aidan asked.

"Yes."

Aidan felt the man's anger burning below the surface.

"How did you come by him?" Faris asked. His face remained impassive, but Aidan didn't miss the dangerous edge to his voice.

"Darcy, Lord Ulrich's son, had bought him, but couldn't lay a hand on him." Aidan relayed the story of winning Kael, careful to leave out any connection he had to the Tormey family. He was glad that here, at least, he could fill in the missing pieces for Faris without compromising their own journey.

When he finished the story, Faris grinned. "You did well in making a fool of that Darcy. I don't know what is worse, Ulrich on the Lord's seat of Glenariff, or the thought of that pompous, self-important idiot that he calls a son, succeeding him."

Aidan nodded, hoping he could avoid any discussions about his uncle and cousin. It was an accident of birth that they were related, and as he was doing his best to forget the fact, he didn't relish the idea of bringing it up with others. To his relief, Faris didn't pursue the subject.

"You have a way with horses."

Aidan flushed. Where Marek had made it into an insult, it was obvious that Faris intended it as a complement.

"I know that horse," Faris continued. "He has more fight in him than most I've seen. I wasn't looking forward to training him to saddle. It seems that you've done the job for me."

No words came out when Aidan tried to answer. He looked away, feeling his face grow hot.

Kael didn't belong to him.

It was as though a chasm opened up at the thought of a world without the black horse. He reached out to the stallion and Kael turned from his grazing and nickered. Mumbling something incoherent, Aidan retreated to where Kael grazed. The horse nudged his chest, snuffing his tunic for a slice of apple or piece of bread. Aidan kept his back to Faris, blinking hard.

He heard Faris shuffling through his pack for food. As much as he wanted to hate the man for owning Kael, he couldn't. If only they hadn't run into him...

"Aidan," Elana's voice broke into his thoughts.

He cleared his throat, trying find his voice again. "Yes?"

"I'm so sorry about Kael." Her arm rested lightly on his.

"If the penalty for having one of their horses is death, then we may not be around long enough to miss him." Aidan's attempt at humor fell flat.

"I don't believe that Faris wants us killed. I don't know about his uncle, but we'll find out soon enough." Elana moved away, busying herself with removing burrs from Kael's tail.

Jealousy flared up in Aidan at the stallion's obvious acceptance of her. He sighed and tried to let it go. It wasn't her fault. She had formed the link with Kael in an attempt to rescue him. He should just be grateful.

"If it's possible, let's not mention anything about being Elder Born. I don't know how the Barras feels about us and we don't need any further reason to raise suspicion.

Aidan turned and met her eyes. "Sounds good. We'll just talk about your parents being captured and trying to rescue them. I think we can avoid the rest."

She smiled and moved back to where Faris was setting out food. Aidan watched the man's face light up when she approached. He couldn't make out their conversation, but it was clear that they were both enjoying themselves.

Elana seemed to have gotten over her indignation at Faris. That was good. They stood a better chance if she was charming than if she was moody and closed. He strode over to join them, rehearsing all the while, what he would say to Varen.

CHAPTER 12

FARIS

Evening's quiet wrapped around the Barras village as Faris led them to the Clan House. Candlelight brightened the windows of the hewn log homes, and through them Aidan caught glimpses of families gathered for their evening meals. The barns stood empty, and across the fields came the occasional lowing of a cow or bleating of sheep. Mares grazed on the open hills, their foals suckling at their sides, or gamboling along behind them on spindly legs.

From what Faris told them, Aidan realized that this represented only a fraction of the Barras population. The greater number of the Barras lived in tents, traveling with the herds. Only the very old, the very young, and the infirm lived year round in the villages. Varen, as leader of the Barras, often returned here to attend to business, hear disputes and mete out judgments.

Kael whinnied, high and shrill, and from all around horses lifted their heads. Some watched as the three approached, some answered. Aidan could feel the excitement threatening to sweep his horse away. He had never felt such longing in Kael before. He clung to the consolation that at least the big horse would be happy here. He'd be doing what was best for him.

Nothing seemed to matter anymore. They would tell their story and then Kael would be taken away. After that, Aidan couldn't bring himself to care what happened.

Faris' voice interrupted his thoughts.

"We're here, my friends. It would be best for you both if we unsaddled the horses and put them out in the holding paddocks. Follow me."

Outside a cluster of houses, a weather tight barn attached to separate paddocks stood against the surrounding woods. Faris stopped there.

"We can leave the saddles and packs in the barn and put each of the horses out in their own paddock. That way they can see each other, but not fight. I can't vouch for Shay's behavior when I'm not around."

Aidan nodded his approval. He loosened the girth and relieved Kael of his burden. With shaking hands he led him to one of the paddocks, slipped off his bridle and let him go. The black horse raced the length of the paddock, whinnying his exuberance to the evening.

When they saw all three horses settled down and grazing, Faris led them to the Clan House. Aidan's throat tightened, and he felt Elana move up next to him.

"Let me do the talking at first," Faris warned. "When Varen questions you, choose your words carefully. He's not a bad man, just fiercely protective of our people, and our horses." He gave them a queer look. "I would leave out anything that might sound too unusual. Varen doesn't trust what he doesn't know. He's not been abroad in many years and some old prejudices die hard."

"Thank you for the warning." Aidan managed to force the words out wondering all the while how much Faris knew or had guessed about what they were.

Faris winked at him, savoring some personal jest. "This will be interesting." He pushed the heavy wooden door open, and led them in.

A mountain of a man sat next to a huge fireplace, absently caressing two lean dogs who lounged at his feet. His light brown hair showed streaks of gray, and lines creased his leathery face. Barrel chested and thick limbed, only the dark blue eyes alluded to any kinship with Faris.

"What have you here for us?" The question was gruff.

Faris' expression never changed.

"Prisoners, Uncle."

242

Aidan bristled at this.

Elana stiffened.

"I ran into them trespassing through our lands."

"They're hardly worth bringing back here." Varen's voice grew impatient.

"I know that they're not." Faris tipped his head in acknowledgment. "But they have an interesting story to tell, and I know how much you love to hear stories."

"What is this foolishness?"

"Uncle, if you will humor me I think you'll be glad for the chance to talk with these two."

"Alright, alright. But I'll tell you right now, that dealing with them is going to be your responsibility. You've wiggled out of enough here, off riding through the outskirts, looking for trouble. Well, you're not going to leave this on my doorstep. You found them, you're stuck with them. Wirt will be back by the full moon and I have more important things to do than chastise errant travelers."

"Your word is my command." Faris bowed his head.

"What have you to say for yourselves?" Varen demanded.

Aidan's face grew hot as he pieced their story together with care. He had hoped for a longer introduction than this, and one that might give him a clearer sense of where to go. He decided that the story he told Elana about family business would be the safest. Other than that, he tried to be as truthful as possibly; keenly aware that he lied miserably.

To his relief Elana jumped in frequently. She was masterful, reading Varen's interest and mood with skill. Frank about her parents capture by the Black Knights, she focused on her attempt to find them and rescue them. They both left out anything about being Elder Born, or any reference to forming mind links with the horses. Every time Aidan went to say something about the horses being stolen, he felt Elana at the edge of his mind pushing him. 'Not yet.'

Though Elana mentioned the animals, it wasn't until she related their meeting with Faris that she shared their dismay at finding the horses had been stolen from the Barras Clan. Aidan had to acknowledge the brilliance of Elana's strategy. She had won Varen over to the point that when she told him of their surprise and grief at finding out that these animals were stolen, he nodded in agreement with her. She reiterated her offer to return Devi to the family who had lost her, and Aidan more reluctantly assured Varen that he had no contest with Faris over Kael's ownership. He was unable though to hide his distress at loosing the black horse.

By the time they finished their story, Varen was sitting at the edge of his chair. "I thought it was only us that those foul brigands tormented! It's an outrage." He pounded the arm of his chair with a powerful fist. "I release you both from the penalty for having a horse of the Barras Clan. You're as much victims as we are in this."

He turned to his nephew. "Faris I'll hold to my word. You will indeed be responsible for carrying out our judgment toward these two. You will accompany them until their mission is accomplished. At that point, you are charged with bringing back their horses to their rightful owners. I have no authority to gift them with animals that aren't my own."

Faris made a sweeping bow. "It would be my honor, Uncle."

Varen lowered his voice. "It would be best if you were gone before the full moon."

Faris kneeled and lay his head on his uncle's knee. The huge man placed both hands on his head. "Don't be gone over long."

Varen turned toward Aidan and Elana. "I have the suspicion that if we don't come together to help one another, the enemy will crush us, one at a time. You have my blessing."

"Thank you." Aidan bowed at the leader of the Barras.

Elana shocked him by going up to the big man and giving him a hug. Aidan saw tears blur the dark blue eyes, though he couldn't make out Varen's words to her. The man hugged her before placing his hands on her head in blessing as he had done with Faris.

When Varen was done, Faris led them back outside.

"Well, that went better than I ever dreamed." He gave Elana an approving smile. "For a young spitfire who doesn't know much, you're quite winning when you want to be. I couldn't have done better myself, and that's saying a lot."

Aidan saw her eyes shining in the darkness.

"Wirt comes home at the full moon, so we've best be long away from here by then. I'd like to leave at dawn. No sense in giving Varen a chance to have second thoughts."

Aidan saw the reason in that, and was glad enough to be on their way. The one part he was trying to reconcile was having Faris accompany them. That was nowhere in his plans. They hadn't told him the half of who they were and what they were trying to do. He might have guessed at some, but he would have to know the whole story sooner or later.

Aidan's jaw tightened. He wasn't used to seeking approval from Valefolk. Faris could be a powerful ally, but if he didn't like what he heard, he could also be a dangerous enemy. Dropping back behind the other two, he watched Elana talking with the man. Faris obviously enjoyed her. Maybe her charm would work as well on him as it had on Varen.

He tried to push thoughts of their trial away. He was sure that Elana had been trying to influence his mind. He could feel her at the edge of his consciousness. How much power did she have, and could he trust her to use it wisely?

Lost in gloomy thoughts, Aidan trudged after the chatting pair.

Faris' voice brought him back. "I think it would be best if we pay a visit to Devi's family. They will have heard of this by morning, and I'd like to obtain their goodwill as well as Varen's consent to travel with Devi."

They agreed to the wisdom of that plan.

"Faris, I'd like to be the one to talk with them." Elana's voice was sober.

"And you thought I'd have it any other way?" He bowed to her with a flourish. Then sobering, he said, "It will be good for both of you."

He guided them through the cluster of houses to a small home across the clearing. Curtains hid the light from inside and a thin line of smoke curled up from their chimney.

Faris lowered his voice. "Falbor and Danae live alone here now. They lost their only daughter less than a year ago. They have not yet rallied from that loss. I can't predict what their reaction will be to this. Please, go gently, for their sakes."

Elana's voice was shaky. "I will. I promise."

Faris knocked on the door and they all waited for an answer. After a long silence, they heard a scuffling on the other side of the door. It creaked open on sagging hinges. Framed in the light of a smoking fireplace, a stooped man with a grizzled beard glared out at them.

"What do you want?" he barked.

"Falbor, it is good to see you." Faris' voice was smooth. "I hate to intrude, but I met someone that I want you and Danae to talk with." He reached an arm around Elana's shoulders, pulling her forward into the light. "This girl has a story that you need to hear."

Aidan had the sense that anyone but Faris would be turned away immediately. As it was, the man opened the door with caution, peering out into the night and scowling when he saw Aidan there too.

"Who is this you've brought? Do you expect us to entertain strangers?"

"These two are traveling together. I met them today and will leave with them in the morning with Varen's blessing. Their story is twined with our own."

The words had their desired effect. The man opened the door. "Only for you, Faris. Come in. Excuse the mess. We've not done much here lately..." His voice trailed off.

"Danae - we have visitors."

246

A shade of a woman slipped out from the back room. Aidan thought that she might vanish completely if he blinked. Her face was gaunt and haggard, framed with long unbrushed blond hair. Pale eyes stared out at them, haunted and miserable. Her shoulders were so bony it looked as though they would poke holes in her tunic. Aidan wondered if it was some wasting sickness or grief that had reduced her to this state. It hurt to look at her.

The woman remained silent, barely acknowledging the visitors. Her husband drew out a chair and motioned for her to be seated. He stood behind her, a hand on her brittle shoulder.

"This is Elana," Faris introduced her, "and Aidan," he added. "I met them this morning in the woods. I want you to hear Elana's story."

Elana inclined her head in a little bow, and as no seats were offered to them, they stood and faced the older couple. She related most of what had happened to her since the day of the letter, much as she had with Varen, only bringing different aspects into focus as they pertained to the couple's situation.

Aidan saw Falbor's face soften and Danae lost her vacant look. By the time Elana mentioned Devi, tears were streaming down Danae's withered cheeks. Elana too had tears brimming in her eyes as she spoke of her parents. She looked younger than her eighteen years, small and vulnerable. She finished the telling and stood silent before them.

Danae rose from her chair and opened her arms to the girl. As Elana embraced the older woman, Aidan could almost see new life imbue her withered form.

Falbor choked back a sob, but made no move toward the two. After a long while Danae stroked Elana's cheek with her bony hand.

"My poor dear," she said, her voice hoarse from lack of use. "We lost our only daughter the night those demons stole our horses. The mare you brought back to us was the light of her life. She raised her from a foal." She turned to look at her husband, a question in her eyes. The man nodded back to her.

"The mare, Devi, you call her, please accept her as a gift from us. I can't bear to keep her when she would only remind me each day of that horrible night and our own loss. If she can help you, then at least in that, we've honored our daughters memory."

Falbor stepped up beside his wife and embraced her. Tears ran into his beard. "Charis, our girl, would have wanted it. She was never content to wait here, hoping to avoid trouble. You ease our grief by doing this in her memory as well."

Aidan felt the surge of Elana's Waking.

She threw back her head and in a clear voice said, "All that I do I will do for us both. Devi will be a living memorial to your daughter's spirit and together we will stand against the growing darkness."

The very walls of the cabin resonated as Elana spoke those words. Aidan turned toward Faris, but he seemed not to have noticed anything.

Falbor asked the three of them to stay for a bite to eat and they accepted the offer. Aidan was glad of the chance to infuse the small house with life. The couple hung on their every word, and Aidan found himself enjoying conversation with Falbor; talking with him about the horses, about farming, and about the land. He knew Falbor wasn't Elder Born, but he felt like kin, and were circumstances different, Aidan would have loved to stay here a while and work side by side with this man and his wife.

For the first time he understood some of his father's passion for the Valefolk. Darian had never held to the Elder Born prejudice that the Valefolk were somehow inferior. Aidan's own experience, however, was limited to those with whom he had little in common. Talking with Falbor and Danae gave him much to think about. He wished he could have more time with them.

Always before, when he thought about his father, he felt a sinking sense of failure. He became tongue tied at the thought of trying to rally groups of people together. As he talked with Falbor though, things appeared in a different light. It would be wonderful to meet people like them and speak with them individually... The thought trailed off, leaving him more hopeful than he'd been since starting the journey.

Too soon, their visit drew to a close. They said their goodbyes to the older couple, promising to return if their journey was successful.

Faris brought them back to check on the horses before inviting them to spend the night in his house. His one room cabin, set apart from the cluster of homes, was smaller than most. Once inside, Aidan saw that each item in the cabin stood meticulously in it's place. No one could be that neat.

"You're not here often, are you?" Aidan asked him.

Faris gave him a shrewd look. "No. Shay and I spend most of our time patrolling the boarders of the Barras."

There was more to that story, but right now Aidan was too tired to press.

Faris offered Elana the only bed, while he lit a fire in the fireplace. Aidan was glad to throw a blanket on the floor and wrap himself up in his cloak. He drifted off to the crackle of the dry wood burning, and the low conversation between Faris and Elana.

When he opened his eyes, their host was sitting, staring into the fire as though he had never slept.

"Good morning," Faris greeted him. The corner of his mouth curled up, though no humor showed in his eyes.

"Good morning."

"We've time for a quick bite and then we'd best be leaving. The fewer folks that see us, the less questions we'll have to answer and the quicker we can be on our way."

Aidan acknowledged the sense of that with a sleepy grunt.

"I have a little food here. Why don't you wake Elana and I'll scrape together something to eat." From Faris, it was an order, smooth on the outside, but backed by iron.

Aidan rankled. He wasn't used to taking orders from anyone. He liked the man, he just didn't like taking orders. He took a deep breath, willing his irritation to subside. He called to Elana who took her time coming out of sleep. She was paler than usual and Aidan could see the strain of last night on her face.

"How are you feeling?" he asked.

She gave him a small smile. "I've been better, but I've also been worse. I feel like I could sleep for a week, though. Why do we have to get up so early? I thought we'd be safe here."

"Faris wants us to get an early start to avoid questions."

She nodded. "I'm getting up." She sat up, her blankets bundled around her. "Aidan?"

"Yes."

"Do you think we'll find Laharan?"

He paused, looking closely at her. More than ever she reminded him of an older version of Arella. It made his chest tighten. "I won't stop until we do."

"Thank you," she whispered.

The morning was damp and gray when they quit the small cabin and retrieved their horses. Aidan was glad to be back with Kael again, though he tried to keep thoughts of a future separation at bay. He watched Elana with Devi, trying not to envy her. The mare was her own now. He could see how that changed the way Elana reached out to her, that, and her sense of kinship with the girl who gave her life trying to save Devi.

Banks of thick clouds obliterated the sunrise. Aidan could smell the rain they carried. At least it wasn't too cold. He was eager to be on their way. They saddled the horses, adjusted their packs and mounted up. Faris led them into the woods and in moments they were lost to the sight of the Clan.

"I appreciate the tales you shared last night," Faris slowed his stallion and twisted in the saddle to face them. "But you will have to be more forthcoming with me if I'm to travel with you."

Aidan caught Elana's eye. She nodded almost imperceptibly. He sighed, breathing a prayer to the Ancient Ones that this wasn't their biggest mistake yet.

"We are Elder Born," Elana started.

Nothing like getting to the point, Aidan thought.

A half smile played across Faris' face. "I know."

Elana's eyes flashed. "Well if you know everything, there seems little point in belaboring it."

Her outburst made Faris laugh out loud. "No offense meant, my lady. Please, by all means continue with your tale. I make no pretense to know all that you would disclose."

"Alright then," Elana continued. "Everything you heard us tell last night is true. It just isn't the whole story."

With more forthrightness than Aidan approved of, she told their new companion about the Ancient Ones' lost Gifts, about Laharan, about the prophecy, even about Marek - with the sole exception of the mind link.

"So, we are searching for Laharan." She looked defiantly at Faris. "I believe that I'm supposed to help bring these Gifts back to the Vale. That's why the Hunter took my parents. They were after me, trying to stop me." Her voice shrunk. "I only hope that we're doing the right thing."

He nodded, his face impassive, taking it all in. After a moment, he turned to Aidan. "Who are you really?"

Aidan started. "I'm Aidan. I told you that."

Faris frowned. "Don't play with me. I'm no simpleton to be trifled with." He gave Aidan a shrewd look. "How did you come to live in Glenariff?"

Aidan realized that Faris wouldn't stop at anything less than the truth.

"Lord Ulrich granted us asylum after my father's murder."

Faris raised an eyebrow. "Why would he do that?"

Ulrich is my father's younger brother.

"Who was your father?"

"Darian. I don't know if you heard of him. He was a bastard son, but Firstborn of the House of Tormey. His mother was Elder Born but died at his birth. There was little love lost between him and Ulrich." Aidan's temples throbbed as he spoke of his uncle. He didn't speak his suspicious of his Uncle playing some part in Darian's death. "My mother told me that Ulrich promised us asylum on the condition that she remain there with me. As the alternative was being hunted down and killed by his men, she accepted and we bided our time. Ulrich wasn't keen on another potential heir to the Lord's seat on the loose. When Ulrich swore allegiance to the Shadow King we had to risk leaving. Staying would have bought us only a guarantee of death." Aidan sighed. "I never intended to challenge Darcy's claim. I am also Elder Born. I wouldn't leave that for all the Lord's Seats in the Vale."

"Who said you'd have to?"

Aidan opened him mouth, but nothing came out.

"No one. It just hasn't been done before." Faris answered his own question. "I knew Darian. He was a hero to the people of Lanreath. I've never met a better man."

Aidan didn't know whether to feel proud, or miserable in comparison.

"It's no mistake that we met." Faris scrutinized him. "I can believe Elana's story about the Lost Gifts, but truth be told, I hold more stake in Darian's son on the Lord's Seat of Glenariff than all the Gifts imaginable popping out of myth or legend to save us. Even if the threat from the West is removed, it'll take more than that to restore the Vale." As he spoke, Faris' hand strayed to the hilt of his sword.

Aidan's stomach sank. He wasn't his father. The phrase, "A hero to the people" seemed ridiculous when applied to him. "After we help Elana I have to get to Farran. I made a promise."

"I'm sure you did." Faris gave him a knowing look. "But you can't put off destiny forever."

Aidan put a hand on Kael's neck to steady himself. His Waking surged out of control for just a moment. He had told no one, not even Elana, about Granny's parting word, "Destiny".

"That's not what's in front of us now," was all the reply he could muster.

Faris urged Shay forward, and led them off through the woods. The clouds made good on their promise and a soaking rain penetrated even the covered paths that their companion chose. Aidan set his gaze on Elana's back, trying to blot out Faris' keen blue eyes that haunted his thoughts.

Rain streamed down Elana's bare head, into her eyes, making it hard to see Faris, just in front of her. She was so wet, she might as well have taken a bath, which, she grinned to herself, she probably needed anyway.

She welcomed the rain. It made it hard to talk, and right now, she needed some time to think. The idea of Faris accompanying them was still new. He'd made her so angry at first she couldn't have imagined liking him, but the longer they traveled together, the more he grew on her. He was shrewd, that was for sure, and although she didn't trust him implicitly as she did Aidan, he intrigued her. He also made her laugh. That was something she hadn't done in too long.

All in all, she was glad for the addition of his company. He knew Lanreath well, by all accounts, and they needed someone to help them navigate their way through these folk.

These people and their customs were foreign to her. Though her parents had traveled through these lands before she was born, when they left Farran with her five years ago, they had followed the Fairway east to Merrion. The Fairway was the only real road through Lanreath, and most of the towns along the road, if you could call them that, were comprised of opportunists, hoping to siphon off some of the silver that passed their way. It wasn't a good living, and the Clans of Lanreath looked down on those renegade towns.

The towns in turn, separated themselves from any fealty to the Clans, forming loose groupings, each wary of the others and of any outsiders. The memories Elana carried of the people there were laced with darkness and distrust.

They chose Merrion at Reeves' urging, hoping to, in a quiet way, plant seeds of trust between the Elder Born and the Valefolk. Using their Skills to teach, and to heal, they attempted, one person, one family at a time, to counter the widespread fear, and the hatred born of ignorance, that the Valefolk harbored toward the Elder Born. Most of the Valefolk they encountered never knew they were Elder Born. Her parents design was to kindle some hope in the hearts of the Valefolk, leaving them more kindly disposed toward others because of their meeting. Hamilton and Madelyn had made a special effort to cultivate friendships with those, who like Farrell, the innkeeper back in their village, were not hopelessly steeped in the narrowness of mind that overran the Vale. Elana knew her parents genuinely loved these new friends and though it didn't seem like much, it was their way of standing against the Shadow.

Thinking of her parents made Elana's chest hurt. She tried not to picture where they were now, or what might be happening to them. She refused to acknowledge that this attempted rescue might be for nothing. Fiercely she shut out those thoughts.

Her mind, casting about for something else to grab onto, turned to the golden mare she was riding. Her fingers twined in the wet mane. She would never forget Danae's face as she spoke of her daughter, or the tears that ran into Falbor's grizzled beard. It wasn't just about her parents. There was something even bigger at stake here. Something she wasn't at all sure she understood.

The rain followed them, soaking them for the remainder of the day and into the night as they set up camp. Elana was now thoroughly sick of it, and Faris' displeasure was palpable. Only Aidan seemed to accept it with equanimity. Reaching out quietly in his direction, the only thing she could feel was the bond between him and Kael. The big horse consumed his mind, and the pain there made her draw back, ashamed that she'd intruded.

She'd forgotten that Kael belonged to Faris now. Her heart ached for Aidan. It seemed so unfair that she should be given Devi, whom she'd just bonded with, while every day brought him closer to loosing the stallion that had become a part of his very being.

She tried to shut him out, to shut everyone out. It just got to be too much sometimes. Each of them remained wrapped in their own thoughts. Even in the thickness of the trees, where Faris found space enough for them to stop, the drip, drip of the rain off the new leaves took all cheer from the small, smoking fire, and made sleep a miserable affair. At least, she consoled herself, she wasn't also trying to keep Marek at bay. She didn't think she would have had the strength to keep him out much longer.

They woke the next morning enshrouded in mist, but the rain had stopped. Neither Faris nor Aidan attempted a fire. They ate a cold breakfast of meat and flatbread in silence and then saddled the horses for the day's ride.

"Where are we going?" Elana asked Faris.

"West." Faris tightened his girth, not turning to answer.

Elana grimaced. "And what lies to the west?" she asked, trying without success to keep the frustration out of her voice.

"Ah, that would be the question."

She glared at him, her hands on her hips until he laughed out loud.

"Easy, my lady. No need to spend your temper on me. We must cross through the lands of the Dundas, the largest and most powerful Clan in Lanreath. Sneaking through like thieves would only raise suspicion. I'd prefer to go straight to Payton, their leader and seek his goodwill. I've had dealings with him in the past. He's a good man. I'd wager he'd be willing to aid our journey, if only by providing information on the whereabouts of the Black Knights and the Hunters."

Elana saw Aidan nod at this, though she caught the undercurrent of worry about him.

"What?" she asked him.

"How close are they to Drumcard?"

"Not that far," Faris conceded. "Cahermore, their main city, is well fortified. Ulrich's soldiers have not dared approach it. The fighting has for now, been limited to the river."

Elana gave him a questioning look. She didn't know much about this part of the Vale.

"Historically, the river has been neutral," Faris explained, "allowing trade from all peoples to pass through. In the last few years Ulrich has attempted to control it, and has paid dearly for his greed. Payton's men are fierce fighters, protecting their own lands. Ulrich's mercenaries care only for gold, women, and strong drink." His lip curled in disgust as though the mention of them left a sour taste in his mouth.

"I'd heard of the boarder disputes," Aidan said slowly. "Of course, they weren't spoken of in that light, but I guessed as much. I just have no wish to draw Ulrich's men after us. I'm afraid I would be a bait they couldn't resist. I don't want to bring trouble to any of the good people here."

"Trouble?" Faris laughed. "I don't think they'd see you in quite that light."

Aidan dropped his eyes and said no more.

"You don't know your own friends, lad," Faris muttered. "But you're about to meet them."

Elana felt the turmoil in Aidan and reached out a tentative thought. She understood his hesitancy. It was only natural. He was Elder Born. It was unheard of for any of their race to hold a Lord's seat, and that seemed to be a hope that Faris grabbed on to.

Aidan turned to look at her and she offered him a small smile. He returned it and she felt his mood lighten. She wished they could talk openly about this, but she didn't want to bring it up with Faris here.

They made better time without the rain, and Faris pointed out landmarks and regaled them with stories of the Dundas. From what he said, they were the fiercest warriors in the Vale. Living under the

Shadow Hills and in proximity to Drumcard, which had become steadily more corrupt through the generations, it was a necessity for them, but a necessity they relished. Faris made no further mention of Aidan's lineage, or the expectations surrounding him.

By nightfall they crossed over the boarder into the lands of the Dundas. They camped in a clearing, taking turns to keep watch. Elana woke stiff and aching in the morning, what little sleep she had taken had been woven through with disturbing dreams; Black Knights following their trail, the Hunter standing in front of her laughing and laughing, and always overhead, almost out of sight, a falcon circling.

"It was a Shadow night," Faris remarked over breakfast.

Elana shot him a questioning look.

"It's a granny's tale. They say some nights the Shadow from the West moves down and stalks these lands. Last night was one of those."

Aidan sat straight up, staring at him. "That's no granny's tale," he said in a low voice.

Faris raised an eyebrow. "What do you mean?"

"That's exactly what happens. I used to see it on our farm. The Shadow would creep down from the far hills. The animals all felt it. Kael always knew. They would be restless. We would have disturbing dreams; wake up feeling like we had never rested."

"You could see it?" Faris' voice was incredulous.

"It's how my Skills run," Aidan explained. "I see things, hear things that most people miss. The animals don't miss them though."

Faris looked at him with a new respect. "That would come in handy."

"I don't know. It doesn't do much good fighting a war, or rallying people. It's an unusual way to be Skilled."

"Unusual," Faris mused, "I'll give you that. But don't sell it short. I've lived next to the land my whole life. I'd give plenty to have a bit of your Skills." He gave a chuckle. "You're going to be a surprise to them, that's for sure, and to yourself too, I'd wager. I'd like to be there to see how it all comes out."

Elana wasn't sure what he was talking about, and from the look on Aidan's face, he didn't know any more than she did.

The sun hadn't cleared the treetops when three men on horseback rode out from the woods and stood in their path.

"Halt. You are riding through the land of the Dundas. State your name and purpose."

Faris raised a hand in salute. "My name is Faris, nephew of Varen, leader of the Barras. I am here at his request, to seek the counsel of Payton. These two are friends of the Barras and are under my protection."

The soldiers exchanged a brief word.

"Welcome, Faris. Your name is known to us, even without your lineage. You are a friend of the Dundas. You are free to travel through these lands. We will allow your friends to pass with you if you will give your word for them."

"It is done then. I speak for them without hesitation, and will take all responsibility for them myself."

The soldier who was speaking bowed his head, then raised it, and in a more conversational tone added, "I would take the northern approach. The fighting has moved closer and I wouldn't want you to find yourselves in the middle of it. Not with two charges on your hands."

Elana felt her face flush. She hated being talked about as though she wasn't there. She was just about to say something, when Faris shot her a quick glare. Taking a deep breath, she contained herself. Her cheeks burned. She didn't want Faris thinking that she would fly in a temper at the slightest provocation. That was not who she was raised to be. She didn't know why her temper seemed so short lately.

Faris led them further north after this, stopping often to check landmarks and confirm their bearings. He seemed pleased with their progress and they traveled until nightfall without incident.

The next morning they rode past the first village they had seen since they left the Barras.

258

"I'd like to stop in and have a word with the smith here. I know him well, and he might have information."

They followed him into the village. People stared at them as they rode through the streets. No children played around the houses and the men and women they saw passed one another in the street with the barest nods, not stopping to chat or pass the time of day. There was no laughter, no smiles.

Faris navigated the narrow lanes, stopping at last in front of a large yard at the edge of the village. Smoke rose out from a wooden shed in the yard, and the ringing of hammer and anvil made Elana's ears throb.

A strapping man, bare chested and soot blackened, raised his hand in greeting. The yard fell silent.

"Faris, my friend! What trouble are you stirring up now?"

His joviality seemed out of place in this village.

"Trouble? You do me an injustice!" Faris leaped off his horse and embraced the man. "Niall, these are my two friends, Aidan and Elana."

"Friends indeed." The smith raised an eyebrow. "You've let the lad ride your horse. When did you get him back?"

Faris' grin evaporated. "He brought him back to me, but a few days ago. Quite by accident, but I don't hold that against him."

The smith tipped his head, scrutinizing Aidan. "Could I press you to stay for lunch? I accepted a barrel of ale in exchange for some swords I forged and there's still some left."

"What are we waiting for?" Faris' face lit up.

Niall led them behind the smithy to a small barn with four ample stalls. An aged gray cart horse with a kind eye stood in one stall, munching cut grass. He seemed used to other horses coming and going, and sniffed the noses of each of the newcomers with equanimity. When the three travelers had untacked the horses and seen to their comfort, they followed the big man to the house.

"It's been dark times here, most all the young men gone to the fighting, and Shadow nights blackening folks' mood more often than not." Niall shook his head. "But you're a sight for sore eyes. The first time I've thought to smile since I can't remember when." He clapped Faris on the back, nearly sending him sprawling in the dirt.

"I could do with a little less exuberance," Faris retorted.

Niall laughed out loud and led them up the stone walk to his home. The house was well built, fashioned out of planed logs. Elana noted the attention to detail on all the iron work. Niall was indeed a gifted smith.

Aidan's face lit up in this place. He turned to the big man. "You have a wonderful feel for the iron. I've rarely seen work that could equal it.

Niall beamed at him. "I love it. It's in my blood. Nothing else I'd rather be doing."

"It shows," Aidan said appreciatively.

Niall insisted that they all sit at the sturdy table while he poured the ale and ladled hot stew from a pot over the fire. He produced a loaf of rich brown bread and a tub of fresh butter to round out their lunch.

"It's simple fare, but it keeps me strong." He patted his muscled chest, by way of proof.

"That and grueling hours in your forge," Faris teased.

"Better than hours in a saddle," Niall shot back. "It's not natural for a man to use legs other than his own. Pulling carts - now that's honest work for a horse. I've no argument with riding in one of them. You can sit down proper like, and walk proper like when the journey's done." He laughed heartily. "To each his own, my friend. I've no more desire to straddle one of your beasts than you've desire to swing my hammer."

Faris lifted his mug to that and took a deep pull of the dark ale. "We always do manage to agree in the end." He winked at his friend, then his face grew serious. "I didn't realize that the Shadow was so heavy on you here. We're farther east, and out of range of Drumcard. It was hard to ride in and see this happy place so somber."

260

Niall nodded. "It was just last full moon Payton called out all the young men to join the boarder fighting. We've lost a dozen of our finest to Ulrich's mercenaries. That's not something you just put behind you. There's many a face I look for by habit and then it hits me all over again that they're gone."

Niall took a slow drink. "Sometimes I think it should have been me. Payton won't let me fight. Says I can do more damage forging swords than wielding one. It doesn't sit right with me though."

Elana could almost see the sorrow wrapping around him. A long silence filled the room.

Faris broke it at last. "What's changed? There's been fighting at the boarder for years now."

"Last month Ulrich swore allegiance to the Shadow King." Aidan's quiet voice answered the question.

Niall stared at him, his face growing pale. "How do you know this?"

Aidan shot Faris a quick look, set his jaw and answered. "I am Ulrich's nephew. My father, Darian, was his elder brother, though a bastard to the line. I have lived as a prisoner on Ulrich's lands for the past five years, since my father's murder." He took a deep breath. "The night Ulrich swore allegiance I left. I only pray that my mother and younger sister got out safely as we had planned."

"Darian's son?" Niall looked at him in awe. "Darian's name is legend with our people. Maybe there is hope after all."

"I am his son. I am not Darian. I could never fill his place." Aidan looked into the big man's eyes. "Don't rest your hopes in me, Niall. I'm afraid I would only disappoint."

Elana bit back a retort at the bitterness in his words. It wasn't true.

Niall shook himself like someone waking from sleep. He ignored Aidan's words and scrutinized the young man as someone would a horse to purchase. "I see it now. I only saw her once, but I could never forget her. You favor your father, but there's some of Bree there too."

Tears welled up in Aidan's tawny eyes, so like his mother's. I'm more like her than my father. Except my Skills are not like either one. I don't really know how I fit in."

Elana winced at such open talk about his Skills. She was still unused to such a thing. It didn't seem to ruffle their host, though. She glanced over at Faris in time to see the corners of his mouth curling up, as if at some private joke.

Niall pushed himself back from the table, nearly upsetting his chair. He pulled Aidan to his feet and embraced him heartily. "It's an honor to have you in my home. If there's anything I can do for you, anything at all, I am at your service."

"Thank you," Aidan managed to gasp out.

Niall topped off Aidan's mug of ale and sat back down shaking his head. "To think I would live to see Darian and Bree's son at my table. I thought you'd gone back to live with the Elder Born. And not that I'd have blamed you if you had. I'd bet my forge that it was that conniving weasel Ulrich that was behind Darian's death. No one else stood to gain as much from it."

The muscles in Aidan's jaw tightened.

"And to think," the big man continued, "that he'd managed to keep you captive these past years." He stopped his ranting. "You said you had a younger sister?"

"Yes. My mother was with child when my father was killed. Arella never knew her father."

"I'm sorry," Niall said. "That's horrible, horrible." He slammed his fist into the table. "We've got to take him to Payton." This last bit was addressed to Faris.

"Yes, that was my thought too," Faris answered. "But I didn't want to go strolling up there without finding out how things stood."

"You won't just go strolling up there alone." Niall glowered at imaginary adversaries. "I'm going with you."

No matter what Faris or Aidan said, there was no arguing with Niall. He was like a force of nature; once his mind was made up you just had to ride out the storm to its conclusion. Elana wondered at the authority Payton carried to keep this man from battle in the first place.

Faris related an abbreviated version of their story to his old friend, leaving out, Elana noted, any mention of her finding the lost Gifts. Either he didn't believe her in the first place, or else he placed little stock in help from that quarter. She rankled at the omission. It felt like wasting precious time, to travel yet farther south just to announce Aidan's presence to some Clan ruler who in all likelihood would try and move heaven and earth to put him on the Lord's Seat of Glenariff. Aidan didn't even want the Lord's Seat. What did these Valefolk know about the choices in front of him?

She paused in the middle of her thinking. Or did he? Aidan, without any hesitation, just about claimed his blood right to the Lord's Seat, here in Niall's house. He didn't hesitate to reveal his Elder Born blood either. Elana knew he was conflicted about filling his father's place, but then Darian wasn't on the Lord's Seat. Maybe Aidan figured this was what he would do. If so, he'd certainly come to the right place.

The only problem was that she had believed him when he promised to help her.

For the first time since leaving Marek, Elana doubted the wisdom of that choice. She was still glad to have Marek's presence gone from her mind, but now with that feeling of invasion removed, she could remember why she had followed him so willingly in the first place. He was the only one who seemed to believe in her almost more than she believed in herself. It seemed like Aidan had believed in her, but now she wasn't sure if he would hold fast to his promise, with the Lord's Seat of Glenariff dangling in front of him.

She scowled. There wasn't anything for it, but to go along. She didn't know the way and it was foolishness to head out alone in these lands. But she resented the delay. Who knew what her parents were going through right now, what they were suffering?

A voice at her elbow made her start.

"What is troubling you, my lady?" Faris caught her eye and held it until she looked away. "Do you think I've forgotten my promise to you? The direct route is not always the fastest."

Elana said nothing and turned away from the challenge in his eyes. She didn't know what to make of this man. If he hadn't made his Valefolk lineage abundantly clear, she would have thought him to be Elder Born. She was unused to someone reading her so clearly. All the Valefolk she'd known, and most of the Elder Born, for that matter, were so much less aware of what people were thinking. Maybe the differences weren't so cut and dried as she'd imagined.

Niall refreshed their supplies and to Elana's amazement saddled his old cart horse an led the party out of the village while their shadows were still small.

"I thought you didn't ride," Aidan said to the smith.

"I don't." That was the only reply he gave.

Faris laughed out loud at this. "You'd best be content with that, young man. If you can explain Niall, you will have solved a mystery indeed."

The road was only wide enough here for two to travel abreast. Niall led the way with Aidan beside him. Elana could hear Aidan asking him questions about his trade and Niall giving explanations far more detailed than she had the patience to listen to.

She dropped back to ride alongside Faris.

"I'm sorry for doubting you." Elana broke the silence tentatively. They hadn't spoken since his words to her in Niall's house.

"Don't trouble yourself, I'm used to it by now." His brusque answer seemed out of character.

Elana looked at him questioningly.

He met her gaze but his eyes were far away. "Nothing," he said, then pressed Shay into a canter, leaving her and Devi behind.

Taken aback, she watched him ride off. Her Waking prickled and she caught a glimpse in her mind of his uncle Varen and a younger man, coarse featured, who she knew must be the cousin Wirt. She forgot about being offended and began to think that she knew a lot less about Faris than she'd imagined.

CHAPTER 13

THE DUNDAS

Two days of hard riding brought them to the gates of Cahermore, the ruling city of the Dundas. A yellow and green flag snapped in the stiff breeze above the iron gates. Elana understood now why Ulrich had avoided an outright assault here. Towering stone walls circled the city, where bowmen, stationed at even intervals, commanded a view of the entire countryside. The only way it could be captured was by siege, and from what Faris and Niall told them, the main strength of the Dundas was out fighting. Any attempt at a siege would leave Ulrich's men trapped between the city walls and the Dundas army.

For the first time since she left Marek's home, Elana entertained the hope of safety. It would be good to sleep behind those stone walls tonight. The further west they traveled, the more uneasy she had become. Visions of the Shadow reaching out to seize her haunted her thoughts, usually in the moments before drifting off into sleep. It didn't make for restful nights. She guarded her Waking now with a vigilance, realizing that it might well be the difference between life and death, should it draw a Hunter to them.

The guards at the fortified iron gates knew both Niall and Faris, and let them through without incident.

"I don't know who'll be happier to reach this journey's end," Niall grunted, "me or Ramble." He stroked his gelding's neck. "It's been years since I've asked him to carry me."

"Wishing you had taken that old cart now?" Faris teased.

"No. I was getting too soft anyway."

Elana stifled a laugh. 'Soft' was never a word she would have associated with Niall.

The smith led them through the tangle of cobbled streets, toward the interior of the city, unperturbed by the stares that they drew from the residents. Cahermore reminded Elana of the old section of Bellport. The buildings were thoughtfully fashioned, with attention to detail in the carving of stone and wood and the working of iron. An agelessness hung about it. The mark of the Elder Born was strong in this place. Not surprising, really, Elana thought. It was close to Drumcard, the city of the Orchard Tree Elders, renowned craftsmen, before the Forgetting.

Elana saw few young men and fewer horses. Most of the people here were women; some with baskets on their arms and small children clinging to their skirts, and many tending stands in the streets where they sold early fruits, fresh baked brown breads, cheeses, and simple woven cloth. Older men, bent and scarred, sat and talked in doorways, stopping their conversation to watch the travelers as they passed. Every now and then Elana would see a younger man, leaning on a crutch, or nursing the stub of an arm wrapped up in bandages. She averted her eyes, trying not to stare.

For all its beauty, Cahermore felt hollow, bereft of vitality. The ache in her chest that never completely left her since the night the Hunter came, grew more acute. It was more than pain though, that she felt here. It was despair. These people had lost their hope. She swallowed hard, regretting her impatience with Faris and Aidan.

In spite of her vigilance, her Waking nudged her again as they approached a massive stone house near the center of the city. Coming here wasn't a mistake.

Niall dismounted Ramble with care, and walked, stiff legged, to the door. Before he could knock, an armed guard opened it.

"We need to see Payton," Niall stated without prologue.

The man looked them over. "Bring your animals round to the back. I'll see that stalls are readied for them."

Niall grunted and led them around to the back of the house where a stable opened up to a generous yard. The only occupants were two heavy boned horses and an old donkey. A flock of chickens scratched at the grass in the yard and a stable lad scurried to ready four stalls for the new arrivals.

Niall raised an eyebrow at the sight of the two horses. "Well, this is a surprise. The gray there on the right belongs to Kenrich, Payton's son. He looked at Aidan. "He's about your age I'd guess, and a fierce fighter. It must have been something urgent to bring him back now. Payton depends on him in the front. The men have given their hearts to that one. He's a born leader."

Elana felt Aidan wince as though he'd been delivered a blow. She scowled, disliking this Kenrich already.

Faris stepped up alongside Aidan, catching his eye. "His strength is on the battlefield, I have to give him that. He's adept with sword, spear and bow. I've seen few his equal." He lowered his voice to a conspiratorial whisper. "Myself, I've more respect for a leader who knows how to listen to his people. It's one thing to command an army, it's another to lead a people."

Niall looked over at them and frowned. "You always did have a way of seeing round things to the other side. Yes, I suppose if you put it that way. But my hat's off to the lad, nonetheless. I'd follow him into battle any day."

"And you wouldn't be misguided to do so." Faris' smile warmed for his friend. "I would fight alongside him, and be stronger for it. There's few I can say as much for."

"Yes, but that's you," Niall said. He turned to Aidan and Elana. "Sometime when he's not here, I have some stories that'd make your eyes pop. He'll never speak of it, and most of his people don't even know. But there's not a man in Lanreath I respect more than this smooth talking horse rider."

Faris shot him a warning look. "Don't get carried away, my friend."

Elana caught Aidan's eye. From the look he gave her, she imagined he'd find a way to get some time alone with Niall. For all the stories of themselves that they shared with Faris, they still knew precious little about him.

When the horses were unsaddled and stalled, they followed Niall back to the big house. The guard opened the door once again for them, ushering them inside. Elana caught his eye by accident and for an instant her Waking flared up. Then it was gone, leaving her with a leaden feeling inside. She positioned herself between Faris and Aidan, drawing comfort from their proximity. She wanted to get Aidan alone so she could talk with him about it. Maybe after the meeting there would be a chance. She tried to push aside her fears. For now, it would be wisdom to concentrate on the meeting before them.

The floors were bare stone, as were the perimeter walls, with no tapestries or rugs to soften or warm them. It was a stark contrast to Marek's home, where every detail spoke of comfort and wealth. Elana could feel the age in this house, its walls seemed to have stories to tell, if only one knew how to listen. She wondered if it had always been this severe, or if that was a reflection of the current situation. Looking over at Aidan, she saw him run his hands over the carved stone of a doorway. His eyes looked far away.

They followed the guard, down the dark hallways where stubs of candles guttered in sconces, until they came to a solid wood door. The man knocked twice and waited.

"Come."

The voice that answered the knock sounded impatient, angry at the interruption.

The uniformed man opened the door and motioned for them to enter. Elana felt like she had swallowed a rock. Of the four of them, only Faris looked unconcerned.

He led them into the room, stopping before two men, who appeared to be in the middle of an argument. The elder of the two, Elana guessed to be Payton. A gold circlet banded his gray flecked hair, and a rich cloak of indigo hung over his shoulders. He was powerfully built, with clear eyes and a firm jaw; a man in his prime, in spite of the gray; well able to wield the huge sword belted to his waist.

The other man was surely Kenrich. As she looked from Payton toward him, it was like seeing a younger double. He was dark haired and broad shouldered, with a face that Elana would have thought handsome were it not red with anger. He was trying with difficulty, to compose himself now, as they walked in. His clothes were well made, though much worn and soiled, as though he'd just ridden in and not taken the time to change.

Faris bowed. "It is an honor, my Lord," he nodded at the older man, "Kenrich," he tipped his head toward the red faced younger man.

Payton's face broke into a smile, and Elana felt as though the sun had just come out in this cold, severe place.

"Faris," Payton cried, and strode toward them, clasping their friend to him in a hearty embrace. "It's been too long, though I'm sure you've had trouble enough on your hands without borrowing any of ours." He gestured to the others with a sweep of his arm. "Welcome all. And Niall, you old scoundrel, don't tell me you're here to try and talk me into letting you go to the front. I won't hear of it. You're the best sword maker in all my land. I've half a mind to order you to Cahermore, where I can keep my eye on you myself."

Niall's smile looked strained. "No, no. No need for that. I'm resigned to shaping iron. It soothes me to know that my blades are bringing down Ulrich's mercenaries, even if I'm restrained from wielding one myself."

Faris grinned at his friend's discomfort, then his face sobered. "He's not here on his own behalf, but on ours. We need to speak with you."

Payton glanced at his son.

"Kenrich can hear what we have to say," Faris answered the unspoken question. "This affects us all."

Elana felt, more than saw Aidan cringe.

"You must be hungry from your travels," Payton addressed them. "Go freshen up, while I arrange for something to eat and then you can tell me what news brings you here." He strode to the door and gave orders to the guard, who disappeared down the dim corridor.

A moment later an elderly woman with kind eyes bustled up and led each of them in turn to their own rooms. Elana's room overlooked the stable and the yard, and the deep set window stood open, inviting in the mild spring air. Tapestries hung from the walls here, lending warmth and cheer to the surroundings, and the bed was made with a beautiful rose colored quilt, the likes of which Elana had never seen before. They left her there to wash the travel dirt from her hands and face, which she gladly did. The pitcher held only cold water, but it was refreshing, and the soft towels were a luxury in themselves.

She curled up on the window ledge waiting for them to return, and watched the goings on in the yard below. Hoofbeats caught her ear and she stuck her head out the window in time to see a man gallop up on a lathered horse, scattering chickens as he flew into the yard. He vaulted off, shouted for the stable boy to take his mount, and ran for the house. Moments later, he appeared again, this time with Kenrich. The two talked briefly, then Kenrich gave the man his own horse and he galloped off once more, as though the Shadow King himself were after him. Kenrich saw that the stable boy looked after the man's mount, and then made his way back to the house, shoulders bent.

A knock at the door interrupted her viewing, and Elana put aside her questions as the prospect of telling their story to Payton loomed closer.

It was Faris this time, and he greeted Elana with slow smile.

"Have you forgiven me for the delay yet?" he asked her.

"You know I have," she answered. "I just don't know what our coming can do for them. There's no hope in this place. It makes my heart hurt."

He gave her a strange look. "Payton's waiting for us. Niall took Aidan down, said he wanted to show him some of the iron work here."

Elana's eyes twinkled, remembering the look Aidan had given her. "I can't wait to hear what stories Niall has about you."

Faris scowled. "That scoundrel. I'll have his tongue from his mouth if he spreads stories about me." He glared at Elana, which only served to amuse her more.

"It's too late now," she said. "Anyway, we told you our story, it's only fair that you tell us yours."

His voice softened. "It is only fair. I just hoped I would be the one to do the telling. Niall embellishes and I don't want you to get a false impression of me."

He offered Elana his arm and led her down the corridor. Clearly, the subject was closed for now.

In silence, Faris escorted her to a great room. The long table in the center of the room beckoned, with steaming plates laid out for them. There was a door set in each of the four walls and an ancient tapestry hung from the far end of the room. Shafts of sunlight from high narrow windows filtered down through the dim expanse and fell in stripes across the flagstone floor. The place felt empty with only Niall and Aidan sitting together at the table. Even their voices sounded hollow, echoing off the bare walls and floor. Elana shivered, feeling suddenly small and insignificant. Before they could sit down, Payton entered from the opposite door.

"Kenrich will be joining us shortly," he said. "We've just had some bad news from the river, but I'll let him share that." He lowered himself into a chair with a sigh, and Elana's heart went out to this man who carried the weight of the Dundas on his shoulders.

The guard appeared once more, bearing glasses and a pitcher of dark ale. He poured a glass for each of them and retreated through the open side door. Payton lifted his glass.

"To friends," he said.

The rest of them lifted their glasses in response and drank in silence. The door on the far side of the room opened once more, and Kenrich joined them.

"My apologies for the delay. I just received word from the river. A Hunter made an appearance at the fighting. It seems that he now has a power over men's minds. Wherever he is, men lose the heart to fight. They have reported afterwards hearing dark words spoken in their minds with such force that they never doubted them. For the first time in all these years, Ulrich's mercenaries routed our men. It was a slaughter. We lost many of our best." He looked at his father in despair. "I have failed you. I shouldn't have come. This is my fault."

Payton shook his head. "No. The fault lies with me. I sent for you. There was no way to know…" His voice broke.

Niall sat with head bent, mourning the news. Elana exchanged glances with Aidan. His face was pale and grim and his mind was closed to her. She could only guess at his turmoil.

"I'm so sorry," Faris said. His eyes traveled from Kenrich to Payton. "But there is no life in blame." He took a deep breath. "I wish I could lend you strength of arms now, but I cannot. I do though, have something perhaps even more valuable to share." He looked long at each of the leaders and then spoke one word. "Hope."

Payton's eyes rekindled. "I have never known you to banter with me. Speak clearly now. What is this hope you bring?"

Faris took a long drink of his ale and turned to Aidan and Elana and nodded. He began weaving the story, telling of his meeting with Aidan and Elana in the woods outside the Barras Clan. At his prompting, Aidan and Elana told their own parts in turn, stopping frequently to answer the questions that Payton fired at them. Elana noted that Aidan shared more than she had heard him speak of before, not holding back either the implications of his lineage, or his consternation at the choices before him.

Kenrich remained silent throughout the telling, but whenever Aidan spoke, Elana could feel the life quicken in him. His eyes never left Aidan's face, and he hung on every word with a fierceness bordering on reverence.

As Aidan finished his story, tears rolled down Payton's cheeks.

"Hope indeed!" He pushed back his chair and took Aidan's hands in his own. "Darian was one of my dearest friends. When he was killed, a part of me died as well. To think that I'd live to see his son standing in my own hall. We all thought that Bree had fled to Farran with you. We feared we'd never hear of you again." He rose, pulled Aidan to his feet and embraced him in a bear hug that left him breathless. "I would have laid down my life for Darian. I will do no less for you. Whatever you need, whatever we can do to aid you, it is yours."

Aidan's face was pale and drawn, but his tawny eyes were bright. "I don't know how to thank you. I'm only afraid I've done nothing to warrant such a reception. My path leads me away from this place for an indefinite time, though it is my heart's desire to return here."

Kenrich stepped forward, and dropped to one knee before Aidan. "My father cannot literally give his life to help you, as he has the lives of the Dundas in his care, but if he will release me, then I can." He looked up at Payton, who nodded slowly. "I pledge myself to help you in whatever way I am able. I will travel with you until your task is completed and then I will return to our people with you, and help you to regain the Lord's Seat that is rightfully yours."

Payton stepped back and beamed. "I couldn't ask for more."

Aidan stammered an unintelligible thanks. This had clearly gone farther than he was comfortable with.

Kenrich sat back down, a fire burning in his eyes. Aidan too, sat down, but like someone moving in his sleep.

Payton turned from him and addressed Elana. "My dear, I am so sorry for the capture of your parents. You are brave indeed to undertake this quest, both for them and ultimately for us all. I'm afraid I understand less of this than I do of fighting and ruling, but something in me tells me that your success is more important to us than even defeating Ulrich's men." He took her hand gently in his own. "Darian spoke of your parents often; they were dear friends of his. He also spoke of their daughter and the unusual strength of her Skills. You are uniquely equipped for what is before you. It is no accident that set you on this path."

Elana's Waking surged at these words and Aidan turned to look at her. Even Payton leaned back. "There are some among the Dundas who would say that the Ancient Ones are a myth, and that the Elder Born but another Clan hidden high up in the Border Mountains. Darian showed me too much to believe that anymore. We will do everything in our power to help you succeed in finding these Gifts that you speak of. I have a premonition that their recovery will be remembered long after all other details are lost." He looked past Elana, as though he saw something outside the confines of the room.

Shaking his head, he brought his focus back to her. "Faris did well to bring you both here. I now know why we are seeing involvement from the Hunter. I'm afraid that it is you he is seeking. You will need both protection and a strategy to cross Lanreath. The Barras gave you their finest - mounts unequalled anywhere in the Vale, and Faris to lead you." Payton threw back his shoulders. "I would not be outdone by them." He surveyed the small group. "I give you my son and only heir, Kenrich. He is mighty in battle and proven against the Black Knights. You will be glad of him if you find yourselves confronted."

Kenrich bowed his head, but his eyes sparkled, and Elana saw him finger the hilt of his sword. She decided she would try and overlook his fervent desire to plan Aidan's future, and just be grateful for his strength lent to their journey.

Payton turned to the smith, a wry smile crossing his face. "Niall's skill at arms is legend, and only his excellence at the forge keeps him here while any of the Dundas draw sword. Well, now I release him. Niall, if you will, I would have you accompany this group and see them safely to their journey's end.

Niall's chest swelled and his eyes flashed. "It would be my honor," he boomed.

Elana was genuinely grateful for his addition to the party, separate from any of his abilities. She had grown quite fond of the huge smith. Faris too, nodded and gripped his old friend's arm, and Aidan's face relaxed for the first time since this meeting began.

Payton called through the open door behind him and the guard appeared almost instantly. He shot her and Aidan a quick look, and Elana winced at the malice she felt from him. Had he been listening in on their conversation? The others didn't seem to notice anything.

Payton gave him orders for the preparations needed to travel. The man bowed, turned on his heel and left.

"Who is he?" Elana asked Payton.

"Excuse me?" he looked at her, puzzled.

"That man. Who is he?"

"Holt. His name is Holt." Payton's brow furrowed. "Why do you ask?"

The question had flown out of Elana before she had time to consider it. She stammered now, "I just... I thought... I had the sense..." Her words trailed off. Payton stared at her, clearly puzzled.

"What did you feel from him?" Aidan's tawny eyes held her own, not letting her look away.

"What do you mean by that?" Niall's voice was incredulous.

"It's Elana's Skill," Aidan answered. "She can sense what's going on inside others. You would do well to pay attention."

Aidan spoke with an authority on her behalf that he would never have been comfortable with on his own. Elana's face reddened.

He glared at her, daring her to gainsay him. "I felt it too, so don't try and deny it."

Faris interrupted them. "You felt what?"

Aidan raised an eyebrow at her. She nodded back.

"I felt something from him when we first arrived. He caught my eye and I had a vague sense, nothing sure. Then when he walked in just now, there was something dark, angry, wanting to harm. I don't know how to describe it." She shrugged her shoulders and raised her hands.

Payton's scowl deepened. "I don't know what to think. He conducted himself with honor on the battlefield, and has always been loyal to myself and Kenrich. We asked him to come back here almost a moon ago. He had been taken prisoner by the Black Knights and fought his way free. He said he saw a Hunter when he was with them and that the man questioned him extensively." Payton lowered his voice. "It's my belief he was tortured. Poor man, came back shattered, didn't know his own name for a while. I promised him a place in my home for as long as he desired it. It was the least I could do."

Elana's insides turned to ice. She tried to push aside the thought of her parents suffering in the same manner.

Payton gave a short order to Kenrich, who excused himself.

"Kenrich will see that the man is guarded until you are well gone."

Elana appreciated his offer, but realized that it was too late. The damage was done.

Aidan's hand on her arm brought her back. He met her eyes and for the first time since she knew him, she felt his mind reaching out to hers. Two thoughts came through. "The Hunter." And, "Mind link."

Aidan tried to ignore the sinking feeling that settled in his stomach. The room itself had cried out a warning when the guard walked back in. Almost as disturbing, was that without thinking about it, Aidan had reached out and touched Elana's mind. After what he'd seen of Marek, he'd sworn to himself that he'd never try and use his Skills in that way. He had pulled back as soon as it happened, but that didn't undo it. He wanted to say something to Elana, to apologize, but with everyone always there, no chance presented itself.

Faris and Niall were overseeing the preparations for their journey, stocking oiled leather sacks with cooked meats, loaves of twice baked flatbread, yellow wheels of sharp cheese, and last year's apples from the ample kitchens. Kenrich however, took it upon himself to shadow Aidan like some devotee, plying him with questions about his life on the farm and his plans for the future. The first accentuated his worry over his mother and sister's welfare, and he had no clear response for the second. Aidan wasn't used to so much company and felt a bit like a trapped animal, growing edgy with all the attention. He did make some good use of the time, asking Kenrich to study the maps of Lanreath with him. There weren't many, but Kenrich dug them all out and the two of them spent hours poring over them.

Payton too, made a point to talk with him, though that was more welcome. The leader of the Dundas shared stories of his father, stories that Aidan had never heard before. Aidan soaked them in, hungry for the connection that was severed so abruptly five years ago. He had been too consumed with his own world then to really understand what his father was attempting to do.

"Darian was brilliant," Payton told him, his dark eyes shining. "He was one of those that made everyone around him feel bigger for his being there. He always seemed to see the best version of whomever he was with."

"I remember," Aidan answered, images flitting through his mind. "At least he was that way with us at home. Our world crumbled the day he was killed." He lowered his voice. "I'm afraid I can never take his place. I tried with my sister, Arella, but I'm not him."

Payton laid a strong hand on his shoulder. "You've done more I'm sure than most young men would have, in your place. You can be proud of that. Your father knew you weren't like him. He loved that about you. He always told me that you'd go places he would never be able to - that your Skills were unique and not even completely understood. His greatest desire was for you to become all you were born to be. He never would have wanted you to try and take his place. It would leave your place empty."

Aidan met the Dundas leader's eyes. He could find no words to express his thanks, but none seemed necessary.

Preparations for their journey took the next two days. Their plan was to make for the city of Holding, in the foothills of the Border Mountains. It was the southernmost city of the Hafwen Clan. Faris insisted on it, saying that of all the Valefolk, the Hafwen alone, maintained contact with the Elder Born of Farran. There, they might find out valuable information, and at the very least, they would be able to get a message to Farran to let the Elder Born there know what was happening. Equally appealing was the fact that no Black Knights had ever been seen that far north before.

The day of departure dawned fair and cool. High wispy clouds scudded over Cahermore, and the green and yellow flag snapped like a pennant against the sky. After a light breakfast the company gathered in the yard. Payton had given his own chestnut gelding to Kenrich, and the smith had set new shoes on the big horse and his own Ramble. The Barras never put shoes on their horses and their rock hard hooves carried them over even the roughest terrain with ease.

Kenrich made a final plea for Niall to accept one of their horses.

"I'm sure your old fellow is fine pulling a cart or going for a stroll along a grassy lane, but we're going through the wilds of Lanreath and may have to ride hard for days in a row. I don't think it's fair to him."

Niall staunchly refused the use of any other horse. "It's bad enough to be riding at all. You're not going to get me on one of your monstrosities. Ramble and I have been together for years. He's got more spunk in him than he lets on to. We'll be just fine."

Aidan, who had been stroking Ramble's face, met the old horse's eye.

"He's perfect." Aidan backed up Niall. "In fact the others will be better for his company."

"Thank you. There... see?" This last was directed to Kenrich. "This old fellow's seen me through some interesting times and he's never let me down."

"Nor will he, if it's in his power to help," Aidan said.

Faris gave Aidan a keen look, which Aidan pretended not to notice. He'd be fielding more questions later. Faris didn't miss much.

Kenrich shrugged and walked off to check his own saddle.

Payton spoke a blessing over them and they swung up on their horses and rode from the yard. Looking back over his shoulder, Aidan caught a glimpse of the guard, Holt, watching them from a window. He ducked out of sight as soon as Aidan looked his way.

There's nothing I can do about it now, Aidan reasoned. Best to be on our way.

The sentries at the gate saluted them as they rode through, and Kenrich returned the salute with a flourish. The last clatter of hooves sounded on cobbled streets and then they were free of the city. The wind whipped over the vast grasslands and the horses snorted and pranced, glad to be beyond the city walls. Faris moved Shay into a canter and Aidan let his big horse fly, glorying in his speed and strength.

Faris let out a whoop and the two of them raced across the plain, their horses running neck to neck. The world fell away and Aidan found himself laughing out loud for the first time in weeks, as they pulled the horses up.

Faris' laugh rang out with his own as they watched the others struggling to catch up. Then the Dundas' face sobered and he leveled his gaze at Aidan.

"He's more truly yours than he ever will be mine."

Aidan frowned. "I'm sorry?" he asked.

"Kael." Faris said. "You reached him in a way I never could. If I were to take him back I would break his heart." The words came out with an effort. Faris shook his head, as though clearing away stray thoughts.

"You will never be parted with him on my account. He's yours now. I could do no less for him."

Aidan realized he'd been holding his breath. It came out in a strangled, "Thank you." His head spun and he blinked back tears, unashamed.

Faris' smile held a trace of bittersweet. "When he was stolen I swore vengeance on whomever had him. I could never have imagined I'd be giving him up. But how could I do otherwise?"

Before Aidan could answer, Elana galloped up on Devi, her hair flying and eyes shining. Kenrich was close behind her, with Niall bringing up the rear. Ramble seemed to be enjoying himself more than the smith, who held on with a grim face. When they had all gathered, Faris raised his hand. He motioned for Aidan to dismount, and then took Kael's reins.

"I vow now, with you as my witnesses, that Kael, mine from birth, now belongs to Aidan. I release all claim upon him and willingly, and freely give him to this man."

The words had a ritualistic sound to them and Aidan guessed that this was the Barras way.

Niall responded. "I hear and witness your vow and will uphold it all of my days."

Kenrich nodded his approval. "A lordly gift indeed. I've not seen his equal, excepting your own mount."

"They're full brothers. You could search the entire Vale and not find their equal. Aidan has won his heart and as I love him, I could do no less for them both."

Elana caught Aidan's eye and her joy for him washed through his mind. "I'm so happy," she said.

He smiled in return, unable to feel worried even about the stirrings of a mind link. He knew he needed to talk with her about it, but right now it felt like nothing could bother him again. He rode the rest of the morning in a daze, savoring his connection with Kael, seeing the world through his eyes; the grasses blowing in the wind, a lone falcon circling high above, and rabbits and quail flushed out of their hiding by the passage of the riders.

They stopped for lunch on the edge of the grasslands. It was a lighthearted affair, with danger feeling far off and distant. Aidan lay back in the warm sun, gazing at the deep blue of the sky, when he noticed again, a falcon circling high above. A chill crept over him and he sat up, trying to listen.

There it was, the faint warning, thrumming through the air.

"Elana." He interrupted her conversation with Faris and pointed up at the sky.

"I know." Her voice grew heavy. "Vian. She's marked our journey since our departure from Cahermore."

For a moment Aidan had a vision of a tapestry, with threads and colors interconnected across the vast expanse. The malevolent face of the man in the castle, raced across his memory, as well as questions about Marek's involvement with the Hunter and the Black Knights. Just how were they all woven together?

Faris interrupted them. "What are you talking about?"

Elana answered him. "Marek's bird. He uses her to send messages. He has a connection with her, he can see some of what she sees. It means he knows where we travel."

Kenrich sat down next to them. "How can he do that?"

"It's one of the ways he uses his Elder Born Skills," Elana explained, her voice cautious. "Not all Elder Born can do that, and most who can choose not to. But he had her from a fledgling and formed an unusual bond with her."

"He told you this?" Kenrich sounded incredulous.

"Not in so many words, but yes."

Aidan refrained from looking at her. She was walking a fine line.

"Is that like what you have with Kael?" Faris' question took the focus off Elana.

"Sort of. Though I don't use it in the same way. Kael isn't subject to me." Anger glinted in Aidan's tawny eyes at the thought. "I could never use him like that."

"I'm glad." Faris studied Aidan's face a while. "But this doesn't bode well for us. I was counting on secrecy." He turned to Elana. "It would have been better if you had spoken of this to me as soon as you knew what was going on. Is there anything else you might need to say?"

Elana blanched at the question. She threw a helpless glance at Aidan who nodded imperceptibly to her. It was time to be honest. In truth, he realized, it should have happened from the first.

Elana's voice was small and her eyes never left the ground as she answered Faris. "Marek opened a mind link with me when I stayed with him in Bellport. When we ran from him, he followed through the link for a while. He said he'd feared that Aidan had kidnapped me, or worse. When I told him I was fine and wanted to go on without him, he said he'd not contact me, but would stay open should I ever need him."

Faris' face looked fierce. Niall had joined them and he was listening with his mouth hanging open.

"I knew because of the mind link, that Marek was planning to kill Aidan in an ambush. He's in some sort of league with the Black Knights and the Hunters. I'm not sure how. That's when we ran away."

She raised her eyes and met each of their gazes. "I'm sorry I kept this from you. I didn't know until our first night at Bellport, that I could even do such a thing. When Orvis and I were attacked I called out and Marek answered." Her chin had a defiant set to it now. "I also used my Skills to repel our attackers. I had no idea that was even possible. Aidan saw the whole thing and because of that he didn't trust me for quite a while. I didn't want the same thing to happen here."

Niall nodded. "I can understand that. There's plenty of folks who repeat stories of Elder witches. Most would likely run you out of town if they knew. That is, if you're lucky. Even in the Clans, folks aren't too keen on anything of that sort."

He reached a calloused hand to her and she took it with her small one. "I can't say that I'd have been easy on hearing that right off. But I don't mistrust you. I'm glad you can share it. It just might come in handy too. Don't throw away any tools at hand when there's a job to be done. That's what I say."

He looked around at the others. "They're going to use everything in their arsenal to stop us. We'd be fools not to use everything we've got to keep ahead of them."

Kenrich said nothing, but glowered in silence.

Faris sighed. "You're right Niall." He looked Elana square in the face. "I'm just sorry you couldn't tell me earlier. I would have thought you were a better judge of character than that."

Turning to Kenrich he said, "You're going to have to put away old prejudices. Elana's not a witch. We're dealing with things that have until now, been legend or superstition. You have a chance to make a difference, not only for the Dundas, but for the entire Vale."

Kenrich's eyes flashed ominously, but he nodded in agreement.

Aidan watched the interchange and his heart sank. He would talk with him later, try to help Kenrich accept this.

Faris led the party northward through thickening woods. He seemed familiar with this land, though it was not his own. Elana followed him, silent since their conversation over lunch. Niall rode behind her, whistling tunelessly to himself. Aidan held Kael back some so that he and Kenrich had a little space from the others.

When they had dropped back out of earshot Aidan spoke.

"It took me a long time to trust her too."

Kenrich looked at him questioningly.

"I actually ran from her the first time I met her in person." He grinned. "It's a little embarrassing now. But after Cecily and I were attacked, Elana, at great risk to herself, saved my life. She didn't have to do it. It took tremendous courage. I started seeing her differently." He caught Kenrich's eye. "She can't help the way her Skills present themselves, any more than I can. And my own path is tied to hers in some way. I have to do all in my power to help her." He paused, letting his words sink in. Then, stopping his horse, he turned to face Kenrich again. "Will you stand with me here?"

Kenrich lowered his gaze. Aidan could feel the young man's turmoil.

"I swore to stand with you. I won't forswear myself. Should your paths separate, I make no promises to her."

"That is enough. You deserve the same chance to weigh her for yourself, as I did. Thank you, Kenrich. It means more to me than you can know."

Aidan didn't plan on those last words, but for the first time he felt a bond with the young leader of the Dundas. He smiled at him and Kenrich, surprised by his warmth, returned the smile.

"Tell me about this Cecily," he asked Aidan.

Aidan reddened. "There's not much to tell. She lives in a different world than me, and in all likelihood, believes me to be a coward, or worse. Her people think I deserted her when we were attacked on the road." Bitterness rose up in him. He'd tried not to think about her.

"She can't be so much a fool as to believe that. Not after what you did for her on the road to Bellport." Kenrich's grin widened. "More likely she's pining away someplace, believing you dead. Who knows, she may even give up and marry that abominable Darcy. It would be an awful shame."

Aidan couldn't find his voice. He'd never considered that possibility. His stomach churned and he was glad he was astride Kael. It would have been difficult to walk.

"I never thought..." his voice trailed off, unable to keep up with the flight of his mind.

"You've been too sheltered on that farm of yours." Kenrich laughed out loud. "You've probably broken the Lady's heart. You ride in, rescue her, sweep her off her feet, and then disappear. I'm sure she's thought of nothing but you since that day."

"You're making sport of me."

"I swear I'm not. I just hate to see you let something like that slip out of your hands."

"But Marek's practically her father," Aidan protested.

Kenrich gave him a funny look. "Yes, for now. But if you were to marry her, than you would become the next Lord, of both Merrion and Glenariff. Not to mention, you'd have the most beautiful woman in the Vale for your wife."

The obstacles to that happening loomed large in Aidan's mind, but for a brief moment, he allowed himself to imagine it as reality. His breath caught in his throat. If she really did care for him...

His thoughts drifted off into pleasant speculation.

"Think about it, my friend," Kenrich said. "I can't believe it was accident that you met her on the road to Bellport."

Kenrich nudged his gelding and the two of them caught back up with the rest.

285

CHAPTER 14

THE EMPTY HILLS

Four long days riding north and east brought them to Rinns, one of the few trade towns on the Fairway belonging to the Dundas. The prospect of warm beds and a hot meal cheered the company. Kenrich was something of a hero here and the townsfolk greeted him with enthusiasm.

"I don't know if this was a good idea," Faris said ruefully. "We might as well have a herald announce our coming." He gathered the company to him. "Speak nothing of our journey. If anyone asks, we can tell the good people here that Kenrich is setting out for the Barras with me to obtain the aid of Varen."

They spent the night at The Beachwood, a cozy inn on the outskirts of town. The proprietor insisted on giving them his finest rooms and would accept no silver for their lodgings. Kenrich made it up by paying double for their meal.

"I can't have anyone believing that I would take advantage of my own people. You give enough, with your sons fighting at the river and the renegade towns encroaching on the trade. I don't want to be the cause of any further hardship in your lives."

The proprietor bowed and accepted the coins that Kenrich offered. The crowd that had drifted in with them cheered for their young leader.

By morning, Aidan was horrified to see a stream of townsfolk visiting the stables. It looked like the town had called a local holiday. If Kenrich being there wasn't enough, Shay, Kael and Devi brought out the rest of the townsfolk. The horses of the Barras were legend and most people outside the Clan never had the opportunity to see one in their entire life.

Aidan volunteered to keep watch over the animals while Niall went out with Kenrich to restock some of the dwindling supplies.

Faris and Elana stayed at the inn. Aidan had noticed them growing closer in the past few days. Elana leaned on Faris in a way that made Aidan slightly jealous. Not that he was interested in her that way, but it bothered Aidan to see her laugh, smile, and relax with Faris in a way she hadn't with him.

The morning passed slowly, with Aidan answering questions about the horses to the remaining townsfolk who came to gawk at them. He was ready to go back to the inn for a bite to eat when a familiar voice spoke his name.

"Aidan?"

His heart clenched in his chest. He turned, knowing immediately who he would see.

Cecily stood framed in the light of the doorway, a pale blue travel cloak wrapped about her shoulders, and her golden hair framing her face.

"How did you... What are you... I never thought I'd..." Words failed him.

"You're alive." She spoke it softly, her green eyes filling with tears. "I thought you were dead and that I was the cause of it. I haven't slept a full night since that awful day. Aidan, I'm so sorry!" Her voice caught in a sob and she reached for his hands.

Without thinking, he pulled her close to him and held her tight, feeling her small frame melt against him.

"I went back to find you and heard the rumors that I had failed you, had put you in harms way." He closed his eyes, not wanting to speak of it. "I feared you hated me. The soldiers at the gate of Bellport would have run me through if they'd known who I was. I knew you were safe and that's what mattered most. So I left, believing I would never again find a welcome with you."

"I could never hate you." She pulled back and looked into his eyes. "I thought you were gone forever. Promise me you won't leave me again."

The reality of his situation came crashing down upon Aidan. "I would never want to leave you, Cecily." He hesitated, not wanting to tell her too much. "But the business I spoke of, I must finish it. It's not for me that I travel, but to keep faith with my entire family, and with those whose lives may hang on the outcome of this journey. I can not abandon it."

Her green eyes cooled for a moment. "Then take me with you," she said.

Aidan's world flung itself into turmoil.

"It's not my decision to make," he said. "I'm not traveling alone and even if I were, the danger is extreme. Some of us may not return. It would be selfish indeed to drag you into this."

"I haven't spoken your name to a soul since that day on the road. I believed I'd killed you. Marek took me with him when he traveled here, hoping the change of scenery would cheer me." She lowered her voice. "He wasn't able to prevail over my father. When I return to Bellport, I'm to marry Darcy. Until this moment, I couldn't even care. But if I go back now, I will not be here when you return."

"Marek is here?" Aidan's blood chilled. Everyone knew they were here, their names and description would be throughout the entire town by now.

"Well, not exactly here. He left me to wait for him at the Hawk's Nest Inn. He's been gone for two days and isn't due back until tomorrow night."

Aidan's mind raced. They had to get out of here before then. He could think of no way to keep Cecily from mentioning their meeting to Marek without raising questions he couldn't answer. It would be one thing for him to hear rumors of their passing through, but another entirely for him to get confirmation from Cecily.

"At least you could take me to your company and let me plead my cause to them. They may not be as heartless as you fear. If any of them knew of Darcy, they surely would let me come with you."

His resistance melted. It surely would keep Marek from hearing directly about them. He tried not to think what Elana would say. He knew there was no love lost between her and Cecily.

"Aidan." Kenrich's voice rang out in the yard. He and Niall were striding toward them.

Aidan's insides twisted around themselves.

"Kenrich, Niall, I have someone I'd like you to meet."

The two men looked from Aidan to Cecily. Niall raised an eyebrow, and gave Aidan a questioning look.

"Cecily, these are two of my friends, Kenrich, heir to the Lord of the Dundas," he motioned toward the young leader of the Dundas, "and Niall, famed smith and warrior of the Dundas." He nodded toward the smith.

Kenrich stood speechless, but Niall gave a graceful bow for one his size and said, "It's an honor to meet you my Lady."

"The honor is mine, I assure you. Any friends of Aidan are well met indeed." She smiled up at the big smith as though she'd never been happier to meet someone in her life.

Aidan wanted to nudge Kenrich who was all but gaping at Cecily. The young leader finally found his voice. "I am at your service, my Lady. If there's ever anything I can do for you, you have but to name it."

Cecily blushed and lowered her eyes. "That's too kind, my Lord. You are the son of Payton, are you not?"

He bowed low. "I am."

"Maybe you could help me," Cecily extended a hand to him.

Kenrich grasped it like a drowning man clinging to a rope.

Aidan didn't know whether to laugh or be offended. He'd never seen his companion loose his composure.

"I had the great fortune of meeting Aidan a few weeks ago," Cecily began. "I had hoped to spend more time with him as we traveled, but on the road out of Bellport we were attacked, and until this day, I believed him dead." Her green eyes filled with tears. "My world ended that day. Until now. I heard of the visitors here in Rinns and the description of them dangled a hope before me. I came to see for myself, and found to my greatest delight that my dear friend is alive. This would be the happiest day of my life, but for one thing." She paused, looking from Kenrich to Niall, letting her words sink in. "My father, Lord Gratton, has insisted on my marrying Darcy, the son of Lord Ulrich. He thinks not of me, but of his own political gain. When I thought Aidan was dead, I couldn't bring myself to care what happened to me one way or the other. But now, when I return home from this trip, the marriage to Darcy will be formalized. I can't live with that."

"My Lady, that can never be!" Kenrich was outraged. "You cannot be made to marry such a brute. I know more of this Darcy than you could be comfortable with. Your life would be torment."

"That is what I fear," Cecily whispered.

"Why not come with us?" Kenrich's face lit up at the thought.

Cecily gave Aidan a sly smile. "I have to admit, that is what I was hoping," she said. "Aidan had concerns about the danger of the journey and my safety."

Niall nodded at this. "He's right about that, my lady. This isn't a jaunt into the countryside. We're pulling danger behind us as we go, and no disrespect intended, but it won't bode well for any of us to have the hosts of Merrion tracking us on your account."

"They wouldn't do that." Cecily's voice was cool, confident. "Marek is my guardian. He is the one who raised me. He finds the proposed match as distasteful as I do and I think he would be delighted to lead my father's men on a wild goose chase to give me the chance to escape."

Niall's face grew alarmed. "You know Marek?"

"Of course. I traveled here with him."

Aidan looked significantly at the smith. Even Kenrich's face sobered.

"He's not here now. He left me to enjoy this town for a few days while he took care of some business. But he's returning tomorrow. I could tell him all about you. I'm sure he'd be delighted for me."

"I'm sure he would," the smith said sardonically.

Kenrich regained his composure. "It might be better if we left now, before he returned. It would avoid questions, complications. Could you leave him a note assuring him of your safety?"

Aidan just about choked. "But we would be assuring her danger, not her safety."

Kenrich leveled his gaze on him. "No. Not more danger than being wed to Darcy. I'm sorry, Aidan. I have to disagree. It is imperative that she come with us."

Niall shook his head. "We'll need to speak with Faris and Elana first. We cannot make this decision without them."

"Are they here?" Cecily asked, her face alight.

"They're in the common room." Niall answered. "We saw them before we came out."

They found Faris and Elana at a small table in a shadowy corner, deep in conversation.

"Faris, Elana," Kenrich called out, steering Cecily by the arm toward them.

A look of horror flitted across Elana's face.

"What are you doing here?" she demanded.

Cecily's eyes hardened. "How dare you talk to me like that." Then recognition dawned on her. "You are the servant from Marek's house. What are you doing here? Seeking your own level, I see."

Aidan's stomach knotted. This would never work.

"Cecily, this is Elana, one of my companions. She was never a servant in Marek's house, that was just a role she was playing, with Marek's

291

knowledge," he added. "She is the most important member of our company."

Cecily frowned as she tried to absorb this new information. Finally, in a cool voice she said, "My apologies, Elana. I had no idea. If I had, I would never have spoken to you in such a way."

Elana's eyes flashed dangerously. "I accept your apology, for what it is. You can't help being poorly raised."

Cecily's face turned red, but she held her tongue.

Kenrich looked from one to the other, confusion written all over him. "You two know each other?"

Elana had not retold that part of her journey, thinking it of little significance.

"Yes," she answered curtly. "We have spoken before."

Kenrich nodded. "Well then, Cecily, this is Faris."

Before he could go into any further explanations, Faris held up his hand.

"It's a pleasure to meet you Cecily," he said, with a smile that never reached his eyes. He rose from his seat and bowed, with all the authority of a Lord, patronizing a lowly peasant.

"It was not my intention to bring discord," Cecily apologized, changing her tactics. "I am a friend of Aidan's and until this hour, believed him dead, and myself the cause. I heard the rumors of the travelers in town and came here straight away with nothing but a thread of hope."

She told the rest of her story to Faris and Elana, though Aidan noticed she never met Elana's gaze. When she was done she asked, "May I travel with you? I know Aidan said it would be dangerous, but I see no other chance for me to escape a marriage to Darcy. I would sooner be dead than marry him, now that I know Aidan is alive."

At this last statement, she blushed again and looked sideways at Aidan.

He could feel the blood rush to his own face. Did she mean what she was saying? Elana gave him a pointed look, which he tried to ignore.

"There's no good answer here," Faris spoke slowly. "Aidan was not exaggerating. We are counting on speed and secrecy. If we were to take you, it would compromise both. You can't believe that your father or Marek would just let you disappear?"

"I know what you're thinking, but Marek is as opposed to this marriage as I am. I believe if he knew I were safe, he'd help divert any searches to see that I could get away."

Elana made a rude noise. "This is utter nonsense. There is no way she can travel with us." She turned to Cecily. "I'm sorry. It just won't work."

Kenrich slammed his fist on the table. "You can't just dismiss her out of hand. Elana, think bigger." He looked at her as though her were trying to convey his thoughts directly to her mind.

"I'm sorry, you'll have to explain yourself."

Aidan cringed at her tone. He'd seen Elana be difficult.

Faris' mocking smile spread across his face. "Now children..." He turned to Cecily. "My Lady, we will need a chance to discuss this among ourselves. As you see, this is no simple request. May I recommend a pleasant stroll through this fine town and upon your return we will have an answer."

She bowed her head, her green eyes cool. "I will take myself out and await your decision."

Aidan caught her arm and escorted her to the door. "I'm so sorry about this. You don't know what you're asking. I'm afraid, even if they agree to this, that you will regret your choice here."

At the door of the inn she turned and whispered in his ear, "I could never regret being with you." She gave him a swift kiss on the cheek, which left his face on fire, and slipped out the door.

He walked slowly back through the common room, his heart torn.

At the table Elana and Kenrich were all but shouting at each other.

"If Aidan feels about her the way I think, it would be the best thing for the entire Vale if they were to wed. He will regain the Lord's Seat of Glenariff, and with Cecily as his wife, he will hold the Lord's Seat of Merrion too."

Elana's pale face flushed. "I don't know what Aidan feels for her, but I won't presume to marry him off for political gain. If she comes with us, we may never accomplish our task and I'm sorry to say it won't matter who holds the Lord's Seat of Glenariff or Merrion." She glared at Kenrich. "Anyway, it's easy enough for you to talk about Aidan now, but I think you're taken with her."

Faris looked at the stricken face of the young Dundas leader. "Elana, he's out of his depth. It's not fair." The Barras roared with laughter, holding his sides.

"No one's marrying me off any time soon, for any reason." Aidan joined his companions, saving Kenrich from having to come up with a reply to Elana's latest barb.

"Well, I'm glad to hear that," Niall interjected. "We've got our hands full without matchmaking."

"But Kenrich does have a point, though I'm not sure if he's seeing it clearly himself." Faris caught his breath and reentered the conversation. "If Cecily does marry Darcy, it would solidify an allegiance between Merrion and Glenariff. The Shadow King could use that to crush the rest of the Vale, before we have time to counter him. If we could keep her from marrying, it buys us time there, and right now we need all the time we can get."

Elana glared at him. "So, we just have Marek and all the army of Merrion tailing us while we escort a spoiled girl through the wilds of Lanreath?"

"The truth is, we have Marek tailing us anyway. It's no accident that he's in the area. My guess is that he wouldn't want Lord Gratton interested in what we're doing. He may indeed, for reasons other than Cecily believes, divert the search from us. We've known since we left Cahermore that we would have to outwit him. Even if she comes with us, that doesn't change that substantially."

Kenrich looked in amazement at him. "It is no wonder my father speaks of you as he does."

"Don't underestimate him," Niall said. "I know a few people who did and it was the last mistake they made."

Faris gave him a warning look.

"So what you're saying is that she'd come with us, but almost like a hostage." A slow smile spread across Elana's face. "I might be able to adjust to that."

Faris looked approvingly at her. "You're better than I thought. I would do well to not underestimate you."

She rewarded him with a dazzling smile.

Aidan shook his head. He didn't like hearing Cecily's fate bantered about so casually. Nor did he like the talk of her as a hostage.

"She's not the awful person you make her out to be," he rose to Cecily's defense.

"No. Not if you're a handsome, eligible young man. I'm sure that if she wants something from you she can be quite charming. Fortunately, I've not had that honor. I get to see behind the façade." Elana smirked at Aidan. "One of the few advantages of being female."

Aidan gave up. He didn't have the heart to fight with Elana, especially as he'd been there when Cecily has abused her in front of him. Right now he didn't want to think too hard about it.

"So, does this mean she's with us?" he asked.

"Given that she knows we're here, I think it's the safest thing to do." Faris gave him an understanding look. "I'm sorry. I know this is not what you'd have wanted. I wish this hadn't happened. Though if all goes well, she won't be wed to Darcy." He surveyed them all. "As far as she understands she is our traveling companion, but we do not take her into our confidence." He looked hard at both Aidan and Kenrich. "Can you agree to that?"

They both nodded. Kenrich looked glazed with happiness and Aidan thought he'd have agreed to stick his boot in the fire just now, had Faris asked it of him.

"We leave in an hour's time. Aidan, find Cecily and see that she writes Marek a note telling him she's met up with an old friend, and is laying low to escape the prospect of marriage to Darcy. Have her say that she'll write again in a fortnight, and post it to Bellport. That may buy us some time."

"Kenrich, Niall, help me pack the supplies. Elana could you pack our personal belongings and bring them to the stable?"

"Women's work?" Elana quipped.

"I could have you reset Ramble's shoe for me," Niall suggested, "If that's more to your taste. He twisted it yesterday."

She grinned at him. "No thank you. I think I'd be delighted to pack our clothes."

Aidan left them, half running out the door. His head was spinning. She was really coming with them! A part of him wanted to shout and dance, yet another part of him wished they'd never stopped in this town.

He found her under a flowering cherry tree, sitting amidst the fallen blossoms.

"You can come," he said, taking her hand and helping her to her feet. "They've agreed. Even Elana."

Relief washed over her face and she flung her arms around his neck. "Thank you, thank you."

Aidan could feel her heart pounding. He couldn't imagine what she was going through, wondering if she would be fated to marry Darcy. He couldn't bring himself to believe she might really want him.

She slipped her hand in his and the two started walking. Aidan explained about the note and their need to leave immediately. They made their way back to the Hawk's Nest where she packed up the clothes most suitable for an extended trip on horseback, and left the note for Marek. Aidan carried her bag and they snuck out the back, where he saddled her gray mare and helped her mount.

"I can't believe I found you again." Cecily rested her hand on his shoulder as he walked beside her. "Are you happy that I'm coming?"

The conversation between his companions replayed itself in Aidan's mind. He tried to forget about it and push away his doubts. "Just seeing you makes me happy," he said truthfully.

That seemed to satisfy her and she chatted to him the rest of the way back about things that had happened since they were parted.

At the inn yard, Elana had the horses packed and saddled, even Kael. Aidan felt the familiar twinge that struck him every time the stallion accepted her attentions.

"Ready?" Faris asked him.

Aidan nodded.

"We head due north from here, avoiding the road at all costs." He checked Shay's saddle and swung up.

The rest followed and Faris led them out of the yard with a clatter of hooves on the cobbled stones.

Elana followed behind Faris. She couldn't bring herself to watch Aidan with Cecily. It's not that she was jealous of her, she reasoned, she just didn't like the girl. There was something more too. Ever since Cecily walked into the common room, Elana felt the outline of Marek's presence in her mind. Not clearly, but enough to put her on edge. She had never liked the feeling of him being in her mind, and it made her irritable to have it back again.

She wished more than ever that she could have a moment alone with Aidan. Kenrich's assertion of his feelings for Cecily shook her. She thought she knew him pretty well, and she didn't believe she'd seen that in him. She would wish them all the best, if that's what he wanted, but she couldn't imagine him being happy with someone like her. Kenrich, on the other hand, was going to make himself ridiculous, and she'd rather not be there to see it.

Her only solace was Faris and Niall.

A smile softened her face as she thought about Faris. It still seemed odd to her that he was not Elder Born. She kept finding herself assuming he was. She'd never met anyone like him. She was glad that he, at least, wasn't swept away by Cecily.

He pushed them hard until after sunset. The horses were lathered and steaming when he called for a halt.

"We'll camp here for the night. No fire."

His tension permeated the company. There was little chatter as they unsaddled and set up camp. Everything hinged on them getting away without pursuit for the next few days.

Cecily's face was drawn, ashen. She looked like a wilted flower. Elana couldn't help feeling smug about it. Lord Gratton's daughter had probably never ridden that hard in her life. Aidan and Kenrich were both solicitous, looking after her every need. There was no use wasting sympathy on her. She'd get plenty from them.

Elana tended to Devi, walking her till she was cool before seeing to her own things.

Faris came up beside her. "Thank you for making this possible. I know it's not to your liking."

She grimaced. "You're right, but your argument was more compelling than my distaste. I'm not doing it for her." She rubbed the last of the sweat off her mare's sides with a piece of supple leather. Devi nosed her, hoping for a treat.

"You get on well with her," Faris remarked, referring to the mare. "I never would have believed you to be a horse person."

"I'm not sure that I am. Not in the way you, or Aidan are. I just have this connection with her."

"Do you use it when you're with her?" he asked.

"Yes. Though not as much as I used to. It's like that was my language, and she's started to teach me hers. I can understand her better now." She glanced over to where Cecily was sitting and lowered her voice, "I don't like using it too much, even with Devi. I'm still afraid that any use of my Skills will draw the Hunter."

"I'm glad to hear it. Keep that fear. It's healthy."

He walked away and Elana felt like somehow she'd just passed a test.

The nights were growing warmer, so losing the fire was no physical hardship. Even so, it was a cheerless camp without one. Over supper, Faris outlined his plan to the company.

They would stay off the road, riding north of the Fairway and west, until they came to the Empty Hills. They would travel through that forsaken land until they reached Holding, which lay half a day's hard riding from the far side of the Empty Hills.

No roads ran through those hills and no people made their homes there. The Fairway gave it wide berth as well, bending many leagues south, so that a vast rocky plain lay between the road and the Empty Hills rising up against the sky. Long standing legend spoke of the Empty Hills as a haunted trackless wild where unsuspecting travelers could get hopelessly lost riding in circles until madness, or something worse, took them.

Elana had never paid attention to these stories, so their name struck no fear into her heart.

Both Niall and Kenrich shifted uneasily.

"I've never questioned you before," Niall spoke to Faris, "But what makes you think that even if we evade pursuit, we can find our way out on the other side?"

Faris turned and gave a long look to Aidan. "He does."

Aidan started. "What do you mean?"

He gave Aidan a significant look. "Let's just say that I think it would be hard for that land to confound you."

The others shook their head, unconvinced.

Faris shrugged. "I've been in there before, and encountered nothing more dangerous than bears, wolves, and an occasional mountain lion. No one lives there and the animals seek it out as a refuge."

Kenrich was unmoved. "But we'll be traveling for days through there. I have no weapon that is useful against a shade."

"I think that the stories have grown in the telling," Faris answered. "The Barras keep a clear memory of their stories, and though they speak of strange and wondrous things there, they speak of no shades, and no evil. Danger to the irreverent, yes. Evil - no. It was a land held dear to the Ancient Ones long ago and the land doesn't forget them as quickly as people do. I would rather face the Empty Hills than the Fairway. It is my hope that they will discourage any pursuit."

The young Dundas leader bowed his head, clearly unhappy, but willing to submit to Faris' leadership.

Niall slapped his friend on the back. "Lead the way and I'll follow. I may not like it, but I'll not back away." He looked at Aidan, as well. "I knew your father and would have followed him anywhere. I'd be dishonoring his memory to not do the same with you."

Aidan looked distinctly uncomfortable at this, but made no reply.

They finished their supper in silence, each lost in their own thoughts. The tree frogs and crickets started up their chorus as the group unrolled their blankets and settled in to sleep. Niall kept first watch. The last thing Elana saw was his thick form, a little apart from the company, outlined in the starlight against a huge oak tree.

Sleep was fitful for her, with disturbing dreams of dark cloaked men galloping, and a falcon circling above them. She woke once to see Aidan's outline, taking the watch beneath the oak. Slightly comforted, she closed her eyes again.

The next thing she knew rough hands were shaking her awake.

"Get up. Now!" Kenrich's voice hissed in her ear. "We're being followed."

She woke instantly, her insides cold with dread, bundled her blankets together and raced for Devi. The mare shied away from her, skittish.

She threw away caution and used the mind link she shared with the mare to calm her. With shaking hands she managed to pack her bags, and saddle and bridle Devi.

Faris had already saddled Shay and he and Niall were talking in short clipped tones. Elana couldn't make out what they were saying. Kenrich was helping Cecily get her blankets together, and Aidan was saddling her mare. Kael stood ready, waiting for him.

Elana swung up on Devi and rode over to Aidan.

"What's happening?" she asked him.

"It was my watch, I could feel it, danger coming. They'll be here soon. We'll have to run for it."

"Who'll be here?"

"I don't know," he answered candidly. "My Skills aren't that specific. But it's not good."

That was enough for her.

Kenrich brought an exhausted Cecily over and all but heaved her up onto her mare. Even the quiet gray mare was snorting and blowing at the night. Cecily clung to her reins, looking haggard.

Faris wheeled Shay and rode over to them. "We're making a run for it. I know this land and we'll stay in the open for as long as we can and make for the Empty Hills. We need all the speed we can get. If they get too close, Aidan, you take Elana and Cecily and lead them into the Empty Hills. Kenrich, Niall and I will stay behind and change their minds about following us."

Elana could sense Aidan's distress at being singled out to guide the women rather than fight.

"You're the only one who won't get hopelessly lost in there," Faris said, as though Aidan has spoken his thoughts out loud. "If they get to Elana, it's all over. Whatever you do, keep her safe. We'll try and track you and meet up as soon as we can. Make for Holding. If we can't find you, we'll meet you again there."

He surveyed the company, his eyes stopping on Cecily. "You wanted to travel with us? This is what it means. Ride now like your life depends on it, because it does. Those tracking us will likely kill you before they know who you are."

She set her jaw and nodded.

For just a moment, Elana felt sorry for her. Then they were off.

There was no room to be frightened of pursuit in the headlong gallop into the night. The immediate fear of falling off, or being scraped against a tree eclipsed everything else. Elana lived in tiny moments: ducking to miss a branch, Devi stumbling in a hole and catching herself just before they both went down, flying downhill, where every stride seemed to put themselves in danger of going head over heels. Soon her whole body ached with the effort of staying astride the mare. They made it to the open land and Devi streaked past Kenrich's chestnut, flying to catch Shay and Kael. She was like the wind itself. Elana had never imagined such speed. She wrapped both hands in the silver mane and prayed she wouldn't come off.

Tears from the wind streaked down her cheeks and Devi's flying mane stung her face. Everything disappeared except for the pounding of hooves beneath her. Then behind her she heard a yell.

Faris pulled up Shay and they almost plowed into him, swerving aside at the last moment.

Niall shouted again.

She wheeled Devi around and in the faint starlight, saw the outline of a company of riders cresting the far hill behind them.

Faris swore and turned to meet Aidan's eye. "You know what you have to do."

Aidan nodded. It only took a moment for Kenrich and Cecily to catch up to them.

"We'll ride in to meet them," Faris said. "Take Elana and Cecily and head out that way." He pointed to a band of trees running along the open land. "That marks the boundary of the Empty Hills. Take them in and if we can't find you, we'll see you in Holding."

He caught Elana's eye. "Don't worry about us if we're not there right away. I don't plan on letting any leave here alive."

As he spoke, her throat tightened. She hadn't let herself imagine anything happening to him. "Be careful." Her voice came out tight and small.

Niall rode up alongside her. "He could probably take them on himself. We'll be fine." He leaned in and whispered, "Don't let our hostage distract Aidan. We need him focused on the job at hand. If you see to her," he gave Elana a sharp look, "he won't have to. It might be better that way."

"I ought never underestimate you," she said. "Distasteful, but necessary. I'll do it." She winked at him and the smith saluted her, riding off on Ramble, who had livened up considerably since their journey's start.

Elana rode up beside Cecily. "Are you ready to go? Keep next to me. We'll be alright."

It wasn't as hard as she imagined to be civil. Cecily's face was drained of all color, but the set of her jaw made Elana believe there might be tougher stuff in her. They'd soon find out.

Aidan led the way toward the band of trees outlined in the dark. The hoofbeats of their pursuers pounded behind them. She checked Devi's speed to stay abreast of Cecily's gray. They had just reached the woods when they heard shouts and the clash of weapons. Elana's stomach clenched. She tried not to picture what was happening back there.

Without looking back they plunged into the darkness of the trees. They lost the benefit of any discernible paths and their pace slowed to a crawl. Aidan stopped occasionally, as though listening for something. Elana stayed by Cecily.

The sounds of fighting faded behind them. It was silent under the close trees, only the thud of their horses' hooves and the crack of twigs underfoot broke the stillness of the night. Here, in the darkness, with nothing to distract her, Elana became more aware of Marek's presence. Never a voice in her mind, never something she could point to exactly, but he was there, just as surely as if he's been standing next to her. She tried to close her mind to him, and it lessened somewhat, but she couldn't make it go away.

Thick underbrush hampered their progress at every turn. They had to dismount, leading their horses through the grasping vines, and tangles of limbs. Ears straining for sounds of pursuit, the three inched their way deeper into the woods. After what seemed like hours, their path opened onto a game trail. The trees thinned here and Elana could make out the velvet blue of the sky. Night was giving way to dawn and they would soon lose whatever cover darkness lent.

They mounted their horses once again and Aidan led them in single file, Elana riding in the rear. The first bird woke and sung his welcome to the coming light. Another joined him. Then, from behind them, came a sound that silenced everything else.

The lone howl of a hunting wolf pierced the early dawn. It was answered, and the cry was picked up and carried as the pack closed in on them.

The horses bolted through the tight, twisted path, running for their lives. Elana couldn't break through the panic in Devi's mind to reach her. She could see Cecily clinging to her gray. The trail opened up into a small clearing. Aidan pulled Kael around, already fitting an arrow to his bow.

"Follow the trail!" He pointed across the clearing to where the game trail reentered the trees. "Don't wait for me."

Elana couldn't hold Devi back. Springing ahead of Cecily's gray, the little gold mare careened into the trees, heedless of any paths. Branches tore at Elana's hair, clothes and limbs. She tasted blood, and felt it's warm trickle on her cheek. She buried her face in Devi's mane, trying to protect herself and just stay with the frantic mare. It was fully daylight when Devi stopped, her sides heaving, sweat running from her.

Elana slid off the mare and looked around. They were completely alone, neither Cecily nor Aidan were anywhere in sight. The trees here were evergreens, tall firs and pines that filled the wood with their scent. There was no sound of the wolves, and no sound of her companions.

We left a trail a blind man could follow, thought Elana, looking back at the broken branches behind them. She just hoped there was someone to follow them. She felt like a fool, letting the mare run away with her and saving her own skin, when her companions were in danger.

The bubbling of a creek caught Devi's ear and the mare strained in that direction. Elana led her down to the water, careful to only let her drink small sips until she cooled out. When they both had their fill, she noticed what seemed to be a clearing at the top of a hill across the creek. They made for it, Elana hoping that maybe she could get a better view of the surrounding land.

It was a steep climb up the hill and Elana was sweating by the time they stepped into the small meadow at the top. A deep stillness filled this place, and Devi, who had been staring at the trees and snorting at every noise, immediately relaxed and started tearing at the fresh spring grass. Tying the reins around Devi's neck so she wouldn't step on them, Elana looked around.

The early morning birdsong which had filled the woods below, was absent. There were no clouds overhead either, though Elana could have sworn that she saw white clouds through the trees on her climb. The back of her neck tingled and her Waking surged. She tried to contain it to no avail.

Great, she thought. I can't find my friends, but I'll have no problem attracting my enemies.

The force of her Waking grew stronger still. Try as she might to fight it, it overpowered her senses. Her eyes seemed to be playing tricks on her. She rubbed them, trying to clear her vision. It didn't work. Looking up across the clearing she saw a shadowy figure; a ghost image of a young woman her own age, running up from the other side of the hill, clutching something that hung around her neck. Faint sounds of pursuit trailed her from the far woods.

The woman ran straight past Elana, giving no sign that she had seen her. Elana called to her but she never turned. Without a backwards glance, she raced for a huge boulder at the pinnacle of the clearing. Gasping for breath and half sobbing, she pulled off some sort of necklace she was wearing. Elana caught sight of something small hanging from its chain. Power emanated from the object, pulsing around the young woman. She kneeled by the boulder and Elana could just make out the words she chanted:

Between the worlds and outside time

Safe from prying hands or eyes

Encased in stone, will Stone set free

When claimed by she who holds the Key.

The young woman held up the necklace for a moment. Swinging in the sunlight on the chain hung a finely wrought Key. Elana's heart pounded. The woman tucked the Key into a crack on the face of the stone and began to chant again.

Here lie till Waking vision quicken

The sight to find, the song to open

Till blood drawn oath will bind her life

No other hand may here alight.

Elana drew a sharp breath. The crack where the young woman placed the Key closed around it, leaving no sign that it had ever been there. The woman looked up and whispered, "Please let me have done the right thing."

Booted feet crashed through the far woods. Men's voices broke the stillness of the clearing. The woman looked back now, blood draining from her face. She raised her hands as if in supplication, though

Elana could not tell to what. Slowly, as if in answer, another form materialized next to her.

A crone, wispy gray hair peering from the folds of a deep blue cloak, reached out her gnarled hands to the upraised young ones.

"Evana, you have done well, my child."

Evana's eyes lit up and tears streamed down her face.

"I never thought I'd see you," she breathed.

The crone's hood fell back and where lines and wrinkles gave the impression of great age, now a fierce look from her eyes at the pursuing men, made Elana alter her perception. Whatever the age of the old woman, it brought no attending weakness.

Three men broke into the clearing. Elana shrunk back into herself, afraid that somehow they would see her and come after her. But the men took no notice of her or Devi, who grazed unconcerned on the sweet grass. They made straight for Evana.

The crone whispered something in Evana's ear, and at her answering nod, took her hands and raised her to her feet.

Elana gasped, horrified. She saw Evana rise and walk away with the old woman, but somehow she had left her kneeling body behind. Now an empty shell, it toppled over on the grass, dead.

The men shouted curses at her and one another, apparently unable to see Evana and the old woman, and rudely searched the body, but to no avail. The thing they were hunting was now hidden.

The vision faded, leaving Elana shaking from what she had just seen.

Her Waking though, surged on. It drew her to the boulder, and the object concealed within. Taking tentative steps in its direction, and afraid that she would encounter the long dead bones of Evana, Elana made her way over to the great rock. No bones lay in the grass. The rock stood guard over the clearing like a sentinel. No moss lined its craggy sides, and no grass grew up around its base. It seemed to Elana, to hum almost, with a presence unlike anything she'd ever encountered. Reaching out her hand she touched it.

The rock tingled under her touch as though it were alive. She traced the spot where she saw Evana lay the Key into the crack. The tingling grew stronger. She believed with everything in her that the Key she saw hidden away in this very rock was the same Key spoken of in the ancient song. This had to be the Key that unlocked the Firestone. There must be some way for her to retrieve it.

She strained to recall the words she heard Evana chant before hiding away the Key. Her Waking, in response to her need, thrust them upon her consciousness the way a wave throws a piece of driftwood onto the shore.

Between the worlds and outside time

Safe from prying hands or eyes

Encased in stone, will Stone set free

When claimed by she who holds the Key.

And then the second verse:

Here lie till Waking vision quicken

The sight to find, the song to open

Till blood drawn oath will bind her life

No other hand may here alight.

But what does that mean? She wracked her mind for some answer to the riddle. "Between the worlds and outside time, Safe from prying hands or eyes..." That probably meant the very stone that stood in front of her. Was it, was she, in Laharan? Had she stumbled upon the island between the worlds?

"Encased in stone, will Stone set free, When claimed by she who holds the Key." She had just watched in her vision, the Key become encased in stone, and if it was indeed the Key that unlocked the Firestone, then it would set a Stone free. Her heart pounded and her hands shook. It was here. Her Waking flared uncontrollably, and her mind jumped to the next verse.

"Here lie till Waking vision quicken..." Well, that just happened. She saw it with her Waking vision. "The sight to find, the song to open..." Elana paused. Her Waking sight enabled her to find the stone, but what song opened it? She didn't know very many songs. And only one that mentioned the Key.

With a shaking voice she intoned the verse of the ancient teaching song her mother sung to her the night before they were taken by the Hunter.

The Three will rise to reunite

When the Shadow's arm grown long,

Together push the darkness back,

The Key, the Seed, the Song.

The humming of the rock grew more pronounced. The deep crack along the side where Elana had seen Evana hide the Key, opened before her eyes. There it was. A small Key, finely wrought from what Elana guessed to be bronze, lay still hooked to a chain of the same metal. She wanted to laugh out loud. It was working! This was almost too easy. She had found the Key. Without a second thought she reached out her hand to lay hold of it. A crack sounded through the clearing and something flung Elana back onto the grass.

The last two lines of the second verse rang through her head:

Till blood drawn oath will bind her life

No other hand may here alight.

Bruised and trembling, Elana sat up. The picture of the woman's empty lifeless body hovered in her mind. Whoever the crone was, who seemed to preside over the Key, she left Evana dead. Elana guessed that the old woman was one of the Ancient Ones. She'd heard of the Ancient Ones all her life, but she imagined them somewhat less involved with the lives of real people. She knew the stories of them giving the Vale Gifts to the first Elder Born and teaching them how to use them, but somehow she figured that they no longer got involved, at least not where anyone could actually see or speak with them. She had a sinking feeling that those comfortable stories were about to be turned upside down. And none of this brought her any closer to figuring out what oath would be required of her.

She closed her eyes and tried to breathe. Tried to think. She couldn't come this close to loose everything now.

"Elana."

Her eyes popped open. There, in front of the boulder, stood the old woman. Elana couldn't stop shaking. It wasn't entirely fear, though she was terrified, but there was something more, something bigger. This woman was one of the Ancient Ones.

The crone had the same deep blue cloak but this time its hood covered her face entirely. She seemed to be waiting for an answer.

Slowly, trying to keep her voice from quavering, Elana asked, "What oath would you have from me?"

The voice that answered was gentle, almost sad. "Only this. That you undertake whatever the Firestone asks of you."

Elana waited for something more, but the old woman remained silent. Well, she thought, At least I'm not going to die now. She was glad the Ancient One hadn't reached out her gnarled hands, because she wasn't sure if she would have been able to take them. But she couldn't imagine withholding anything from the Firestone. It was her dream and deepest desire to unlock it.

Her strength returning she said, "I swear to you, to undertake whatever the Firestone asks of me."

"Well spoken, my child."

The warmth of those words flowed throughout Elana's entire being. Gathering her courage, Elana asked the old woman, "What happened to Evana?"

"That is between Evana and I," the old woman answered. "She followed me faithfully and was rewarded for that."

Elana couldn't help but wonder how dying was a reward. That wasn't one she was keen on receiving.

"That is not your path, little one," the Ancient One answered, as though Elana had spoken her thoughts aloud. "Yours is more difficult, but I will help you walk it."

Elana didn't want to try and guess what that would mean. Pictures of the Hunter darkened the edges of her thoughts.

"Reach out and take the Key," the Ancient One continued. "You will seal this oath in your blood."

She got up, reached out, and though she was cringing inside, took hold of the Key. It rounded edges sliced into her hand as though they were shards of cut glass. Hot blood covered the Key and where the blood touched it, the Key took on a red hue. Her hand burned and it took all her focus not to drop the Key.

"It is sealed." The Ancient One's words rang out through the clearing. "You alone are bound to this Key to unlock the Firestone."

"Where is the Firestone? How will I unlock it when I find it?" Elana asked, afraid that the old woman would disappear before she learned everything she needed.

"This is the Key to Laharan, the land now hidden between the worlds. Your Waking has taken you here now, but only the Key will open the door to the part of Laharan where the Firestone is hidden. After that, follow your Waking. It will show you. Just remember, whatever the Firestone asks of you, you must do. It will give you the strength to carry it out."

Elana shuddered and tried to push from her mind images of single combat with the mind of the Hunter. It wasn't today's task.

"Will I ever see you again?" she asked the old woman.

"That is not for me to say, but I give you my blessing, Elana, leader of the Firestone Eldership."

A breeze stirred through the clearing, and the Ancient One melted away.

Elana stood speechless, still shaken by the encounter and the woman's parting words. She studied the Key in her bleeding hand. Even when she wiped the blood off it, the Key held its reddened hue. Like someone in a dream she caught Devi, tore a piece of cloth off her blanket to wrap her hand, slipped the Key on its chain over her neck, tucked it under her tunic, and made her way down the hill. She turned one last time to look at the clearing, and as she did, a breeze blew through the trees and the clearing vanished.

CHAPTER 15

SHADOW ON THE FAIRWAY

For all Aidan could figure, the pine woods had swallowed Elana and Devi whole. He'd followed their trail without difficulty. Devi had plowed through the trees in her panic to escape the wolves, but at the top of this hill the trail simply vanished. Cecily sat hunched over on her horse, not looking at him, and not speaking. She was hardly recognizable as Lord Gratton's heir. He knew she needed to eat and to rest, but he couldn't just give up the search. He looked up through the trees to where the sun was making its way down toward the western horizon. It would be sunset in a few hours and they needed a safer place to camp for the night. Five wolves lay dead, their bodies pierced with his arrows, but there were more out there and he wasn't keen on being attacked while he slept. Reluctantly, he led Cecily back down the hill to the creek. Something kept tugging him back, but he couldn't ignore the danger to them if they stayed.

At the creek bottom Kael turned and whinnied, staring back up the hill.

"I know fellow," he said to the stallion. "I don't want to leave them either."

A higher pitched whinny answered. It was Devi.

"Elana!" Aidan called and sprinted back up the hill.

She half ran, half slid down to meet him. "You're here, you found me. I have so much to tell you."

Excitement bubbled out of her. She seemed heedless of the anxiety she'd caused him.

"I've only been looking all day for you. Where have you been? Your trail just disappeared." All his worry and frustration turned to anger. "How could you just run off like that? What were you thinking?"

Hurt registered on her face for the briefest moment and then her black eyes flashed dangerously.

"Well, I'm so sorry to inconvenience you. I'll consult you first, the next time I think of having my horse run away with me." Her small shoulders stiffened and she turned away.

"Elana." Aidan immediately regretted his outburst. "Forgive me. I didn't mean to yell."

She gave him a sideways glance, not giving in right away. Finally she said, "Alright. I forgive you. But I didn't do it on purpose."

"I know. I was just afraid something happened to you." He held his hand out to her in truce.

She took it and then surprised him completely by throwing her arms around him and giving him a huge hug.

"I have so much to tell you," she whispered to his shoulder. "I have it. The Key."

He pushed her back from himself, staring hard at her as if that would help him make better sense of what she was saying. "What?"

"The Key. The Key from the prophecy. I was in Laharan and I saw the Key being hidden ages and ages ago, and I met one of the Ancient Ones and she made me swear an oath and after that I got the Key."

"Are you sure you're alright?" Kenrich's worries about shades came back to his mind.

She glared at him.

Yes, she was still herself, thought Aidan. Better take this one slowly.

"You were in Laharan? How did you get there?"

"I don't know. I climbed the hill and there was a clearing at the top." She pointed to the top of the hill, now thick with trees. "My Waking was so strong there I couldn't stop it. I saw the last Firestone Elder to hold the Key and she ran there, chased by men like the Hunter, only she was able to hide the Key before they got to her. She saw the Ancient One too, and she followed her..." Here Elana paused, looking uncomfortable. "She took the Ancient One's hands and died.

Just stepped out of her body and left it empty. Only she seemed happy to follow the Ancient One even if it meant leaving this world. A faraway look came over Elana. Tears stood out in her eyes. "But this means that Laharan is not just been a crazy notion. Aidan, I might be able to help my parents and the whole Vale. The Ancient One said that I was the one to unlock the Firestone." With careful fingers, she reached down and pulled the chain out of the front of her tunic.

Aidan gaped at he Key. He could feel the power emanating from it. There was no doubt about what Elana was saying.

"Put it away. I don't want Cecily to see it." He frowned at her, a troublesome thought occurring to him. "Elana, that thing radiates power like you do when your Waking runs strong. How are we going to get it across the Vale without acting like a beacon to the Hunter?"

She blanched. "I don't know. But we have to."

"Let's go back down. We can think about it as we travel. Right now we've got to get away from here. The Key won't do us any good if we're eaten by wolves." He grinned at her, hoping to convey more reassurance than he felt.

Cecily was waiting for them at the bottom of the hill, practically falling asleep in the saddle. "I'm glad you're alright," she said to Elana. Her voice was soft. Weariness stole some of the beauty from her features, but Aidan noticed that much of the arrogance was gone as well. His heart went out to her. She'd probably never had a day like this before in her life.

Apparently Elana was moved as well. She reached out and touched Cecily's arm. "Lets go find a place to camp and you can get some rest."

Cecily smiled wanly, unable to conjure up the strength to answer, and they set out, following Aidan. As the light mellowed toward sunset, he led them to the clearing where the wolves first attacked. After dragging the dead bodies of the wolves out along the perimeter as a warning, he and Elana gathered wood for a bonfire.

"It's our best protection at night," he told her. "Let's make sure we have enough wood to carry us through to morning."

For Aidan and Elana it was a backbreaking hour of gathering deadwood from the forest before the light left the sky and they retired to the fire to wait. The horses shifted nervously, staying within the ring of firelight, and blowing at every strange noise in the trees. They ate a hurried supper, with their backs to the blaze, watching for eyes in the surrounding woods. Aidan kept his bow out with an arrow at the ready.

Cecily, who hadn't offered to help them, fell asleep over her food and Elana took out the girl's blanket and wrapped her up against the night chill.

The stars glittered in the clear sky and Elana lay back staring up at them.

"Aidan," she said, "Do you think the others are alright?"

"Yes."

"How far are we from Holding?"

He tried to remember the maps that he'd studied with Kenrich. "About three day's ride, I'd guess. It's not far off the Fairway and I'd like to stay close to the road in case we can get any word of the others." He saw her nod. "You miss Faris, don't you?"

She propped herself up on an elbow. "Yes. I've never met anyone like him."

"I know what you mean," he answered.

She looked over at the now sleeping Cecily. "Do you love her?"

Aidan blushed furiously, grateful for the dark to cover it. "I don't know," he answered truthfully. "She's really special, but I've only known her a short while and she lives in a different world from mine. I don't think she's figured out that I'm Elder Born."

"That could cause problems," Elana said dryly.

"You're not kidding." Aidan sighed. "Why does it have to be so complicated?"

Elana was silent for a while. Aidan looked over at her, wondering if she fell asleep.

316

"Aidan?" Elana asked in a quiet voice, "Do you think Orvis is healed by now? I still think about him all the time. Everything happened so fast when I left Bellport, and I feel like I betrayed him." She sat up, pulling her blanket around her shoulders. "I should never have left him behind. He wanted to go back to Farran. His dearest friend, Brenna, is there." The firelight reflected in her tears. "I believed we were going together. It's almost like I saw it with my Waking, Aidan, when I looked ahead, I saw him with me, and now he's gone."

There was another long silence.

"I saw Faris with me too, after we met him. And he's gone now." She turned to face him. "And the worst of it is, I don't know what bothers me more, loosing their company, or feeling that I can't trust my Waking."

Aidan felt lost. His Waking worked so differently, he didn't know what to say to her.

In the cover of darkness her fears came tumbling out. "Marek's in my mind all the time now. I think it's Cecily - somehow since she joined us I can't shake him." She paused, as if weighing her words. "Aidan."

"Yes."

"I still see Marek with us too." She raised her hands in a helpless gesture. "I don't understand anything anymore."

A shiver ran through Aidan. "Neither do I," he answered. He cast about for another topic, hoping to draw her attention away from Marek. He didn't know quite how their mind link worked, but talking about him out here where they were far from any help seemed foolhardy.

"Tell me more about Orvis," he said, "I never knew him."

Elana had given him a brief description when she first told her own story to Aidan, but now she pulled out her memories of him, bringing to life his wry sense of humor and grim demeanor.

"I could trust him the way I could trust the tide to come in. I've never known anyone so solid. When I first met him he frightened me, he was so fierce and seemed angry all the time, but that's just his way. It took me a while to realize he was teasing me." She gave a strained smile. "Then I could tease him back and he never got mad for it. He's had a hard life, harder than I imagined possible."

She sat up and faced Aidan. "He didn't want me to go off without him. He didn't entirely trust Marek." Sighing she said, "I just wrote it off as his suspicious nature."

She yawned and lapsed into silence.

Aidan sat, listening to the song of the tree frogs and crickets, and wishing he could say something that would help. He struggled with his own nagging doubts about leaving his mother and Arella. There was nothing he could do about it now, he reasoned. When he looked back over at Elana she had fallen asleep, her face still strained and uneasy.

The night passed without incident, and when morning dawned cool and damp, Aidan woke Cecily and Elana. He was exhausted, having only slept in fitful spurts, ever vigilant for their safety. They ate a hurried breakfast and he led them through the tangle of woods back toward the road. He hoped to meet back up with the other three and the chances of finding them improved if they didn't have to stray too far into the Empty Hills.

An urgency pushed him forward. They had to reach Holding soon. He could feel the power pulsing from the Bronze Key that Elana held, and tried not to picture it drawing the Hunter to them.

Since Elana returned with the Bronze Key he felt his own Waking heightened. Not since he left Bellport had he so clearly heard the land speaking. He would have enjoyed it more except that he felt the land responding to the presence of the Bronze Key. It was as though they were being heralded as they traveled.

He stretched the reach of his Waking, searching through the rhythms that washed over him, for some hint of Faris, Kenrich, and Niall. By mid afternoon he found it. They were farther along the road to Holding, but how far, he couldn't tell. Aidan decided to risk the open road to gain time. The three of them rode out of the Empty Hills, pushing their horses to catch up.

The sun was hanging just above the treetops when Aidan spotted their companions up ahead. His heart lightened at the sight. He gave a shout and the three figures in the distance wheeled their horses around and then raced toward them.

Faris reached them first, a smile softening his features. He reached out and clapped Aidan on the back.

"I'm so glad to see you, you can't know..." he began.

Before he could continue Kenrich and Niall joined them. Everyone began talking at once in the exuberant chaos of reunion.

Faris was the one to bring order. "Let's find a place to camp and then we can exchange stories."

Hearty approval met his suggestion and before the sun was down, they found a likely spot in a clearing well off the road.

Aidan couldn't help but notice that Kenrich had appointed himself Cecily's special guardian. Guilt and jealousy warred in him at the sight. He had been less than attentive to her since they separated, but then they had never been out of danger until now. She was certainly regaining her bloom under Kenrich's care. He felt his face burning and he turned away, not wanting to make a fool of himself.

Niall got the fire lit, and Elana and Faris pooled the food stores and set out the first solid meal Aidan had seen in days. In the midst of all the bustle he felt strangely alone. A melancholy tugged at him and the old fears and doubts started whispering in his ear. He reached out to Kael, seeking the comfort of the stallion's presence, but Kael was full of his own reunions, only partially aware of Aidan. A heavy hand on his shoulder brought him back.

"Come help me gather wood for the night watch." Niall's voice was rough, but his eyes met Aidan's with understanding.

Once they were out of sight of the camp, the big smith started talking.

"Afterwards is always the hardest part. Give me a fight, or a search, or an ambush, or even a retreat. Something to do. It braces a fellow somehow. But after... that's when it all catches up. It takes more courage to live through that sometimes, when you have to face in cold blood what's happened and what may happen..." His words trailed off.

Niall shocked Aidan out of his gloom. He just couldn't imagine the smith ever being afraid of anything.

"You get afraid?" he ventured.

"Only a simpleton doesn't." The smith's eyes held his own, searching them with an intensity Aidan didn't fully understand. "I've lived through many a battle, and will tell you now, the best fighters know fear. Only the ones capable of courage wrestle with doubt. Those who don't know the fear are like brittle iron. Can't trust them under pressure. They'll snap just when you need them to be strong."

Aidan shook his head, amazed.

"Don't be ashamed of it. It's part of the forging."

A shout from Faris, calling them to supper, cut short the questions forming in Aidan's mind. Niall's generous smile lit up his face for a moment before the big man turned back toward the camp. Aidan followed him, his thoughts tumbling around inside his head.

When they all had served themselves supper, Elana opened the questions.

"The last we heard, you were engaging the Black Knights. What happened?"

Faris sat silent, not offering any explanation, and Niall tended the fire. It was Kenrich who volunteered the details.

Eyes shining like a true Dundas, he recounted the skirmish.

"There were seven of them and they overtook us where we stopped. I could tell by their faces that they thought us easy prey." The young lord's face hardened. "It was their last mistake. We cut three of them down as they rode and then had to pursue the remaining four to finish the job. We didn't want reports of our whereabouts leaving with them."

"It was well for us that The Hunter was not in their company," Faris interjected. "It might have gone much different if he were."

Kenrich scowled. "You don't have to remind me."

Cecily looked at him questioningly.

"The Hunter holds a power over the minds of men," Kenrich explained. "He drives the courage out of them in battle, using sorcery. I have met none who could stand in battle when he was there. For all our prowess, we would have been helpless before him."

Cecily paled, her green eyes widening. "Is he Elder Born?" she asked.

Aidan felt his cheeks burn, and he saw Elana bite her lip. It was Faris who answered the question.

"Not all Elder Born are evil. I don't know what prejudices fester in Bellport, my lady, but you would do well to learn differently."

Cecily's eyes flashed at his tone.

Aidan saw that she had recovered more than her bloom. The arrogance was there again as well. His heart sank.

"Then maybe you could instruct me," she parried.

Faris' mouth curled in his mocking smile. "Very well."

He slowed the cadence of his speech as though he were speaking to a child.

"The Shadow King hates and fears the Elder Born. They are his ancient enemies. To overcome them, he must do one of two things: kill them, or turn them to his service. Those who turn become what we know as Hunters. They hunt down other Elder Born, forcing upon them the same bitter choice. This betrayal of their own kind has grown slowly over the years."

He paused, making sure she followed.

An arched eyebrow from her invited him to continue. "About five years ago, an Elder Born of tremendous power turned to the Shadow King. Rumor of him has been spreading through the Vale. It is my guess that he hails from Drumcard. He is known only as The Hunter. Whatever his true identity, he has kept it close."

"This does nothing to set my mind at ease," Cecily retorted. "Your lesson only increases my distaste toward them."

Kenrich shifted uncomfortably, throwing a glance toward Aidan.

"Are there good men in Bellport?" Faris asked her.

"Of course." Cecily bristled at this slight against her city. "The city is not entirely corrupt."

"Should those good men carry the taint of the unsavory?"

"Certainly not." She stopped abruptly, recognizing what Faris was doing. "But none of the Valefolk, good or evil, is capable of cursing another with sorcery."

"True." Faris nodded. His hand toyed with the sword at his side.

Cecily gave him a triumphant look.

Without changing expression Faris rose, drew the blade, and held the tip against Cecily's throat.

Kenrich gasped and reached for his own blade, but Niall's huge hand pushed him back down. The smith's eyes were twinkling.

The mocking smile disappeared from Faris' face.

"The Valefolk cannot use sorcery, yet with a drawn blade they can empty a man of his life's blood. Is that not horror enough for you?" He met her eyes, his gaze unwavering.

"Should we judge you by your father? Your own flesh and blood? Should the spilt blood of the sons of Airth be on your hands, daughter and heir to the House of Gratton? Would you have us weigh you on the same scale you weigh the Elder Born?"

All color drained from Cecily's face and her voice trembled. "Speak not to me of Lord Gratton. I am nothing more to him than a cargo ship of silks, to be traded for gold or power. It is but an accident of birth that left me as his daughter."

"And the same accident left others as Elder Born, my lady. They had no more choice over their birth than you did over yours." Faris held her eyes until she looked away. "I do not judge you by your father, and I will judge no man or woman by the accident of their birth." He lowered his sword. "You would do well to follow my example."

Cecily raised her head, her words cold, measured. "It will take more than clever words twisted into arguments, or threats to convince me. I have not to date met an Elder Born that I could trust. Until such a day, you will have to excuse me."

Faris' eyes blazed. "Such a day has come and you have no excuse. You speak of what you do not know."

Elana nodded at him.

Aidan looked away. He had known he would have to tell her eventually, but this was not the way he would have chosen.

"Aidan?" Faris inclined his head toward him.

His stomach in knots, Aidan turned toward Cecily. A wary look haunted her green eyes.

"I am Elder Born, Cecily. I'm sorry I did not say anything sooner. I meant to tell you, but the time never seemed right."

"But you are of the House of Tormey," she protested.

"My father was the eldest son of that line, but a bastard. His mother was Elder Born and died at his birth. His own heritage didn't show until he was almost a man. Ulrich, his younger half brother, took the Lord's seat instead of my father, and there has been little love between our families."

Cecily turned away from him, refusing to meet his gaze. "You lied to me. You deliberately deceived me."

"And he also saved your life, my lady," Niall interjected. "He told you no lie, though he held back the full tally of truth. He could have left you on the road to Bellport." Niall shrugged at her. "It would have been the more prudent course."

"It was my own selfishness that held the truth from you." Aidan straightened his shoulders and faced her. "I ask your forgiveness. I have spent the last five years in hiding, reviled by those who would keep me prisoner. Your company was a sweet contrast to the life I'd lived. I only hoped for a chance to be known for who, not what, I am."

A long silence lay over the party. It was Kenrich who broke it.

"Surely lady, you know some of what he speaks. I know, for truth, that I do. How many in your acquaintance appreciate the woman, Cecily, rather than Lord Gratton's heir? Does it not get tiresome to be known and judged only by your position? Do you not long for someone to enjoy you for yourself?"

Aidan wasn't sure if he saw or imagined some struggle within her. She sat withdrawn, as though listening to something only she could hear. When finally she spoke it was with the icy voice of disdain.

"There has been one, Kenrich - ever faithful to me, ever vigilant for my well being. He has proven his faithfulness through long years of care. I betrayed his trust when I ran after Aidan." A faraway look stole over her face. "I only hope he can forgive me," she whispered.

A lump formed in Aidan's throat, making it impossible to speak. He felt as though she had kicked him. She refused to even look in his direction, as though the sight of him would taint her.

Elana broke the silence. "I too am Elder Born," she said, her voice low. Aidan could hear the rage trembling behind the words. He felt the force of her Waking surge.

Cecily's eyes widened and she drew back.

"Stay away from me," she hissed.

"If I had wanted to harm you I could have left you in the Empty Hills. The wolves would have thanked us for an easy meal."

"What do you want with me?" Cecily asked.

"Nothing," Elana said. "I want nothing at all. I have never wanted anything but to be far from your presence. You have yet to recommend yourself as a worthwhile companion. Yet I suffer you, your airs, your presumptions, your intrusion into our lives, your ignorance - because I think somehow that you can't help how you were raised, and I shouldn't hold the circumstances of your birth

324

against you." Her face softened for a moment. "I hold out the hope that you are not all that you seem, and that you might not be beyond help."

Panic flashed across Cecily's face as Elana grew suddenly quiet.

As if by reflex, Aidan reached out to Elana in his mind and felt her searching, probing Cecily. For the briefest moment he felt what she was searching for.

Marek.

Horrified at what he'd just done, he withdrew himself. But not before Elana turned and acknowledged him with a nod. Her voice sounded clear in his head. "He's there."

Faris gave him a keen look.

"*Not much gets past him,*" Aidan thought.

Elana turned to the company. "Cecily is not entirely herself," she said, her words carefully chosen and measured. "I think it best if we disregard anything that might bring offense or division. If all goes as planned, we might see a very different outcome for her than she could ever have imagined."

Cecily drew herself up and glared at Elana. "Do not speak of me as though I were not here," she commanded. She cast a withering glare over the rest of the company. "When we arrive at the next town, I will leave you and return to Marek. I was foolish to have ever doubted his ability to help me."

"That may not be one of your options," Niall growled.

"Rest assured, smith, Marek will help me," Cecily said. "Nothing you can do will prevent him from rescuing me if I call for his help."

"Cecily," Elana spoke so softly that silence fell over the company as they leaned forward to hear her words. "Marek is Elder Born, too."

"You lie." Cecily's eyes blazed. "You would destroy all that I've ever held dear. I hate you. I hate all of you!"

Kenrich's face was clouded, a mute agony playing over his handsome features. He gave Aidan a helpless look.

It was Faris who responded. "We warned you of the dangers of our path, and gave ample evidence to dissuade you from joining us. At this late hour, leaving our company is no longer your choice. We will see that you are as well protected as any of us, but to let you depart would put our lives at greater risk. I'm sorry lady, if our company wearies you." With iron in his voice he continued. "But seeing as how your life depends on our goodwill, you would do well not to make your presence a burden. I will not judge you by the accident of your birth, but trust me - I will judge you by your own actions. There is a limit to our generosity."

For a moment Aidan resented him. As awful as Cecily had been, he could never bring himself to threaten her. He knew, from one look at Faris' face, that he would sooner leave her dead on the trail than suffer her to compromise their quest.

"The day may come when you regret those words," she said. Turning her back, she wrapped herself in her cloak and pretended to sleep.

Aidan sighed. The joy of reunion lay trampled on the ground. No one had the heart to talk anymore. One by one, each of the companions settled into a spot by the fire and let sleep carry them away.

Elana tossed and turned, sleep eluding her. There was some bitter satisfaction in confirming that Marek was indeed linked to Cecily, but the bitterness outweighed the satisfaction. She knew Faris was right. It was less dangerous to keep her with them, but the whole thing stank.

It wasn't enough to have the Bronze Key announcing their presence to any with the ability to hear? Now there was Cecily calling out to Marek for help. Elana could feel her reaching out to him. It was only a matter of time before he responded. What she couldn't predict was how or where he would act.

She lay seething, resenting the need to pretend sleep. The look she had seen on Aidan's face when Cecily turned away from him, haunted her. It was almost enough to make her want to harm the girl, but her own experience with Marek diffused the anger. With all her power, she could barely stand against Marek's passion and hatred without having it consume her as well. There was no way Cecily would have had a chance. She felt bile rise to her throat. Marek raised her from a child. Did she even know who she was separate from him? She had been a victim of the worst kind of abuse an Elder Born could commit, and yet she didn't even realize it. The horror of that eclipsed her offensiveness. In truth, she had true cause to hate the Elder Born. She was just hating amiss.

Elana wished in vain that she could speak privately with Faris or Aidan. Faris appeared to be sleeping. She reached tentatively toward Aidan in her mind. Nothing. He was an enigma, his mind closed tight to her. How had he touched her mind earlier? Why had he done that? Her head ached from all that had gone on. She dozed on and off, her thoughts running in circles until Niall woke Faris for the next watch.

Seeing the chance for some quiet talk, she waited until she was sure the smith had fallen asleep and then stole quietly toward Faris. The shadows from the firelight played over Faris' features, highlighting the stern lines in his face. For a moment Elana quailed, nervous about approaching him, and then he turned to her, his blue eyes bidding her welcome. She sat down next to him, wrapping her cloak around her to ward off the night chill.

"You never told us your story," Faris said, his voice low.

Elana wanted to speak more about what had happened, but thought it best not to push. Anyway, there was much she needed to tell him. She recounted as best she could, the happenings of the last few days, pulling out the Bronze Key to show him.

"Put it away, and don't let anyone else know what you have here," he warned.

"Aidan knows," she said.

"Good. He must know. I would trust Niall as well, but I don't yet know about Kenrich. He means well, but that isn't always enough."

Elana nodded, glad that she wasn't going to be pushed to reveal it. "Aidan said that it acts like a beacon, the way my Waking acts when I let it go unchecked."

Faris grinned at her. "You do tend toward the dramatic, don't you?"

Elana tried to return the smile, glad at least, that he wasn't frightened off.

"There's something else, too. Marek is linked with Cecily. Those weren't empty threats she was mouthing tonight about him helping her. I could hear her calling out to him before she fell asleep. He will answer. It's just a matter of where and when."

"I was afraid of something like that," he said. "What can we do about it?"

"Nothing that I know of." Elana frowned. "I've had enough trouble keeping Marek out of my own mind with her around. She's like a door left ajar that he seeps through. I can feel him there on the periphery."

"Could you contact him and hold him off?"

"I don't know how I'd do that."

"What if you threatened Cecily's well being?" Faris suggested. "He wouldn't have to know that we have no wish to harm her."

Elana shook her head. "I don't know if he cares that much about her. She's just a means to an end for him. If he saw it as necessary, he might be willing to sacrifice her." She felt sick. "I almost feel sorry for her."

"You said that she might not be past help. What do you mean by that?"

"I don't know how much Marek has invaded her personality." She looked away, ashamed to speak of her link with Marek. "He can be very persuasive and she would have no defenses against him. I don't know if anyone knows who Cecily really is."

"Did he try that with you?" Faris asked, his blue eyes glinting with suppressed fury.

"Yes." She found it hard to say more.

Faris waited silently for her to continue.

"I found a place where I could hide from him, search his own mind while he was trying to dominate mine. He couldn't detect me there. I think my Elder Skills are more powerful than his. He suspects they might be, but doesn't know that for sure. If he didn't need me for something I don't know what my chances of surviving would have been. You know that he tried to have Aidan killed. Twice."

Faris spat on the ground, as though no words could express his distaste for the man.

His expression turned inward, homing in on a new thought. "And what does he need from you?"

"I don't know."

"Don't you?" He looked at her, the mocking smile that never reached his eyes, curling up along the edges of his mouth. "I think you're wearing it around your neck right now."

"The Firestone," Elana breathed. She felt her blood run cold. Why had she not seen it before? Probably because she only half believed it possible herself. If Marek had control of the Firestone...

Faris nodded, his face grim. "We underestimated him. Do you think he knows you have the Key?"

"I have no idea."

"It's a race then, to find Laharan," Faris said. "Speak nothing of this to any but Aidan. I will fill in Niall as soon as I am able. We ride for Holding before first light. It will be a few days ride yet, if we make good time and are not troubled on the road. My heart tells me that there we will find news of how to proceed next."

Elana's heart hammered in her chest. She tried not to picture Marek swooping down on them from one side as the Black Knights and the Hunter swooped down on them from another. The one consolation that she had was that she didn't believe that Marek was entirely in league with the Black Knights. Marek served Marek. He wasn't above using them, but it would thwart his plans to have her fall into their hands.

"Try and sleep Elana. We have a long day ahead of us." Faris reached out and touched her cheek. "You've done well. I'm proud of you."

She blushed at the compliment, so uncustomary from the Barras.

"Good night Faris." She rose and made her way back to her blanket.

Kenrich grunted and rolled over in his sleep, calling out unintelligible words. Crickets scraped out their night songs and the bullfrogs from a nearby pond answered them. She felt Faris' eyes on her, though instead of making her uncomfortable, she felt unaccountably safe again. Curling up in her blanket and cloak she let sleep take her.

It seemed only moments later, hands were shaking her, telling her it was time to wake.

"I'm sorry Elana, but you must get up now." Niall was bent over her, his face apologetic.

It was so black that the world outside the dying firelight disappeared completely.

Elana struggled to smile at the smith and pushed herself up. "Thank you Niall."

She felt eyes on her again, and turned to see Faris watching her from across the fire. She wasn't sure, but she thought she saw worry flit across his face.

"He said we need to start now, before the light," Niall explained. "I've never regretted following his lead before, and I'd do more with a good heart, were he to ask it."

"Elana gave his arm a squeeze. "I'm not grumbling, just sleepy. I'll be ready in just a moment."

She grabbed a piece of flat bread from her pack and forced herself to chew on it. Everyone was packing their things; horses shuffled and snorted in the dark, and muffled curses jarred the pre morning stillness.

Elana noticed that Kenrich had not abandoned Cecily, but had all her things packed and her mare saddled before he saw to his own. The tight lipped expression on the young Lord's face betrayed the conflict of heart he was suffering.

Aidan was the only one who made no stir. Silent as a shadow, he packed up his things, readied Kael and then helped others wherever necessary. Elana felt his mind firmly closed to her.

The morning's ride passed like a feverish dream. They pushed the horses as hard as they dared. It was all Elana could do to stay awake; the pounding of hooves made a steady rhythm that threatened to carry her back into sleep again. She clung to Devi's mane, unable to focus on anything past staying upright on the golden mare.

By the time they stopped in the afternoon, every muscle ached and her head pounded with fatigue. Only Faris seemed in good spirits.

"We're closer than I realized," he told the company. He pointed to a rock formation high above the road to the north. "I thought we were at least a day's ride from here." His buoyancy revived the group some. "We can stop for a few hours rest and then press on."

They saw to their horses, grabbed some cold food, and one by one caught whatever sleep they could. The sun was setting when Elana woke. A vague uneasiness made her look quickly into the surrounding woods. Before she had time to think about what was happening, she felt something else - Marek.

She jumped up, half expecting to see him, but all she saw was Cecily sitting alone, with a small triumphant smile on her face.

Elana's stomach turned over. Only Aidan was awake, keeping watch at the other side of their camp, staring doggedly away from Cecily. He turned when she sat up and beckoned her over with a nod.

"It's all wrong," he said when she sat down beside him.

"I'm so sorry about Cecily," she began.

"No, not that." Aidan shook his head. "That's wrong too, but it's worse. There's danger all around, but I can't make anything out clearly. It's as though something was interfering with my Waking."

The hairs on the back of Elana's neck stood up. "We have to wake the others." The foreboding that woke her threatened now to explode into panic."

She half ran to Faris, who sat up before she even reached him.

"What is it" he demanded.

"I don't know." She couldn't keep her voice from shaking. "Something's not right though and Aidan feels it too."

Faris was on his feet without another word, and woke the two Dundas. After a brief council, they agreed to press on. This place was not defensible in the event of an attack, and if they could reach Holding before anything happened, they could find help.

There was no temptation to sleep on this ride. Fear drove them forward, their horses picking it up from the riders and pushing themselves without urging. Even Niall's old gelding kept pace, drawing from resources Elana wouldn't have imagined he possessed.

They rode by moonlight until the animals were lathered, their sides heaving, their heads hanging down. Then they dismounted and walked the horses, not daring to stop yet.

Elana kept looking back to Cecily. It seemed as though she were almost in a trance. She could feel Marek's presence so strongly in her that there was no room for Cecily. As much as she disliked Lord Gratton's daughter, seeing her like this made her sick to her stomach.

The road passed through a thick wood that blotted out most of the moonlight. Elana could barely make out Aidan and Faris talking together, heads bent toward one another in council, as they walked. Niall had loosened the sword in his belt and was glancing around suspiciously. Kenrich's face was set in hard lines. He had ridden like one stricken all day, stealing furtive glances at Cecily. Elana felt sorry for the young Lord. He was going to make himself ridiculous with her sooner or later, and she had little patience for that, but even so, she hated to see him so torn.

The uneasiness that had pursued them all night continued to mount. Faris called everyone to a halt and told them that they would make camp at the next likely spot. Though Elana didn't like the idea of stopping in this wood, she recognized the wisdom of it. It would be worse to face an attack while on the road. They walked on in silence. No crickets called, and no frogs sounded. The night birds were silent. A heaviness lay over the wood. Their horses, exhausted though they were, spooked and snorted at shadows.

Elana made her way up to Aidan.

"What is it?" she whispered to him.

"It's all a jumble," he answered. "Something's very wrong, but I can't pick up where it's coming from. For all I know we could be walking straight into a trap."

The heaviness grew until it became a tangible fear. Only Cecily seemed impervious to it. She walked on oblivious to her surroundings and when Elana reached out toward her, the only presence she felt was Marek's. Focusing her Waking, she tried to determine if the fear was coming from him. It wasn't. It was more like he was shielding Cecily from whatever was out there.

Even Faris looked uneasy, glancing over his shoulder and starting at the crack of a broken branch. Elana felt a fog settle in over her mind. It became hard to think straight. It took all of her determination just to put one foot in front of another and keep walking. She felt as though she had stumbled into a nightmare. With what little sense she had left, she saw that the others also seemed aimless, struggling with internal shadows and no longer focused on finding a place to camp. Something inside her was screaming out a warning, but it sounded faint and far away. It felt hard to take a breath. She reached her hand to her throat, as though to push away whatever was suffocating her and brushed against the chain that secured the Bronze Key. Her fingers closed over it and by instinct reached down and pulled the Key out of her tunic.

Instantly her mind cleared. Her Waking surged and she recoiled from what she saw. The Shadow that she'd seen from Orvis's boat, it's fingers reaching for her, was swirling around them. A presence was driving it forward. A presence she recognized. The Hunter.

Recognizing her in the same instant, the Hunter slammed against her mind. Everything went black for a moment before she regained her senses. She clutched the Bronze Key and willed her Waking to rise. Hiding was no longer an option.

A shout rang out just ahead of them and another answered it. Hooves pounded on the road. The company staggered to a halt as a band of Black Knights, led by the Hunter, rode down upon them.

Elana watched in horror. They would be massacred. Faris and Aidan struggled to draw their weapons. Niall and Kenrich stood staring, unable to fight.

She slammed back against the mind of the Hunter. She felt him quail, and the Black Knights slowed their charge. Then he rallied and made straight for her.

Time slowed for Elana. She could see the raw boned bay, nostrils flared, eating up the road between them. The Hunter held a naked sword aloft, swinging it through the air, his eyes never leaving her face. It was only a matter of moments and she would be dead.

Without stopping to weigh the consequences, she cried out for help. The answer almost knocked her off her feet. Marek was there, pouring his power into her mind, strengthening her Waking until her body shook with the force of it. She assaulted the Hunter's mind once more and this time something in him broke. His horse veered away from her, throwing him onto the road.

The fog lifted from everyone's minds and she saw her companions collect their wits just as the Black Knights reached them. One, seeing what happened to The Hunter, rode toward her, sword loosed. Without hesitation she unleashed her Waking on him, knocking him senseless. He tumbled off his horse, only to have Niall's blade make a short end to his life. Elana's stomach heaved and her Waking wavered. A part of her shouted a warning, but before she could consider it, The Hunter regained his feet. He walked toward her, slowly, deliberately, a strange smile playing along his face.

The ring of iron blades and the shouts of wounded men sounded faint in her ears. Her Waking surged strong again, fueled by a sudden

334

hunger for revenge. This was the man she saw kidnap her parents. Anger pounded through her, adding its power to her Waking.

Marek's voice sounded in her mind, "You are more powerful than him. With my help, there would be none who could oppose you. I'm very impressed, little one."

She considered the words for a moment, and then as though a door went click, she knew what she wanted to do. It felt as though she stood at the center of a whirlwind. Gathering all the power of her Waking, she spoke directly into the mind of the Hunter.

"What have you done with them?"

His smile wavered and she saw pictures in his mind of her parents, gaunt and haggard, but alive. They were heavily guarded in a large cave. Above it stood a bare rock mountain with two blackened peaks.

The Hunter tried to answer back in her own mind, but she slammed the force of her Waking against him again. Hatred flickered in his eyes.

He spoke aloud this time. "You will come back with me and my Master will decide your fate. Your parents are lost to you."

Blind rage burned through Elana. It consumed her, feeding on itself and multiplying until there was nothing else left in her world.

The Hunter's expression changed. Fear ghosted across his face. It served only to spur her on.

In a voice not her own, she spoke into his mind. "I will kill you first."

The Hunter looked away from her for the first time. Most of his men lay dead on the road and the remaining few were battling for their lives. His face went ashen. Throwing her a last furtive glance, he raced to the raw boned bay, flung himself on, and galloped down the road away from Holding.

The whirlwind inside her grew, unabated by his absence. It became harder to see what was going on around her. Even the sounds of battle seemed far away, unreal. She could no longer control the whirlwind's force, now it turned on her, pulling at her mind, threatening to undo it. Again, the far away warning screamed. Something in her quailed, afraid now, for the first time since the power poured into her. Clinging to the Bronze Key, she fought the whirlwind. She felt it tearing at her, worse now, with her resisting. There was a voice inside it, a voice that wasn't human. It was laughing at her, mocking her fear, claiming her for its own. With the last of her strength she called out once more. From far away she heard an echo of an answer, but it was too faint to tell. Despair pulled away the last shreds of her awareness and she wandered in swirling blackness, unable to remember anything, even her name.

CHAPTER 16

CITY OF THE HAFWEN

The muscles in Aidan's arm burned. With each swing of his sword the weapon grew heavier. Fear pounded in his chest, stealing the breath from his lungs. He fought with desperation, having no more plan than to stay alive one moment more. It was his Waking that saved him. With that other sense guiding him, he jumped aside as the swarthy faced Black Knight lunged toward him. Spinning around he drove his sword into the man's back. It made a sickening thud as iron pierced flesh and he yanked it back out again, bright red with the man's life blood. His attacker crumpled to the ground.

A part of him watched, sickened, from somewhere far away. How could people think there was glory in this? Did this man have any family? Would anybody miss him? The whole thing was surreal, first the fog and then regaining his senses just as the Black Knights bore down upon them. This was a nightmare he couldn't wake from. He was a farmer, a craftsman... not a warrior. What was he doing here?

His Waking flared again. Whirling around he spotted Kenrich at the edge of the road, holding off two Black Knights who circled him like wolves before a kill. The Dundas was at the edge of his strength. Aidan ran toward him, fear for his friend kindling a slow burning anger.

The anger fed his Waking. He melted into the rhythms of the land. The huge man on the right raised his sword to finish Kenrich as the young Lord dueled with the other Black Knight. Aidan's sword found it's mark before the man could utter a cry. Now it was two on one against the remaining Black Knight. Kenrich shot him a grateful look and with renewed energy made short work of his assailant.

There was a moment's reprieve. Aidan looked around, taking stock of the situation. Niall fought with an agility that belied his great size.

Three Black Knights lay dead by his sword, and two others were backing away from him, harboring second thoughts.

Faris's bloody sword had bought Cecily's life. The girl had revived from whatever trance held her. Her green eyes stared wide with terror and she kept herself between Faris and a huge old oak at the edge of the road.

Aidan wondered if it was duty or a native kindness that drove Faris to protect her. He knew there was no love lost between them. His heart warmed toward the enigmatic Barras. Here, he thought, was a leader worth following.

In the reprieve from immediate attack, he scanned the darkness, looking for Elana. It took a moment to locate her and when he did, his blood ran cold. Her Waking was stronger than he'd ever seen it, but instead of the clear light he'd witnessed before, it was a roiling darkness. He knew now why he hadn't spotted her right away. It wasn't Elana. With his own Waking he felt only Shadow and rage pulsing out of her. He saw The Hunter approach her and saw him speak, though he couldn't make out the words. Then, before Aidan had time to react, The Hunter turned away, sprung aboard his horse and raced back down the road. Elana stood for a while, oblivious to all that went on around her and then for no reason that he could discern, crumpled to the ground, one hand clutching the Bronze Key around her neck.

Fearful of the worst, Aidan was at her side almost as she reached the earth. Her face was pale, but she was still breathing, though with some effort. Her eyes stared into the gloom of the wood, not comprehending anything they saw. She wasn't there. Her body was there, but there seemed to be no Elana inside it. With all the force he could muster, he threw himself into her mind, desperate to find some echo of her there. It was like throwing himself into a tornado. The force of that dark whirlwind tried to rip away all remembrance of who he was and what he was doing. With a convulsive effort, he broke the link before his mind was torn to shreds.

He lay gasping for breath, not daring to open his eyes. She was there. He'd felt her, only ever so faintly, and she was fighting the Shadow that raged through her. Tears of frustration stung his eyes. He was watching her drown just out of his reach. How could she possibly hold on?

The fog, that had lifted so suddenly before the battle, crept back over his mind. He tried to fight it, but a hopelessness gripped at him, refusing to release its hold.

A shout jarred Aidan partially back to the world around him. Kenrich lunged toward him, cutting down a Black Knight that would have made a quick end to both Aidan and Elana's life. Everything around them fell silent. The Black Knights lay dead, their bodies scattered along the road and surrounding woods.

"You picked a strange time to daydream," Kenrich chided him. "But I'm glad I could return your favor. Those other two would have finished me if you hadn't stepped in."

Aidan could only nod.

Kenrich looked from him to Elana, his handsome face suddenly etched with worry. "What happened? Is she..." He didn't finish the question.

"No. She's alive, but only barely. She's fighting the Shadow King."

Aidan stared at Kenrich, amazed at what he'd just said. How did he know that?

Kenrich's eyebrows lifted. "She's what?"

A strange reluctance to speak of it anymore gripped him. He forced himself to answer Kenrich's question, the fog slowing his thoughts.

"In her mind. She's fighting the darkness. If she can't hold on, we'll loose her."

Faris knelt down beside them. He placed a hand on Elana's neck, feeling for the faint pulse there. "What did you just say?" he demanded.

With extreme effort Aidan repeated what he'd only just realized.

Faris looked hard at him. "Can you reach her?"

He recoiled from the thought. "I tried. It almost tore my mind apart. I don't know how she's holding on." The fog grew thicker. Helplessness opened a door to a yawning chasm of despair. It was lost. Everything was lost. They might as well give up now. Elana would never make it and without her there was no hope of any victory.

From what seemed very far away, a hand grabbed his shoulder. Strong fingers boring into him brought him back again. Faris was staring at him, and for the first time ever, Aidan saw fear in his clear blue eyes.

"Don't try and reach her again. It's too dangerous. We need to get both of you to someone who can help." His tone was harsh. Aidan bridled at it, suddenly angry. The world around him grew cloudy. It was hard to make out the faces of his companions. He heard Faris shout something and a moment later a soft muzzle was blowing warm air into his face.

Kael.

The stallion's presence filled his mind, seeping in through cracks in the darkness, dispelling it the way the sun dissolves the morning mist. Aidan felt, more than heard, a howl of rage as the Shadow withdrew.

He reached up and threw both his arms around Kael's neck, letting the horse's mind fill his own, half afraid to try and come back to himself. The rhythms of the land that were clear to Kael, that Aidan shared only through his Waking, grew stronger. He felt the deep quiet within the horse and rested in its peace, trusting himself to the anchor of the stallion's presence.

He didn't know how much time had passed when Kael nudged him, forcing him back into himself. The worst of the Shadow was gone, though he could feel it circling, like a falcon, almost out of sight, on the edge of his awareness.

"You share an extraordinary bond with your horse." Faris' eyes were wistful as he looked from Aidan to Kael. "I believe he just saved your life."

Aidan pushed himself to a sitting position and leaned against Kael's forelegs. "He did." It took a monumental effort to speak. He still felt the strange reluctance to speak of the Shadow at all. "What do we do now?" he asked, changing the subject.

"We ride for Holding immediately. The Hafwen have healers there who may be able to help Elana. It's our only chance. If they can't then we must bring her to Farran."

Faris' words brought back the weight of their situation. If they lost Elana...

He couldn't bear to think of it. Clinging to Kael's mind with all his strength, so as not to be sucked back into the Shadow, Aidan went through the motions of getting ready to ride.

Faris carried Elana with him on Shay and Niall led Devi behind his quiet gelding. They rode through the night, skirting the Empty Hills, riding along hidden paths that only Faris remembered from his travels through this region. For once Aidan felt as blind as one of the Valefolk. It took all his concentration to keep the Shadow at bay. He had nothing left over to navigate with. Grateful for Faris' guidance, he let himself drift with Kael, wandering in the safety of the stallion's mind.

A deep velvet blue that whispered of the coming dawn, crept in from the east by the time Faris halted. They stood on the top of a ridge overlooking a narrow valley. The early morning light revealed houses and small farms huddled together under the sheltering hills. They'd reached the land of the Hafwen.

The horses were stumbling with fatigue as they drew near the first dwellings. A tall lean man waved to them, set down the buckets of milk he carried, and ambled over.

"Can I help you folks?" he asked, his face shining with goodwill.

"We're riding for Holding," Faris answered. "We have two here that need an expert healer."

The Hafwen furrowed his brow. "You've a few hours ride yet to reach Holding." He pointed to the far side of the valley. "It's through that pass and just on the other side. I'll send a messenger bird ahead to let them know you're coming. Then at least you'll have no delay once you arrive."

He asked Faris to repeat his name and their situation. With a salute he waved them off. Moments later they saw a pigeon winging its way toward the Hafwen city.

"Are these people always this kind to strangers?" Kenrich asked Faris.

"Most are," Faris answered. "They live far enough away from the skirmishes of the Vale to maintain a gentler outlook on the world. They are also the only Valefolk left who seek out contact with the Elder Born of Farran. Some say there's Elder Born blood running in their veins. I don't doubt that myself. Whatever they are, they are renowned for their skill with healing. Though that is not all they do."

A far away look stole over Faris' face. "They have no army, nor defenses, aside from the land itself. Refugees from across the Vale, seeking another way of life, find their way here and are welcomed. There are as many artists, musicians, and craftsmen here as healers."

"You've spent some time here then?" asked Kenrich.

"Yes. If it were my choice, I'd spend more. It's more of a home to me even than the lands of the Barras." Faris gave him a sad smile.

Niall shook his head. "Only the Ancient Ones know why you keep your word to a man who neither understands nor loves you. Varen doesn't know what he has in you. I'm sorry my friend. You deserve better."

Kenrich looked from one to the other, obviously confused at the exchange. Aidan thought for a moment that he was going to ask further, but the look on Faris' face silenced him. He changed subjects instead.

"Do you know the Lord of the Hafwen? What kind of man is he?" Kenrich tried to get the conversation back onto grounds that he could understand.

Faris' laugh rang out, surprising Kenrich and Aidan both.

"A poor man, my friend. A very poor man indeed."

The young Dundas lord stared at him in puzzlement.

Faris, still chuckling, explained himself. "The Hafwen are not ruled by a Lord the way the rest of the Valefolk are. They have a council of twelve men and women, two from each of the six districts of their land. The leader of the council, is not a man at all, but a woman. From time out of mind they have been governed by a woman. They call her The Wise One. Once she is chosen she holds that position for life."

His grin widened at the shock in Kenrich's eyes.

"A woman leads them? Buy why? What sort of man would let himself be governed by a woman?"

The laughter died on Faris' face. "A peaceable man, my friend. A man that doesn't live by weapons and war. It's a privilege we've never known."

Kenrich frowned, clearly not agreeing with Faris' take on this.

"Did you not know that the Firestone Elders are always led by a woman?" Faris asked. "The Hafwen have remained in close contact with them through the long years of The Forgetting. They learned more than just healing from them."

Kenrich made a derisive sound. "Healing is well and good, but leave ruling to the men."

Aidan watched the two, concerned that Kenrich was going too far. Before Faris could respond, Cecily interrupted.

Her brow was furrowed and she gave Faris a wary look. "Are you saying that the Elder Born are ruled by a woman?"

Faris nodded to her, his face inscrutable.

"And these people, these Valefolk are also ruled by a woman and a council, not a family determined to drive all others out of power?"

"Yes, my Lady. They have found a different way of doing things."

Aidan looked at her, taking her in for the first time since the night of their reunion. She made no further reply, though Aidan could see she was turning over that piece of information. It seemed to him that

343

whatever darkness had held her was no longer there. He tried to blot out the memory of Marek's presence through his link to Elana. His stomach twisted into a knot. He couldn't help being drawn to Cecily, but there was no guarantee that Marek wouldn't be back to turn her again at his whim and fancy. The Shadow in his own mind grew stronger and he let all those thoughts go and clung to Kael; letting himself be swept up in the scents and sounds of the morning. It was too dangerous to even think about her right now.

By mid afternoon they had crossed the pass. Holding opened up before them, gateless, borderless, and much smaller than Aidan had imagined. His own fatigue was heightened by Kael's. All he could think of was finding a safe place to sleep.

As they navigated the narrow road down to the city, Aidan saw three riders come galloping up to meet them. The companions drew closer together from instinct and stopped to meet the riders. Two were women wearing unbleached tunics and riding mountain ponies, their long hair tied back in braids and streaming out behind them. The third Aidan felt to be a man, though he was cloaked and hooded, so his face wasn't visible. They pulled up alongside the companions.

Faris, from his saddle, bowed deeply to the women. "Thank you for helping us in our hour of need."

"The Hall of Healing is open to all," the eldest of the women replied. Her voice was low and confident, washing away some of the strain in Aidan's mind.

"We had more than one message of your coming," she continued.

Faris gave her a questioning look.

The man who was riding with them came alongside and threw back his hood, revealing a shock of flaming red hair.

Aidan almost cried for joy. It was Reeves.

Reeves nodded to Aidan, catching his eye and holding it with his penetrating gaze. "Well met, Aidan, son of Darian. You have done well to have made it this far."

344

"But Elana..." he stammered. "She needs help. HE has her."

"I know," Reeves answered. "She cried out in the midst of the struggle, before she lost contact. I tried to answer her cry, but I was too late. I followed its echo and guessed that if any were with her, they would bring her here. If you hadn't shown up by this evening, I would have ridden out to look for her. I didn't want to risk missing you on the many paths into the land of the Hafwen."

He turned to the others of the company. "I am remiss in introductions. My name is Reeves. I am the leader of the Bells Eldership."

Faris nodded in acknowledgment. "I am honored to meet you," he said. "I am Faris, from the Barras of Lanreath."

Reeves flashed him a brilliant smile. "The honor is mine, I assure you. We have much to speak of together, you and I."

Kenrich bowed in greeting. "I am Kenrich, son of Payton, Lord of the Dundas."

"Greetings Kenrich, and well met." Reeves looked at him with a warmth that caused the young lord to flush. "It has been years since I visited Cahermore. Your father is an old friend of mine."

Niall inclined his head to the red haired man. "I am Niall. A smith of the Dundas."

Reeves' broad smile embraced the smith. "Not just any smith, my good man. Your reputation has traveled throughout the Vale. It is my great pleasure to meet the man behind the legend."

Cecily face was strained as she studied this new Elder Born. She didn't offer her name.

Reeves turned to her, a pained look haunting his eyes and then vanishing in his kind smile. "The Captive Bird of Bellport. Lady Cecily, I have long hoped for an opportunity to speak with you. We share a mutual friend."

His gentleness seemed to pierce some defense in her and Aidan saw her lip quiver, though she gave no response.

Looking back to Faris, Reeves continued, "With your leave, I would like to tend to Elana immediately."

Faris nodded, handing the limp form of Elana down to the red haired man.

Aidan didn't want to watch, afraid that his worst fears would be confirmed, but he couldn't tear his eyes away. The Shadow that held Elana still swirled too close to his own mind. Reeves knelt on the ground beside Elana, cradling her face in his hands. Staring into her vacant eyes he started singing soft and low.

The song stirred Aidan's Waking and in it he could feel the ripple of power coming from the leader of the Bells Eldership. Aidan could feel the echo of Elana's name sounding in a mind cry through his own mind as well. He couldn't catch any of the words, but it seemed to him that the song itself wove a cocoon of light around Elana, keeping the Shadow at bay, though she still lay motionless in the center of that light.

Sweat poured down Reeves face and he paled from the strain of the singing. The companions encircled them, watching, silent.

At last Reeves straightened up.

"This is all I can do for her. She's out of the worst danger, but I can't call her back. I'm going to need more help."

Faris nodded, his mouth still set in a tight line. He lifted Elana as though she were a child and they followed Reeves and the two Hafwen women into Holding.

Reeves led them in silence to a low thatched-roofed cottage with wide windows. He knocked on the door and motioned for the companions to wait.

A boy's face appeared at the window; his white blonde hair standing out from his head like a halo. Aidan looked into his pale blue eyes and caught his breath. Baird. He'd almost forgotten about the boy. It seemed a lifetime ago since he met him and Granny on the road to Bellport.

346

Baird flashed a quick grin at Aidan, disappeared from the window and reappeared at the door. His pointed features sobered when he saw Reeves.

"What's wrong?"

"It's the young lady. She needs our help. Get the others."

Reeves had no energy to spare for politeness and Baird, sensing the urgency, disappeared again.

He reappeared in a moment and looked out at the company.

"They won't all fit in here," he declared with candor.

"No, I suppose not." Reeves' words were curt.

Faris motioned for Niall, Kenrich, and Cecily to wait outside with the horses.

He carried Elana into the house. Aidan and Reeves followed.

An old woman sat by the small fire, knitting. She didn't look up at their approach, and didn't slow her stitches.

"Welcome again, Aidan, son of Darian," Granny greeted him.

"Hello Granny," Aidan answered her. He felt his world tipping. The Shadow around him receded in her presence.

"The rashness of youth," she said, shaking her head. "It's not yet your place to challenge Him."

Aidan bristled at her words. "I didn't do that. It was Elana. She was in trouble."

Granny didn't respond.

Aidan bit his lip, embarrassed that Granny had gotten a rise out of him so easily.

From out of the shadows of the back wall, an older man got up with difficulty from a bench where he had been sitting. Though his face was gaunt and his breathing labored, Aidan recognized this as the old man he'd seen out his window in Bellport, the night of the attack. It was Orvis.

"What's there lad?" The grizzled old man directed his brusque question to Reeves.

Faris frowned at his tone.

"We have her, my friend," Reeves answered, laying a hand on the old man's shoulder to steady himself. "But she needs your help."

Faris' frown deepened at this, and Aidan tried to imagine what this old sailor could do that Reeves could not.

Reeves turned to the boy.

"Baird, fetch Orvis' flute."

The boy returned with the ancient instrument.

Orvis looked up, puzzled. "What? Am I to play her a song? You and the lad are better for that than me. And she's sleeping pretty enough. I think it'd take something more like a shout to wake her."

His calloused hand reached out, touching Elana's arm.

Granny answered him from her rocking chair, without turning or slowing her knitting. "She's lost at sea, old sailor. She needs someone familiar to steer her home."

Orvis gave an awkward cough and looked in desperation at Reeves.

"You know I'd do anything to help her, but I have no training in the Skills."

Reeves answered him, "It's not your Skills she needs, but your heart. She trusts you. She may follow you back."

Baird handed the flute to the old sailor. "It'll bring you to her. Play a song that makes you think of her and call her in your mind."

Reeves shot the boy a quick look of surprise and then nodded. "Baird's exactly right. Just play a little tune that puts her in your mind and call her back home. It'll be like a lighthouse for her, she'll hear you and find her way back again."

Reeves spread a blanket out by the fire and Faris lay Elana's small frame down; her hand still closed over the Bronze Key.

Red with embarrassment, Orvis took up the ancient flute, his gnarled fingers curling awkwardly over the holes. Bringing it to his lips he blew a tentative note and then another.

Slowly, haltingly, the notes shaped themselves into a simple tune; bittersweet and melancholy.

Aidan closed his eyes and images floated through his mind: the sea after a storm, a lonely strip of sand with a gray green ocean stretching beyond it as far as the eye could see. There were two people with kind faces, that he'd never seen before, and then, with the two strangers, he saw Elana, running along the beach, her long black hair blowing in the wind. He saw her laughing with the old sailor and the other two people, who he realized must be her parents... sitting with Orvis on the beach as he showed her the night stars... teasing the old sailor, sharing meals with him and her parents. Aidan felt the warmth of their companionship.

He heard the old sailor calling to her, with a tenderness he would never have imagined from one so gruff. He followed the call, straining to hear some answer.

The song played on and on. As it played, Aidan felt the last clinging of the Shadow loose its hold over him. For the first time since the attack, he felt completely himself again. There was no Shadow circling at the edge of his awareness. It was gone. He was free.

He opened his eyes and saw Reeves watching him. In his head he heard Reeves' voice.

"Go with him. You're safe now. She trusts you as well."

Nodding, Aidan closed his eyes again and let himself follow the song. Now his own Waking surged and he heard so much more than the simple tune. He heard the discord of the Shadow, fighting against the music of the flute, and somewhere, far off, he heard Elana's voice. Without stopping to think what he was doing, he reached into Orvis' mind, adding his own strength to that of the sailor. He felt Orvis' momentary surprise, and then felt the old man's thanks. Together they called to Elana and this time they both heard her answer.

A nightmare tore at Elana's mind. She wandered lost in a maelstrom. One hand clutched the Bronze Key and the only thing she knew was that she must not let it go. It was an anchor to something, though all remembrance of what that something might be, was gone.

After what seemed an eternity, she heard someone singing. The song tugged at her, nudging her to remember, to come back, but every time she was just about to grasp hold of what she was trying to remember, it slipped away. The song silenced the whirlwind, but she was floating, lost, unable to find any way out of this emptiness. There was no fear here, but a nagging pull that she didn't know how to answer.

Then into the emptiness came the faintest tune. It was beautiful and she latched onto it. With the tune, pictures formed in her mind. She saw the ocean and remembered that she knew of such a thing. She heard a voice calling. It sounded familiar, stirred a longing inside her, but it all remained nameless. She saw pictures of people, faint and far away, too far away to see who they were. Then another voice joined the first and suddenly she heard her name.

"Elana!"

That was her name! She was Elana. The pictures grew, cleared. and she saw her parents and Orvis together with her. She called back with all her might and felt the old sailor's joy at her answer. She clung to him, pieces of the past months coming back. There was something she didn't want to remember.

"Elana, it's me, Orvis." The gruff voice in her mind anchored her.

"Where am I?" she asked.

"Don't worry about that, just follow my voice. I'll get you back."

She wanted to cry with relief. He sounded closer and clearer. Something in her was saying that he couldn't be there, but she pushed that away. She didn't want to remember anything that would stop her now. She was going back home. Orvis would be there, and her parents, and she would be safe again. No more nightmares.

She felt the other presence with Orvis and wondered at that. No one else in their village would be with her family.

"Elana."

The other voice spoke her name. She saw pictures of a black horse, with a tawny eyed man astride him.

"It's me, Aidan. Do you remember me?"

It all came back – who she was and what she didn't want to remember. There would be no family to greet her, no Orvis - nothing but a fool's hope and a desperate journey.

"I'm here lass." Orvis' voice broke through her despair. "Don't give up now. I've walked half the Vale to see you."

The music stopped and she felt a hand on her face, rough and calloused. She opened her eyes and saw the old sailor's clear blue eyes filled with tears, looking into her own.

"I thought I'd lost you lass," he choked out, grabbing her into his arms. "Don't ever do that again."

"I'll try not to," she said, clinging to him with all her strength.

She closed her eyes again. It was enough just to be back with the old sailor. She didn't want to think about anything else.

Her mind and body both felt battered. Sleep. She just wanted to sleep. Low voices rose and fell in the room around her, and she knew vaguely that they were talking about her, but she was too exhausted to care. She rested her head against Orvis' shoulder and let herself drift, this time in safety. The last thing she remembered was hearing a man's voice singing, and the song seemed to wrap itself around her, cradling her in a web of light.

Embers from the dying fire glowed on the hearth, giving the room its only light. Elana sat up, trying to piece together where she was. It was silent around her- save for the steady creaking of a rocking chair, and the labored breathing of Orvis, sleeping on a pallet next to her bed.

An old woman sat in the rocking chair, eyes closed and hands folded over the knitting in her lap.

"I've been waiting for you to wake."

Elana started. She assumed the old woman was sleeping.

The woman opened her eyes and turned toward Elana.

Even in this light, Elana could see the milky white of her pupils staring blindly in her direction. She swallowed hard, her heart beating in her throat. "Who are you?" she asked.

"You can call me Granny," the old woman answered in a graveled voice. "I'm an old friend of Reeves. I had the pleasure of meeting Aidan this spring on the road to Bellport."

Though the old woman's voice betrayed her age, Elana felt an unmistakable surge of power from her. She sat up, suddenly needing to talk.

"Granny, what happened to me?"

"Why don't you tell me?" Granny countered.

Slowly, piece by piece, Elana recounted the events leading up to the ambush, not holding anything back, even the finding of the Bronze Key. Her face burned when she admitted receiving help from Marek, but Granny said nothing; just sat rocking, her bony fingers folded over the knitting.

When Elana had talked herself out, Granny let the silence fill the room for a while.

"You're going to need help," she said. "Reeves and I are shielding your mind right now, but we can't be with you always to do that. You're still untrained, and the raw power of the Skills can be as much liability as an asset, as you've experienced.

"Will you train me then?" Elana asked, hope rising in her. She didn't doubt that Granny had more than ample power and experience to train her.

The unseeing eyes made the old woman's face unreadable. "I may play a part in that, but this isn't the time. No. There's work that will not wait, not even for training. Lives are at stake, and we must be willing to walk in new ways if we're to rise to the task."

Elana saw a flash of her parents held hostage by The Hunter.

"I have to find them. I know where they are now. I have to go save them!" Her voice quavered. "I know they're alive."

The bed felt confining now. She wanted to be up, out and on her way to them. The picture of the bare rock mountain with its two blackened peaks, burned in her memory. Surely, it wouldn't be that difficult to locate such a place.

"Child," Granny said, her voice firm, "Don't you understand, the Hunter knows that you pulled those images from him. It's his great hope, to lure you to them."

"But I can't just leave my parents. "She tried in vain to hold the anger back. "You don't understand." She gave up trying to fight the resentment coursing through her. The anger had a power all its own. It promised strength - strength to help, strength to fight, strength to go find her parents.

Without warning, she felt like she'd been hit by a bolt of lightening. She was thrown back onto her bed, her mind raw and quivering from whatever had just happened. The anger was gone.

Granny's voice spoke in her head. It was not the voice of a feeble old woman anymore.

"Is that what you want? You almost invited the Shadow back in. That's what He's hoping for. Entertain the strength of your anger again and I may not be able to save you. We will have this lesson here and now."

The mind link with Granny was so much clearer than the one she had experienced with Marek. Granny showed her places in herself, her anger and bitterness, her fear and need to prove herself. Behind each she saw a door and on the other side of that door, the Shadow swirled, it's tendrils reaching for her, willing her to open one of those doors and let it in."

Elana felt cold down to her bones, cold and sick. She had almost gotten herself lost again. Despair clung to her, but before it could suck her down, Granny showed her the Shadow behind it as well.

"You must fight, Elana. But not with His weapons."

Unbidden, her hand reached for the Bronze Key, hanging around her neck. She remembered The Ancient One's words. She must promise to obey whatever the Firestone directed her to do. So this was it. This was how the Elder Born were meant to fight. She had to find the Firestone and with it, defeat the Shadow King. She swallowed over a thick lump in her throat.

As if in confirmation, Granny spoke into her mind. "Follow the Bronze Key. Find the Firestone. It's your only hope." There was a long pause. "It's the only hope for us all."

A picture flitted through Elana's mind, of herself, holding the balance of power that would free or completely enslave the entire Vale.

It was gone as soon as she saw it, and Granny spoke out loud. "You are the only one who can do this thing. You must not fail!"

An indignant snort broke the ensuing silence.

"That's no way to talk to the lass," Orvis growled. "She's flesh and blood, not just some pawn in your plans."

Granny's chin went up, but Orvis plowed through.

"And don't you go lecturing me, old woman. I've seen too many winters to be impressed by your age. Sure, you can see things what we can't, but let me tell you, I can feel things that you never have stumbled on."

Orvis pushed himself up to a sitting position, breathing hard. "What Elana needs is folks around her, helping her. Just because you lived your life alone, doesn't mean everyone else has to. She has to do what's before her, but she doesn't have to face it with no one at her side."

Orvis turned and faced her. "See here lass, Aidan told me most of what happened since that night on the docks. I don't blame you for accepting Marek's offer of help. How were you to know? What you did know was that you couldn't do this by yourself. And you were right. I let you down." He looked away. "I don't know that I could have given you what you needed anyways."

"No Orvis," Elana interrupted.

"Hush lass." Orvis scowled at her. "When have I ever gone soft with the truth?"

He took a deep breath. "When I was calling you back from that dark place, I couldn't do it by myself. I could find you, but it wasn't enough to bring you back. It wasn't until Aidan joined me that we had the strength. Maybe if we all worked together, we could help you face whatever's in front of you?"

Hope hurt, and Elana wasn't sure that she wanted to go there.

"Well, old man, you surprise me sometimes." Granny sat nodding at Orvis. "I do believe you have the right of this thing. We'll have to speak to Reeves of this in the morning. Good night."

Her dismissal left no room for further comment.

Elana looked over at Orvis. "Thank you," she said.

He smiled at her, his face unreadable.

Reeves joined them after breakfast, with Faris at his side. Elana felt awkward with the leader of the Barras. She felt the fool, and didn't meet Faris' questioning eyes. She didn't feel much like talking with anyone and stayed close to Orvis, letting the old sailor play watchdog over her. She even avoided Aidan, not wanting to think about what he'd done for her.

Only the strange boy with the shock of white hair didn't seem intimidated by her silence. He followed her every movement with his pale eyes, and when she stopped and stared back at him, he laughed.

"What do you want?" she finally asked in exasperation.

He didn't answer, just pulled a small shepherd's pipe from his pocket and began to play, ignoring her completely. The tune was both intricate and achingly beautiful. She'd never heard anything like it before, yet if felt somehow as though it had been with her for as long as she could remember.

He stopped playing suddenly, and just sat watching her, a question in his pale eyes.

"Where's the rest of the song," she asked him.

"You haven't found it yet," he said.

"Me? What? I'm sorry, I don't understand." She frowned at him, trying to make sense of this.

"Well done, Baird," said Reeves, a warm smile shining on his face. "Your Skills are extraordinary."

He turned to Elana. "He just put all he could sense of you into song. That's what he played. He stopped because the rest is yet to be lived. Beautiful, isn't it?"

Elana blushed so hard her ears throbbed.

Baird continued grinning at her. "I thought you needed a little help. You've been moping all morning."

She didn't like being called to task by a child, but he was so disarming about it that she couldn't be mad. "I know. It's just that I feel like an idiot, who wouldn't know enough to get out of the rain. It's a little embarrassing."

Sighs of relief rippled across the room. She hadn't realized how worried everyone had been about her.

Aidan flashed her a smile, and Faris gave her a slow nod, holding her gaze until she looked down, blushing again.

"Elana," Reeves began, looking seriously at her. "You know Granny and I have been shielding your mind since you've come back."

She nodded.

356

"We won't be able to continue doing that for you, and you need it. You'll need it more as time goes on."

He let his words sink in before continuing.

"I won't be coming with you."

Elana's heart sunk into her belly. She had so hoped he'd join them. The promise of finding Reeves and him making everything alright had never quite left her.

"I am going after your parents. You found out where they are and I don't want to loose that advantage."

Granny scowled at him.

Elana jumped up, knocking her chair over, and threw her arms around Reeves' neck. "Thank you, thank you!" For the first time since she came back, it felt like everything just might work out all right. "I'll do anything you need me to if I know you're going to try and help them."

"I need you to form a mind link with Aidan." Reeves' words hit her like a tree branch across the face.

"What?"

"He's the only other one powerful enough to help you." A spasm of anger twisted across Reeves' face. "What Marek did with you was wrong. He knew that untrained, you wouldn't be able to sever the link with him, once you entered into it. And there was no precedence for him to take you there." He looked at her sadly. "If there was any other way, I would never ask this of you."

Across the room, Aidan looked anguished. The irony of this did not escape her. She didn't know who this would be worse for, her or him. She caught his eye and for the briefest moment, he was in her mind.

"I'm sorry," he said, and was gone again.

"It's all right," she spoke out loud. "We'll get through this."

He gave her a feeble smile.

"When do we do it?" she asked.

"Now. There's no time to loose and I want to help you both manage this before I send you out into the wild." Reeves shook his head. "If there were any other way, Elana..."

Reeves had them stand in front of the fireplace, facing each other, palms touching, just like when she formed the link with Marek. Elana felt herself brace against the onset of the link. She didn't like the feeling of someone else trying to take up space in her mind. With reluctance she met Aidan's eyes, waiting for the push that meant he was trying to reach in. There was nothing. No push, no forcing, just him standing in front of her waiting.

The knot that had tightened in her stomach released a fraction. Still nothing pushed at her from him. An invitation hung in the air between them. He had always been walled off from her, save in rare moments when he spoke directly to her mind and then vanished again. Curiosity overcame fear and she reached out tentatively.

He didn't reach back, only let her come closer. Slipping into his perspective was effortless and startling. Kael met her immediately, surprise giving way to equanimity at her presence. She hadn't realized what a big part of Aidan the stallion shared. She moved carefully, fearful of intruding, but still the invitation stood. Pictures flashed in her mind; a woman her mother's age, with Aidan's tawny eyes, looking drawn and tired, a little girl, who could have been her own sister, they looked so much alike, a tiny cottage by a marsh.

Tears burned Elana's eyes. He was sharing the things most precious to him with her. Not once had he asked for anything in return. She knew now why Kael had trusted him, bonded with him. She didn't want to intrude any farther without also letting Aidan see who she was.

She invited him into her thoughts, showing him her parents, the village they'd spent the last years in, Farrell, the innkeeper, Orvis, and the sea in the early morning when she'd slip out to try and make sense of her Waking. She felt his compassion at her loss and the last of the knot in her stomach melted away. This wasn't going to be anything like it was with Marek.

"Thank you," she spoke to his mind.

"Friends?" he sent back.

"Friends," she said.

CHAPTER 17

IN SEARCH OF THE DOOR

Exhaustion muddied Aidan's thinking, which, he supposed, wasn't even entirely his own anymore. It had been two days now since he'd formed the mind link. Reeves promised him it would get easier as he got used to it, and Aidan tried to believe him. The only problem was that he hadn't been entirely honest with Reeves. He'd kept himself busy, hoping that what he refused to look at, would just go away. Half formed fears buzzed around his head, like deerflies on a hot summer's day. He did his best to ignore them, but the effort was wearing him down.

Though he tried to keep his worries to himself, he felt wisps of reassurance, as well as unspoken questions, reaching out to him from Elana. He sent back a quiet thanks, embarrassed that she'd picked that up. They hadn't been alone since they'd formed the link, and Aidan was reticent to use it to talk with her. It felt too invasive. He wanted to sit down and talk, out loud, using words. He'd hoped to catch her after lunch, but Granny had commandeered her and was delivering a lecture about her Skills. Aidan tried hard not to listen in. Seeing as no one else needed anything in particular from him, he went out to find Kael. Maybe some space away from everyone would help.

Tensions in the company were running high. Kenrich and Niall had turned their house upside down, packing provisions and readying the horses to ride out. Cecily hovered around them, comfortable now, only with Kenrich. Aidan had successfully avoided her since they'd arrived in Holding, and though he knew he'd have to face her sooner or later, he put it off. She seemed happy enough in Kenrich's care. He tried to keep his thoughts of her to himself, not wanting to imagine Elana's reaction if she stumbled upon his musings over Cecily.

Aidan grimaced. Reeves had shown him how to guard his mind from Elana venturing in. He was not yet able to do that as completely as Reeves or Granny. Even with what guarding he could accomplish, the mind link with Elana shook him. He could feel her presence so clearly. He'd never imagined having that with someone before. He could also pick out the breaches where Marek was hovering, trying to infiltrate the torn pieces of Elana's mind. The very thought made Aidan's skin crawl. He shut Marek out with vehemence, relishing his enemy's shock and disorientation.

Elana's gratitude was tangible, but there was something else there too. She expected him to reach all the way into her mind, share her thoughts, her feelings. He could feel her confusion at his reticence. After her initial fear when they first formed the link, he'd let her in, shown her parts of himself that he hoped would reassure her. Then he left, giving her time to get used to the mandatory contact between them.

It dawned on him that her idea of a mind link was very different from his. That could only have come from what Marek had done. Aidan hadn't given much thought to the appropriate use of a mind link, when she first told him of it. He just hated the whole business. Now, after being instructed by Granny and Reeves on how to shield her without invading her person, he was horrified at what Marek had done. What was worse though, was how tempted he was to respond to her invitation and experience the full depth of what a mind link could be. He broke out into a sweat just thinking about it. Shaking off the thought, he brought his mind back to Kael. That was a safe topic and he could use the reassurance of equine companionship right now. He was a mess.

Unfortunately, he wasn't the only one with that thought.

Aidan opened the stable door, breathing in the sweet smell of cut grass and horses, and almost walked into Faris, who was pacing up and down the aisle. The leader of the Barras looked older than his years, his face haggard in the shadows.

"I'm sorry to disturb you," Aidan said, backing out of the stable.

"No. Stay. I suppose apologies could extend both ways." A thin smile flitted across Faris' face.

Aidan nodded. He hadn't seen much of Faris since the morning he and Elana forged the mind link. He had supposed the Barras was attending to the company, but now he had second thoughts. Something seemed amiss.

Aidan lowered himself to the dirt floor in front of Kael's stall. The stallion reached his head over the half door, lipping his hair. Aidan stroked the horse's soft nose. Before he could think of something to say, Faris turned to him.

"How is the shield coming with Elana?"

"The shielding is easy. Everything else is harder than I expected." Aidan's answer surprised him. He'd not acknowledged the full extent of his concerns to anyone, but here, in the quiet of the stable, it suddenly seemed like the right time to speak of them. His heart pounded.

Faris' eyes followed him, questioning.

"I'm getting more adept at holding the shield around Elana. My link with Kael has given me some practice at that sort of thing." He stopped, working up the resolve to get closer to what was disturbing him the most. He didn't know why he would speak of this to Faris when he could not bring himself to say anything to Reeves. He blurted out his next thoughts before losing his nerve.

"What Marek did to Elana - Faris, it was more wrong than I ever imagined. And I don't think she realizes it."

Faris nodded, all trace of a smile gone.

"When we forged the link, she was so scared. It was like she expected me to..." He trailed off, unwilling to put words to his thoughts. "If she weren't so powerful, she'd have been lost completely to him, like Cecily." His voice choked and he cleared his throat. "I'm so afraid that I'm going to reopen a wound, or somehow hurt her in the same way."

He met Faris' eyes for the first time. They were unreadable. The Barras waited.

Aidan continued, "I've heard stories of life partners among the Firestone Elders who have the Skill, and share this link. Outside of that, it was only done between the leaders of the Elderships, and only with those fully trained."

He felt his face burn. "Reeves and Granny can shield her without intruding on her mind, or her reaching theirs. I'm not that good. I feel like Marek violated her and now I might end up doing it again. The worst of it is, she doesn't even know it's wrong. She would let me in and think she was doing the right thing."

A long silence hung between them.

Faris broke it, speaking slowly. "You are not Marek. You do not have his motives. That would be an unfair accusation. You are doing this to protect her, not possess her."

Aidan nodded, still miserable.

"Does she invite you in?" Faris asked, a strange look in his eye.

"Yes." Aidan took a deep breath. "When I didn't push my way in at the beginning, she opened the door herself, but I've never walked through it."

"You want to though, don't you?"

Aidan looked down, staring hard at a the rusted tines of a pitchfork leaning against the opposite wall. "Yes, sometimes, but I don't even know why."

"Do you love her?" Faris watched him closely. "Might she be your life partner?"

Aidan swallowed hard over the lump that suddenly lodged in his throat. He hadn't meant for things to go here.

"I don't know. I care for her, but love? I'm not sure. We've mostly just fought or worked together out of duress. I don't even really know her, who she is outside of this nightmare journey. And both of us have things we have to do. We're not free to follow our own desires."

"But that door stands open, and it's sweet, at least for the moment." Faris didn't let him off the hook. "What if you walked through it? What if you accepted her invitation?"

Aidan writhed inside. This is why he didn't wanted to go here, to speak any of this out loud. Once said, he couldn't deny what he was doing. He wanted to link fully with Elana, to experience her the way he'd only experienced Kael. It was an intimacy that made bedding a woman seem paltry in comparison. And she had offered it.

A picture grew in his mind of his cousin Darcy, using his title to command young women to his bed. Some went willingly, some only by force, but it was their faces in the markets afterwards, that haunted Aidan. He swore years ago, that he would never use his Skill or position to take advantage of a woman. Elana hadn't sought this link. It was forced on her by expediency. Maybe this was for them to share, but how could he know it? And how could he live with himself if it wasn't?

"I can't," he whispered, finally. "I would be no different than Marek, than Darcy. I couldn't live with myself." His stomach knotted and he could feel his face burn. "Faris, I don't know that I am any better than them. I haven't said anything to anyone, because I keep thinking that maybe it wouldn't be so bad to go there. If I don't tell anyone, no one would have to know. But I'd know. And she would. Eventually, she'd know I'd taken from her what wasn't mine to take. Or even if it was, I would have taken it out of season."

"Yet you told me," Faris replied. "Reeves' confidence in you is not ill placed. I know few who would turn from such an opportunity."

There was a bitter edge to his words, and Aidan had a momentary flash of aching loneliness from the Barras. His own turmoil kept him from probing deeper.

"What if I go back on what I know I must do? How do I maintain my resolve?" He looked up at Faris, anguished. "Would you help me?"

"Any way I am able," Faris answered with fervency.

"Then I would make a vow, with you as my witness, on my father's name, that I will honor Elana the same way I would my own sister." A picture of Arella appeared in his mind, and he smiled, wondering again at how much Elana reminded him of her. "I will not take advantage of the mind link - either by letting her in where she need not go, or by going where I need not go. If we have such a thing to share, it will happen in its own time, and not this way."

He took a full breath, suddenly feeling lighter than he had in days. "Faris, if you have any question about my conduct, say something. It helps me so much to know I'm not carrying this alone."

Faris extended a hand and pulled Aidan to his feet. He clasped him in a quick embrace, before answering.

"You have my word on that. And may I make a suggestion?"

Aidan nodded.

"Tell this to Elana. Tell her everything. I think she needs to hear it."

Of course, Aidan thought. That was the right thing to do. He could never have done it though, without first talking to Faris. He wouldn't have been willing. He owed the Barras so much.

"Thank you," he said.

Faris met his gaze, and once again there was a moment of aching loneliness, before the Barras changed the subject.

"I was speaking with Reeves about Cecily," he said. "What you said about her being lost to Marek, it may not be her fate."

Aidan stared at him. The words didn't make sense.

"Reeves thinks that Geri might be able to help her get free from Marek's hold. At the very least, Geri might be able to shield her and she would always be welcome to claim sanctuary in Farran. It seems that Marek has insinuated himself into her very being, and that it would be dangerous in the extreme for Reeves to try anything. Geri has more Skill here than any Elder Born living. If anyone can help her, she can. That is his hope, and the reason she's coming with us."

Faris shook his head. "It explains much and enables me to forgive her behavior. I can't say I look forward to her company, but now I do pity her."

The sky outside the stable shone a bright clear blue as Aidan ran back to the cottage Granny shared with Baird, Reeves, Orvis, and Elana. He couldn't imagine a more wonderful day. Throwing open the door, he burst in on Elana and Granny.

"Sorry Granny, but I need to talk with Elana," he interrupted them.

"Apparently so. Badly enough that you've forgotten all your manners," Granny answered, her voice tart.

Aidan laughed and kissed Granny on her wrinkled cheek. He grabbed Elana's hand and pulled her out of doors. He had to do this now, or he might squirrel out completely. Her questions were pressing in on him, but he held her at bay.

"Elana, I need to talk with you."

"We can talk any time we want to, you know," she said, obviously confused at his urgency.

"No, we can't."

She frowned, not understanding.

He took a deep breath and jumped in, explaining the things he had seen and felt since their mind link. There were so many ways she could take this wrong, and he breathed up a prayer to the Ancient Ones that she would understand.

She sat listening, her brow furrowed as Aidan spilled out all that had tormented him for the past two days.

"I just talked with Faris," he ended. I told him everything and made a vow that I would not use our link in any way it should not be used. He counseled me to come and talk to you. It's what I should have done all along. I'm sorry I didn't see it sooner."

He stopped and just watched her. Her expression was far away.

"Elana, I'm so sorry for what Marek did. And I'm sorry that when you first told me I didn't understand. I never offered to help, or even saw how he'd taken advantage of you. All this time you must have thought what he did was normal. That's horrible."

She stood like someone in a trance, shaking her head. "I didn't know, I knew it felt awful at first, but I got used to the bad part, and I've always been able to read people, so..." Her voice trailed off.

She wouldn't meet Aidan's eyes and she bit her lip until it went white, before speaking again. "What do you think of me?"

Aidan was so afraid he'd just done more harm. He cupped her face in his hands. "Don't you see? It's not your fault at all. All of that is Marek's doing. He told you he was training you. How could you have known? And you had to trust him with your life. It's so unfair to you."

He couldn't bear to see the pain in her eyes. He wrapped his arms around her, holding her like he would hold Arella when she fell down and scraped herself.

"I think that you are an amazing woman, brave and generous. And I don't warrant the things you offer. You don't have to go there, Elana. I can shield you from Marek without ever intruding on your person. I don't ever want to do anything that would reopen the hurt Marek caused. That part of you is yours to share when you choose. You never have to give that under duress. I just want you to know that you're safe with me."

She took a great shuddering breath and he felt her body relax against his. Part of him was kicking himself for doing this. It seemed crazy that he was holding her in his arms while he firmly closed this door. Maybe someday it would be open between them, because she chose it, not because she thought she had to. He felt the door to her mind disappear as though it had never been opened. Her conscious presence in his mind also vanished. There was no longer a clear sense of her emotions. Her absence left an emptiness that surprised him. He looked down, startled to feel her crying.

"Aidan, please don't tell anyone else," she said, her voice muffled against his tunic.

"I won't. I promise," he assured her. "I know Faris doesn't think any of this is your fault. He was furious at Marek."

Elana looked up, her expression conflicted. "I have a lot of sorting out to do," she said.

"Me too," Aidan answered. "I'm just so glad we can talk about it." Not really knowing why he added, "I think Faris would be someone else you could talk to."

Elana smiled and sighed. "Yes, I think that would be good, too."

Aidan felt a pang of jealousy, but brushed it off. She deserved all the help and understanding she could get, and if it hadn't been for Faris, he wouldn't be here right now.

She pushed herself back and brushed her hair out of her face.

"Thank you, Aidan. For everything."

Standing on her tiptoes, she leaned forward and gave him a quick kiss. "Whoever you choose to partner with will be a very fortunate woman."

His heart raced, but he forced himself to smile. "We have to live long enough to make that an option."

Elana's hand reached reflexively for the Bronze Key hanging under her tunic. "It's time," she said. "I can feel it pulling me. I just don't know where to go."

Aidan tucked his hand under her elbow, leading her back to the house. "I think I can help you with that. That is something my Skills are useful for."

Her smile was all the reward he needed.

Aidan escorted Elana back to Granny. Baird was sitting in the corner, sorting colored balls of yarn. The boy shot him a pleading look.

Catching the hint Aidan asked, "Granny, could I borrow Baird for a bit?"

She grunted her consent. "I know you've been itching to get out all afternoon. You can go with Aidan, so long as you promise to be of help."

"Thank you Granny!" The boy leaped up, spilling the yarn about the room. With a furtive glance at the old woman, he gathered it back into the basket, wrapped his arms around her in a quick hug and giving Aidan a fierce grin, raced for the door.

The boy's exuberance infected Aidan. The two raced to the barns and on impulse Aidan saddled Kael and offered to let Baird ride together with him. Baird's pale eyes lit up, and without fear, he wiggled onto Kael, behind Aidan, holding on tight with his skinny arms.

"Don't kick him," Aidan warned. "He'll toss you right off."

Aidan could feel Baird's heart pounding against his back. They set off at a walk to let Baird get accustomed to the feel of riding.

Kael shifted under the added weight, and change of balance, but soon ignored the boy behind Aidan. The horse was itching to move. Being confined to a stall and small paddock was not his idea of fun.

Aidan released the horse into a swinging trot and when he was confident that Baird wouldn't fall off, nudged Kael into a canter. Baird's arms squeezed Aidan's ribs so hard they ached, but he could hear the boy's laughter whipping away behind them in the wind. The three of them raced to the far side of the valley and then circled around the small city. Around the other side of Holding, a deep lake reflected the high green mountains.

Kael stopped there to drink and Aidan helped Baird down, untacked the horse and proposed a swim. The water was still winter cold, and after a quick dip with much splashing around, they flopped down on the grass to let the warm sun dry their clothes.

Baird intrigued Aidan. He found himself drawn to the lad, and was glad for this chance to pry him away from Granny's strict oversight. Very little escaped the boy's pale gaze, and Aidan would give a good gold piece to know more of what went through his mind.

"Baird, I still haven't heard the story of how you and Granny got here." He hoped an open ended invitation would encourage the boy to talk.

Baird didn't need much prompting. Propping up on his pointed elbows, he gazed past Aidan, collecting his thoughts. "A few weeks ago, Reeves came to visit us again. He comes every year and plays music with me." Baird's eyes shone at the memory. "Nobody plays like Reeves."

Aidan nodded in encouragement.

"This time though, instead of staying with us for a fortnight, he told us that it was time to go to Farran. He was going to take us up there with him." Baird leaned over, reached deep into his pocket and pulled out a set of small pipes. Seeming to forget his story, he blew a few notes in the damp pipes and then wove it into a simple melody that flew, danced and spun with joy. With a satisfied smile, he set the pipes down and continued.

"I've been wanting to go for forever." His pale eyes grew big and he gave Aidan an emphatic nod. "My Waking's started."

This last statement was a surprise. He was very young to start his Waking.

"Granny said she knew it would come early. She said when there's a need, sometimes things change. We have to change with them."

Aidan nodded. He could accept that.

"Reeves promised me he would take me through my training." Again, the pipes came out and this time Baird got lost in the music, closing his eyes and letting himself go to a place he had no words to express.

Aidan lay back and let the music wash over him. Excitement, elation, fear, hope, stirrings of something deeper just out of reach, the music encompassed all these things. It closely echoed Aidan's own emotions on this trip. He felt a kinship growing with the boy. How could one so young be aware of so much?

With a great sigh, Baird put down the pipes again. "I'm sorry. I just can't say it all in words yet. I had the feeling you would understand me better with the music."

"You were right." Aidan answered. "But tell me more of what happened on your trip."

370

"Well, Reeves had to go back to Bellport," Baird began, "and that made Granny mad. She didn't say it, but she was afraid for him. He came back after a week, with an old man on a donkey riding beside him. That was Orvis, you know." Baird sat up, a fierce scowl lining his face. "Granny said that Marek's physician was poisoning Orvis. She made him drink some awful smelling stuff and Orvis threw up and threw up, but then he started getting better."

Baird glowered. "That Marek better hope he never runs into me. I'll show him what I think of that."

"I wouldn't worry about Marek," Aidan said. "There's plenty of others who would be glad to take care of that for you."

"Orvis has an old flute that he plays," Baird continued. "I got him to play it with me while I played on my pipes. He played songs of the ocean and taught me some too. I think the music helped him to heal faster. Music goes into places that nothing else can reach."

Aidan raised an eyebrow. Baird just continued on, oblivious.

"Orvis told me stories of the sea, and of Lars and Brenna. I played them into songs and even though he growled at me for it, I could tell he liked them. I'd catch him humming them when he didn't know I was listening."

The boy's eyes grew wistful. "I never knew my parents. I wouldn't mind having Orvis for a dad."

Aidan swallowed hard. "*Some things never stop aching,*" he thought.

"Can I play you some of the songs I made for him?" Baird asked.

"Please." The music took him away, back to the moment when he first looked out over the sandy shore at the ocean, the waves crashing in and the gulls riding the swells behind them. The longing and loneliness brought tears to his eyes. He was no longer Aidan, but Orvis, spending years alone, finding solace on the open water, unexpected grace in his friendship with Lars and Brenna, and then, long years later, having to let go and say goodbye to them both. Fiercely self-sufficient, untrusting of anything save the call of the sea;

and as Baird played, Aidan became the old sailor, sharing an understanding with him that he'd never imagined possible.

Baird stopped playing and they sat in silence until Kael wandered up to nudge at Aidan.

While he tacked up the big horse, Baird finished his story.

"Reeves sold Granny's goats and the cow and bought a donkey for her to ride." The boy grinned wickedly. "She didn't want any part of that. It was Orvis who finally talked her into it. He's not bothered by her ways."

Aidan had to smile imagining that conversation.

"We packed our food and left once Orvis was strong enough to make the journey. Reeves kept us off the roads and really it was a bit boring, just walking all day every day, with only small stops for meals." Baird shrugged. "Reeves told me that boring was good right now. Well, I could do with a little less good, myself. Though when we got close to Holding, Reeves said that someone was in trouble and he had to find her. It was Elana, but I didn't know that then. After that, you know the rest." He ended matter-of-factly.

Aidan laughed. "I think I took your share of interesting as well as my own. I would have been glad to trade it away for some boring. But I wouldn't wish that kind of interesting on you."

He pulled the boy up behind him once more, and the two trotted back to their cottages. Aidan made another promise to himself to take whatever time he could with Baird, should they all reach Farran. It wasn't just pity, either. He liked him. He'd never met anyone similar, and though it could be disconcerting, Baird exuded a different kind of power than he'd ever been near before.

Faris called a meeting over supper that night. All of them, save Cecily, crowded into the larger house where Reeves, Faris, Kenrich, Niall, and Aidan lodged. Orvis, Granny, Elana, and Baird joined them. The meal was sumptuous; roast pork, new potatoes, boiled greens, fresh baked bread, and red wine from grapes grown in the valley. After they'd eaten their fill, they leaned back in the sturdy wooden chairs, sharing small talk as they waited for Faris to address them.

Aidan was warmed that Elana took a seat next to him. Orvis stationed himself on her other side, always attentive to her every need. The old sailor spent almost every waking moment with Elana, and to Aidan's eyes, this seemed to have done him a world of good. With Elana here, Orvis had no more patience for taking things slowly. He moved without pain most of the time now and in the last few days his step was regaining some spring.

Baird sat next to Orvis, totally undaunted by the sailor's harsh ways. He adored the old man, hanging onto his every word and lighting up like a beacon should Orvis praise him.

What Aidan didn't know, was how things were to take shape now. An urgency was growing in him and he felt as though they were readying themselves for the last great race. He didn't have a clear idea of where they needed to go, but he knew the general direction, and it would lead them straight back into the Empty Hills. The thought was not comforting. He hoped that they would be able to travel light, and with as few extra people as possible. The threat of danger throbbed in the background. It seemed unlikely that they would meet no resistance on this leg of their journey.

Faris stood up, putting an end to Aidan's musings. The Barras waited silently for everyone to finish their conversations. His blue eyes rested on each of the companions in turn, before he spoke.

"Tomorrow we leave the safety of Holding," he began.

Kenrich shifted in his chair, his eyes alight with anticipation.

"It was my thought to travel light and fast. From what we've seen, pursuit is inevitable." He stopped, looking now at Orvis, Granny, and Baird. "I cannot guarantee the safety of anyone traveling with us."

Orvis growled something unintelligible.

"We are not traveling to Farran, as some of you may have imagined." Faris glanced at Kenrich. "We will be following Aidan's guidance from here on, as we search for the Hidden Door to Laharan."

Niall gave a quiet cough, and Kenrich looked startled.

"I thought Laharan existed only in fables," Kenrich said.

"So did I for many years," Faris answered. "But I was mistaken. Elana has been to Laharan and must return there."

Kenrich's eyes widened.

Faris glanced over at Elana, and she nodded to him.

"It is for her to unlock the Firestone," Faris said, his voice low.

Niall's eyebrows shot halfway up his forehead. "You never did back down from a challenge, did you?"

"The Firestone?" Kenrich almost choked.

Niall clapped him on the shoulder. "There's a reason his uncle sleeps easier with him gone."

Elana stood up and pulled the Bronze Key out from her tunic.

All voices stilled.

Speaking low, she retold the story of its finding for the benefit of those who had not yet heard.

Kenrich gave her a candid look. "Do I have to believe all of this to ride with you?" The young Lord shook his head. "I'm not sure I can swallow it all at once." He bowed to Elana. "But I gave my word to help Aidan and you both, and I don't need to agree with everything you believe to do that."

"I'm honored and grateful to have you ride with us." Elana said. "I've thought I was half crazy for a long time now. It's only just starting to sink in that all this is real."

Aidan only realized he'd been holding his breath, when he started breathing again. Neither Kenrich nor Elana were overly fond of the other and he was relieved to see them each give ground.

Elana took her seat and Faris continued.

"We won't be as small a party as I'd like. Cecily will accompany us, though it is imperative that she know nothing of our mission. For her purposes, we are traveling to Farran. Orvis too, will travel with us. After we are gone, Granny and Baird will have an escort to Farran. Reeves will ride west and search for Elana's parents. We will, in all likelihood, draw enough attention to ourselves to buy him some time to find them."

"Why are we taking Cecily out into the wild again?" Kenrich asked. "She needn't go, and it's just an unnecessary danger to her."

"If we leave her in Holding, she will eventually draw Marek or the Black Knights here. She would be lost to Marek, and these peaceable folk would suffer horribly at the hands of the Black Knights. Reeves believes there's hope for Cecily if we can get her to Farran, which is where we will go after Elana accomplishes her task." Faris shook his head. "It's not my first choice either. But it's the only choice left."

"But she could travel straight to Farran with Granny and Baird, Kenrich argued.

"That would be easier for us and for her, except that the escort the good people here have offered is unarmed. The Black Knights have searched for years for both Granny and Baird. Sending Cecily with them would be as good as signing their death warrant." Faris gave him a sympathetic look and shrugged. "There are no easy answers here for any of us."

The rest of the evening was spent hashing out the particulars of the journey. It passed in a blur for Aidan. Talking didn't help him now. He wanted to be out of the city, away from all noise. Somehow he had to find the Hidden Door. This was going to be a test of his Skills like no other.

Morning dawned warm and fair. Elana picked at the fresh berries and brown bread laid out for breakfast. She had no stomach for food.

Granny came and sat next to her, for once not lecturing. She lay a gnarled hand on Elana's arm.

"Our love goes with you."

Tears stung Elana's eyes. She clung to Granny's hand like a small girl.

"But what if..." Her words died away.

"The Ancient Ones are not capricious. And we can't understand all ends."

That wasn't exactly comforting. Elana swallowed hard.

"You'll understand in time," Granny said. She went back to her knitting as though nothing special was happening.

"Elana." Granny didn't even look up. "You could try being nicer to Cecily. Unless we can build a bridge to her, even Geri won't be able to help. She has to trust us, and want our help."

Elana muttered something unintelligible and pushed away from the table. She didn't have time for this.

"Think about it..."

Granny's words followed her out as she left to find Devi.

Aidan was at the stable, saddling her mare. She felt him there at the periphery, keeping Marek at bay, and she blushed again, still embarrassed at how she'd responded to their mind link.

"Please don't be offended," he said, gesturing toward Devi. "I needed to be out here with the horses."

His expression was strained, and she realized that she just took for granted his Skill to find the Hidden Door.

"You have everything you need, Aidan."

He gave her a doubting look.

She slipped her arm through his. "I'll believe in you if you'll believe in me."

His tawny eyes met hers and held her gaze, a hint of a question in them that she was unwilling to probe.

"I've got the easy part." He smiled and the question vanished. "Thank you."

"Aidan," she said, "if we have to use the mind link, don't be afraid of it, or afraid of hurting me."

He wrinkled his brow in a frown.

"I'm not saying we will, I just don't want to lay aside any advantage we might be able to use."

"Fair enough. But only if we have to."

She smiled, feeling a little lighter inside, and took Devi's reins from him.

The company headed out without fanfare. Only Baird waved them off, his pale eyes following Orvis' back as the old sailor rode out of Holding. Reeves had left that morning, at first light.

Now that they were on the road again, the Bronze Key pulled relentlessly at Elana. When she mentioned it to Aidan, he said that he felt it too.

Once out of the valley, Aidan turned them back toward the Empty Hills. The company rode in silence, each lost in their own thoughts. Aidan led on Kael, followed by Orvis, Elana, Niall, Kenrich and Cecily. Faris rode as the rear guard. More than once Elana turned to find the Barras' piercing gaze fixed on her. She dropped back to ride next to him.

"Don't be afraid to face what lies ahead," he said, without preamble.

More than Aidan, or even Orvis, Faris seemed to understand what was happening with her. It still was hard to believe that he was not Elder Born.

"Easier said than done," she answered. "It would help some to know what this task was going to be." She lowered her voice. "I just hope I don't have to confront the Shadow King, like I did before. I don't know that I would survive that one again."

"You can't fight the enemy when the enemy is within," Faris replied. "I spoke with Reeves about that. When you accepted Marek's help, Marek's power... something of the Shadow King came in with it. Now, you probably would have been killed if you hadn't, so I'm not blaming you." A fleeting smile belied the worry in Faris' eyes. "But, you won't get caught in that whirlwind again, so long as you don't open that door."

"Do you ever get scared that the enemy is too strong for you?"

"Sometimes. I'd be a fool not to. But I can't think along those lines. I've got to focus on what I can do." Faris sized her up. "You've got to use everything you're given, and believe in yourself. If the worst happens, you will have fought with honor. What do you bring to this?"

"Nothing. Not like that, anyway."

"I wouldn't say that. You're not here for your prowess with a blade, but that doesn't mean you're not dangerous to an enemy."

Elana thought for a bit. "I stopped those men at the docks with my will. Though I'm not sure exactly how I did it."

That's right. And you didn't need Marek's or anyone else's help for that, did you? You had Aidan running for cover for a while too, and who could blame him?" Faris' eyes twinkled.

"I got Kael back from the thief at the inn at Pikeman's Crossing. I guess that was on my own too."

Faris nodded. "What else?"

"Well, when we had to tell our story to Varen, I knew how to talk with him, so that he would by sympathetic to us."

"That's right."

"And I have the Bronze Key, though I'm not really sure what it does."

"I might spend a little bit of time looking into that one if I were you. Understand all your potential weapons before the battle. Gives you a bit of an edge."

"I never really thought of that. I was mostly trying to keep it quiet. It kind of broadcasts itself to anyone who can hear."

"You did right, but I don't think secrecy is much of an option anymore. I'd open your Skills to it, find out what it does to you, or does for you."

Elana flashed a smile at Faris. "Thanks. I will."

The first time she reached out with her Skills toward the Bronze Key, both Aidan and Orvis turned around and stared at her.

"What?" she asked them.

"Even I can hear that," Orvis said. "It's singing some kind of song, bringing back something too beautiful to hold for long in this world. Makes me want to play it on that old flute. Wish Baird were here. That lad would be spinning harmonies around it fit to make you cry."

"Aidan looked hard at the old sailor. "That's not what I heard at all. I heard a herald's blast, announcing a king. I kept getting this push to unpack the robe Granny gave me and wear it, like for some honored occasion."

They all looked puzzled at one another. It was Faris who broke the silence.

"Why don't you both do just that. Orvis, get out that flute and find the song on it. Play it out for everyone to hear. And Aidan, put that robe on. If there's anything to this, it's worth acting a little ridiculous to find out."

The Barras winked at Kenrich, who had overheard, including the young lord in the conversation. "It's not like anyone could accuse us of being rational at this point."

Kenrich returned his smile with genuine warmth.

The company halted for lunch and Aidan and Orvis followed Faris' suggestions. Elana found that the Bronze Key was almost reaching back to her, as though it had a consciousness of its own. She welcomed it in, thinking of Faris' words about understanding any potential weapons before a battle. It didn't feel very warlike, though. If anything, it made it hard for Elana to concentrate on what was going on around her. She had to remember to worry, otherwise a peacefulness flowing out of the Bronze Key, permeated her thoughts.

Orvis sat by the packs, picking out the tune he heard, on the worn flute. One by one, each of the company gathered round him, their faces reflecting the longing that the music stirred. Cecily stood a little apart from the rest, her face unreadable. Granny's words about her, drifted back to Elana. She edged herself around to where Cecily stood. The peace that flowed out from the Bronze Key encouraged a sympathy toward Lord Gratton's daughter.

"I'm sorry things have gone this way for you," Elana offered.

Cecily sighed. "I don't know what is real anymore." She met Elana's eyes, with none of the haughtiness that usually marked her expression.

Elana gave her a shy smile. "I know what you mean. Most of my ideas have been turned on their ear in these past months, too. It's not very comfortable, is it?"

Cecily returned the smile, but a sadness hovered over her. "No, it's not."

Orvis' music played on, permeating the atmosphere of the camp. The longing in it was palpable. Niall sat on a rock next to the sailor, staring off into the woods, tears glistening in his bushy beard. Kenrich too, looked like he wanted to cry, but couldn't allow himself.

Aidan stood apart, looking regal in the deep green robe, his expression unreadable. Elana didn't want to pry. Just looking at him stirred her Waking, strange visions of another man wearing that same robe, running through a courtyard built around a dying tree, carrying something wrapped in the folds of the cloak...

She shook herself free from the vision, her Waking still surging. The Bronze Key called to her stronger than before. It almost felt like it was asking her to form a mind link with it. She pulled back, afraid that if she did this thing, she would not be able to retrieve herself. Remembering what Faris said, she looked for him, hoping to have a quiet word with the Barras. He might not be Elder Born, but she trusted his council implicitly.

He was tending to the horses, the only one not enthralled by Orvis' playing. When she caught his eye, the ache inside of him made her step back. She hadn't wanted to intrude. It was gone in an instant, only a murmur remaining. The thought returned to her, that she still knew little of his life, of his struggles, hopes, or dreams. This wasn't the time, though.

"I need to talk to you," she said.

He motioned her to sit with him, behind the horses, out of sight of the company.

She jumped right in. "I feel like the Bronze Key wants to form a mind link with me. I didn't know such a thing was possible. It's so powerful, I'm afraid that I might loose myself completely in it."

Faris sighed. "Reeves said that it's capable of far more than he could hope to understand in such a short time. He believed that the Key saved your mind from the Shadow King. Had you let go of it, we might have lost you. That physical contact alone, enabled it to protect you."

He gripped her shoulder. "I don't have any clear answers for you, and I could not live with myself if I said something that brought you to harm. Even so, I trust this thing. If we are to walk forward here, there can be no holding back."

The intensity in his eyes caused her Waking to surge once again. She had her answer.

"Thank you. You're right. I'll do it, now." It was easier somehow to take that leap with Faris right there.

She closed her eyes, opening her mind up to the presence of the Bronze Key.

Peace. It was peace, freedom from fear, and freedom from something else. As that presence swept through her, she felt the push from Marek at the edge of her mind, wash away. Aidan's mind touched hers for an instant, questioning, reaching out to her.

She spoke directly to him, mind to mind, without fear or embarrassment. "It's the Bronze Key. I've let it in."

Faris interrupted her thoughts. "Aidan needs this too."

He rose and returned with Aidan.

"What's going on?" Aidan asked out loud. He hadn't responded directly to her link.

Elana repeated what she already told him, and added that this was somehow for him, as well. When she said the words, she felt the presence of the Bronze Key leap out toward Aidan.

He gave her a startled look. "Alright. I'll let it in."

She knew he wasn't happy about it.

He closed his eyes and reached out to touch the Bronze Key. With a yelp, he pulled his hand back. The Key had burned him.

He gave Elana an accusing look. "What are you trying to do to me?"

"I didn't know it would do that. I know it was reaching out to you. I felt it."

"How was it reaching out?" Faris asked.

Elana thought a moment. "Through our link."

"Then you might try that," he said.

"But that means..." Aidan left his sentence unfinished.

The Barras looked grim. "If you stop now, we might as well turn around and go home."

"It's not like that, Elana tried to explain to Aidan. "It's not like before. You'll see."

She opened herself up to the Bronze Key until she felt it filling every fiber of her. All the worry melted away in its peace. She reached out tentatively to Aidan, encouraging him to reach back. The instant he did, the Bronze Key arced across their link to him. His elation soared with her own as the Key's presence filled him. The lines on his face smoothed out and his Waking surged. Bits of the Waking spilled over to her. She could feel the land singing, whispering, teaching its secrets to Aidan. With a slight pang of jealousy she realized that she walked through life blind compared to him.

She felt ashamed too, realizing that she had always assumed that his Waking wasn't as strong as hers. It was just so different. He caught her eye and with that glance she saw that he'd always known, and had already forgiven her.

His thought raced past that though, drawn by the urgency of the Bronze Key.

"I can do it now," he said. "The Key will take me to the Door."

The company pressed on, following Aidan's lead. They cantered wherever the terrain allowed, slowing only to navigate the narrow, rocky paths that traversed these hills, or to rest the horses. The urgency coming from the Bronze Key drove all fatigue from Elana. She wondered if it affected the others as well.

They traveled this way for the next few days, stopping only to eat hurried meals or to catch a few hours of sleep on the hard ground. No one volunteered any chatter. A cloud of foreboding settled over the riders. The longer they traveled without any sign of their enemy, the worse it grew. On the evening of the third day, Elana felt something shift in the land. Aidan scanned their surrounding, searching for signs of danger. She followed his gaze upwards. High in the cloudless sky, a falcon circled. It cried out once and plummeted down toward the woods nearby. It was Vian.

Niall hurried over, having seen the same thing. "I wondered when we would meet with company. If you want to know the truth, I'd rather know where my enemy is, than wonder if he's going to pop out from behind every bush."

"How close to the Hidden Door do you think we are?" Faris asked Aidan.

"Close. Less than a day's ride."

"Do you think we can beat him?" Niall looked over his shoulder as if expecting Marek to come riding into the clearing.

"It's hard to say. I can't tell where he is."

"Are the Black Knights with him?" Elana asked.

"I don't think so." Aidan shook his head in puzzlement. "I don't understand, really."

"I think I might," Elana said, a sudden awareness flooding her mind. "This is the final race. If the Black Knights get hold of the Bronze Key, Marek would loose all hope of keeping it for himself. They still owe primary allegiance to the Shadow King. I think Marek is playing both ends against each other for his own gain."

"So he sent them off, in the hopes of waylaying us himself?" Faris asked.

"That's my guess, but I don't know how he hopes to overpower a company of this size." Disturbing thoughts interrupted the flow of peace from the Bronze Key. Elana wasn't able to pin them down, though.

A strangled cry cut their meeting short.

Kenrich hollered to them as Cecily's crumpled form tumbled from her saddle.

A single word hung between Aidan and Elana's minds.

Marek.

CHAPTER 18

LAHARAN

Kenrich cradled Cecily in his arms, his face anguished. She wasn't breathing. Her lips were tinged with blue, her green eyes open and staring.

Aidan vaulted off Kael and in three strides was at her side, searching with his Skill for signs of life.

"She lives, but only just." He scanned the area, looking for a possible cause.

Niall swung off his old gelding and drew his sword, circling in a crouch, prepared for an attack. Faris had his bow out, an arrow at the ready.

From out of nowhere a voice rang through the clearing. "Drop your weapons or the girl dies."

With a flare of anger, Elana recognized the disembodied voice as Marek's. What she couldn't make out was why the company looked so terrified.

Niall's sword clattered to the ground. Faris lowered his bow, but still gripped it in his hands.

"What is this devilry, that you speak inside our minds?" he asked.

Now Elana understood. She didn't know how he managed it, but obviously, he'd forced himself upon their minds. His Skills were formidable and he'd had many years to hone them.

"Her blood will stain your hands, Barras," Marek's voice continued.

Elana noticed in passing that she only heard him from the outside. He wasn't able to get through to her.

In slow motion, Faris let the bow fall from his fingers.

"That's better. Now we can talk."

A cry of relief broke from Kenrich. Cecily had resumed breathing. Her eyes still stared, blank and unknowing, at the world around her.

"I have shown mercy to you," Marek said, stepping now from behind a copse of firs, leading a thick boned chestnut. "I could easily have sent the Black Knights to finish you off, but I believe we can come to a more agreeable arrangement."

Faris reached for his bow.

"That would be unwise," Marek motioned to the Barras. "What I've done to Cecily, I can do as easily to any of you."

"Not any of us," Aidan countered. He rose, his face red.

"No," Marek answered evenly. "I'm speaking of the Valefolk. The un-Skilled, untrained masses, whom your father so delighted to befriend. Did you think in the end they could save you?

Marek's eyes blazed at Aidan. "Fool! Like your father before you, but without any semblance of his Skill. You're an embarrassment to the Elder Born."

An inarticulate cry of rage burst out of Aidan and he lunged at Marek.

"No!" The pleading in Kenrich's voice stopped Aidan cold. Cecily gasped for breath in his arms, as though an unseen hand choked her.

"You're a monster," Aidan spat. "How could you?"

"You know nothing of what I could or couldn't do. I'm not a spineless fool, spinning fairy tales for the ignorant. I learned early just what these Valefolk are. Give no quarter. For surely you'll get none from them."

"What do you mean?" Elana's only thought was to keep him talking long enough to think up some plan.

He turned to Elana for the first time.

"There was much I hoped to protect you from," he began. "But you'll discover the truth for yourself." A spasm of pain twisted his face. "I grew up in a small village in Merrion. Both my parents were Elder

Born, but without any training. They were different enough though, to be hated by the villagers. When I was nine, a wasting sickness fell on the village. It spread from home to home, leaving many dead in its wake. Because we didn't associate with the other families, we did not catch it. One night, I was wakened from sleep by a pounding at the door. Men with torches and knives dragged us from our beds, accusing my parents of cursing the village with this sickness. They were satisfied with nothing short of my parents' murder. I escaped by the kindness of the butcher's wife, who though she had just lost her own son, refused to believe that a mere boy could be guilty of such a thing. She took me to raise in the place of her child, but not more than a week later, caught the wasting sickness herself and died. The villagers seemed to have lost their taste for blood, but the butcher kept me for the next five years, determined to make me pay in every other way for the sin of being Elder Born."

The company listened in silence. Elana's heart ached at the pain Marek could not conceal.

"I escaped when I was just fourteen. I lived for the next three years, traveling the Vale, practicing my Skills, using whatever means I had at my disposal just to stay alive. I swore that I would grow strong enough to one day restore the Elder Born to their rightful position as rulers of this land. With that in mind, I searched out Farran, and at last found it. I received training there from Geri, and when I set out again, I vowed to return to Merrion and begin my rule there."

Out of the corner of her eye, Elana saw Faris nod, as though putting something together. She looked from Marek to Cecily, her stomach twisting in knots at the thought of this girl's life being sacrificed to Marek's vengeance. Not that she entirely blamed him. She couldn't imagine the horrors he lived though, and five years traveling the Vale had left her jaded about the Valefolk. But she knew those feelings were wrong. After these past weeks, it was hard to think of them in different terms than she thought of herself. She looked again at Faris. She had never met anyone she respected more. She turned back to Marek.

"I'm so sorry for everything you've been though. That's horrible." She met his eyes, willing her sympathy to reach out to him.

It must have, because she saw him start, looking at her for a moment with unspeakable longing. She could feel him reaching back to her, but the presence of the Bronze Key kept him from touching her completely.

Something in him wavered. Elana could feel it. He spoke to her in a strangled voice. "Let me travel with you. Please." The air of command vanished. When she looked at him, she saw the little boy, still hoping to find a safe haven.

Reaching out a hand to him, she said, "Of course you can." She could no more refuse him than she could have refused the child whose parents had just been killed.

Faris and Aidan both stared at her.

"What are you doing?" Aidan demanded.

"Please trust me," she answered. Through their mind link, she added, "There's something here. I don't know what, but he's not beyond help."

Reeve's words in the letter to her father rushed back. He believed it too. She felt the presence of the Bronze Key reach out to Marek. Not in the way that it had to Aidan, but in a gentle, soothing way. She knew that she'd made the right choice.

"You must release your hold on Cecily," she told Marek. "You're here because I believe you're supposed to be. No hostages."

Marek nodded, his face contorted with some internal struggle. Anger flashed for a moment in his eyes, and then was gone. He smiled at Elana and the smile held a shy warmth. "For you, my dear," he said.

A warning sounded inside her, but with nothing more than that to go on, she took no action. She would watch and wait. The presence of the Bronze Key grew stronger and with it, the assurance that Marek held no danger for her now.

Cecily's eyes came slowly back into focus. She looked from Kenrich, to Aidan, to Marek.

"What happened?" she asked.

Everyone looked at Elana, unwilling to attempt an answer.

"You fell off your horse," Elana answered. She gestured to Marek. "Marek has joined us for this next portion of our trip." She didn't want to lie outright, but it was cruel to say anything to make Cecily's situation more difficult. She felt absurd.

Cecily must have suspected something. She narrowed her eyes, giving Elana a wary look. Marek broke the awkward silence.

"My girl, look at you," he exclaimed, holding his arms out to Cecily. "Who ever would have imagined you traipsing around the countryside like this."

She struggled to her feet and walked over to him, accepting his embrace like someone in a trance.

"You've given me quite a start, going off like you did. I'm only glad I've found you at last. Your friends have agreed that it's best that I accompany you. I can offer you a greater degree of protection than they are able." He frowned at Lord Gratton's daughter. "Did you really believe that I would allow you to be married to Ulrich's beast of a son?"

Cecily hung her head, chagrined.

He lifted her chin with a finger. "I don't tell you all of my plans. An old man can't give away all of his surprises."

"I'm sorry to doubt you," she said. "I'm not sure what I think anymore."

"There's time enough to sort things out. Let's get going now. The sooner started, the sooner finished and back to the comforts of home."

Cecily looked like she relished that thought.

The Bronze Key tugged at Elana. She felt a new urgency from it. Looking at Aidan, who appeared to feel it too, she said, "Let's get going."

Everyone mounted and rode off, Aidan leading the way.

Faris maneuvered himself next to Elana.

"Will you please give me some explanation?" he demanded, his eyes hard. "All it takes is one arrow and we can be rid of him."

"I know," Elana answered. She looked at the Barras, aching at the mistrust she saw in him.

"What are you playing at?"

"I'm not playing, Faris. You have to believe me. I just have this feeling. I can't explain it. He doesn't have to be evil. I feel the Bronze Key reaching out to him too," she added. "He can't get to me now. I know it. His voice wasn't able to reach my mind when he pulled that little trick."

"Well, one of those little tricks could kill us. We don't have your protection against him."

Elana frowned. She hadn't thought that one through.

"This may be the stupidest thing I've done, but Faris, if I stop following these feelings now, what else do I have to go on?"

She wanted so much for him to believe her. His good opinion meant the world. She looked away, trying to hide the tears that came unbidden.

Shay drew up right next to Devi, and Faris' leg brushed her own. His hand reached out and tipped her face back toward him, forcing her to look into his eyes. After a long moment, he released her.

"I'm sorry," he said, a strange look on his face. "I just had to be sure he wasn't influencing you. I didn't know there for a while..." His blue eyes bored into hers. "I'm with you. I'm just going to have to trust you to watch our backs with him around."

He pulled ahead of her and cantered up to Aidan.

They navigated the Empty Hills, following Aidan's lead. He took them on a straight path, blazing a trail through scraggly woods and rocky slopes, rarely stopping or turning. Once again, he pushed them all to the edge of their endurance.

The urgency of the Bronze Key drove all other thoughts from Elana's mind. She noticed at times Marek watching her with a fierce intensity. He must be able to feel it too.

Aidan pulled up Kael, and waited for her to catch up. His face shone.

"We're almost there," he whispered.

Her heart raced. "How are we going to do this?" she asked. The others were still a little ways away. "I don't want Marek trying to go in with me."

"I don't think you'll have to worry about that," Aidan said. "Somehow, I don't think the Door will allow anyone in who's not supposed to be there. But it would be nice if we could find it alone. I'd rather have to explain things after it's all wrapped up, than stave off hysteria while it's going on."

They both knew he was referring to Cecily.

"Do you think everyone will be able to see the door?" she asked.

"I have no idea," he answered. "Let's ride up ahead a bit and see what we might find."

They nudged their horses into a trot and came to the top of a rocky rise. Just down the other side they both saw it. A thick wooden Door stood alone on the far slope. It's frame was not attached to any building, just the empty sky. Finely wrought ornamentation, matching the Bronze Key, curled around the planks of the Door. They could see the bronze lock on it's right hand side.

Without thinking, Elana drove Devi into a gallop heading straight for the Door. The Bronze Key sang out, filling all her senses. She pulled Devi up in front of the Door, her heart hammering in her chest. Jumping off the mare, she approached it, unaware that the company had joined Aidan at the top of the ridge. With trembling hands she drew out the Bronze Key and fit it to the lock. It slid in as though it were made yesterday. The lock turned with a deep click, and the door swung open.

Elana hesitated for a moment and then stepped through the door. She heard a cry from behind her, but the sound vanished in an instant. When she turned to see who it was, expecting to see Aidan outlined at the top of the rocky slope, she saw only a level sweeping lawn of green grass. The sky was a deeper blue than she remembered it, and the grass a brighter green. Everything smelled fresher and sweeter than she ever remembered smelling. She felt like she had landed in the middle of the most marvelous dream she could imagine. Reaching for the Bronze Key, she realized it was still in the Door, and the Door itself had vanished. Some part of her wondered how she would ever return. The thought didn't bother her as much as it might have.

She wandered through the grass, searching for something that would give her direction. It seemed hours that she wandered, at times forgetting her own name, or why she was here at all. She lost all track of time and lay down and fell asleep, waking later with a terrific thirst. The sound of a fountain led her on, up a shallow hill. At the top, a stone fountain spilled over with clear blue water. Elana plunged her head in it and drank and drank. The water quenched her thirst, and cleared her senses. For the first time since the door opened, she remembered clearly who she was and why she was there.

She had no idea how much time had passed. The land was silent. No bird sang, nor insect buzzed. There was no sun in the sky, though the whole place was lit as though on a bright spring afternoon. Looking around her, Elana realized that she was hopelessly lost. Fear tingled around the edges of her mind. She was in Laharan, the island between the worlds. It was beautiful, but it's beauty was neither warm nor comforting. There was a wildness, a pureness, that made Elana feel small, insignificant. Somehow, here, she had to find the Firestone. She scanned the horizon. Past the fountain lay a huge hill, and at it's peak, a tower. It was the only landmark anywhere, so she headed for it.

She tried to recall everything she had heard about the Firestone, and what she might be expected to do. The fear tingling on the edges of her mind, grew. Finding Laharan was Aidan's test, unlocking the Firestone, would be hers.

The Ancient One told her that she was to do whatever the Firestone asked of her. She had sworn that she would. Images of her fighting the Shadow King filled her mind. She no longer felt the presence of the Bronze Key, so she wondered if she still had its protection. She trudged on, feeling smaller and smaller as she approached the huge hill. Climbing it's side, she reached the tower. It was ancient, made of moss covered stone. An arched doorway stood open at its base. Elana hesitated, before stepping into the dark interior.

As she stepped inside, a shadowy figure swirled around her, making the hair on the small of her neck stand up.

"We meet at last, Elana," a smooth voice said. "I've come to help you in your task. Look," a dark hand directed her to a narrow window next to the doorway. "The battle gathers outside. The enemy awaits you, little one."

Elana looked out the window, and to her shock, the landscape was dark, with clouds blocking the light from the sunless sky, and a fierce wind whipping the grasses. An agonized howl moaned over the hilltop as dark shadows raced around the stone tower. Elana pulled back, frozen.

"No. I can't do this," she stammered. She felt the malicious presence of whatever was outside, searching for her. Like on the beach, out on the boat with Orvis... She was trapped here, alone, cornered like a small animal against a pack of wolves.

The shadowy figure spoke again. "Not alone, little one. Not while I'm here. How do you expect to leave this tower without defeating the enemy outside?"

He let the words sink in.

She didn't see any other option. She didn't like the shadowy figure, but she knew with a certainty, that if she stepped foot outside the tower, she would be consumed by the evil that stalked her.

"A wise man once told you," the shadowy figure whispered, "that in battle you have to use everything you're given."

Elana remembered Faris' advice to her, and with that, she remembered more. The Barras believed in her. He believed that she had everything she needed within herself to accomplish her task. He had warned her not to accept help from Marek, or any other power outside of herself. Faris' steel blue eyes and quick smile burned themselves on her mind. She felt his faith in her and held onto it like an anchor.

Turning to the shadowy figure, she gathered herself up and spoke in as clear a voice as she could muster. "Go away! I reject all offers of your help or aid. I will have no part of you and you will have no part of me."

An earsplitting shriek shook the tower and drove Elana to her knees. The shadowy figure grew until it filled the room.

"You will regret this, Elana. I will make sure of that!"

Red eyes blazed at her from within the figure's cloak. The figure swept it's arm up and vanished in a whirlwind.

Elana sat down, every muscle shaking. The darkness outside grew more fierce, and the tower trembled at it's onslaught.

In the dim light, Elana made out a stair at the back of the room. She groped her way toward it and started to climb. It seemed to go up forever. When at last it opened into a small anteroom, she paused to catch her breath. The stairway continued on up, but she sat on the cold stone floor, waiting for her heart to stop pounding.

She felt so alone. Getting up, she peeked out the window at the palpable darkness outside. She wished with all her heart that someone was here to share this with her.

Without warning, she felt Marek's presence in her mind.

"Dear one," he said, his voice warm. "I had so hoped to protect you from this. Are you alright?"

"Yes," she whispered back, to stunned to block him out.

"Let me in, and I can be with you. I can help you face the task before you. I too, am of the Firestone Eldership, and I know something of what lies ahead."

Pictures of a vague future floated through Elana's head. With the Firestone unlocked, she would be called upon to rule the Vale. No longer would her life be her own. She would be unable to do anything she wanted, and the burden of the entire land's well being would rest on her shoulders alone. She saw Faris going back to the Barras, alone, estranged from her. Aidan and Orvis left to live their lives, and she would be alone, trying to rule. No one respected her, no one realized what she had done for them.

"Let me come with you, Elana. I can change that. I know what you're doing, and have ruled Merrion well for many years. I can get you the respect you deserve."

Now the picture changed. All her friends were looking up to her, and the nobles of the land were bringing her exotic trinkets as tokens of their goodwill. She was dressed in robes of crimson velvet, that set off her black hair. No more did the Valefolk sneer or gossip when she walked passed. They parted in the streets for her, bowing and throwing flowers at her feet. She looked and saw faces she recognized; fishwives from the village on the coast, Farrell, bustling out of his inn to pay homage to her.

That's when it hit her. She liked Farrell, respected him, and the look of fear on his face soured the picture. This wasn't what she wanted at all. She never wanted to rule, and if for some reason it was thrust upon her, it wouldn't look like that. That was Marek's dream, not hers.

She steeled herself for the loneliness that she knew would follow. Drawing herself up once again, she spoke out loud to Marek.

"I will not allow you to come with me. This is not your task, and you will have no part of it."

Marek slammed into her mind with a rage that almost made her black out, but she held on. She gathered all her strength to close herself to him. He railed against her, and she thought she would be forced to give in. When all was almost lost, she felt Aidan's presence there with her, closing the door to Marek. He never intruded, never spoke to her, just offered his strength and support, asking no questions.

As quickly as it had begun, it was over. Marek was gone. Aidan was gone too, and Elana started once again up the stairs.

Growing more narrow as they wound upwards, the stairs were no longer all the same height. Elana groped her way in the semi-darkness, climbing now on hands and feet, to keep from falling backwards. When she was sure that she could not force herself up another stair, a small landing opened up. Grateful for a more secure place to rest, Elana sat with her legs stretched out, rubbing her sore muscles. She leaned against the cold wall and closed her eyes.

A soft voice roused her.

"Elana."

She looked around. It was her mother's voice.

"Mother!" she called.

"Oh honey, you're alright. We've been so worried about you."

"Where are you?" Elana asked, searching frantically for her parents. Hope soared up in her. They were here. She had found them at last.

"We're here, but only the Firestone can set us free. We can see you, but you can't see us. The Shadow King has us under His spell."

"How can I help you?"

"You must go up these stairs and claim the Firestone for your own. You are the rightful heir to it, you know. Your father and I suspected this for years and we're so proud of you."

Elana could feel the love pouring from her mother's voice.

"You have to claim it for your own before you do anything else. It will be forced to obey you then. Only then will you have the power you need to set us free. If you don't do this, we will soon die." Her mother's voice gave a catch and a small sob.

"Where's Father?" she asked, hoping to hear his voice as well.

"I'm right here, Elana," her father's voice answered. "Your mother is right. We both hoped you would be heir to the Firestone. You have brought our family back to its rightful place of honor within the Elder Born."

She frowned. That didn't sound like her father. He had given up a place of respect in Farran to travel through the Vale, teaching people who, for the most part, feared or despised him. He had never, for as long as Elana could remember, cared about being honored by others. The only honor he cared about, was doing what was right, regardless of the cost.

"Promise me," her father's voice continued, "promise me that you'll do as your mother instructed you. You must claim the Firestone for your own. Once you do, come back down here and we will tell you how to use it to set us free."

Tears ran down Elana's face. Hearing her parents voices again brought back the grief, the despair, the tiny thread of hope that had started her on this harrowing journey. She had done all this for them. What if it was them here? What if she went all this way and in the last moment, let them down?

"Promise me, Elana!" her father's voice was tinged with anger now. "Do you want us to die here?"

Her father had never spoken to her like that. That little feeling inside, the one she had been so afraid to trust, spoke to her now. This was not from her parents. Sobbing, she spoke out, "I will make you no promises. This is not your task. I will obey whatever the Firestone asks of me. It is not my servant, but I am servant to it."

She ran for the stairs, before she had to hear any answer.

The only sound in the room below her, was the soft sobbing of her mother. Matching the sobs with her own, she climbed the last flight of stairs to the top of the tower.

A small circular room opened up before her, with a dais in the center. On the dais, rested a clear stone that flickered in its depths as if harboring its own fire. It was big enough that Elana didn't think she could wrap her arms completely around it if she tried. The stone's light filled the room. After the darkness of the stairs, it made Elana blink.

She was wrung out. There was no more fear, or pride, or hope for her own gain. She heard the darkness rage outside, and accepted the fact that she probably wouldn't get out of this tower alive. But she would do what she came here to do, even if it meant fighting the Shadow King herself, becoming estranged from those she loved, or losing her parents.

The presence of the Firestone filled the room, and with a gentleness that made Elana smile, in spite of herself, it reached out to her. She reached back, opening up all of herself to it, inviting it in. Bit by bit it filled her, searching every corner of her mind. It unnerved Elana, to be almost probed by this thing, but she felt no malice in it, only questions. The same peace that accompanied the Bronze Key, flowed in with the Firestone.

After the initial search a wordless request formed in her mind.

"Will you pour your Skills into me?" the Firestone asked her.

"Is this what you're asking me to do?" Elana asked it.

"Yes. Will you give me all of your Skills, holding back nothing for yourself? Will you content yourself to go from here and live as the Valefolk do?"

Elana swallowed hard. This was the last thing she imagined. She might as well gouge out her eyes, or silence her ears.

"Is it forever?" she asked the Firestone.

"Will you trust me with them?" the Firestone answered.

Elana sensed that she would get no further explanation.

She thought of Aidan and Faris, and Orvis, of Niall, and Kenrich. If she made it back there, she would have to tell them she failed. She never unlocked the Firestone, or passed any test. It was all for nothing.

The face of the Ancient One floated before her. She had made the vow that she would do whatever the Firestone requested. Somehow, she didn't imagine this was an option, but a promise was a promise.

"I will do it," she said.

The Firestone pulsed brightly once and Elana felt it open itself up to her. She focused all her Skills toward it and willed the Firestone to take them. There was a moment of glorious touching and then she was empty. Her Skills were gone. She could no longer see the glow of the Firestone, or the walls of the tower around her. She felt a last momentary touch from it, and then all went black.

Aidan watched Elana gallop toward the Door. He wanted to cheer her on, to see her safely through to the other side before anyone else realized she was gone. Hoofbeats pounded behind him. Marek galloped up, his face drawn.

"Where is she?" he demanded.

Before Aidan could answer, his eyes found her. She had just opened the Door, and stepped through.

Marek howled, like an enraged animal, but Elana and the Door vanished.

Faris rode up behind them.

"What's happening?"

"This sorry excuse for an Elder Born just let Elana go through the Door unaided. She could be killed," Marek ranted.

Faris smiled a slow smile and turned to Aidan. "Well done. She has everything she needs. She need fear no attack, nor turn to any outside help."

"But she will need help with the Firestone. Don't you realize the burden of ruling the Vale falls on her alone? She must have help with that!"

Aidan looked at Marek. He trusted the man less now than ever. Whatever Elana saw in Marek, escaped him. With her gone, he was going to trust his own instincts. He felt Marek reaching out toward Elana, and felt her respond to him. Then when she tried to shut him out, Marek assaulted her with such rage that any lesser Elder Born would have been driven mad. Aidan, reaching out to her through their link, joined in with her, until Marek was unable to find any chink into her mind.

There, Aidan thought. I can at least do that for her. Whatever she might need, it isn't him.

Marek collapsed to the ground, and lay there unmoving. Aidan kept an eye on him, but as long as he wasn't making any threats, he'd leave the man alone.

He could still feel echoes of Elana's struggle, but refrained from intruding, unless she called for him, or for help.

Niall and Kenrich rode up with Orvis and Cecily. Faris gave them a brief update, no longer caring that Cecily knew what was happening. Elana's task was beyond all of their reach.

They rode down to where they guessed the Door had been and camped there, fixing supper as they waited for Elana to return. Marek had revived enough to ride down with them, but sat in silence, refusing to eat or speak.

Orvis paced the encampment, and to Aidan's surprise, it was Cecily who went to the old man. She encouraged him to sit with her and take some supper, and she listened while he talked on into the evening.

Everyone was quiet and moody. Aidan never thought beyond finding the Door. He had no idea what was to happen next. One by one, the companions dropped off to sleep. Aidan took the first watch. At some point he realized that he couldn't feel Elana's presence at all. The thought disturbed him, but seeing as how there was nothing he could do about it, he kept it to himself.

Just as he was preparing to wake Niall for the next shift, he heard a rustling in the dark.

"Who's there?" he whispered.

"Aidan?" Elana's voice whispered back.

"I'm here. Follow the light."

In a moment, Elana stumbled into the circle of firelight. She looked awful - empty and haggard.

Their voices woke Faris and Orvis. The old man wrapped Elana up in his arms like a child and held her. She clung to him, burying her face in his shoulder. Aidan saw her back shaking with sobs.

"What's wrong, little one? Are you hurt?" Orvis asked.

By this time, the rest of the camp was up.

"I failed." Her voice was flat.

Marek raised his head, a queer light in his eyes.

"What do you mean?" Orvis pressed.

"I didn't unlock the Firestone."

"What did you do?" Aidan asked.

"I obeyed it," she answered, a wisp of defiance in her voice for a moment. "But it came to nothing."

"I don't understand." Faris said.

"Why don't you start at the beginning," Niall suggested. "I, for one, am going to need a more thorough explanation than this." He gave her a gentle wink and stroked her cropped hair.

She smiled up at the big smith.

"Could I tell the whole thing later? I'm so tired now."

"Of course," he said.

"The main part is that I failed," she repeated. "The Firestone wanted me to give it my Skills, so I did. I don't have them anymore."

Aidan stared at her. That's why he couldn't feel her anymore. She couldn't forge a mind link. The company waited in awkward silence.

"I couldn't even see it after it took my Skills. The next thing I remember is waking up here in the dark."

Aidan didn't know what to say. She had done what she promised to do, but it did look pretty bleak. He couldn't imagine the courage it took to give up her Skills. He couldn't even imagine living without them. It was a horror just to contemplate.

Marek was staring at her, his face unreadable. Aidan went to head that one off.

"Faris, will you and Orvis watch Elana?" he asked the Barras.

He motioned Marek to follow him. "Don't say a word to her," he demanded.

Marek gave him a slow smile. "I don't think any of you simpletons understand. No, I won't say a word." Turning his back on Aidan, he walked off into the darkness.

Aidan heard soft footsteps behind him. Cecily touched his shoulder.

"Can I speak to you?" she asked. "I want to apologize for how I've acted toward you. I woke up just before Elana came back. I felt like I was somehow a different person than I'd been. I don't know what's been going on, but I want you to know that I feel so badly about how I've treated you and Elana."

Aidan tried not to gawk. This was not a Cecily he'd ever known. "Thank you. Apology accepted." A sudden question hit him. "Cecily, how do you feel about Elder Born?"

"I don't know," the girl answered. "In fact, I don't know how I feel about most things. Except that I feel like I've been living in some sort of dream or haze, especially lately. It wasn't very nice," she added.

"But you're alright now?"

"I think so."

402

"Good." He gave her a grin. "I've got to talk to Elana for a moment. Will you come with me?"

Elana sat staring numbly into the fire. She didn't look up when Aidan and Cecily sat down next to her.

"Elana, I think that more happened up there with you and the Firestone than you realize," Aidan began.

She looked up at him, her eyes listless.

With some encouragement from Aidan, Cecily tried to explain what had happened to her.

A little life came back to Elana's face.

"I don't think this is an accident," Aidan said.

He left Elana with Orvis and turned the second watch over to Niall. Whatever mysteries remained, could wait until morning. The last thing he remembered before falling asleep, was Marek grumbling to himself in his blanket.

Aidan's Skill woke him in the wee hours of the morning, warning him of danger. He stirred, reaching for his hunting knife. He looked around, noting that Kenrich was keeping watch and Marek seemed to join him, pacing fitfully around the perimeter of the camp. As Marek drew near to where Elana slept, the warning inside him screamed. He yelled for Orvis, who was next to her, and the old sailor was in motion before Aidan's shout was stilled.

With a crazed look on his face, Marek sprang at Elana, brandishing a long knife. Orvis was quicker. Before Marek could reach the girl, Orvis jumped in between them, receiving the thrust intended for her.

The old sailor crumpled to the ground, blood seeping out from the wound in his side. Marek looked at him in horror, the crazed expression gone. He ran for his horse and galloped off before anyone realized what was happening.

CHAPTER 19

FARRAN

Without a second thought, Aidan whistled for Kael. Marek didn't stand a chance. There was no place the man could hide where Aidan couldn't track him, and Kael could outrun the chestnut with ease. He would make that cold blooded Elder Born pay for what he'd done to Orvis, Elana, and Cecily. Aidan's slow anger kindled now to a blaze.

Niall's heavy hand on Aidan's shoulder stopped him short.

"I want to slit the weasel's throat too," the smith growled through clenched teeth. "But you're the only hope Orvis' got."

Aidan twisted out from under the hand.

"Don't let us down now, my friend."

Niall's words were cold water on Aidan's rage. He knew the smith was right. His shoulders sagged as he followed the big man back to Orvis, giving up for the moment, the hope for vengeance.

Now it was Elana who cradled Orvis in her arms. By her blank stare, Aidan guessed she was in shock. This was too much, too close together.

Kenrich stripped off Orvis' shirt, inspecting the wound.

"It's missed anything vital," he reported, "but he's no youngster, and he's loosing blood fast."

He bandaged the old sailor, with expertise learned on the battle field.

"How far do we have to ride?" he asked.

Faris looked at Aidan who shrugged. Neither had ever been to Farran.

Kenrich gave them a grim look and shook his head. We'd better start now. I don't know how much time we have.

They packed camp in a hurry and mounted up; Faris holding Orvis in front of him on Shay. Niall ponied Orvis' horse, his quiet gelding not minding another horse bumping alongside.

Aidan strained his Skills to their utmost. Orvis' life hung in the balance.

To his surprise, the land delighted in revealing itself, giving Aidan a clear picture of the route they needed to take. Moving through the Empty Hills, Aidan could almost believe that the trees shifted for them, creating paths that led in a straight line to Farran.

Somehow, since Elana's return, his Skills had grown stronger. The land felt eager to cooperate with him, like a willing horse under saddle, and they covered more ground than Aidan thought possible. Toward morning Faris confirmed this.

"Do you see what's going on?" he whispered to Aidan. "I've traveled for years, and never seen anything like this. We might as well be flying, yet we've not moved beyond a walk."

"Something's changed since Elana's come back."

Aidan told the Barras about the change in Cecily. "I don't know what it is, but I don't think Elana failed. Something's different."

"You've got that right." Faris answered. "Haven't a clue what she's done, but let's keep our eyes and ears open. It may make the difference for Orvis."

When the sun lifted over the trees, the path opened up to reveal a fertile valley below them.

"Farran," Elana breathed. It was her first word since Marek's attack. She turned to Aidan, "I didn't think we were this close."

"We weren't," he said.

A mist shimmered over the valley, and for a moment, he thought he saw the steep road before them level out to an easy descent.

Kenrich rode up to join them, giving the gentle road an appreciative nod. "I was worried how we were going to make it down to the valley with him." He gave a worried look in Orvis' direction. The old sailor lay unconscious in Faris' arms. His face had a pasty cast, and blood oozed out of the bandages.

They navigated the road to the valley, arriving sooner than Aidan thought possible. Maybe it was just the land around Farran that was different.

Two horses galloped up to meet them.

"Hail, and welcome to Farran," a young man said, raising his hand in salute. "Geri sent us to help you. She said you came with special urgency."

"Thank you, friend," Aidan answered. "One of our company is wounded. He needs immediate care."

The man looked over at Orvis and motioned to his companion.

The old woman riding with him threw back her hood. Blue-green eyes, the color of the sea, twinkled with youth and daring. Aidan thought them mismatched to her white hair and wrinkled skin. After a moment of watching her though, he changed his opinion, deciding that the years had betrayed her and the white hair and wrinkled skin were more out of place than the twinkling eyes.

She dismounted with a fluid motion and made her way to Orvis and Faris.

"What do you bring, my friend?" she asked the Barras.

"Our companion, Orvis, is gravely wounded," Faris answered, inclining his head in respect for the woman.

For a moment, the woman's age seem to catch up with her, and she steadied herself with a hand on Shay's shoulder.

"Did you say, 'Orvis'?" she asked. Her bright eyes clouded over.

"Yes." Faris looked at her with concern. "Do you know him?"

"He's the brother of my heart," the woman replied. "I have wondered long years if I'd ever see him again."

Elana, who had been watching the exchange in silence, spoke.

"Brenna?"

406

"Do I know you, child?"

"I am a friend of Orvis, and he told me about you. He so wanted to see you."

The woman took a deep breath. "Then we've work to do. I wouldn't want to disappoint him."

The young man rode ahead while Brenna led the company to a house on the edge of the valley. Once there, she instructed Faris to lay Orvis on a bed, while she unwrapped his wounds.

Two healers, one young and one older, appeared at the door and took over Orvis' care. Brenna hovered over them, refusing to leave the old sailor's side. After putting up the horses, the company crowded into the outer chamber, awaiting some word of his condition.

When the healers came out, their faces were sober.

"I won't lie to you, it isn't good," the elder woman said.

Brenna turned to Elana. "Did Orvis mention an old flute?"

"He has it here." Elana dug through the old sailor's pack and retrieved the flute.

Brenna fingered it with fondness, then, looking at the younger healer, said, "Go get Baird."

The boy rode back behind the healer. He threw himself off the horse before the beast had stopped and ran into the house.

"Where is he? What happened to Orvis?"

Brenna caught him by the arm. "He needs your help, Baird. Can you play for him on his flute? It's time."

She led him to Orvis. Baird looked from Brenna's face to the instrument.

"Call him back to us. He doesn't have to leave yet, if he can find the strength to stay."

Baird picked up the flute and put it to his mouth. He played as though his heart were breaking, putting all his longing into the music.

Aidan never heard anything so sad.

Brenna leaned over to the boy. "He's not gone yet. Help him remember why he'd want to stay."

 The tune changed, still with the sadness in the background, but now it brought back to Aidan the sound of the sea; the wind and the gulls and the bright, hard, sunshine over the water. The tune shifted again, and Aidan felt the warmth of sitting in front of a fire with his family, snug together while the winter wind blew outside. Again and again the song shifted, each time the pale boy captured a piece of life, turning it into song and calling all that was in Orvis to join with it.

There wasn't a dry eye in the room. Each person stood lost in their own memories, each face etched with the longing of what still might be.

Orvis stirred on the bed.

Baird didn't cease his playing, but slowed it, calling to the old man, willing him to fight.

A blush of color returned to the sailor's face.

Elana bit her fist, watching him.

The old man coughed painfully, then opened his eyes.

"You're not going to let me go in peace, are you boy?" His raspy voice barely topped a whisper.

A lone tear spilled onto Baird's cheek.

"I guess it's not my time yet." Orvis tried to smile, though it came as more of a grimace.

Brenna moved to his side. "No it's not, old sailor."

Orvis tried to turn his head. "Brenna?"

The two grasped hands, eyes beaming at one another.

Aidan could feel the life in Orvis growing stronger. For the first time since they arrived, he took a deep breath. The recovery may be long, but the old sailor would make it.

Worry over Orvis had driven all other thoughts from Aidan. Now he turned to Elana. The girl looked horrible, drained of life. None of her flash and fire remained. He interrupted one of the healers.

"Could we get another bed?"

The healer followed his glance to Elana.

With a quick nod, she shooed everyone else out of the house and made up a bed next to the fire.

"Come lie down here," she instructed Elana.

She poured some musky smelling liquid into a cup of tea and sat next to Elana while the girl drank it. Within minutes Elana was asleep.

Aidan felt on the verge of collapse himself, but he wanted to speak to Geri before he let himself rest.

Faris caught up with him outside.

"How can I help you, Aidan?" he asked.

"I need to speak with Geri."

Faris cornered the older healer and after a few low words, the woman approached Aidan.

"Geri is waiting for you," she said.

Aidan nodded in thanks, and looked over at Faris.

"Will you come with me?" he asked the Barras.

Faris raised an eyebrow.

"This is your story too," Aidan said, unable to put his feelings properly into words right now.

While the younger healer attended to the needs of the company, Faris and Aidan followed the older woman into Farran.

They stopped at a tiny cottage and followed the old healer to the door. The woman knocked and opened it up without waiting for an answer.

The room was sparsely furnished. A small fire crackled in the stone fireplace, with a kettle of water simmering over it. Sitting in the only chair at a worn table, an old woman pored over a roll of parchment by lamplight. She looked up as they entered and her smile embraced them both.

"Welcome," she said, rising and flinging her arms wide. "I have waited long for this day."

Her black eyes made Aidan think of an ancient version of Elana; they were almost impish. Thinking about Elana made his insides hurt all over again.

Aidan remembered his manners and introduced himself and Faris to Geri.

"It is my honor to meet you at last, Faris" the head of the Elder Born said. "We are in your debt."

"The honor is mine," Faris answered. He took Geri's offered hand and held it for a moment, in both of his own.

"Aidan," she turned to him. "Your mother and Arella arrived less than a week ago. They are both well and strong. Eli brought them without incident."

Aidan wished there was another chair in the room, because he needed to sit down. He hadn't let himself think of them for so long now. They were safe. He didn't know whether to laugh or cry.

Geri smiled and offered him her chair. "When we are through here, and you have rested, you will see them."

"Now," she said, "tell me what happened."

The tiny woman paced back and forth as first Aidan then Faris filled in pieces of the story. She interrupted occasionally, to check a detail, or clarify some point, but mostly she listened. At last, Aidan ended with his worries about Elana.

"She's lost all her Skills. I can't imagine what she's going through. She feels barely alive." Aidan choked on the last words.

410

"I had no idea, no idea at all," Geri muttered. "I had hoped to spend time with her before she set out, to finish her training myself, but we ran out of time. The Hunter found her first."

Geri tapped the parchment on the table. "Reeves brought me some ancient records from Bellport. We've lost so much knowledge..." She brought herself back with a shake. "It seems that the Firestone isn't a tool, or a weapon, but more like a personality. I don't fully understand it, but something did change last night. I felt it too."

She peered out the window and spoke in a quiet voice. "Something is awake, stirring. Something beyond my comprehension, yet kindly disposed toward us. Just as I've felt the Malice from the West stirring for years, growing in strength and malevolence, now something is awake in the land to challenge it."

Faris set his jaw and his hand reached instinctively for his sword. "I pledge my strength to that battle. I've waited all my life for this."

"We'll be glad of your strength before the end. That I know," Geri said.

The thrill that first coursed through Aidan at Geri's words, fell flat. It should be him saying that, not Faris. He should be the one rising to the occasion, going out to do battle with evil. He searched within himself, but it wasn't there. Not that he'd shrink from a fight, but he had no desire to seek one out.

He'd hoped that this journey would somehow shape him into the person he needed to be to help the Elder Born. For a while, it seemed that it might. But not now. Since last night, his Skills more than ever were calling him to the land. He wanted to explore it, to speak with it, to hear its secrets and learn from it. Hardly a warrior or leader of any sort...

The rest of the meeting passed in a blur. They took leave of Geri, followed the healer to a cottage prepared for them, and fell into their beds, exhausted.

Aidan woke to the sound of Baird's music. The intricate tune danced and tumbled through the open window, filling the room with life. An orange glow lit the far wall, telling him the sun was just going down. Aidan stretched and yawned, refreshed for the first time since they left Hafwen. His stomach growled, reminding him that it had been too long since his last meal. It growled again, and Aidan got up, pulled on his clothes and stepped outside.

His cottage lay grouped in a cluster of small guest homes, forming a courtyard in the center. In that courtyard a group of children played, rolling a wooden hoop with a stick. Baird sat in a low branch above them, like a gangly white bird, playing the flute. The sight made Aidan laugh.

At the sound of his laughter, a small girl burst from the group and ran for Aidan, nearly knocking him over as she crashed into his legs. It was Arella.

He swung her up and spun her in circles, laughing as she screamed with delight.

"I told you we'd see you again," she said.

When he put her down she pulled at him, leading him to their mother.

Bree was preparing supper. Aidan thought she looked older than when he'd left. Her face was more serious than ever, the lines around her eyes deepened.

"Momma, look who I've brought!" An exuberant Arella danced around her mother.

Bree turned, gave a small cry, and Aidan wrapped her up in his arms.

The three of them ate together that night, sharing stories of the road and soaking up one another's company. When Arella went to bed Aidan excused himself to check on his companions. He didn't want to face his mother alone. She knew him too well, and there were still questions he'd rather not answer.

The company was gathered in Orvis' cottage, talking quietly with the old man, and one another. Only Elana was absent. The healers moved her to her own cottage, and asked that no one disturb her.

Cecily sought Aidan out.

"I spoke with Geri today," she said. She was shy with Aidan, hesitant to meet his gaze. "She told me what Marek did."

Aidan didn't know what to say. He hated the man.

"Geri offered me sanctuary here for as long as I want," Cecily continued. "She said that what Elana accomplished with the Firestone broke Marek's link to me. That's the difference that I felt." Cecily paused. "She also said that she didn't know what damage Marek might have caused. She offered to work with me, to help heal the places he hurt." She looked away, her face troubled. "I don't know what to think anymore. I don't know who to trust."

"Cecily, please trust her." Aidan reached out for her hand. "She'd sooner die than hurt you in any way, and she is the most able to help. I so want you to be free from every trace of that man."

"I hardly know who I am, Aidan. Bellport is the only home I've known. And I have responsibilities there."

He felt her wavering. "Don't make any decisions yet. Stay here a while and see. Everything has happened so fast. Just give this a little time."

The thought of her leaving, left him with a strange emptiness. He knew that he wasn't free to say more, so he held his peace.

"Geri did say that it was possible that I could reinitiate the link with Marek. From what she guessed, the Firestone now prevents Elder Born from intruding on the minds of the Valefolk. If there's an invitation though..." she didn't finish her sentence.

"Do you want it back?" Aidan asked, appalled.

"Sometimes," she said, ducking away from him. "It's so lonely now. I never knew that life was any other way. He was always there for me; helping me, taking care of me, making decisions for me. I feel so empty now."

Aidan saw what Geri meant by the damage Marek caused.

"Please don't, Cecily. Please, please... Give Geri a chance."

"I'll think about it," she said.

After that conversation Aidan sought out Niall. The smith's solid presence always comforted him.

"So, what's going to happen next?" the smith questioned.

"I have no idea. I guess you and Faris and Kenrich can go home now."

Niall scowled. "You're not getting rid of us that easily." The man laid a calloused hand on Aidan's shoulder. "I pledged myself to help you, and as far as I can see, your task hasn't even begun."

The knot that twisted up in him after his talk with Geri, tightened another notch. He'd better face it now. It obviously wasn't going away.

"I'm not a warrior, Niall. I'm not even a good leader. I thought I might get there, but it's not in me. You're wasting your time."

"Of course you're not a warrior, you fool. You're handy enough in a fight, but that's like hitching a racehorse to a plough. It's not what you're made for. Any idiot can see that. That's what we're here for. What you do have, with the land, hearing it and all, and what you bring out in others, that's your part. You work on being what you're meant to be. Don't know how it all fits together yet, but I'd wager good gold on it, there's no mistakes in the mix."

The smith snorted, growing more indignant as he gathered steam. "You're not the swaggering up front type of leader, but that's a bonus in my opinion. You get men to work together, you inspire loyalty, and you're humble enough not to take all the credit."

Aidan reddened. "That's because it's not mine to take! Faris is the leader here. He always has been. I'd lay down my life for him. I've never respected a man more."

"You see, there you go. You recognize the strengths of your men and don't need to make them smaller to puff yourself up in comparison.

The only thing you don't recognize is your own strength." Niall smiled. "That's alright. It'll come in time."

Kenrich walked in on the tail end of the conversation. "He's right, Aidan. We'll see this thing through to the end. I may not be Elder Born, but I know some things, and the caliber of men is one of them. It's an honor to serve you."

Aidan blushed furiously. He had no reply for any of this, and seeing as how he couldn't talk them out of their opinions, he was profoundly grateful for their promise of companionship.

The night deepened and as Orvis grew weary, the companions filed out to their own beds. Aidan found himself bone tired again, amazed that he needed sleep so soon. Elana still hadn't returned. He thought to ask Faris about her, but the grim look on the Barras' face made him think better of it. He wondered about Faris and Elana. The Barras shared a bond with her that Aidan, even with their mind link, never approached. It seemed that the fierce leader saw her more clearly than anyone else. Maybe he could help her come back. With that thought floating through his mind, Aidan collapsed into bed and deep sleep.

The next morning, Baird hunted Aidan down before breakfast.

"Granny wants to see you," he said.

Then, as though it took some working up to say it, "Can I see your horse again?"

Aidan laughed. "Of course."

They went to feed Kael, and then Baird took him to Granny's cottage.

The old woman sat rocking on the front porch, just like she had been at her home.

"Welcome to Farran, Aidan, son of Darian. You've accomplished the first part of your task."

Aidan grit his teeth. He wished for once she'd speak plainly.

"I'm not sure what you mean, Granny." He tried to be polite.

"Where's the cloak I gave you?"

How could she tell he wasn't wearing it?

"It's with my things," he answered.

"I didn't give it to you to live bundled in a pack."

Aidan's patience was running thin. "Granny, I can't just wear it everywhere. It's looks like it's for royalty."

"That's because it is."

He changed the subject. "What's the second part of my task?"

"Do you know who you are?" she asked.

Aidan wondered briefly how Baird turned out as well as he did, growing up with her. It was amazing that the boy could hold a conversation.

"Yes, I know who I am. And if I forgot, you seem to delight in reminding me," he retorted.

Granny chuckled, her brittle laugh crackling like dried leaves. "I like you, boy. Sorry you can't stay around longer."

A chill curled up Aidan's spine. "What do you mean?"

"You have to find out who you are. Not going to find it here. Pity, too."

Her sightless eyes fixed on him. "There's those that helped you get here. You owe something to them. Don't be afraid to follow where they'll take you. Your father didn't fail. He opened the way for you. Payton's son pledged himself to you. Your journey's bound to his. The smith sees you clearer than you see yourself. You can trust him."

She stopped talking and turned away. "I've likely gone and said too much again, but you seem to pull it out of me."

Aidan held back a snort of laughter. That was a long speech for her, but hardly saying too much. "Thank you, Granny." Affection for the prickly old woman bubbled up in him. He bent down and gave her a hug.

"Stop by sometime boy," she said, returning his hug with quick fierceness. "I've been a long time waiting for you."

Tears stung Aidan's eyes. A picture sprung to his mind of her standing in the darkness, holding hope like a tiny flame, guarding it from any drafts. Somehow, she too, was tied to him. He had the sense that this unusual old woman had been protecting him, even watching over him. The thought comforted him. Although he had no idea where he was headed next, he resolved to see her every chance he had.

Elana wanted to die. It was all for nothing - some horrible, twisted joke, with her at the butt of it. She'd lost everything. Her parents were gone, the Firestone was lost. She didn't even have the Bronze Key anymore. The worst of it was, she lost her Skills. It was like waking up blind. Here she was in Farran, the place she'd dreamed of being since her Waking started, surrounded by Elder Born, the place she was supposed to belong, and now she was some kind of freak. She wanted to hide. The friendly faces, the pitying looks, the whispers when they thought she was sleeping... Just being here hurt. She gave in to self pity, buried her face in the pillow and sobbed herself to sleep again.

The cottage door clicked open. Voices whispered in the outside room, beckoning her out of fitful dreams. Candlelight flickered shadows on the wall beyond her bedroom door. She recognized the healer's voice, but there was another there. Unable to fall back asleep, she climbed out of bed, wrapped a quilt around her shoulders and steeled herself to face the visitors.

An old woman stood talking with the healer. Her bright black eyes and warm smile greeted Elana, bringing back memories from her childhood. It was Geri.

Her throat went dry and sticky. All the hopes of making it to Farran and being trained by Geri, taunted her. She was ashamed to meet the old woman's eyes.

The healer let herself out of the cottage.

Geri held out both her hands to Elana.

"My dear..."

She was the closest to a mother that Elana had now. All the fears and doubts that tormented her poured out to Geri's sympathetic ear. The old woman listened, offering nods, and words of encouragement when Elana faltered. Never once did she reprimand, or even appear disappointed.

After what seemed like hours, Elana finished in a dead voice. "I've lost my Skills. I gave them to the Firestone. But I didn't manage to bring the Firestone back. I'm not even an Elder Born anymore. I failed."

For the first time, Geri looked stern. "I know it looks that way to you now. But it couldn't be farther from the truth. If you've told me all your story, it might be time for me to tell you some of what I've found."

In spite of herself, hope flickered somewhere inside Elana.

"It's my fault you were ever put in this position," Geri began. "I underestimated the danger. I should have sent for you last year." Her voice broke and she paused to gain control. "Your parents are some of my dearest friends. If anything happens to them... " Taking a deep breath, she continued. "Elana, whatever else happens, I want you to know that you did not fail."

"How can that be?" Elana interrupted.

"The Firestone isn't just a tool, or a weapon. It's been so long since it was hidden that most of what we believe about it is little more than myth or legend. Reeves brought me manuscripts from Bellport that shed more light." Geri lowered her voice and her eyes twinkled. "Elana, I don't understand all of what happened when you found it, but there is no doubt that you wakened the Firestone." An odd smile played across her face. "Actually, if you would know, I believe that this makes you head of the Elder Born. The Ancient One knew what she was talking about."

418

Elana didn't know whether to laugh or cry. This was ridiculous!

"Something has changed since you've come back. I spoke at length with Cecily, and searched the perimeter of her mind to see if I could detect any presence of Marek, and he's not there. More than that, there's not an open door for him to access her anymore." Geri shook her head. "Do you know how difficult that would have been to do for her, if it were even possible? I would have been in danger the entire time of destroying the integrity of Cecily's mind. Yet from the moment you came back, it was accomplished. What did that?"

Elana didn't answer. She knew Aidan had said something like that, but in her despair, she discounted it.

Geri reached a hand out to her. "The Firestone isn't a rock. It's an entity unto itself, and a doorway to the Ancient Ones."

The hair on the back of Elana's neck stood up.

"In the past when the Vale was threatened, the Firestone forged a link with the head Elder Born. The Ancient Ones don't directly interfere in the affairs of the Vale, but through the Firestone, and the selflessness of the head Elder Born, they will sometimes move in unusual ways to protect and care for this land. That link gives the Ancient Ones access to act on our behalf."

Elana's head swam. This sounded like a fairytale.

"I've talked with Aidan and Faris. Do you know how far you were from Farran when Marek wounded Orvis?"

"I thought we were just a day's ride," said Elana.

"You were at least four days hard riding, through some of the roughest country in the Vale."

Elana didn't understand.

"Yet you made it in a day. Both Aidan and Faris noticed." Excitement mounted in Geri voice. "I can't tell you exactly why, but I have a very strong sense that it was because the Firestone knew how much Orvis meant to you. You gave your best to the Firestone, and though you may not recognize it, the Firestone has forged a link with you."

She grew sober. "I don't know why you don't have your Skills now, Elana. I wish I had an answer for you, but the best I can do is guess. My guess is that the need is so great, and with the other two Gifts from the Ancient Ones lost to us it asked more from you than any Elder Born has ever been asked to give."

"Do you think that I may get my Skills back someday?" Elana could barely get the words out.

"I don't know, child. It's not impossible, though. But whether you do or not, you are the head Elder Born."

"No. That's not right. I couldn't take that place. Please don't ask me to do that, Geri."

"I won't ask you to do that, but not for the reason you're thinking. It wouldn't be safe for you. I don't want to draw any attention to you, Elana."

"Why not?"

"Do you know why Marek attacked you that night?"

Elana had no idea.

"He realized something that I only just put together. The power of the Ancient Ones in the Firestone is linked to you. If something happens to you, the Firestone is rendered powerless. Worse still, it reopens the possibility that it could fall into the wrong hands."

"What do you mean?" Elana asked.

"The Shadow King is also one of the Ancient Ones. Unlike the others though, he wants to possess the Vale for himself."

Elana remembered the shadowy figure that met her when she entered the Firestone's tower. A chill ran up her spine.

"What would have happened if I had listened to any of the voices in the tower?" she asked.

Geri gave a shiver. "If you had claimed the Firestone for your own, you would have become the servant of the Shadow King, and his puppet. He would have forged an unbreakable link with you, and through you used the power of the Firestone to secure the Vale for himself.

"I didn't know..." Elana's blood ran cold.

"Neither did we," Geri said quietly.

"Is Marek in league with the Shadow King?"

"At least to some extent," Geri said. "But I still hold out hope for him."

"You do?" That was the last thing Elana expected to hear.

"Yes, I do. He's been through so much pain, but there's something good in him still. I can feel it there at times." She stroked Elana's cheek. "You weren't wrong to give him the chance to come with you in the end. The Firestone knew it too. That may be another reason why your journey here was so unusually short. You said you felt the Bronze Key reaching out to him. You trusted that. I believe the Firestone honored that trust."

Geri grew serious. "Marek is not your only danger, Elana. The Hunter is a bondservant to the Shadow King. He will do all in his power to carry out his master's will." Geri's voice grew sad. "I knew him years ago. He too, was not always like he is now. He was one of our most powerful Elder Born. The greater the Skills, the greater the temptation to ill gotten power," she concluded.

"Where can I go?"

"I don't know yet," Geri said. "There's much to be decided. I want to wait for Reeves' return before making any definite plans. I don't fully understand all the ramifications of what's happened." She frowned at Elana. "What I do imagine though, is that anyone who's looking for you will look first and hardest here. So, it makes sense to me, that you not be around when they come to call."

Elana gave her a small grin. Then, without thinking, she tried to reach out again with her Skills, as she always had, to gain a sense of what would be best.

The shock of their absence was like getting to the bottom of a flight of stairs and putting your foot down for the next step only to have the ground slam you, jarring all the way to the top of your head. Her stomach turned.

Next to her, Geri winced.

Panic's cold fingers gripped Elana's chest. "Geri, I can't do this. I don't know how to live this way."

Geri stroked her hair, wordless.

Elana took a deep breath, trying to still the frantic beating of her heart. Her thoughts replayed their trip, looking for something that might make sense. She remembered riding through Cahermore, down the empty streets of the fortress city and seeing the maimed men slumped in doorways, or hobbling along on crutches, the light gone from their faces. They too had lost their strength, their dreams, to the fight with the Shadow King. The realization braced her, pushing back the panic. She thought of Falbor and Danae, the daughter they lost, and the gift of the golden mare. There was Gwyth, whose dreams died with Darian, and Aidan's family who had lived these years alone in exile without husband and father; no, she was not alone.

"I don't know how to do this, but somehow, I must." She looked at Geri with new resolve.

Tears wet the old woman's wrinkled cheeks. "I would give you all of my Skills, if I could." She kissed Elana's forehead. "Anything I can do to help you, know that I will."

Elana still avoided Aidan. In fact, she avoided most of the company. The only one she could bear to be with was Faris. He didn't speak much, or press her to talk. Mostly, the two of them rode through the valley, or took long walks, commenting on the view from this ledge, or the discovery of a blueberry bush in full fruit. With him the intuitive ability to read others that she carried from young childhood grew clearer. The bond that had always existed between them seemed to draw that out in her. They never spoke of it, but then, it didn't need words. In those moments together, Elana almost felt normal again.

Until now she assumed that her ability to perceive what others were thinking was a part of her Skills, but it had remained, while everything else vanished. She had to use it differently, but it was still available. And now that she stopped to think about it, Faris had always shared that with her. More than anyone she had ever met, he seemed to know a side of her she never voiced to anyone. She was grateful now that he showed up at her door whenever she was feeling lonely or disoriented; never asking questions, just offering his presence as solace against her malaise.

Time slowed down. Orvis healed faster than anyone imagined he would, and Elana visited him and Brenna briefly each day. Baird was usually with the old sailor, playing Orvis' flute now, whenever the old sailor wasn't sleeping.

One morning Cecily knocked on Elana's door. The arrogant look that Lord Gratton's daughter had always worn, was gone. For the first time, Elana saw a glimpse of what Aidan and Kenrich must have found beautiful about her.

"Come in," Elana opened the door and offered her a seat.

Cecily sat down, looking shy. "Can I talk to you?" she asked Elana.

Granny's admonition about reaching out to Cecily, came back. "Yes, of course," Elana answered, wondering what they would find to talk about.

Cecily spilled out her story of Marek and talking with Geri and Aidan. She told Elana about her ambivalence around her new freedom, and the difficulty in trusting anyone.

"I'm so sorry for how I behaved to you," she finished, reddening as she met Elana's eyes. "I understand if you don't want to have anything to do with me."

Elana nodded. She had forgiven Cecily when she first realized Marek's power over her, but she never imagined there being any connection between the two of them.

"It's all forgiven," she told her. "I know more than anyone else, just how powerful Marek is. I'm amazed and thrilled to see you free."

"It's because of what you did," Cecily answered. "I wouldn't have myself back, but for you."

Elana blushed. She never looked at it that way.

"I heard what happened to your Skills," Cecily said. The words tumbled out fast, as though she were forcing them past her awkwardness. "I'm so sorry. I don't know what you're going through exactly, but I know it can't be easy."

"Actually, you're going through something a little similar," Elana said, not missing the irony of this. "You're having to learn a new way of being, too."

Cecily gave her a shy smile. "Maybe you, more than anyone, can understand me."

The unlikely twosome shared lunch and when Cecily left, it was with the promise to visit Elana again, the next day.

That evening, after supper, Aidan came running to her cottage. He burst through the door without even knocking, scaring Elana half to death.

"What's wrong?" she asked him, afraid that something awful had happened.

"Nothing. Nothing's wrong," Aidan gasped, trying to catch his breath. "Reeves is back. He's brought your parents. They're here." Aidan stood panting, his face glowing.

Elana gasped and the room spun around her. Aidan grabbed her before she fell down.

Then, picking her up like she was Arella, he swung her around, beaming from ear to ear.

"They're safe, they're all safe," he crowed.

She was laughing and crying at the same time, and so dizzy she thought she'd faint.

Finally he put her down and looked at her. His tawny eyes held a tentative question.

For the first time since reaching Farran, she let down her guard around him. She had to force herself not to try and use her non-existent Skills to reach out to him. She didn't need that horrible jolt. She just let herself look back into his eyes, allowing him to see all she'd been trying to hide.

He didn't say anything for the longest time; just held her face in his hands.

"Please don't lock yourself off from me again. I've missed you so much."

The hurt in his eyes made her want to look away. How could he understand?

"But..." she began.

He put a finger on her lips and shook his head. "Your Skills aren't what made you who you are. It's you that's so special."

"Thank you," she whispered.

She didn't deserve his friendship. He'd been there for her when she needed him the most. It didn't take Skill to recognize the doubts that tormented him now. She hoped with all her heart that someday she'd be able to return the support he'd given her.

She smiled at him, stood up on tiptoes, and gave him a kiss on the cheek.

He grinned back at her and blushed.

"Let's go find your parents," he said.

Cheers and shouts rang through Farran; rising up from the joyous procession heading their way. Elana clung to Aidan's hand, searching the crowd for her parents faces. She spotted Reeves first, looking tired but satisfied. It took a moment to realize that the haggard, emaciated couple with him were her parents. She steeled herself, not wanting them to see her horror at their condition.

They were safe now, she kept repeating. That was what mattered.

Aidan squeezed her hand and then released her. The crowd parted and silence fell as she approached.

Reeves broke the silence. "You did it, Elana. You woke the Firestone!" Pride and gratitude shone from his eyes. "And to this story at least, I can offer you a happy ending."

Elana winced. He didn't know about her lost Skills. This wasn't the time.

"Thank you, Reeves."

"Elana," her mother's choked cry broke her heart. "What happened to you?"

There was no room to answer as both her parents caught her up in their arms. Elana was crying and laughing all at the same time, and from somewhere in the crowd she was sure she heard Baird's flute singing out the song of her own heart.

That night Elana slept in a cottage with her parents for the first time since the night of The Hunter. The others left them alone, giving them time together. More than once when she looked at them, she saw shades of Falbor and Danae. She hadn't thought about the fact that they were afraid for her life. She had been too preoccupied with being afraid for them. They didn't go into detail about their ordeal, but pressed her to share all she could of her journey. Her mother brewed tea for them and sat next to Elana as she drank, stroking her shorn hair. Her father's eyes glistened with tears as he sat across from her and listened.

"I'm so sorry, Elana," he said. "Sorry for all you've been through. I should have brought both of you back here last year. This is my fault."

"No." Elana laid a hand on his arm. "Nobody anticipated this." She straightened her shoulders. "I may have lost my Skills, but Geri said that I did forge a link with the Firestone, and somehow, though it's not what I imagined, I succeeded. It's presence is here now, in the Vale."

Hamilton's eyes shone. "I know. We felt it the moment you succeeded. The Hunter could no longer assail our minds. He also lost his hold on the minds of his men. Chaos ensued, and in the midst of it, Reeves accomplished our rescue. So, you did save us, you know."

Warmth crept through the ache in Elana's chest. That's what she set out to do - free her parents and wake the Firestone. It was done. She thought of Orvis and Brenna, spending their days in one another's company, each savoring the preciousness of this time together. None of it looked like she had imagined in her daydreams, but yet each promise stood fulfilled.

They stayed up late into the night, talking and soaking in the sweetness of reunion.

Yet, after her parents closed the door to their bedroom and she to hers, she knew something had changed. She wasn't the girl who set out for Bellport with Orvis. She didn't know who she was.

Not wanting to disturb them, she snuck out her window, hoping a walk in the moonlight would help clear her head.

Her feet found their way to the stables, where Devi gave her a soft nicker in greeting.

"Who's out there, little girl?"

Faris' voice floated out from Shay's stall, to the golden mare.

"It's me," Elana answered.

Faris' head appeared above the stall door.

"I thought you'd be with your parents."

"I was. They went to sleep. I needed to get out." She leaned next to Shay's stall, staring over the moonlit valley. "It's different than I thought it would be. I've changed."

Faris chuckled.

"Not just loosing my Skills," she started.

"I didn't mean that," he said, his voice low.

"I always assumed that I'd stay with my parents, if I could get them back. But now..."

She told Faris what Geri had said about her not being safe in Farran. "I don't know what I'm going to do, or where I'm going to go."

Faris joined her in the moonlight. "I was wondering some of the same things myself."

He grew quiet.

"I thought you'd be traveling with Aidan," she said.

"I thought you would be, too," he countered. "I don't doubt that I will at some point, but I promised Varen that I'd see you through to the end of this quest and then return to the Barras. There are certain obligations I must attend to."

"Elana." His blue eyes held hers. "Would you come back to the Barras with me? I can't promise you an easy time of it, but if you need to disappear..." The corners of his mouth curled in a hint of a smile. "I have some experience with disappearing."

Elana's pulse quickened. For the first time since she returned from Laharan, she had the distinct sense that this was the path for her to walk.

"I know Aidan will need our help before this is through," Faris continued, "but if what Geri said is true, I'd like to buy you some time out of sight. When it's right, we'll rejoin him. I promise."

Elana breathed in the cool night air, full of promise. She smiled up at the stern Barras, a tingle of excitement running up her spine. She never imagined he would allow her to accompany him. In the place where she used to feel her Waking, the presence of the Firestone thrummed through her like a whisper, and then was gone.

"Whenever you're ready, I'll go with you," she answered.

The flash of warmth in his eyes was all the response she needed.

She sighed and relaxed against the sturdy wooden stable. A lone whippoorwill called once, from across the field and then the steady

428

sound of horses chewing hay filled the silence of the night. Faris slipped out of Shay's stall to join her. She couldn't imagine what lay before her, or how she would navigate life without her Skills, but now, in this moment, none of that mattered. She felt right, clear down to her bones. For tonight, it was good to be Elana.

The Elder Born:

The Firestone Eldership

- Elana - daughter of Hamilton and Madeline, untrained in her Skills, woke the Firestone
- Hamilton - Elana's father, Skilled in teaching
- Madeline - Elana's mother, Skilled in healing
- Marek - right hand to Lord Gratton, ruler of Merrion, Vale born, trained by Geri, Skilled in mind to mind contact, and wielding power
- Granny - guardian of Baird, Skilled in visions and wielding of power
- Geri - longstanding leader of the Firestone Eldership, Skilled in teaching, mind to mind contact, healing, and wielding power

The Bells Eldership

- Reeves - leader of the Bells Eldership, Skilled in music
- Orvis - friend to Elana's family, Skilled in connection with the ocean
- Baird - lives with Granny, not completed his Waking yet, powerfully Skilled in music

The Orchard Tree Eldership

- Aidan - son of Darian and Bree, companion to Elana, Skilled in the land, animals, and craftsmanship
- Darian - Aidan's late father, was leader of the Orchard Tree Eldership, Skilled in leadership
- Bree - Aidan's mother, Skilled in the land, and craftsmanship

The Valefolk:

Merrion:

- Farrell - innkeeper in a coastal village, friend to Elana's family
- Cecily - daughter and heir to Lord Gratton, ruler of Merrion
- Braxton - servant to Marek

Glenariff:

- Ulrich - ruler of Glanariff, uncle to Aidan
- Darcy - Ulrich's son and heir

Lanreath

Barras

- Farris - nephew to Varen, ruler of the Barras
- Varen - ruler of the Barras
- Falbor and Danae - Barras clan, lost their daughter to the Black Knights, gifted Devi to Elana

Dundas

- Niall - renown smith and warrior of the Dundas
- Payton - ruler of the Dundas
- Kenrich - son and heir to Payton

About the author:

Elizabeth Love Kennon develops and teaches equine facilitated coaching programs, is a natural horsemanship trainer, and a master life coach. Her home is in Raleigh, NC where she enjoys time with her husband Jeff, their sons Joshua, Jonathan, and Cayden, and the ranch where she works as Equine Manager at Hope Reins. There she coaches people and trains horses; helping them pair rescued horses with hurting kids to provide opportunities for hope and healing. She believes in the power of story and uses it in her work, to help people access places within that are difficult to reach directly. She can be found at www.elizabethlovekennon.com

For more information about Hope Reins go to www.hopereinsnc.org

www.ingramcontent.com/pod-product-compliance
Lightning Source LLC
Chambersburg PA
CBHW071637260626
47170CB00001B/132